C000196600

Ar....

The Inheritance

The Guernsey Novels – Book 7

Sarnia Press
London

To my mother, Janet Williams, with love

Believe in a love that is being stored up for you like an inheritance, and have faith that in this love there is a strength and a blessing so large that you can travel as far as you wish without having to step outside it.

<u>Rainer Maria Rilke</u>

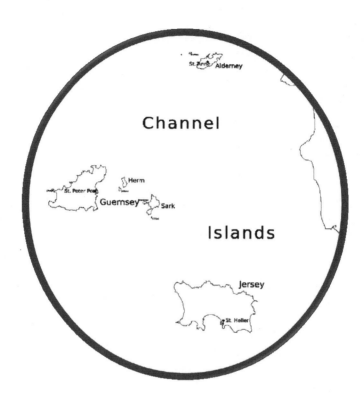

CHAPTER 1

Eugénie's Diary – Guernsey March 1862

My heart is so full of grief and my body so burdened by pain that I find it hard to write of the events of the past few days. But I must try.

The day that was to change my life began with no hint of what was to occur. I rose late after another fitful night and dressed reluctantly in my newly acquired widow's weeds. The black made my skin appear even paler than normal and when I caught a glimpse of myself in the bedroom mirror, I drew back in shock at the change in my appearance. Not quite nineteen, I looked, and felt, like an old crone. I forced myself to walk down to the bustling market to buy provisions; the stalls of winter vegetables, meat and fish providing splashes of colour against the granite walls. I caught pitying looks from those who would normally have nodded or spoken a greeting. It seemed young widows were objects of pity, to be shunned rather than embraced and consoled. Not lingering over my shopping, as once I would have done, I dragged myself back up Horn Street and into Hauteville, keeping my eyes averted from passers-by. There was only so much pity a person could stand.

My luncheon was meagre; bread and cheese and an apple. I ate only for my child's sake, not mine. The house was colder than it was outside as I had not the strength to replenish the fires in the kitchen and parlour. The view of the white-capped waves crashing onto the shore of Havelet Bay was an added torment and I trailed upstairs to our – my – bedroom and huddled under the blankets for warmth and comfort. After a short rest I felt somewhat stronger and decided a walk might warm my body and offer sustenance to my heavy heart. Wrapping an extra shawl around me I ventured out to take what had been my favourite walk to Fermain Bay. The joy I used to feel on striding out was replaced by an unutterable sadness as I considered how I was to survive without my beloved husband.

I had not walked far when a vicious pain rippled through my body, causing me to double over and cry out. It was nothing like any pain I had experienced before but I knew with dreadful certainty what was happening. As I leaned against a tree to stop myself falling to my knees I became aware of an open carriage pulling to a stop and a woman calling to me.

'M'dame, are you hurt? Can we help?'

Through eyes blurred with tears, I took in the familiar figure of M'dame Juliette Drouet approaching me, followed by her companion and lover, M'sieur Hugo. Oh, how unfortunate! To have my predicament witnessed by these of all people. They were not likely to know me, but all of Guernsey knew them. More tears fell. I hastily brushed them away with my gloved hand as she drew close.

'My dear, you are *enceinte*? Is something wrong?' Her voice was kind and she touched my arm with the gentlest of gestures.

'Yes, I…I fear I am losing my baby, m'dame. The pain…' I gasped as another pain, like the squeeze of a vice, swept through my abdomen and across my back. Something sticky slid down my thighs. She held on tighter and called to M'sieur Hugo for help.

'*Mon cher*, we must take this poor lady to my house at once. She is in need of a doctor. Can you help me get her in the carriage?'

I glanced up to see the great man staring at me, wide-eyed and white as if with shock.

'Léopoldine! Can it be you? Risen from the dead?' He stood as if transfixed and I wondered which one of us had lost their senses. M'dame Drouet, still supporting me with her hands, gave me a keen look and gasped.

'I hadn't noticed before, but you're right. She is indeed the image of your poor daughter. But I have seen this lady before and she is a neighbour of ours and in sore need of help. Come, let us go directly to *La Fallue* and send for Dr Corbin.'

M'sieur Hugo seemed to recover his composure and, each taking one arm, between them I was conveyed to the carriage and helped aboard. The driver flicked his whip over the horse and within minutes we arrived at the house of M'dame Drouet in Hauteville, a little up the road from my own home and one I had passed many times as I walked along to Fermain. As I was about to descend from the carriage I must have succumbed to a faint as the next thing I remember is waking up in a bed with M'dame Drouet on one side and a woman I recognised as her maid on the other.

'The doctor's on his way, but I fear you may be losing your child, as you suspected. You have lost a lot of blood and we've had to remove your outer garments.' M'dame Drouet brushed my hair back from my face with a gentle touch, her care-worn face creased in concern. 'I'm afraid I do not know your name, M'dame, even though I have seen you about. And you are now in mourning, I see. Surely not your husband?'

I nodded, clenching my teeth against another spasm tearing at my innards.

'My name…Eugénie Sarchet. My…my husband, Arnaud, a captain…merchant navy, drowned…collision at sea ten days ago. Died trying…save…sailor. Telegraph.' Between each spasm of pain Arnaud's face floated into my mind causing more tears. The maid silently passed me a linen handkerchief.

'You poor, poor child! Do you have anyone here who can care for you? You shouldn't be alone at such a time,' M'dame Drouet said, squeezing my hand.

'No. I…I am quite alone. I am a Frenchwoman. My maid left…her mother is sick.' I noticed the women glance at each other and the maid nodded.

'Then you must stay here until you recover. Ah, here is Doctor Corbin. I will leave you for a moment.'

A middle-aged man with a kind expression and a beard even bushier than M'sieur Hugo's approached me as M'dame Drouet left, leaving her maid in attendance.

'Now, M'dame, let us see if I can help.'

No man had touched me since my marriage to Arnaud and I flinched when his hands rested on my swollen belly, straining against my linen petticoat. I told him I was about seven months pregnant and had suffered cramping pain and loss of blood all afternoon. He looked grave as he examined me and as he turned back to speak I already knew what he was going to say.

'I fear your child has died in your womb, M'dame, and it's now most urgent you expel the infant as quickly as possible before you lose more blood. You must be strong and allow me to help if you are not to die also.'

At that moment, with my body and mind in torment, I would gladly have died and joined Arnaud and my unborn child in heaven. But God – or whoever – had other plans for me.

CHAPTER 2

Tess – Exeter 2012

Tess stared in horror at the face of the young boy on the trolley. It was clear he was dead.

'You all right, Doctor? It's not someone you know is it?' The paramedic's voice sounded concerned.

Tess looked at him, trying to stay calm, but struggling. Surrounded by the perpetual noise of Accident and Emergency with the constant flow of trolleys carrying patients of all ages and injuries, the sight of the dead boy had hit her like a physical blow.

'No, not really. He…he came in last week after a road traffic accident, knocked off his bike by a car. Nothing serious. What…what happened?'

The paramedic, known for his cheerfulness, looked solemn.

'He was playing in a football match at school and, according to whoever called us, just keeled over as he was about to score.' He touched the boy's head. 'There was nothing we could do, Doctor. Poor kid. But we had to go through the motions, like. Recorded as DOA, I suppose.' She nodded as he handed her his report.

'What about the parents?' She held her breath, knowing she would find it difficult to face them now. What if it was her fault?

'Away. The lad's been staying with friends.' He nodded towards an ashen-faced woman with her arms around a boy wearing the same football kit as Gary. Both looked as if they were about to be sick. Tess called a nurse over and asked her to take them into a private room and give them tea.

'Thanks, Tom, would you mind taking the…body – Gary – downstairs? I'll just sign the report and they can carry on from there.' She dashed her name at the bottom of the report, trying not to look at the pale, unmarked face of the thirteen-year-old boy who had been so chirpy only a week ago. And alive.

'And what can we do for you, young man?' It had been a busy day in Accident and Emergency and Tess was looking forward to the end of her shift but she smiled at the boy propped up on the trolley in the cubicle. He looked dazed, with scratches and a bruise on his face. Glancing at the file handed to her by the nurse, she saw his name was Gary Saunders and some speeding driver had knocked him off his bike.

The boy, who reminded her of her brother at that age, was clearly putting on a brave face, but she saw his mouth tighten in pain. His tousled hair stuck up on his scalp and his eyes were wide.

'My ankle hurts, Doctor, and I was told it had to be checked in case it's broken. It isn't is it? Only I've a big match coming up next week and I'm the best scorer in the team.' His look was beseeching as she lifted the blanket.

'Let's look, shall we?' Running her hands over the swollen and bruised ankle she soon realised it was a sprain and told him he needed to rest it, use ice packs and take painkillers.

'It's what we call a Grade One sprain and should heal within a week if you're careful. No cycling or football for the next few days, though. Understood?'

His face lit up.

'That's great, thanks, Doctor. Can I have a sick note for school?'

Tess laughed.

'Hey, I said nothing about missing school! If it hurts to walk on it we can lend you some crutches. I'll just check the rest of you to make sure we've missed nothing.' Tess knew the paramedics would have examined him, but she wanted nothing left to chance. Better to be safe than sorry, was her mantra.

And now, a week later he was dead. Had she missed something after all?

Later that day Tess sat with her boss, Dr Grant, in his office as he went through the report of Gary's earlier visit to A & E. It was usual procedure after a sudden death so soon after recent treatment. She sipped water from a plastic cup, willing herself to stay calm and professional. Like anyone in the medical profession, she had always strived to remain emotionally detached from patients, or risk being unable to carry out her work. But haunted by the sight of Gary's pale, lifeless body, she had almost convinced herself it was her fault. The sick feeling in her stomach tribute to her guilt.

Dr Grant looked up and rubbed his chin.

'Well, Tess, from what I've read here, there seems no connection with what happened a week ago and today's sad event. You checked all his vital signs, including his heart and pulse, and all was normal. Confirmed by the paramedics who brought him in.' He sighed, closing the file in front of him, and added, 'We'll know for certain after the PM, but I suspect it was an hypertrophic cardiomyopathy, or something similar. It fits the description of how the lad collapsed, without warning. It's rare, but happens in young men who are otherwise fit, as I'm sure you're aware.' His expression was sympathetic and Tess relaxed a little.

'So, if it was an HCM, for example, I wouldn't bear any responsibility for Gary's death?'

'Absolutely not. Is that what you've been worried about?' His eyes widened. 'I know it's an awful thing to happen and it was bad luck you were on duty today when he came in, but please don't blame yourself. Whatever killed the lad, it wasn't anything you did or didn't do. Okay?'

'Okay, thanks.' Tess gulped down the last of the water, feeling the knot in her stomach ease.

'Good. You're a great doctor, Tess, and I don't want you worrying yourself unnecessarily.' Dr Grant stood up and she did the same, keen to leave and go home, suddenly aware of how exhausted she was.

They shook hands and he promised to keep her informed of the results of the post-mortem.

Once out of the office Tess ran to the staff car park, planning to do a quick shop at the supermarket for pizza and wine. She hoped she'd sleep that night with a couple of glasses inside her.

By the time Tess arrived at work the next day she was hungover and a bundle of anxiety. Unfortunately, she hadn't stopped at two glasses and slept fitfully most of the night. Telling herself 'never again', she headed straight for the staff canteen and a double strength latte. Keeping her eyes down she avoided the usual morning chit-chat with her colleagues and pretended to be engrossed in something on her phone. It would be a long day, not only because of her shift, but because the result of the PM wouldn't be known until late afternoon. No matter Dr Grant's reassurance, Tess wanted – needed – to know Gary's death was not her fault. She was nearing the end of her placement in the hospital and wanted to leave without a cloud over her. With an inward groan, Tess swallowed the last of the coffee and headed for A & E and whatever that day would bring.

The regular assortment of road accidents, falls, suspected heart attacks and chest complaints kept her busy and unable to think of anything else and Tess barely had time for a quick sandwich and another strong coffee at lunchtime. Short-staffed, there was no choice but to focus all her energy on dealing with those in pain or afraid. It took her by surprise when she received a message saying Dr Grant wanted to see her. Her watch said it was five fifteen yet she could have sworn it was only about three. After passing on instructions to a junior doctor, Tess made her way once more to Dr Grant's office, her hands sticky with sweat. Wiping them on her scrubs, she knocked and went in.

'Ah, Tess, thanks for coming,' Dr Grant said, with an encouraging smile, from behind his cluttered desk.

'The PM results are back?' Her heart was beating so loud she was sure he could hear it.

'Yes, and it's as I suspected, HCM. Poor lad.' He shook his head, frowning. 'No prior indications and no known family history. But as it's hereditary I shall insist the family get checked out soon as. I believe there's a younger brother,' he said, glancing at the open file, 'and we don't want another tragedy in the family, do we?'

Tess felt her own heart slowing down again and shook her head.

'So, I'm not at fault, sir? I checked his heart as a routine, but...'

'No, you wouldn't have picked it up with a stethoscope. You did everything right, Tess, so you have a clear conscience. It was just an unpreventable tragedy.' He stood and reached to take her hand. 'The only good thing is we can now monitor the family and prevent it happening again.'

'Yes, that's something, I guess. Thank you, sir.'

Once outside the office Tess didn't know whether to cheer or cry. Cheer for herself as not being responsible for Gary's death, or cry for the boy lying cold in the mortuary.

By the time Tess arrived back at her flat all she wanted to do was have a quick supper and slouch in front of the television. She knew her boyfriend, Steve, would be unhappy if she didn't ring and suggest they went out for a drink, but she wasn't in the mood. As she chewed on her pasta, she wondered if she wanted to see him again at all. She didn't think he was the proverbial 'one', and he hated her working long hours. Tess was still thinking about what to do when her phone rang. Hoping it wasn't Steve, she picked it up and saw it was her mother. Not much of an improvement as her mother always had something to moan about; she answered warily, 'Hi, Mum, everything all right?'

'Depends which way you look at it, Tess. I'm afraid your great-aunt Doris has passed away,' her mother said, with a deep sigh.

'Oh, I'm sorry to hear that, Mum. But she was a great age, wasn't she? In her nineties? And I didn't think you were close, although I thought she was quite a character.' Tess hadn't seen Doris for years, not since her family had left Guernsey and moved to Devon for her father's job. But she remembered visiting her as a girl and she always had stories to tell and sweets to give.

'Yes, she was getting on, and at least she died in her sleep, I'm told.' Her mother sniffed. 'It's not her death so much I'm upset about, it's that according to her advocate, she's left her house to you and not me.'

❧ CHAPTER 3 ❧

Tess – April 2012

Tess gazed through the plane window at the island of her birth and which she hadn't seen in over twenty years. From this height she couldn't be sure what changes had occurred, but had seen photos on Facebook from old school friends showing places she had not recognised. A fluttering in her stomach bore witness to her excitement, with a mix of trepidation. And sadness. It seemed an unhappy way for her to return, to be the only relative at her aunt's funeral and to meet with the advocate before seeing the house. Her inheritance. Tess frowned at the memory of her mother's flat refusal to come with her.

'Why should I bother? It would be hypocritical of me to go. Doris knew I didn't really care for her, she was an embarrassment to the family, she was, living in that mess of a house as if she hadn't a penny to her name.' Elaine stomped around her immaculate sitting room and Tess, who had come round to try and make her change her mind, realised it was a lost cause. She had never understood why her mother hadn't liked Doris, her grandmother's elder spinster sister. Maybe it was to do with the fact that Doris had inherited the house in Hauteville, and not her grandmother. It would then have passed to Elaine, an only child. And as it turned out, her father, Ken, had risen up the ranks of the police, retiring as a Chief Superintendent, so her parents weren't short of money. And Elaine's late parents had left her a decent sum, as well as a bequest to Tess and her brother, Clive. Her share had helped to buy the flat.

Elaine came to a halt, her chest heaving with emotion.

'And I expect you'll sell the house and make a pretty penny. Although it's not been looked after, it's in a good area and must be worth a bit.' Her eyes flashed at Tess who wished she'd never come. She didn't like confrontations but her mother thrived on them and not for the first time, Tess questioned why she lived in the same city as her mother. But the answer was simple. She adored her father who, she thought, was a saint to put up with her mother's constant bitching.

'Actually, Mum, I might keep the house and move back to Guernsey.' There, she'd said it! Saying it out loud made it seem more real, somehow. She had been mulling it over since hearing about the house, but only in a fanciful kind of way. Like a daydream when life isn't going according to plan. She had finished with Steve and she was growing tired of city living and – and it was a big and – the shock of young Gary's death had rattled her. As an A & E doctor she'd seen plenty of people lose their lives over the years, but his had touched her in a different way. Possibly his resemblance to her brother. Whatever it was, Tess knew you had to grasp life and live it and if that meant a major change, then so be it.

'You're what? You must be mad! That house is cursed, or haunted, or both. Apart from Doris, who always was an obstinate fool and wanted to live forever, no-one who's lived there has achieved much of an age.' Elaine's face was flushed and Tess worried about her blood pressure.

'That's just a load of nonsense, Mum. You know what Guernsey's like for superstition. And as you say, Doris lived into her nineties, which disproves that theory.' Tess took deep, calming breaths, not wanting to get into an argument. Her father had disappeared to his study soon after she arrived. He referred to it as his 'strategic withdrawal'.

'And what about your job and your flat? And Steve? Just going to chuck them all up, are you?' Her mother's face was heading for beetroot.

'Well, if I do decide to move back to Guernsey, then yes, I'll give my notice in at the hospital and look for a job on the island. And I've already chucked Steve.' Tess pushed her hair back behind her ear, wishing she hadn't said anything about moving yet. Anything might stop it happening and in the meantime she had riled her mother. With an inward sigh, she stood, saying, 'Look, Mum, let's leave it shall we? I only came to ask you to come to the funeral with me next week. I have to go now and I'll ring you later.' Quickly kissing her mother before she could say anything, Tess left, not even saying a proper goodbye to her father, something she was sorry about but wanted to avoid a full-blown row with her mother. Not for the first time Tess thought Clive had emigrated to Canada for more reasons than he'd offered at the time. She missed him, but could hardly blame him. Growing up he'd been the proverbial blue-eyed boy who could do no wrong in their mother's eyes. Tess should have been jealous, but he had realised what was happening and made a point of spending time with his big sister and was genuinely proud of her when she qualified as a doctor. He worked in IT and considered it no more than a means to earn mega bucks, nothing compared to saving lives, as he had said, hugging her as he left for his new life.

The plane circled its descent and Tess peered out of the window looking for familiar landmarks. They came in over the west coast and she recognised the unmistakeable white top of Fort Grey, set between long golden beaches. Then over fields surrounded with more houses than she remembered and soon they were bumping gently onto the runway. The airport building was much bigger and more contemporary than the one she remembered. Nevertheless, an inner voice whispered, 'home' and Tess smiled. Whether or not she came back, this would always be home.

It was eight o'clock in the morning and most passengers seemed to be businessmen on a day flight and Tess only waited a few minutes for her case to appear on the carousel. She had come over for a long weekend, Friday to Monday, using a couple of holiday days to lengthen the trip. The funeral was mid-afternoon and she had plenty of time to settle in to her hotel and have breakfast before seeing the advocate. As she walked to the exit through revolving doors, Tess experienced a moment of doubt. The concourse was big and airy with a curved flight of stairs in the middle and windows filled one wall. If the airport had undergone such a transformation, what may have happened to the rest of the island? Would it no longer be as beautiful? Would the islanders, her friends, have changed beyond recognition? Hoping other changes would not be as dramatic as the airport's, Tess wheeled her case to the waiting line of taxis. A smiling driver hopped out and grabbed her case.

'Been away, have you, eh?'

'You could say that. Can you take me to Hotel Pandora, in Hauteville, please?' Tess grinned, pleased the driver assumed she was a local rather than a tourist. Although locals didn't need to stay in hotels, so that's probably confused him, she thought. He was chatty and she gave him a brief version of her reason for leaving Guernsey and her return. When she admitted to not having been back for over twenty years he took it upon himself to tell her of the most notable changes.

'Town has changed the most, and not for the better neither, in my opinion. Too much emphasis on trying to make money, that's the problem nowadays.' He shook his head and sighed. 'Us older ones preferred things as they was, but younger ones like you want progress and lots of modern stuff so perhaps you'll like what you see. Anyways, we can't do much about it, can we, eh?'

Tess agreed, wishing he would stop talking and let her concentrate on what she was seeing through the window. So far, apart from the airport, she hadn't seen much change. They went from St Peters towards St Martin and only the occasional new building marked the passage of time. More changes were visible in the centre of St Martin, with the addition of a new M&S food store and other buildings she didn't remember. Tess recognised some shops from her childhood but a number had changed. It was inevitable in over twenty years, but part of her wanted to see it as it had been. As they drove past the fancy iron gates of Saumarez Manor, she was pleased to see that at least looked unchanged. By the time they reached the top of Le Val des Terres, Tess was more relaxed and she caught her breath at the glimpse of the harbour and its iconic castle down below. The steep winding road down into the western side of Town took them through a wooded area on both sides, and she spotted a hint of early bluebells amongst the grass. The driver was silent as he concentrated on negotiating the bends and Tess was drawn back to the past, a waving and noisy spectator with her father at the motorcycle races which took place every year on the steep road in to Town. Happy times.

All looked as she remembered as they drove past the bus terminal on the left and the road on the right leading up to the model yacht pond and on to Castle Cornet. The streets were busy with early morning traffic and the taxi edged slowly forward as they approached the Albert Memorial forming a mini-roundabout. Then it was up narrow Cornet Street and into Hauteville. Tess had a fleeting glimpse of her aunt's house and it looked shabbier than she remembered, surrounded as it was by other Georgian houses in tip-top condition. A few yards further up, Tess recognised the large house flying a French flag as the one owned by Victor Hugo. For a moment, Tess thought about the old family legend concerning the great man, but was distracted by their arrival at the hotel at the top of Hauteville.

'Here you are, miss, hope you have a good weekend and here's my number for your pick-up on Monday,' the driver said, handing her a card. After paying him, he took her case up the steps to the entrance. Once checked in, Tess, hungry after an early start, was directed to the restaurant to join other residents for breakfast. She found an empty table by the window and gazed out at a view very similar to that from her aunt's house. While she ate, Tess felt a tremor of excitement at the possibility of living here and enjoying the amazing view of St Peter Port harbour, Castle Cornet and the islands of Herm, Jethou and Sark on the horizon. A big contrast to her view from the flat in Exeter, namely a boring block of flats. A lot would depend on the condition of the house. Too dilapidated and she might have to reconsider. Sighing, she concentrated on her food, keen to go to her room and hang up the navy suit she'd brought for the funeral.

Half an hour later Tess left the hotel to walk into Town. Her appointment with the advocate was for eleven, and it was now nine thirty, so she had time for a quick recce and a cup of coffee beforehand. The early April weather was mild, with a soft breeze and she wore her favourite leather jacket and jeans tucked into boots. As she walked past Hauteville House Tess paused, remembering what Aunt Doris had told her so many years ago.

'Has your mother mentioned the family legend, Tess? About Victor Hugo?' Doris, a sprightly seventy-year-old, was perched

14

on the sofa in a sitting room hardly worthy of the name, any chairs or sofas piled high with newspapers, magazines and books. Tess was curled on the floor in front of the sofa, cuddling Doris' cat, Spook. Well-named, thanks to his black fur and green eyes which shone in the dark, spooking Tess when she was about six and had entered a room before the lights were switched on. Now, at eleven, she was used to him.

'What legend, Aunt? Wasn't he the Frenchman who lived up the street from here about a hundred years ago. The writer?'

Doris sniffed.

'I don't think your mother believes it, but I do and think you should be told.'

Tess was all ears.

'Told what?'

'You know this house has been handed down through the family since the 1860s?' Tess nodded. For some reason, her mother was upset about this when she told her.

'Well, it originally belonged to a direct ancestor of ours, your great-great-great-grandmother, Eugénie. She had inherited it from her first husband, Arnaud, who died young. Some years later she remarried and had a son and the line has carried on through each generation.' Doris paused to take a sip of her tea and Tess, wide-eyed, waited impatiently for her to continue.

'Nothing unusual in that, you may think, young Tess, but what makes our story more interesting is that Eugénie, recently widowed, started working for Victor Hugo as his copyist. And carried on for several years until she remarried.'

'Ooh! You mean she copied out his books and poems before they were published? Did she work in his house?' Tess waved her hand in the direction of Hauteville House, yards up the street. How exciting to have an ancestor who knew such a famous man!

'Yes, I believe she did work in his house, but there's more to the story. Even more exciting,' her aunt said, eyes sparkling. 'Legend has it Eugénie had an affair with Victor and her son, born less than nine months after she remarried, was actually Victor's child.'

❧ CHAPTER 4 ❧

Eugénie's Diary – Guernsey March 1862

The hours that followed are burned in my memory as some of the worst in my life. There were moments when I felt myself slipping away on a wave of excruciating pain and I yearned to be allowed to go. But the doctor and a hired midwife fought back with a combination of strong drugs and a desire to rid my ravaged body of my poor child. One final push and he eventually slid onto the bloodied sheets, his tiny but fully formed body pale and lifeless. I turned my head away and shed tears of relief, pain and sorrow. Doctor Corbin gave me a draught of something to make me sleep – laudanum, I think – and left as the midwife finished her ministrations. I vowed I would never bear another child and then fell into a blessed oblivion.

'Good morning. How are you feeling, m'dame?'

I opened leaden eyes to see the face of M'dame Drouet hovering inches from my own. Shifting cautiously under the covers, I was aware of a throbbing ache in my belly and between my legs.

'Better, thank you. My...my son?' Tears gathered at the memory of his lifeless body being swept up swiftly by the midwife. He would be with his father now.

She coughed.

'We weren't sure what to do for the best. A miscarried child isn't buried in a churchyard and we wondered if you would want him buried in your garden? Discreetly, naturally.' Her eyes held a deep compassion and I was touched at her thoughtfulness.

'I would like that, m'dame. But I'm not sure if I can walk yet...' My legs were heavy and lifeless beneath the sheets.

'Oh, do not concern yourself now. When you are able, I will organise someone to dig a grave for your child and, if you wish, you can offer a prayer for him. The doctor has left instructions you must rest for a few days before attempting to leave your bed and I am happy to let you stay as long as needed.'

I was touched by her generosity. Why would someone like her, the confidante of such a tower of literature, known throughout the world, take me under her wing? I was a nobody. All we had in common was our mother country, France.

'*Merci*, m'dame. That's most kind of you, but I don't wish to intrude on your hospitality for longer than absolutely necessary.' I tried to sit up, conscious of a lack of dignity when one is lying down, particularly in someone else's bed, but found I was too weak. Madame Drouet leaned forward and supported me while she plumped up the pillows and eased me up against them.

'It's no hardship, I can assure you. I shall enjoy having the company of a fellow Frenchwoman to talk to when I'm not needed elsewhere.' Her gaze faltered and for a moment I sensed the sadness underneath her confident exterior. A woman in her fifties, her beauty was fading as her body thickened, and she was unmarried. I knew little of her except for her liaison with M'sieur Hugo. I arrived in Guernsey less than two years ago and it was only when I married Arnaud and moved to this street that I learnt of their presence and how scandalised the islanders were when Hugo arrived in 1855 with his wife and children, his mistress making her home nearby. Being French myself, I knew these arrangements were somewhat accepted in Paris, but had quickly discovered how puritanical the islanders could be. I imagine it had not been easy for her to make friends.

'Now, enough talking! You must be hungry and I'll arrange for my maid to bring you *un petit déjeuner*. You need to build up your strength. I will call on you later.' She rose and patted my arm before leaving the room. I gazed around me, taking in the room I'd hardly noticed previously. Heavy velvet curtains shut out the day and I had no idea what time it might be, the gas lights casting strange shadows on the walls. Dark wallpaper and carpet added to the gloom. If m'dame had not referred to it being morning, I would have guessed it was evening. The effect of the laudanum was easing and my emotions rose to the surface, bringing more tears for my poor Arnaud and his son. My husband had been so happy to learn he was to be a father.

'What wonderful news! I'm the luckiest man alive! Not only do I have a beautiful wife, but I'm about to become a father,' Arnaud cried, lifting me up and swinging me around until I became dizzy and begged him to stop. At ten years my senior, he had, he told me, begun to despair of finding a woman to love and settle down with. Being away at sea weeks at a time had put off other ladies, he told me when we first courted.

'But your absences will make me love you the more when you return,' I replied, as we embraced. After his proposal weeks later, I was giddy with happiness and looking forward to spending the rest of my life with him. And bearing his children.

The memory of those early days together in our home, planning our future as a family, was like a physical pain and I cried out. The door opened and the maid bustled in, carrying a tray heavy with covered plates of food, a small carafe of red wine and a pot of coffee. Placing the tray on the bedside table, she took my hand.

'Are you in pain? I heard your cry.'

'No, I was remembering my husband and our time together. I'm sorry, I don't know your name?'

'Suzanne. Let's get you sitting up a bit more, shall we? My mistress wants you to eat and drink as much as you can since you've lost so much blood.' She added another pillow behind me and placed a shawl around my shoulders before offering me the wine.

'I don't drink wine for breakfast–'

'Perhaps not, and rightly so, but it's good for the blood and M'dame insists. There's also eggs and ham and bread. Can you manage if I leave the tray here?' Suzanne frowned, looking as if she didn't trust me to eat if she left. Her ample figure belied her own appetite.

'Yes, thank you.'

A sniff and she was gone. I reached for the plate of ham and eggs, suddenly ravenous and began eating, accompanied by sips of wine. The food was delicious and soon all that was left was the coffee. Strong and black, as I liked it. Replete, I lay back on the pillows and, before I knew it, was asleep.

Over the following days I slowly regained my strength, aided by my youth and the excellent care provided by m'dame and Suzanne. I still slept for hours at a time, but was able to sit out on a chair without much discomfort, looking out through the window at Havelet Bay and Castle Cornet. The grey skies were replaced with blue, dotted with fleeing clouds and it appeared spring was on the way. I yearned to be out in the fresh air, away from the confinement of my fetid room. Despite Suzanne's best efforts, there remained the smell of stale blood, and the air had a metallic taste. A constant reminder of what had occurred here which tore at my heart and soul. The doctor had returned and declared himself satisfied with my progress, but urged me to be patient before venturing downstairs.

Finally, the day arrived and m'dame came smiling to guide me down to her parlour. Suzanne had been sent to my house for fresh undergarments and my dress had been sponged clean ready. At my behest she had also brought me my journal as I was now strong enough to write again. Much as it pains me to relate what has happened these past days, I am pleased to have progressed this far. My legs had little strength and I leaned on m'dame for support and was relieved when we reached the chaise longue and she pushed me down gently.

'There! Well done. Now you can rest if you wish, or I can stay and we can talk.' She took both my hands in a warm clasp and her bright eyes searched my face.

'I shall be honoured to talk to you, m'dame,' I said truthfully.

'*Bien*. I know so little about you and yet you have been my guest these past five days. Would you be willing to share a little of your past? Not from idle curiosity, but because I would like to help you.'

I inclined my head in agreement. There was nothing of which to be ashamed in my life.

She smiled. 'Perhaps you can tell me about your birthplace and your family?'

'I was born and raised in Cherbourg, and my father was the head teacher at the local school. We lived in the large schoolhouse next door. I had a brother and two sisters and we appreciated the space. My mother was a dressmaker who had worked in Paris for noble patrons and I think she found moving to Cherbourg and losing that patronage quite difficult.'

'How interesting. But what brought you to Guernsey?'

Pain flicked through me at the memory.

'My parents and siblings died of a fever which took many lives in the town. I…I came to Guernsey to seek work as a governess and met Arnaud and…we fell in love and married last summer. His parents…died of the tuberculosis some years ago and left him their house.'

'Oh, I am so sorry about your family. And now your husband!' She patted my hand, her face creased with sorrow. 'To be a governess you must have received an education, *n'est ce pas?*'

'*Oui.* My father was a great believer in equality for girls and insisted we studied as hard as my brother. For me, it wasn't a hardship, I enjoyed learning but my sisters were not as keen.' I hesitated, feeling myself flush. 'My father was a great admirer of M'sieur Hugo, reading all his works and passing them to me. He would be most amazed to know I am a neighbour of his and have had the honour of meeting him.'

'You made quite an impression on him, my dear. You bear such a strong likeness to his dearly loved daughter, Léopoldine, that I was afraid for his heart. You know she died tragically at nineteen, soon after marrying?' I nodded, my father had told me. 'A lovely girl, Victor adored her and was thrown into a deep depression when she drowned. Her husband tried to save her, but he also died. *Très tragique, n'est pas?*'

'*Oui*, m'dame.'

'Such a loss! It was years before M'sieur Hugo recovered enough to write again. You can imagine his shock when he saw you! And your stories bear several similarities, it seems providence has brought you to us. He has been most anxious about your health and is impatient to visit you, if you are agreeable?'

I felt my mouth fall open in surprise. Surely such a great man would not bother with one such as me?

She laughed.

'You will find as you get to know him, *ma chère*, that M'sieur Hugo loves talking and mixing with all who he finds interesting. And he will be delighted to hear you are acquainted with his work. May I suggest he call on us this afternoon, if you are not too tired?'

'I would be honoured, m'dame.'

She clapped her hands. 'Good, that is settled. Suzanne will take a note to him.' She stood up, smoothing her skirts. 'I have work to do. Rest here and I'll ask Suzanne to bring in some hot chocolate before she goes. Please feel free to ask her for anything else you may need.'

After she left I sat alone with my tumultuous thoughts. The pain of losing my baby lay heavily on top of the pain of losing my husband and I was afraid of the future. Amidst this sorry tale of woe, I am to be visited by M'sieur Hugo himself. Under different circumstances I would be ecstatic, but…I assume he is coming to offer me his condolences and then departing back to his eyrie in Hauteville House to pen another literary masterpiece. In the meantime I will continue to recover sufficiently to return home. Gazing around the room, it was clear M'dame Drouet had particular tastes in her furnishings and *objets d'art*. Bright silks hung on the walls contrasting with the heavy dark furniture. In spite of thick brocade curtains adorning the windows and a fire burning in the elaborate fireplace, there was an air of dampness, a chill, in the room. I had noticed how she swathed herself in numerous shawls and was glad of the thick woollen one she had lent me.

A painting caught my eye and I went over to study it in more detail. It was of a beautiful young woman, with long, dark hair twisted into ringlets cascading down one side of her neck, her hands clasped in front of her as she gazed serenely ahead.

'That's the mistress, that is, painted when she was a young actress and caught the eye of M'sieur Hugo.' Suzanne came through the door carrying a small tray bearing a jug of steaming chocolate, a cup and a plate of buttered gâche, a Guernsey fruit bread I have come to enjoy. She placed it on the table nearby and joined me in gazing at the portrait.

'She was a beautiful woman indeed. How long have you worked for her?'

Suzanne folded her arms across her stomach.

'Must be twenty years or more. Mam'selle Claire was still alive so it must be.'

I was puzzled.

'Who was Mam'selle Claire?'

'Why, the mistress's daughter. Sad it was, her dying, and only twenty. Tuberculosis.' She shook her head. 'Died a few years after M'sieur's Léopoldine drowned.'

'Oh.' I thought of how kind Madame had been to me since the loss of my baby while she carried the burden of her own loss.

'If there's nothing else, I'd best be off to deliver a note down the road.' Suzanne was halfway to the door and I nodded, saying, 'No, that's all, thank you.' I poured a cup of the thick dark chocolate, a real treat when you have to watch the francs as I do. As I savoured each mouthful, I compared the portrait with the more matronly lady I knew. The eyes were her best feature, bright, displaying a keen intelligence and her hair was still dark.

I picked up a leather-bound book lying on the table and read the gold-lettered spine, *Les Contemplations – Victor Hugo*. Opening the book I saw a handwritten dedication, '*To Ju-Ju, you are my life, and you will be my eternity. From your Toto*'. It was a collection of poems and I began to read as I drank my chocolate. So enthralled was I by the lyrical and romantic verses that an hour must have passed without my being aware of it until m'dame appeared at the door.

'Ah, you have found my favourite poems. I'm pleased. Do they not sing to your soul, *ma chère*?'

'Indeed they do, m'dame. My apologies for not waiting for your permission–' I closed the book hastily, aware of a flush spreading over my face.

She waved her hand dismissively and sat down.

'You are welcome to read any of my books. That is something we are not short of here,' she laughed, nodding towards a bookcase crammed with volumes. 'You are well rested, I trust?'

'Yes, thank you.'

'Good. We shall have luncheon shortly and then Monsieur Hugo has agreed to visit at two, before he and I leave for our constitutional. Do you feel strong enough to take a short walk in the garden? The fresh air would be so uplifting.'

I felt a flutter of excitement. To venture outside after so long indoors would be wonderful and I agreed eagerly, though concerned how I might fare. My cloak was fetched and Madame guided me through a room at the back leading to the garden. Not large, given over to lawn and flower beds, it was on a level, which was a relief.

'There, now. Hold onto my arm and we'll take a gentle stroll towards the far end and you must take deep breaths of air as we admire the view. Similar to your own, is it not?'

I hung on gratefully, drawing strength from her sturdy body as we took small steps along the path. Beyond was the ever-present sea, looking smooth as silk on this windless day with the pale sun glinting off the granite walls of Castle Cornet guarding the harbour. The salty air smelt clean after the mustiness of *La Fallue* and I took care to draw in as much as I could. I wanted to store it inside me, filling my lungs and veins to capacity, eking it out during the time I would be spending back indoors. My legs, like jelly at first, began to regain their usual strength and by the time we returned I was much re-energised.

'Well done! You have so much colour in those pretty cheeks of yours, it is hard to believe you nearly died only days ago. M'sieur will be pleased, he's been so worried about you.'

I couldn't envisage M'sieur Hugo being worried about a virtual stranger, but I did appreciate her concern. Suzanne had set out our meal in the dining room and I ate greedily, my usual appetite much restored. As we finished eating, m'dame looked up, frowning and asked, 'I don't wish to pry, *ma chère*, but are you able to support yourself financially now you have lost your dear husband?'

'There's a little money left from Arnaud's inheritance, and I had formed the idea of taking in lodgers to bring in a regular income once I have recovered my full strength.' My tone was light, but my heart heavy at the thought of having strangers under my roof, expecting regular meals and their laundry taken care of. I'd never been particularly domesticated, much to my dear mama's annoyance, preferring instead to help my father with his paperwork. With Arnaud away so much, I had been able to take my time over the chores, aided by my erstwhile maid.

Madame pursed her lips in what looked like disapproval.

'That is certainly a consideration, but perhaps not the most suitable for someone so young.' With a smile she stood, saying, 'Come, M'sieur Hugo will be here shortly, let us go and refresh ourselves before welcoming him in the drawing room.'

The walk up to my room was easier than the walk down and my reflection in the bedroom mirror showed the improvement in my complexion. I brushed my hair and swept it back into a heavy twist at my neck before sponging my face with water and a little eau de toilette. I was ready to face the great man.

CHAPTER 5

Eugénie's Diary – Guernsey March 1862

'Ah! *La pauvre petite*! And how are feeling today? You have some colour in your cheeks, which is good.' M'sieur Hugo strode into the drawing room and came straight to the chaise longue where I waited, nervously twisting my fingers. Lifting up a hand, he kissed it, accompanied by a slight bow. I lowered my head in acknowledgment.

'I am much improved, m'sieur, thank you. Madame Drouet has been a wonderful nurse.'

He sat in a chair opposite me while she took a seat on the chaise. He looked like a genial grandfather, his thick white hair and beard in need of a trim while his oddly black moustache virtually erased his mouth. Two small, dark eyes studied me and I dropped my gaze.

'Yes, she has indeed.' He leaned forward and patted her hand. Turning to me he went on, 'I owe you an apology for my reaction when we met the other day. The shock of seeing a young woman the very image of my deceased daughter affected my brain for a moment. Do you believe in spirits, the afterlife?' He sat, his hands placed on his splayed legs, looking very much the great thinker and writer.

'I...I don't know, m'sieur. Although I was raised as a Catholic, I am not particularly religious and not in awe of a God who allows so much death and misery to be endured on this earth.'

His eyes sparkled.

'Well said! I am of a similar turn of mind and it has been many years since I entered a church, except for burials. But spirits cannot be so readily dismissed. Why, my own house is haunted and I regularly have conversations with ghosts who seem to frequent my bedroom. Which is why I thought, for a moment, you were the spirit of my dear Léopoldine, come to be reunited with me.' He sighed and his eyes clouded with sadness.

'I am sorry to have disappointed you, m'sieur. I can understand how much it would have meant to you if it were true.' For a moment I allowed the idea of Arnaud returned from his watery grave to fill my mind, and I felt a momentary uplift of my spirits.

He waved his hand.

'It was a foolish old man's whim, nothing more. And for me it's a pleasure to be in the company of one so like my lost daughter. M'dame Drouet informs me you are well educated and are acquainted with my works, which is an extra delight. Do you have a fair hand as well? Would you mind copying a few lines of my book for me?' He indicated the volume I had been reading earlier.

Although puzzled, I agreed and m'dame fetched paper, pen and ink and set them out on a small desk. I took a seat and M'sieur Hugo selected the lines to be copied. My father had always praised my writing skills, both in form and content, and I had no qualms about the result.

'Thank you, *ma petite*, you write beautifully, does she not, m'dame?' He handed her the page and she was as effusive in her praise.

'It is as I told you, I believe she is an excellent choice.' She looked pleased with herself, her broad smile offering a glimpse of the youthful beauty which had captivated Monsieur Hugo. I was left wondering what they had in mind for me.

'Don't look alarmed,' M'sieur Hugo smiled at me, 'we mean you no harm. I'm nearing the end of a work which has consumed me over the years and I need a copyist to aid my dear m'dame as the labour involved is too great for one person. There will be other works too, and we thought it would suit you to be employed in this way rather than be at the beck and call of lodgers.'

My head reeled. To work for Victor Hugo! Reading and copying his masterpieces as they poured from his mind onto the page. Infinitely better than taking in lodgers.

'I am honoured, m'sieur. It would be a great pleasure to work for you.'

M'dame Drouet clapped her hands, saying, 'Wonderful! I think we shall all get along famously and another pair of hands is most welcome.'

'Yes, I believe it was serendipity that we came along when we did the other day. We are able to help each other, yes?' He leapt up, striding around the room, adjusting pictures and flicking open *Les Contemplations.*

'May I enquire whether it's a novel or poetry you are writing? I did so enjoy *Notre-Dame de Paris,*' I ventured to say as he whirled around the room.

He thrust his hands in his pockets, rocking back on his heels, and frowned.

'It is more than a novel. *Les Misérables* is my account of the injustices I've witnessed in my beloved homeland and have long railed against over the years. I hate the inequality suffered by those less fortunate in their birth and believe everyone should have a chance to better themselves. My work addresses all that I feel most strongly about and, I believe, in all modesty, will strike a chord among many. Not only in France, but in all Europe.' He threw out his hands, as if to emphasise the reach of his words.

I glanced at M'dame Drouet and saw her nod her head in agreement, her eyes shining with approval.

'I have had the privilege of reading and copying this work which M'sieur Hugo has laboured on for about twenty years and think it will be remembered as his masterpiece, his greatest work. And the end is in sight, is it not?'

He gave a little bow.

'Only a matter of months before it will be ready for publishing. I am being sent a constant supply of proofs from my publisher, which is why your help would be invaluable, *ma petite.*'

'How wonderful! When do you wish me to start?' Much as I was thankful for the work, I still felt far from well and my voice faltered.

'Oh, not until you are quite recovered. We don't want you suffering a relapse, do we?' He patted my hand, beaming and I smiled my relief. We then discussed the terms of my employment, including the remuneration and likely hours each week. I would have agreed to anything, but the terms were more than favourable and I experienced a lifting of the weight in my chest. As long as I could continue working for M'sieur Hugo, I would be able to support myself with dignity. At least some good had come out of my tragic loss.

❧ CHAPTER 6 ❧

Tess – Guernsey April 2012

Standing outside Hugo's house, Tess had to acknowledge she was piqued by the idea of being a descendant, albeit through an illicit liaison. When Doris had told her, it had been exciting, something which made her 'different', but her mother had soon squashed the idea, telling her Doris was delusional and although the story had been handed down over the generations, there had never been an ounce of proof. Tess had been told, in no uncertain terms not to mention the subject again. She hadn't dared say anything to Clive in case he snitched on her. It was what eight-year-old brothers did. Fortunately, as he grew up, he became her ally against their mother but by then Tess had forgotten about the family legend. Until now.

She forced herself to stop imagining her three times great-grandmother in bed with Hugo, and carried on down the street towards what had been her family's home. All the houses on this side were of a similar type, either early Victorian or late Georgian, she guessed. Some had been rendered and others left in their natural granite state. Most looked well cared for and were substantial properties in what was considered a good area. Then she arrived at her aunt's house. This was plain granite, looking dark against the neighbouring white houses, and its peeling window frames and front door did little to help. The decorative stonework of the ground floor bay window and front door were badly in need of repair and the three sash windows upstairs looked rotten, as did the attic window. Standing back, she could see the roof had slipped tiles but didn't look too bad. She remembered it as a large house, although Doris only used part of it. Rooms had been filled to overflowing with books and papers of all description and Tess had never ventured upstairs. All the windows had drawn curtains, giving the impression of a house asleep. Do not disturb. The words flashed through her mind and Tess shivered. She didn't believe in ghosts and was sure Doris hadn't said anything about the house being haunted. It was probably her mother trying to put her off.

She was about to move on when the neighbour's door opened and a middle-aged woman looked at her somewhat warily.

'Can I help you?' Her tone not the friendliest.

'Don't worry, I'm not planning to burgle the place,' Tess replied, with a laugh. 'Not that it looks worth burgling.' She stretched out her hand. 'I'm Tess Le Prevost, and my great-aunt Doris left me her house. I'm over for the funeral.'

The woman's face split into a broad smile and she shook hands with a strong grip.

'Oh, I'm so pleased to meet you. Doris told me she was leaving you the house. Please accept my condolences.' Her smile faltered.

'Thanks. I hadn't seen Doris for years, but we did keep in touch by letter and card. Birthdays, Christmas, you know. I have fond memories of her from my childhood.'

'We've been here ten years now and I hardly ever saw your aunt, she was quite independent, but she did come in for a cup of tea sometimes.'

Tess stole a glance at her watch.

'I'm afraid I have to go, but I'd love to catch up later, Mrs…?'

'Barker, Heather Barker. I'll see you at the funeral and we can arrange something then.' Heather shook her hand and Tess continued her walk into Town, looking forward to talking more with Heather. Anything she could learn about Doris over the past few years would be a bonus. Minutes later she stood, open-mouthed, in Market Square gazing at the transformed old market and the rest of the area. The lovely old market building had been hijacked by, among others, a national clothes chain, a sports shop and a supermarket. Tess was horrified and began to understand why her local friends weren't happy with the result. It just wasn't Guernsey. No lovely stalls selling fresh produce, the smells tingling the senses as you walked around. Shopping here with her mother had always been a delight, never knowing what might be bought for dinner that night. A choice of fresh fish and shellfish competed with the offerings of the butchers, complemented by the colourful fruit and vegetable stalls.

In some ways it reminded her of Exeter centre, where the beautiful, medieval buildings jostled for space with the modern, characterless malls. She loved shopping there, it was a vibrant city, but this was dear old Guernsey. Keeping an eye on the time, Tess decided she could grab a coffee before her appointment and turned into Commercial Arcade, which, thankfully, looked as she remembered. Dix Neuf Bistro, which had seemed so sophisticated to her twelve-year-old self, was still in situ and she found an empty table by the window and ordered a latte. Shoppers and tourists walked past and Tess half-expected to see someone she recognised. But after twenty years realised it wasn't likely.

The coffee finished, Tess walked up High Street, which still had some shops she remembered, and at the top, by Boots, turned left into Smith Street and up to the small street housing several advocates' offices. Less than an hour later, she left the office with a bunch of keys for what was now her house, and various legal papers neatly collated in a file, together with a letter from a local property developer offering to buy the house. For quite a substantial sum. Much more than the cost of a similar property in Exeter. Tess would be able to pay off her mortgage and still have money over to buy a house instead of a flat. Apart from the value of the house, she had been surprised to learn her aunt had been a canny investor, amassing a decent sum of money from her shares when the advocate sold them. Tess was delighted, but at the same time wished Doris had spent money on herself and the house, *St Michel*. She could have lived out her days in comfort instead of what appeared to be near poverty. Taking a deep breath, Tess retraced her steps to Hauteville and *St Michel*.

'Oh my God!' Tess said out loud, surveying the entrance hall and stairs. It was worse than she remembered. The staircase, a once beautiful mahogany she guessed, was to the right and some of the spindles were missing, which wasn't a big deal, but piles of books on the treads almost blocked the way upstairs. In the narrow hall books were stacked along the wall and along what could be glimpsed of the panelling under the staircase. Wallpaper peeled off the walls and a strong, musty smell caught the back of her throat. The advocate had tried to warn her; he had been to the property shortly after Doris's death but had left after the briefest of visits.

'I'd known your aunt for several years, and she always insisted on coming to my office even when her legs were painful. She was never what you might call smartly dressed for someone of her means, but she was always clean and neat so I had no reason to expect what I found at the house.'

Tess opened the door on her left to the sitting room and found it had been converted to a bed-sitting room. The sofa had been replaced by a single bed but there was still an old armchair nearby facing a television. Everywhere else books and papers covered tables and chairs. Tess recognised the pervading air of sickness hanging in the room and had to gulp down tears for her aunt. Why hadn't she sought help? She could have afforded it. Easily. Must have been pride. And stubbornness. Tess wrenched at the sash window, managing to open it enough to let a small stream of fresh air mingle with the stale within. A door on the further wall led into what had been a dining room originally. The bay window looked out over the garden and towards the harbour and was a much lighter room. Again, books and papers were the main occupants, covering a large table groaning under their weight, and a couple of dining chairs. Tess struggled with the window and this time managed to push it up about a foot. The salty tang of sea air which rushed in provided a welcome relief.

Back in the hall, Tess opened the door to stairs leading down to the basement and the kitchen. She had been here as a child and found it a dark and dismal kitchen from the 1950s that would have horrified her mother who, wherever they lived, insisted on the latest gleaming kitchen of the moment. Switching on the light, she saw it hadn't changed. If anything, Tess thought it was worse. Two more decades of use had dulled the Formica units and worktops and caused cracks and splits to spread. The doors of the battered fridge stood open, revealing an empty interior, for which Tess was grateful. A modern electric cooker, about five years old, she guessed, looked out of place at the end of a run of units. A wooden kitchen table and chairs sat in the middle of the room and Tess checked the larder (empty) and the WC leading off. At the end of a dark passageway was the door to the garden and she unlocked it with the key hanging on a hook to the side.

The door was stiff and Tess wondered how long it had been since her aunt had ventured outside. Judging by the state of the garden, it had been some time, she thought, gazing at the overgrown grass looking more like a meadow than a lawn. Shrubs and weeds vied for space and over it all hung an air of neglect. She couldn't see a clear path to the bottom of the garden, about forty feet away, so she perched on a garden chair propped against the house. The garden sloped down to the end, allowing a sliver of sea to be visible beyond the houses in The Strand, the street running parallel below. Glad to have a chance of fresh air, Tess sat still, with her eyes closed, trying to imagine what the house and garden could look like if renovated. It proved difficult so she returned inside to see the rest of the house.

Watching her step as she negotiated the obstacles on the stairs, Tess made it to the landing and wasn't surprised to find overflowing book shelves between the bedroom doors. There were two double bedrooms at the front, but with only basic single beds and wardrobes in each. Surprisingly, no piles of books or papers but the rooms looked unused and unaired. At the back Tess found her aunt's room, a huge double with wonderful views over the harbour and islands from the bay window. The biggest surprise was the bed. It looked antique, a mahogany four-poster with a threadbare canopy and curtains. There was also a chest of drawers, bedside table and a chair. Opening a door, Tess found a deep cupboard used as a wardrobe, with only a few items hanging from the rail. The bedroom looked as if it hadn't been used for some time and dust caught in her nose and made her sneeze.

Tess had toyed with the idea of living in the house before any renovation, but now realised it was a non-starter, particularly after viewing the bathroom. Like the kitchen, it was in a time-warp, but of indeterminate age. Possibly pre-war, Tess thought, eyeing the loo with the high-rise cistern and bulbous pan; the cracked wash basin with taps rubbed clear of their original chrome finish; and the chipped enamel bath with taps matching those of the basin. All set against walls covered in yellowing paint which might once have been white and complemented by a brackish smell which left a metallic taste in her mouth. No, as temporary living went, it was far worse than any student accommodation she had lived in. She needed a plan B. Assuming she still wanted to live in Guernsey.

CHAPTER 7

Tess – April 2012

There were only a handful of mourners at the Foulon crematorium; hardly surprising, Tess thought as she sat in the front row with the others. She smiled at Heather Barker, accompanied by a man presumably her husband, and nodded at the advocate. A couple of women of indeterminate age sat further along. The service was brief and impersonal and Tess, a lump in her throat as she sang the final hymn, 'Abide with me', was upset that a long life could be so little acknowledged. The casket disappeared behind the curtains and she led the way out into the spring sun, ready to shake hands with her fellow mourners.

'Please accept my condolences. You must be a relative of Doris's?' one of the unknown women said, her hand outstretched.

'Yes, her great-niece. Thank you. And how did you know my aunt?'

'Maureen and I,' she said, indicating the other woman at her side, 'were taught by your aunt at the girls' grammar school. The old one, in Rosaire Avenue, in the sixties. Lovely woman she was, taught us history, didn't she, Maureen?' The other woman nodded. 'It's thanks to her I became passionate about history and went on to university, coming back to teach until I retired.'

Tess was touched.

'I'm so pleased you came and that you have fond memories of Doris.' She waved her hand at the emptiness. 'It's sad to see so few here, but at her age, I suppose her friends have passed on.' The woman nodded and she and her friend moved away.

Tess turned to see Heather Barker waiting with her husband, introduced as Neil. He shook hands, then excused himself, saying he had to return to work.

'What are you doing now, Tess? I thought we might go to my place and have a cup of tea or something stronger, if you like. Unless you'd rather go somewhere else?'

'I'd love to, thanks. I wasn't looking forward to being on my own after…' she gestured towards the chapel.

'Understandable. I've got my car so let's go.'

Ten minutes later Heather was ushering Tess inside her house, a mirror image of her aunt's. Except inside it was anything but.

'This is lovely, Heather. Was it like this when you bought it?' Tess stood in the hallway, admiring the polished mahogany staircase, the treads carpeted in a soft green to tone with the painted walls hung with a mix of paintings and photos. A console table bore a vase of stylishly arranged flowers and a couple of small ornaments. The wooden doors gleamed as if freshly waxed.

'Kind of. We made some changes to make it more us. Come on, let's go through and I'll show you around later. I think we need a drink first, yes?'

Tess followed her into the sitting room, opened up to the back, offering a view of the sea even from the door. The room was painted in soft cream and traditionally furnished with a polished wood floor. Heather waved her to a chair in the far window, saying, 'Tea? Or a glass of wine? And I have cake.'

Tess chose a glass of white wine and Heather disappeared to the kitchen, leaving her to soak up the vastly different atmosphere of the room compared to the one next door. At least it showed her how it could be. Calm and elegant and so much lighter with the middle wall removed.

'Here we are. I know it's a bit early for wine, but, hey, this is Guernsey! And it's traditional after a funeral, isn't it?' Heather said, depositing a tray bearing cake, glasses and a chilled bottle of wine on the adjoining table. She poured two large glasses of wine, saying, 'Always keep a bottle in the fridge. There, let's toast Doris, may she rest in peace.'

Tess clinked glasses and took a sip, admiring the smooth taste of a quality Chardonnay.

'Thanks, I needed that. I hadn't realised how tense I was until now. It's been a full-on day.' She let out a deep breath and let the wine begin its work of relaxation.

Heather's eyes narrowed.

'I can imagine. I gather you haven't been back since you were a child? Doris told me you were reluctant to leave the island.'

Tess told her how her parents, particularly her mother, were ambitious and felt Guernsey wasn't big enough for them to achieve what they wanted. Which was a big house, good income and easy access to London and the cultural life missing on the island.

'Dad was a policeman and managed to get a transfer to Exeter and Mum was an office manager who soon found a new job in the city. Clive, my brother, and I hated leaving, but had no say in it.' She sipped more wine and Heather offered her a slice of carrot cake.

'Homemade. I'm not the greatest cook, but I can make a decent cake,' she said, passing over a plate.

Tess took a bite. 'Delicious, thanks. Are you a Guern, Heather?'

'No, 'fraid not. Neil and I are here for his job. He's in finance and we moved here from London for the more relaxed lifestyle and have loved every minute of it. In effect, we've done the opposite of your parents, but we do spend several weekends a year back in London, catching up with friends and seeing the latest plays.'

'Sounds a good mix. What about your children? Did they mind moving?'

Heather frowned.

'We never had any, so no problem there. I can understand how hard it must have been for you and your brother. Leaving friends behind.'

Tess could have kicked herself. By the look on Heather's face, not having children wasn't her decision. Infertility problems? Neil not want them? Sad, whatever the reason. She judged Heather to be in her forties so it was too late now.

'It was. I was twelve and about to start my second year at grammar school so it hit me harder than Clive in junior school.

I'm thinking about coming back now I've inherited my aunt's house, but it's a big decision.'

Heather smiled, lifting her glass.

'Well, I'll drink to that. Would be lovely to have you as a neighbour, although I'd imagine it needs a lot of work. I've only ever been in the hall but...' she shrugged.

'It's awful and I was beginning to think I might be mad to consider it. But, now I've seen your house I can see it could be equally as gorgeous. Depending on the cost.' Tess pursed her lips. The million dollar question. 'How did you get on with my aunt? She was pretty much a recluse, wasn't she?'

'Yes, I hardly ever saw her outside the house. She managed to walk down to the supermarket until about a year ago, then her legs got worse and I and another neighbour would buy her groceries for her. Before that, she wouldn't accept any help from anyone. Fiercely independent. To be honest,' Heather hesitated, 'when we moved in, I was unhappy about having such an...eccentric old lady next door. She was rumoured to be a bit,' she twirled a finger at her head, 'but she was one of the sanest people I've met. Eccentric and reclusive, yes, but on the ball. Not that we talked a great deal in the early years, just the occasional greeting as we met in the street.'

'What changed?'

Heather topped up their glasses and Tess relaxed back in the chair, happy to learn more about Doris.

'Old age, really. She became so frail and had to sleep downstairs, only managing the steps down to the kitchen and the old loo. I had noticed Doris hadn't been out for a while so popped round and was shocked by how thin she was. She admitted not being able to shop anymore so I took round a cooked meal and some essentials like bread and milk. When she was a bit stronger she came round for a cup of tea and cake and she would talk to me about the past.' Heather bit her lips. 'I became quite fond of her, she reminded me of my late grandmother. People of that age have such stories to tell, don't they?'

Tess nodded.

'Did Doris ever mention the family connection to Victor Hugo?'

'Oh, yes. Exciting stuff, if it's true. Fancy being the whatever-great-granddaughter of such a famous man!' She laughed.

'Not everyone in the family believes it and, to be honest, I'm not convinced until I see some proof. That's the scientist in me talking. The romantic part is happy to daydream. We know Eugénie *did* work for Hugo, so that part's true. It's whether or not, you know...' Tess grinned.

'Well, he was a bit of a skirt chaser, by all accounts, even though his mistress lived a few doors down from us. You've seen it, I suppose? *Le Faerie?*'

'Yes, Doris told me. She thought it hugely amusing that the two "mistresses" should live so close to each other.' Glancing at a nearby clock, Tess saw it was nearly five thirty and guessed Neil would soon be home. 'I should go, but could I see the rest of the house first? To help visualise what mine could become.' She drained her glass and stood.

'Of course, and you must pop back before you leave.' Heather led the way downstairs to a modern, glossy kitchen which segued into a conservatory, bringing light and airiness into what, Tess was only too well aware, would have been a dark and depressing space. After admiring this, and the immaculate garden laid to lawn and shrubs, and bursting with spring flowers, they went upstairs to the bedroom floor. Again, the layout was the same as next door, but beautifully decorated and furnished and somehow an en suite had been squeezed in to the master bedroom. By the time they arrived at the top floor, the old attics, Tess was considering what she could copy in her own house. Her head buzzed with ideas. There were two bedrooms on the top floor, sharing a small shower-room, and with even more far-reaching views over the sea and islands than the other floors.

'This is amazing, Heather. Your home is gorgeous and it makes me feel more positive about doing up mine. At the moment it's in dire need of fresh air and a clear-out and not suitable for visitors let alone occupation,' Tess said, as they returned to the downstairs hall.

'I'd imagined it would be as poor Doris was almost bed-bound near the end.' She sighed. 'Not the way to go, is it?'

39

Tess shook her head. 'No, but I do appreciate all you did for her. It was kind of you.'

'No problem. Now, remember to call round, won't you? More wine and cake,' Heather said, with a grin.

'Will do.'

They parted on the doorstep and Tess strode uphill towards the hotel, giving Hauteville House a wistful look. Maybe, if she were to take up residence in what had been Eugénie's home, she would discover what really happened between her and Hugo. If anything had.

❧ CHAPTER 8 ❧

Eugénie's Diary – Guernsey March 1862

The day before I returned home, M'sieur Hugo's gardener, Henri, dug a grave for my child, named Arnaud after my lost husband. My heart was heavy as I left *La Fallue*, knowing I would miss the motherly ministrations of m'dame and Suzanne. They accompanied me on the short walk to my house and stayed with me when baby Arnaud was placed in the ground. M'dame had kindly commissioned a carpenter to fashion a small oak coffin to hold his tiny body and we stood arm in arm while he was laid to rest under a eucalyptus tree at the bottom of the garden. No words were spoken. I said a silent prayer and placed a camellia bud on top of the little box before Henri took a shovel to the small pile of earth and quickly filled in my son's grave. Clouds scudded across the pale blue sky and a breeze caused me to shudder, pulling my shawl tighter around my body.

'There now, you've been very brave, my dear, and I suggest we go inside and you must have a hot drink. Suzanne will make us some coffee; she has brought some along especially,' M'dame Drouet said, taking my arm and guiding me towards the back door. 'If you can provide a list of provisions needed, Suzanne will purchase them from the market for you as she is also going on my behalf.'

I thanked her, grateful that I wouldn't have to face the enquiring, and perhaps pitying, looks of others quite yet. We settled in the kitchen where Suzanne had already fired up the range, which offered some warmth after the outside chill. The coffee, thick and strong, seemed to race through my veins, bringing a much-needed energy to my weary body. I gazed around at my neglected kitchen, uncared for since the news of Arnaud's death. Like the rest of the house. Shame washed over me as I wondered what m'dame would think. She looked up from her cup and smiled.

'You have a fine house here, my dear, but I can see you may find it difficult to cope on your own at the moment. Suzanne,' she nodded to her maid, wiping over the range, 'knows of a local girl from a large family in need of work who wants to leave home and is said to be a hard worker. You wouldn't need to offer much of a wage beyond her bed and board. Would it suit you to see her?'

I thought quickly. With the little left of our savings and my new income as a copyist, I should be able to support a maid if I lived quietly. As the wife of an officer from a good family, it wasn't seemly for me to be without domestic help. Why, even my mother had had a maid, though she expected us girls to do our fair share around the house.

'It would indeed, m'dame, as long as she is a fair cook. My own abilities in that department are a little limited, I confess.' I glanced across at Suzanne.

'Oh, Sophie's a good little cook, she is. Her mother, a friend of mine, has taught her well and she's eager to practise her skills in her own kitchen, so to speak.' Suzanne crossed her hands over her own ample stomach and I wondered if she'd sampled the girl's cooking.

'In that case, please arrange for her to come around tomorrow at ten and if she's as suitable as you say, she can start immediately.' The thought of having someone to take on the housework and also to keep me company was cheering. The house was large, spread over three storeys, and I rattled around it like a single pea in a pod.

'Excellent!' M'dame exclaimed. 'You will be able to spend more time helping m'sieur with his manuscripts, which will please us both.' She toyed with her cup, looking hesitant. 'Would you be willing to start later this week? I know you aren't entirely well, but—'

'That would suit me, m'dame. I think being busy at such a great undertaking will take my mind away from…unpleasant thoughts. I am eager to repay you both for your kindnesses as soon as possible.' My hand went involuntarily to my almost flat stomach and I had to stifle a sob. My mother had drummed into me how the best cure for overcoming upsets of any kind was to keep busy at a task which allowed no time for brooding. I was beginning to understand how right she was.

M'dame Drouet stood, brushing down her dress, a dark mauve in keeping with the sad event of the morning.

'I'll tell M'sieur Hugo you are happy to start soon and will call around tomorrow. Don't forget to give Suzanne your list for the market. Goodbye, my dear.' She gave me a hug and kissed my cheek as she left and I duly sat and wrote my list and gave it to the maid with the appropriate francs. After she'd gone I huddled by the range, suddenly alone and missing the warmth and security of Arnaud's strong arms around me. His smile. His kisses. The tears flowed unheeded, held in over the past days spent at M'dame Drouet's. The emptiness and silence of the house to which Arnaud had brought me only a year ago as his wife, was in stark contrast to that day, when he spun me around the parlour, showering me with kisses. We had been full of plans and hopes.

'Another three or four years and I'll leave my ship and look for something based ashore. There will always be opportunities for experienced officers to run an import or export company. In fact I was approached only the other day by a wine importer.' We sat embraced on the chaise, still in our wedding finery.

'Why did you not take the offer? I can think of nothing better than having you here beside me every day.'

Arnaud curled his fingers in mine.

'Don't doubt that I feel the same, my darling. But if I stay in the navy a few more years, I'll have saved up a goodly sum for our future. Shore jobs are less well-paid and I want you and our children to have the best. It will pass soon enough and then you will complain I am under your feet too much!' he laughed and I joined in with him, happy my new husband was intent on securing a comfortable future for us. And I would have our children to keep me busy...

The tears finally dried, leaving me exhausted and with an ache in my belly. I forced myself to get up and fill the dying range with wood before splashing my face with cold water. Suzanne wouldn't be much longer and I didn't want her reporting to her mistress that I was a tearful wreck. My eyes swept around the room, taking in the large old table in the middle, scrubbed and pock-marked with many years of use. Only the servants would have eaten here, the family ate in the formal dining room upstairs, so Arnaud told me. Shelves held the china while pots and pans hung from the hooks hanging off a large pole above my head. The pantry was off to the side, kept cool with tiles and marble shelves. On my own I had gravitated to the kitchen more than the parlour, glad of its warmth and the comfort of the old chair placed such that one could warm one's feet by the bottom oven. Old Mrs Sarchet, Arnaud's mother, had two live-in servants, a maid and a cook, and seldom ventured down to the kitchen, he said. She was a gentlewoman, brought up in a grand house in St Martins and considered to have married beneath her when she became Mrs Sarchet. Arnaud told me it was a love match, and his parents adored one another. His father was a popular doctor who could have been wealthier if he hadn't spent some of his time attending to the poor of St Peter Port. But he had done well enough to build this house and have his son educated at Elizabeth College. Arnaud was an only child and his father expected him to become a doctor and was disappointed when he refused.

'I told him I had the greatest respect for medicine, but didn't consider myself cut out to be a doctor. I had loved the sea since a child and wanted nothing more than to sail on the latest ships that put into St Peter Port harbour.' Arnaud's eyes were shining with an inner passion as he told me this on one of our walks early in our courtship. Needless to say, he had headed for the harbour, eagerly pointing out the steam ships newly arrived from England. His own ship sailed out of Southampton and made trips to the Mediterranean ports, loading and unloading a mixture of goods, including olive oil, wine, leather goods, exchanging for British manufactured iron and steel goods.

Although he had been away weeks at a time I survived, only feeling lonely in the evenings. And at night in our big four-poster bed. We bought a new mattress and I enjoyed sewing new bed linen and making a bright patchwork quilt to brighten up what had been a dark bedroom. Sometimes Arnaud brought back mementoes of his travels and the house was dotted with beautiful blue glazed vases, hand-painted Greek pottery, colourful Maltese glass and embroidered linen from Spain. The thought of his lovely gifts propelled me up the stairs to the dining room where they brought splashes of colour to the oak dresser. I found myself stroking each of his gifts, chosen with such love and care. Tears threatened to fall, but I hastily wiped them away with another of his gifts; a fine linen handkerchief from France. Taking a deep breath, I resolved to control my emotions or I would be in no fit state to work for M'sieur Hugo.

Suzanne returned with my provisions, giving me a keen look as I followed her to the kitchen, offering to make me a hot drink. I said I was fine and would rest for a while. With that she left, promising to call in the next day on the way to Market Street to check if I was in need of anything. I took myself upstairs to my bedroom. The dimness of the room suited my mood. Thick, heavy clouds obscured the sun and I drew the curtains even though it was only midday. The room was chill but I had no energy to light a fire and crept under the sheets in my underclothes and closed my eyes, intending to enjoy a short nap.

It was early the next morning when I awoke and the long sleep left me refreshed – and hungry. After washing and dressing I went down to the kitchen, putting more wood in the range, which was close to going out. The loud ticking of the clock was the only sound as I moved around, setting out bread, butter and cheese and heating the water for coffee. I lingered over the meal, drinking more coffee to warm and revive me. There was more than an hour before the girl Sophie would arrive and I planned to test her abilities by setting such tasks as lighting fires in the drawing room and my bedroom and preparing soup from the ingredients bought by Suzanne. My energy was still not what it was and the doctor had warned me it would take time to return to full strength after such a difficult birth and loss of blood.

At ten on the dot a loud knock at the door proclaimed the arrival of Sophie Le Clerc. Her appearance was encouraging. Of average height and build, a round, open face and smiling brown eyes, she was dressed plainly in a green woollen dress and brown cloak. I led the way to the kitchen to begin my interrogation. Sophie shuffled on her chair, twisting her gloved hands, but appeared to relax as I asked the questions.

'I'm sixteen, m'dame, and I believe I have the right skills to be useful as a maid. My mother taught me how to cook and clean and I've often run errands for her in Town. I promise I'll work hard and you'd find me honest.'

She spoke French with a local accent, but I was used to this after two years on the island.

'Good. Can you read and write?'

She beamed.

'Oh, yes. I attended the local parish school and was praised for my letters and sums.'

After verifying for myself that the girl could indeed complete these tasks satisfactorily, I set her to making the soup, and took a taste, which was delicious. I then offered her the position of general maid and cook and she happily accepted my terms. Then I showed her around the house, explaining what would need doing in each room and then took her up to the attic and the servants' quarters. To my eye the rooms were poky and poorly furnished but Sophie declared herself content.

'It will be wonderful to have my own room, m'dame. At home I have to share with my two younger sisters and they're a right nuisance, I can tell you.' She sighed deeply.

For the first time in a while I found myself smiling.

'I sympathise as I had to share with my sisters, also.' I sensed that in Sophie I had found a girl I could relate to and would be a friend as well as my maid. 'Please feel free to bring what you wish from your home to make it more amenable to you. Come, let's go downstairs, it's chilly up here. There's coal for the fires stored outside. I'll show you.'

After showing Sophie the garden and coal-store we agreed she would start the following day. Her father, a farmer in St Martins, would bring her into Town in his cart with what belongings she needed. After Sophie left, offering a cheery wave, I headed back to the kitchen which would be my domain for only a little longer. As I poured Sophie's soup into a bowl, my heart felt lighter. Not only was I soon to begin working for such a person as M'sieur Hugo, but I would have a companion and helper at home. My life, so bleak only days before, was surely set to improve.

❧ CHAPTER 9 ❧

Tess – April 2012

Exhausted, Tess had an early night after a quick supper in the hotel bar. She woke on Saturday morning with her mind replaying the events of the previous day and her stomach crying out for sustenance. Showered and dressed, she went downstairs to the dining room to satisfy the hunger while she sifted through her thoughts. Two priorities emerged: making a start on decluttering the house while tackling the rubbish and arranging to catch up with a friend from school for an update on Guernsey life. Black sacks, boxes and Marigolds were needed for the first and going through her Facebook friends for the second.

Back in her room Tess logged into Facebook and the first name to jump out at her was Colette Simon, previously Mauger. They had been friends since primary school and both went on to the grammar school. Tess remembered she had a gorgeous older brother, Nick, who was now, according to Facebook, married with a family. Tess messaged Colette to say she was on the island and could they meet. She then grabbed the keys to her house and walked down to the Co-op in the market to buy what she needed. Back at the house she opened doors and windows on all floors to create a much-needed flow of fresh air. The first task was filling the sacks with obvious rubbish and stacking them outside. While in the middle of this her phone rang. Colette.

'Hi, it's great to hear from you. How are you?'

'Good, thanks and I've so much to tell you! Would you like to come round for supper tonight and meet Jonathan, my hubby?'

'Love to. Can you text your address and I'll get a taxi. I'm staying in Town.'

'Sure, no problem. How about seven thirty?'

Tess agreed and seconds later Colette's address pinged through. She smiled, looking forward to catching up with her friend. Turning back to her task, Tess carried on filling bin bags as she tried not to inhale the stale air clinging to every surface, including, she feared, her hair and clothes. Once the basement was cleared she tackled the ground floor. Here, the problem wasn't as much rubbish as too many piles of books, magazines and papers, which needed boxes. She was on the way upstairs when the doorbell rang. Thinking it must be Heather, she opened the door with a broad smile and a welcome 'Hi' on her lips. Her smile faded as she took in the stranger on the doorstep.

'Can I help you?' she asked, conscious she must not only look dusty but probably smelled.

'I'm looking for a Miss Le Prevost. Is she in?' The man, tall and muscular, flashed a smile at her.

'You've found *Doctor* Le Prevost. And you are…?'

'Oh, I'm sorry, *Doctor* Le Prevost. I expected someone older, Miss Guilbert's niece and heir.' He looked less sure of himself. 'My name's Jack Renouf, I contacted your aunt's advocate about…'

'Offering to buy my property, I know. She was my great-aunt by the way. I'm afraid, Mr Renouf, this house isn't for sale, so you've wasted your journey. Although why you should think I'd be here now, I can't imagine.' Tess was annoyed, hating to be taken unawares by what she thought of as a coffin-chaser. Had the man no scruples? She was about to shut the door when he pushed his foot forward, stopping the door closing.

'I'm sorry if I've annoyed you by turning up like this, but I happened to be driving past and saw all the windows open. I knew the funeral was yesterday and guessed you might be in the house. I thought it wouldn't hurt to introduce myself.'

Tess clocked the dark green Range Rover in the street.

'The answer is still no, Mr Renouf. I'm planning to live in the house once it's…habitable.' Thinking of the mess behind her, Tess wondered if she was mad, but wasn't going to give this man the satisfaction of knowing that. She pulled herself up straight and fixed him with a glare known to unnerve young medical students.

He removed his foot and stepped back.

'In that case, Doctor Le Prevost, I'll leave you to carry on your…cleaning. But here's my card, in case you change your mind.' He proffered the card, tilting his head as if to challenge her.

Tess grabbed it and closed the door. How dare he! Not even bothering to offer condolences, just keen to make a deal. At least she'd surprised him by being young and intelligent enough to not be sweet-talked into selling. He'd probably imagined a niece to be a pensioner and only too keen to take the money. Energised by the encounter, she shoved the card in her pocket and continued upstairs to tackle the rest of the house.

Once she had gone through the bedrooms and bathroom she took the stairs to the attic, not having seen it the previous day. She was surprised to find two proper rooms, probably used for servants in Victorian times. They were virtually empty, with only a couple of boxes holding old clothes and broken household gadgets. The air was heavy and musty and Tess forced the cobwebbed windows open. Dust motes danced in the weak sunlight highlighting the cobwebs arched across the exposed beams. Tess waved her arms about to forge a way through. A single bare bulb hung from the ceiling in each room, offering a faint light but leaving the corners in shadow. Heaving a sigh, she stuffed the contents of the boxes into bin bags and returned downstairs, badly in need of fresh air.

In the garden she surveyed what was in reality a jungle and slumped onto the chair. The sickly smell of the house still filled her nostrils and cobwebs clung to her clothes and she had barely touched the surface of what needed doing. Her plan had been to clear the rubbish then pack all the books, magazines and anything that appeared important into boxes which could be stored somewhere for checking when she had time. Then assess what to do with the furniture. Some might be worth keeping, like the four-poster and the big table downstairs, but most would need to be dumped. Tess hated to think what it would cost to pay someone to do this, but what choice did she have? Any prospective builders would want a clear space to view before offering quotes. And how long would it take her to sift through all the packed boxes? She groaned. It was a nightmare.

Forcing herself to go back inside, Tess grabbed a pen and paper and made a note of all the moveable furniture in each room, highlighting anything worth keeping. As she had thought, not a lot. She also needed boxes, and lots of them and went next door to see if Heather could help.

'My! I assume you've started a clear-out,' Heather said, gently removing a cobweb from Tess's hair.

'Yes, and it's a thankless task. I'm trying to pack up the books and stuff piled everywhere, you don't have any boxes do you?' She stood on the doorstep, not wanting to pollute Heather's clean and polish-scented home.

'As it happens, we kept a load after we moved in and they're stacked in Neil's shed at the bottom of the garden.' She eyed Tess and grinned. 'Best if you stay there and I'll ask him to fetch them.'

'Thanks, you're a star.' Tess perched on the low boundary wall while she waited, thinking she seemed to have struck lucky with her neighbours. Assuming she did make the move. There was so much to sort out before that could happen, including a job. Just a minor problem, she told herself, pulling more cobwebs from her hair and T-shirt. She was roused from her task by the sight of Neil appearing at the door with a pile of flattened boxes and a roll of tape.

Like Heather, he grinned at her appearance and offered to carry the boxes round for her, saying there were more in the hall.

'No, thanks, I'll manage. Just leave them there and I'll do it in two trips. Do you have the number of the removal firm in case I need more, please?'

Neil wrote it on one of the boxes before carrying out the second load and calling 'Good luck' as she took a load to her house and stacked them in the sitting room. Once she had all the boxes stacked, Tess taped a few ready to start filling them after she'd had a break for lunch. Time for the 'meal deal' from the Co-op and another spot of fresh air. It wasn't long before she was back and keen to fill the boxes. As she was packing books, Tess noticed there were a large number either by or about Victor Hugo and it dawned on her Doris must have been fixated on him. Not sure whether this was a good or bad thing, she continued before focusing on papers and newspapers, not wanting to make the boxes too heavy to lift. It seemed Doris had kept every issue of the *Guernsey Evening Press* for years, and Tess decided to recycle them unless the headlines suggested otherwise. Black sacks soon began to fill with them and she set them outside, separate from the rubbish. It was a wonder the house had never caught fire, Tess thought, glancing at the open fireplace, one of many through the house. Without central heating it must have been difficult to keep warm in such a large house. Even though it was a mild day, now Tess was sitting still she felt the chill in the air.

Over the next two hours she made good progress packing books and throwing out old newspapers, and slower progress with sifting through reams of papers which were a mix of handwritten notes and printed sheets of references, both in English and French, relating to Guernsey and French history. Tess's initial inclination was to bin the lot, but she held back, wondering if, together, they would explain what Doris had been researching, and for what purpose. She might need an historian to check them out before scrapping them. Local parish magazines and various organisations' newsletters were also in the mix and these she had no qualms about binning.

By mid-afternoon Tess called it a day. Her back ached, her head ached and all she wanted to do was have a hot shower and change into clean clothes which didn't reek of musty, ill-smelling houses. Easing herself up from the floor, she stretched and surveyed the room. Most of the books were now in stacked boxes with the kept papers and she had a clearer view of what the room could look like. The bed had been stripped of the stained bedding, now in a bin bag with the rubbish, and the room smelt slightly fresher than it had hours earlier. Result. As Tess went round closing all the windows on the ground floor, but leaving the ones higher up open, she hoped Guernsey still enjoyed a low rate of burglaries. The thought then crossed her mind that if a burglar were to come and empty the place, it would do her a favour. Smiling, she locked the front door and retraced her steps to the Pandora.

'Hi, how are you? You haven't changed a bit!' Colette beamed at Tess as she opened the door.

'I'm good, thanks. And you…you're pregnant! Congratulations.' Tess smiled at her friend who, being short, looked especially rotund at her obviously advanced stage. Eight months, she guessed.

'Thanks. We're thrilled, particularly Jonathan, poor lamb, who's hitting the big four-oh this year and desperate to be a dad before then.' Colette giggled, giving Tess a hug before ushering her inside.

The house, a traditional Guernsey cottage in Rue de Bordeaux, was near where Colette had lived as a child and not far from Tess's old family home. It was as if the years since she'd left had melted away and they were giggling schoolgirls again. Laughing, they linked arms as Colette led the way to a modern conservatory facing a large garden mainly given over to lawn. As they entered the room, a tall, bespectacled man rose from an armchair and came forward, a broad smile on his face.

'Hi, Tess, I'm Jonathan and very pleased to meet you. Colette's been bursting with excitement since you got in touch so you must be someone special.' He kissed her cheek and she saw the dance of laughter in his eyes.

'I don't know about special, but we were great friends as children and as we haven't seen each other for yonks, we've a lot of catching up to do,' Tess said, grinning at Colette, who punched her husband playfully on the arm.

'I'll leave you to it as I'm in charge of the kitchen this evening, to give Colette a break. Dinner should be ready in about thirty minutes.' Jonathan kissed the top of his wife's head and left.

'Make yourself comfortable and I'll get you a drink. Wine okay? I'm stuck with juice, thanks to this,' Colette pulled a face as she patted her bump. 'Can't risk even a little glass with two doctors in the house, can I?'

'Oh, Jonathan's a doctor, too? I didn't know. And wine's fine thanks, dry white if you have it.' Tess couldn't help thinking he might be a useful contact.

'All my local friends know he is, so I assume everyone knows,' Colette said, pulling a bottle of white wine and a carton of juice from a small bar fridge in the corner. 'We met years ago as he's a friend of my brother, Nick, but we didn't start going out until I split with Scott and Jonathan was also single.' She poured a glass of wine for Tess before filling her own glass with juice and sitting down awkwardly on a nearby chair. 'I feel like a beached whale now, and there's a month to go. Men get the easy bit, don't they?' She grinned at Tess.

'Sure do, but there's nothing to beat knowing you have a little person growing inside you. Or so I've been told,' Tess replied, a little wistfully.

'Ah, no-one special around at the moment?'

'No, I've given the latest his marching orders and now I'm young, free and single again.'

'Well, if you do return here to live, which would be fantastic, I'll have to draw up a list of eligible guys.' She screwed up her face, then giggled. 'Can't think of any at the moment, but give me time.' Colette sipped her juice, looking enviously at Tess's wine. 'What's the house like? Able to move in?'

Tess shook her head.

'It's a mess. Doris hadn't touched it for years…' she went on to describe what she had found and Colette's jaw dropped.

'Oh dear, that sounds as if it needs masses of dosh spending on it. Like my brother Nick's place. Although actually it was his wife Jeanne's cottage, inherited from her grandmother. It's gorgeous now with the most fab garden, down in Perelle. I–' she was interrupted by Jonathan sticking his head round the door to announce dinner was ready. He came in to help her out of the chair and Tess followed them into the dining room, next to the kitchen and overlooking the side garden.

'Love the flower arrangements. I guess that's your department, Colette?' Tess sniffed the delicate bowls of freesias on the table, set among sparkling plates and cutlery.

Colette eased herself into a chair, beckoning Tess to sit beside her while Jonathan ferried in the food.

'It's about all I feel like doing at the moment. I'm mentally and physically well below par and I think my staff were glad to see the back of me this week. I hired a new chef to cover for me while I'm away but I'll pop in every day to keep an eye on everything.' She sighed. 'You know, starting up my restaurant was a lot easier than being pregnant, even though it was a huge gamble and I had to work eighty-hour weeks.'

Tess patted her arm.

'Hey, it's normal to feel like this in the last weeks. You'll get back to your usual dynamic self once the baby's born. And sleeping through the night,' she added, with a grin.

'That's what I've told her, Tess, but it doesn't cheer her up,' Jonathan said, bringing in the final dish.

Colette rolled her eyes.

'Honestly, two flippin' doctors! What chance do I have? Shall we eat and you can tell us all about what you've been up to, Tess.'

They piled up their plates with chicken casserole, mash and vegetables and as they ate Tess gave them a short version of her life since qualifying.

'I decided early on I wanted to be a GP and have nearly finished my hospital training prior to taking up a post in a medical practice.' She paused, and took a sip of wine. 'Now that I've inherited a house here, it's made me think about looking for a post here. What do you think, Jonathan?'

He had been looking thoughtful as she spoke and Tess hoped he wasn't going to pour cold water on her hopes. Without a job she couldn't come back. Her stomach clenched at the unwelcome thought.

'Well, I think your timing might be fortuitous. I'm at the St Sampson Medical Practice and one of my colleagues is due to retire in about three months. We'd ultimately be looking for a new partner, but might be prepared to take on a newly qualified doctor on a trial basis, with the option to become a partner later. It's a plus that you're local and we don't have to faff with housing licences.' He smiled at her. 'I'd have to check with my partners, of course, but would you be interested if everyone agreed?'

Her stomach turned over. Would she be interested! She'd be mad not to be.

'You bet! I've got two months to complete in A & E in Exeter and then I'm free. Oh, thanks, Jonathan, this could be wonderful.' She gave him her brightest smile.

Colette looked from one to the other of them, her eyes shining in excitement.

'Wow! I can hardly believe it. I'd hoped you two would become friends, but I never thought of you working together.'

'Nothing's agreed yet, darling, so don't get too excited. We'll need to see your CV, Tess,' he said, turning to her, 'and then, if the partners are happy, we'll arrange an interview. Are you coming back soon?'

'In a couple of weeks. I need to sort out a builder for the work on the house so if you have one of those up your sleeve as well...' she laughed.

'Well, I don't but our friend Andy knows the best builders. He's an architect and would be useful for you to meet anyway. Give you some ideas about your house.'

'Ooh, yes, Andy's lovely, and so is his wife, Charlotte. They have a little boy and we've become great friends. In fact there's a bunch of people I can introduce you to if – when – you move back.'

Tess, swept away by Colette's enthusiasm, was already imagining herself enjoying a vibrant social life on the island. Her long and unsociable hours as a hospital doctor had meant a fragmented personal life, hence the lack of a serious relationship. Few men were prepared to play second fiddle to her work. And she couldn't blame them. But here, in Guernsey, as a GP, all that would change and a bubble of excitement welled up inside her.

'All this sounds marvellous and I can't wait!' She smiled at Jonathan. 'I'll email my CV to you on Tuesday. I'm here until Monday late afternoon and it would be great to meet Andy before I leave.'

'I'll call him tomorrow morning and ask him to get in touch with you asap. Right, has everyone finished? There's pudding if you have room.' He stood and began collecting the plates as the girls said they'd finished and would like some pud.

The rest of the evening was an enjoyable mix of good food, wine and company for Tess and she realised she hadn't enjoyed herself as much for months. It helped that she wouldn't have to get up at the crack of dawn the next day and work a twelve-hour shift. Although whether that was worse than clearing through Doris's accumulated stuff was debateable. But as she waved goodnight to her friends before slipping into the taxi, Tess was hopeful her life was about to change. As long as she passed muster with the local medical practice.

CHAPTER 10

Tess – Guernsey April 2012

Tess opened her eyes and groaned. The bedside clock said it was seven o'clock and she had planned a lie-in. But once awake it was hard to go back to sleep. Her active mind wouldn't allow it. She pulled herself up in the bed and yawned. At least she would have more time at the house, she thought, in an effort to see the bright side. Still yawning, she padded across to the window and peeked outside. Light clouds hid the sun, but at least it was dry and mild. While in the shower Tess went over the previous evening's meal and the promising outcome. Possible architect/builder and even better, possible job. The thought made her smile and banished the last traces of tiredness. Things to do and people to see, and all that jazz.

A full English breakfast completed the transformation to eager clearer of dusty, clutter-filled houses and Tess set off briskly down the road towards the house. Her house. It still felt strange to call it that, and she sent up thanks to her aunt. Had she known Tess needed something to jolt her out of her old life? Or was that a fanciful thought? Ever the scientist, she was wary of anything psychic, but Doris had had a reputation, according to her mother, of being a 'white witch'. Her mother had preferred the epithet 'mad'. Islanders were drawn to stories of witches, fairies and ghosts and Tess had read, wide-eyed, a couple of books on Guernsey folklore as a child, given her by Doris, which had caused her a few sleepless nights. Once living in England, she had put such 'foolishness' as her mother called it, behind her. Now, approaching her front door, the old memories stirred and Tess remembered what Elaine had said about the house being considered unlucky. Telling herself it was only her mother's annoyance at being overlooked by Doris, she unlocked the door and went in.

The trapped air still smelt musty but not as sickly as it had, which was a relief. Once she had opened the downstairs windows, there was a welcome draught of fresh air and Tess eyed the remaining piles of books and papers in the dining room with less hostility than the previous day. She only had a few boxes left and once they were full she planned to sift through the papers in more detail, looking for she knew not what. But there must be something here, surely? Connecting her to Eugénie? Tess was engrossed in trying to decipher her aunt's scribblings when her mobile echoed around the room.

'Hi, Tess speaking.'

'Hello, Tess, Andy Batiste. Jonathan asked me to call you. Is this a good time?'

'It's fine, thanks for calling. Jonathan's told you about my house?'

'Yep, and actually I worked on a similar property in Hauteville a few years ago. You're a lucky woman, they're great houses.'

Tess grinned as she looked at the state of the room she was in.

'I hope this can be, it's not at its best at the moment. Would you be free to come round and give me some advice, please? Tomorrow, ideally.'

'Sure, no problem. Shall we say nine thirty?'

'Great. See you then.' Tess clicked off her phone, relieved she was going to have professional advice. She then dialled Colette's number to thank her for the dinner and to say Andy had called. Then it was back to the sorting and filling more bin bags with rubbish.

By mid-afternoon Tess had had enough. Without more boxes she was limited in what she could achieve anyway, she told herself. The sun had finally made an appearance and it was time to get out for a walk and breathe the ozone-laden air instead of the musty, stale air of the house. Once outside she took a deep breath before heading down towards Cornet Street and the harbour. There was hardly anyone about when she reached the front and for a moment Tess wondered why. Then she remembered. It was Sunday! And Guernsey was closed on Sundays. Or as good as. Shops, restaurants and cafés offered silent windows as she walked past and she could only hope there would be a café somewhere for a cup of coffee. In compensation she had the area around the harbour virtually to herself and she enjoyed strolling around the Albert Pier and looking at the few visitors' boats moored alongside. A gentle breeze carried the invigorating smell of the sea and Tess felt her shoulders relax. She then set off around Havelet Bay towards the bathing pools and the iconic Half-Moon café she remembered from her childhood, perched on the edge of the bay with one of the best views of the area. With a bit of luck they would be open and as she drew nearer the parked cars outside made her smile. Minutes later she was inside, coffee in hand and gazing out at Castle Cornet and the islands beyond. A close-up of the view from her house. She let out a deep sigh of satisfaction. Yes, she was coming home. And not before time.

The next day Tess was on the phone to the removal company ordering a delivery of boxes when the doorbell rang. She finished the call, confirming a load would be dropped off within the hour, and went to open the door.

'Hi, I'm Andy. And you must be Tess?' A tall, slim man in his early forties smiled at her.

'Yes, do come in.' She opened the door wide, suddenly conscious of the mess she was inviting him into.

He must have sensed her discomfort, saying, 'Don't worry, I'm used to surveying rundown houses and you wouldn't need me if it was in good condition, would you?'

She laughed.

'You're right. Just excuse the mess, as my aunt was a hoarder extraordinaire. Let's start in here.' She led him around the various rooms and Andy made notes on a clipboard, making the odd comment about original features and great potential. Once back downstairs Tess suggested they go into the garden while they talked.

'Sorry I can't offer you a drink, but you've seen the kitchen,' she said, with a grimace.

'No worries. Well, the house could be gorgeous, but will cost a lot of money if you want to go to town,' he paused. 'Or you could also bring it up to modern standards without spending as much. Essentials would include rewiring, new plumbing, heating and new bathroom and kitchen.' He cast his eye upwards over the brickwork and what could be seen of the roof. 'As far as I can tell at this stage, the house is sound – no signs of damp or rot – but has had little spent on it for decades.'

'That's what I'd thought, or rather, hoped. What would you count as "going to town"?'

'You may have spotted your neighbours have a conservatory?' She nodded. 'Well that and an upgrade of the attic rooms would be pricey, but result in a spacious and elegant family home.' He gave her a questioning look.

'I see. To be honest I'm not sure what I want. I'm single but that might change and I do like the thought of lots of space.' She chewed her lip.

'Even without the extra rooms you'd have a good sized house. You could always add a conservatory later. And the same with the attic rooms. We could allow for that with any designs we draw up now.'

'Sounds good. I don't know what I can afford until I've spoken to a builder, which leads me to my next question. Jonathan thought you'd know the good ones.'

Andy nodded.

'I can certainly give you some names. A lot depends on who would be available, if you're looking to proceed quickly. What's your time frame?'

'I'm looking to move here in about three months, but I realise a builder might not even have started by then, so will have to rent, or buy a tent!' she laughed.

'At least it'll be summer!' He scratched his head. 'I know one guy who might be free soon. He had a big project lined up, but there's been a delay. He's actually a developer but might be willing to come on board. Name's Jack Renouf and...'

'No!' She surprised herself with the vehemence of her reply. Andy's eyes opened wide.

'You know Jack? Is there a problem?'

'No. Yes.' She frowned. 'I mean I've met him briefly. He sent a letter to the advocate offering to buy the house to develop it, and then turned up here out the blue Saturday morning, hoping I'd sell.' She began to feel a bit foolish as Andy stared at her, a puzzled expression on his face.

'I see. Or rather I don't. All local property developers keep their eyes open for possible projects. On a small island they don't come up that often.' Andy's eyes drew together. 'He didn't threaten you, did he? Because if he did...' His expression darkened.

'Oh no, not at all. Actually he was quite polite.' Tess realised she was digging herself further into a hole if Jack and Andy were friends. She took a deep breath. 'To be honest, I resented someone turning up so soon after my aunt's funeral, like a...a coffin chaser. It felt...indecent.'

Andy's face cleared.

'I can see how it would look to you, and perhaps Jack should have waited. You're right, it wasn't good timing. He's known to be a bit impatient, likes to get his own way. But he's a decent bloke and a damn good builder so it might be a shame to write him off.'

Tess struggled to clear her thoughts. The guy had been insensitive, but from a professional point of view, it seems he was only doing what was normal here. And not as bad as the ambulance chasers back in England. Maybe she had been a bit hasty to say no so vehemently. But if she were to consider him as the builder, she would be the boss, not him. Her project, not his.

'I don't suppose it would do any harm to let him quote for the work, but shouldn't I have more than one quote?'

Andy nodded.

'Yes, of course. At least two, ideally three. Would you like me to ring around and see who else might be willing to consider the job once you've decided what work's to be done?'

'Sounds good, thanks, Andy. Can we go over the options now?'

'Sure, let's go round the house again and I'll explain it in more detail.'

As they explored all the rooms Tess began to see Andy's vision for the house and excitement bubbled inside her. The rough figures he mentioned were daunting, but it was good to know she could do the work in stages. At the end they agreed he would draw up initial plans and a list of works required to get the house up to a good standard, ready to pass on to prospective builders. They agreed to liaise by email and phone and meet up again on her next trip.

'Builders can wait until I come back, Andy, but I'm happy for you to have a key to pop in as needed.'

'Thanks. I'd like to get professional damp, rot and roof specialists round to make sure we don't miss anything.'

Tess gave Andy a key and he left as a van turned up with the packing boxes. No rest for the wicked, she thought, stacking them in the hall.

Hours later, after a shower and a change of clothes, Tess was on the plane to Exeter. As she looked down at the rapidly disappearing island she felt as if she had left a part of herself behind. In less than four days Guernsey had reminded her of what she had been forced to leave behind twenty years ago and she was determined to reclaim her heritage. The only thing which could stop her would be not finding work as a doctor on the island. But surely it had been a good omen that Jonathan's practice was soon to have a vacancy? And there were other surgeries on the island if that didn't work out. Thoughts whirled around her head as exhaustion claimed her and she fell into a doze.

Half an hour later the bump of the landing gear unfolding brought her awake from a weird dream in which she seemed to be in the sitting room of the house in Hauteville and having tea with Aunt Doris and two men. One who looked suspiciously like Victor Hugo, in Victorian attire, and the other who looked like Jack Renouf, in jeans and T-shirt. Tess shook her head, wondering what on earth had triggered such a dream and hoping she wasn't coming under the alleged family curse of becoming odd if she lived in the house. She could understand dreaming about Hugo and Doris as she'd spent many hours poring over his books and her aunt's scribblings. But the builder? Now, that was odd.

CHAPTER 11

Eugénie's Diary – Guernsey March 1862

Sophie was on my doorstep at nine this morning, her father grunting as he unloaded a small trunk and a large box from his cart. The grey mare shackled to the cart wheezed in sympathy. The roads around here are notoriously steep. I exchanged a brief greeting with Mr Le Clerc before he and Sophie manhandled her possessions upstairs. It looked as if she planned to stay and I could only hope she proved a good worker. On their return downstairs her father stopped and shook my hand.

'M'dame Sarchet, thank you for offering my girl work. Her ma and me will miss her, but it's only right she should start to make her own way and we've been assured by Suzanne that she's found a good mistress in you. Best be off,' he added gruffly, with a quick squeeze of Sophie's shoulder. She was all smiles, as if leaving home for the first time was something to celebrate. I remembered when I left my home, the fear and grief causing me to stumble as I mounted the cart taking me to the harbour. With all my family dead there was nothing to stay for and a French friend of my father's had written from Guernsey, saying they needed a governess for their daughter.

Mr Le Clerc turned round as he picked up the reins.

'Nearly forgot. Please accept our condolences, m'dame. It's hard to be widowed so young. Good day to you.' He clicked his tongue and the mare shuffled forward.

So began the first day of Sophie Le Clerc's employment.

Later this morning M'dame Drouet arrived and was shown into the parlour by a smiling Sophie. I asked her to bring us coffee and she bobbed briefly and left.

'Well, it seems the girl has met with your approval. I'm glad, as that will relieve you of any physical labour, allowing you to recover your strength,' m'dame said as she kissed my cheeks.

She studied my face, adding, softly, 'It's uncanny how much you resemble dear Léopoldine, even more so now you have regained some colour in your face.' After making herself comfortable on the sofa she asked me if I still felt able to begin my copying duties the following day.

'I know we promised not to rush you, my dear, but I'm plagued with problems with my eyes at the moment and need to rest them as much as possible. M'sieur Hugo is being pressured by his publisher for the next part of *Les Misérables* and I hate letting him down.'

She did look strained, her eyes quite puffed up. And the thought of being needed on such an important manuscript sent a thrill down my spine.

'Of course I'll start tomorrow. As you see, I'm much improved and writing will not be a strain.'

Her face lifted.

'Thank you, *ma chère*, I'll send a message to him and let you know what time you are to report to Hauteville House. You'll be provided with pen, ink and paper and, for the first few days, we thought it best if you work at my house in case you have any questions. It will take time to decipher his handwriting,' she said, smiling, 'and I want to be certain you're not making errors before you are left on your own.'

The enormity of my task hit home. If I made a mistake, it might ruin the book! M'sieur Hugo's reputation might be compromised. My throat grew dry at the thought. I coughed.

'Will I then complete the copying here once you are satisfied with my competence?'

She shook her head.

'No, that would not be possible. I am the only person allowed to have the manuscripts in my house and other copyists, and there have been a few, work at Hauteville House. There can be no risk of such valuable work being...mislaid.'

I understood. An unscrupulous person might seek to sell sections of his writings for financial gain. I was, quite rightly, to be always supervised.

We continued to talk while we drank our coffee and then she left, after a brief embrace.

After informing Sophie of her tasks for the day, I ventured out, keen for some fresh air. The day was mild and the soft white clouds allowed the sun to shine through, warming my face as I walked down Hauteville and into Horn Street towards the Town centre. I avoided Market Street, glad that Sophie was now responsible for purchasing our provisions, leaving me free to wander at leisure for as long as suited me. Initially I made for the harbour, cutting through Fountain Street and in front of the Town church, barely visible amongst the encroaching buildings and tenements and along Coal Quay. A lonely rigged sailing ship was moored in one corner while men scurried down the gangplank laden with crates and barrels. It was becoming less usual to see old sailing ships since the advent of steamers. The sight of ships and sailors brought a lump to my throat and I realised it was too soon for me to view their comings and goings with the joy it used to instil in me. Keeping my head averted, I turned left up Pier Steps to arrive in the relative safety of High Street and its shops.

Turning left, I paused outside Madame Chofin's, a fellow Frenchwoman and milliner who came over from Jersey with M'sieur Hugo and whose hats were much admired. Arnaud had purchased one as a surprise for my last birthday and I treasured it and looked forward to wearing it when my mourning was over. For the moment I was forced to wear an indifferent black bonnet from the second-hand shop in Market Street. I gazed longingly at the confections of feathers and lace in pastel shades suited to spring. Women bustling past had swapped their heavy dark winter ensembles for neutral lightweight fabrics of cotton, silk and wool. With a deep sigh I tore myself away from the window and walked down High Street towards the Town church. My destination was Mr Barbet's stationers and booksellers a few doors down. I was an infrequent customer, but he still recognised me and wished me a good morning with a slight bow. I returned the greeting and asked if he had any copies of M'sieur Hugo's *Les Contemplations*.

'Of course, m'dame. It is one of our best sellers. I'll fetch you a copy.'

He disappeared behind a nearby set of shelves and emerged with a plain green leather-bound book.

'We do have more elaborate editions if you prefer?' he asked quietly, his eyes taking in my mourning garb.

I flicked through the book and although it was quite plain, it was nicely printed and bound and would serve my purpose.

'This will suit me, thank you. And I need a journal, if I may…' I waved my hand in the direction of a display of such on a table behind me.

He nodded and I took my time with my choice. From a young girl I have kept a journal religiously, writing in bed by the light of a candle before going to sleep. I have continued the habit since arriving in Guernsey and my current journal is nearly filled. It is unlikely anyone would ever read my humble scribblings, but no matter, it is a useful exercise for me. I chose a thick red cloth-bound journal with heavy cream paper, similar to that in use.

Mr Barbet wrapped my purchases in brown paper and string and I counted out my francs. It is an extravagance to buy such objects, but my heart felt lighter at the thought of immersing myself in M'sieur Hugo's lines of poetry. They would be balm to my grieving soul. Leaving the shop I came face to face with a neighbour who was kind enough to ask after my health. We had never exchanged many words but she is a pleasant, middle-aged lady who seems genuinely shocked to hear of my misfortunes. As we parted she told me to call on her at any time if I needed either company or some assistance. I was happy to accept such an offer and went on my way wondering if I had been too quick to judge people. Clutching my precious parcel, I retraced my steps homewards, determined to be more open-minded in future. I have been guilty of keeping people at arm's length since my arrival from France and must try to mix more or face a lonely future.

I rose early this morning, eager to start my new employment. I dressed with care, even though I loathed my mourning dress adorned with black crepe, and attached my black widow's cap. Not being religious and without family, I saw no need to hide behind a traditional crepe veil. Queen Victoria, of Great Britain, overcome with grief after the untimely death of her husband, Prince Albert last year, has been in the deepest mourning and set the strictest of instructions for those about her. Fortunately, I am of no consequence and do not need to abide by such rules. The royal couple visited Guernsey only three years ago, before I arrived here, and were, I understand, greeted warmly by the islanders. A bronze statue of the prince has been commissioned and is to be erected by the harbour to honour him. My thoughts turned to my own lost beloved, threatening to disturb the calm I needed to meet M'sieur Hugo and I hurried downstairs for a hasty breakfast prepared by Sophie. Fortified, I set out.

Mere yards separated our houses but Hauteville House is much the grander, with many windows facing onto the street and a black arched doorway surrounding the almost forbidding black painted door. For a moment I hesitated, wondering if I should approach by a servants' entrance. As I stood on the step the door swung open and a woman dressed in housekeeper's garb called out, 'M'dame Sarchet? Come in, you're expected.'

I followed her into a hallway the like of which I'd never seen before, nor since. It reminded me of a cathedral. A carved dark oak portal spanned the hall, topped with bottle-bottom panes of glass and engraved with lettering I could not decipher. Beyond stretched a passageway towards a rear door, lined with oak cupboards and further on, displays of china. A staircase ran off to the left and the woman beckoned me on to a room on the right and ushered me inside. I gasped. The high ceiling and two walls were covered in intricate, and probably antique, tapestries. I had never seen such richness before and stood like a gawking schoolgirl as my gaze tried to take it all in.

'You're to wait here and m'sieur will be along presently,' the woman said and left.

Glad of the chance to explore further, I became engrossed in the huge oak carved panelling on the third wall, inset with an unusual porcelain fireplace. The whole effect was both overpowering and alien, unlike anything one would expect to find in an ordinary street in St Peter Port.

'Are you admiring my handiwork, *ma petite*?'

I turned, startled by m'sieur's silent entry. He stood a few feet away, his hands in his pockets as he watched me. I dropped a swift curtsy.

'Indeed, m'sieur. You are responsible for this intricate carving?'

He moved forward, waving his hands at the panelling.

'Yes, I love working with my hands and have carved most of what you see in the house and designed everything. A real labour of love, *n'est ce pas?*' He stood by me, his eyes twinkling.

I nodded, and listened while he pointed out various panels and the statue of Saint Paul holding a book, a statue of Saint John looking towards heaven and the engraved names of Socrates, Columbus, Washington among others. As we encompassed the room, he explained the inspiration behind his designs.

'It may be hard for you to believe, but this is the first house I have ever owned, and I wanted to create something so unique, and so rich in design to pay homage to those I consider to be geniuses in their field, whether it be literature, like myself,' he said, striking his chest, 'philosophy or discovery, for example. This is my temple to genius, if you like, and has proved to be as great a passion as my own writing.'

'You leave me speechless with admiration, m'sieur. You have accomplished so much.' I felt even more insignificant in comparison, and again wondered if I was worthy to be entrusted with copying out his words of genius.

'We are all called on in different ways, are we not? And you, how are you now? Your cheeks have more colour, I think.' His stare was so intense, I felt blood rise to my face. It must be odd for him to be reminded of his daughter.

'Better, thank you, and glad to have something to occupy me now...now I'm alone.' I bit my lip, determined not to give into tears in front of him.

'And I will keep you busy. Come, follow me.' He led the way through a door in the corner into a room lit by large windows, bright after the dimness of the room of tapestries. Again a heavy carved oak structure filled one wall, but I had no time to examine it as M'sieur Hugo picked up a pile of papers on the table. He explained what was required of me and asked if I could decipher his writing, handing me a page of his manuscript. There were crossings out and scribbles in the margins, and as I read it out he nodded or shook his head according to whether or not I was right. After spending some time explaining his method of working so that I might understand better how to transcribe his writings, he collected up the manuscript, a bundle of blank paper, and pens.

'Suzanne is here to help carry these to M'dame Drouet's where you will begin your work. In a few weeks' time, it will suit me if you work here. You will have a wonderful view over the garden and will be undisturbed. Is that agreeable to you, *ma petite*?'

To work in these hallowed, extraordinary rooms! How could I not be pleased?

'Yes, m'sieur. Your…your family is not here?'

He snorted.

'They are not. My son Charles is now settled in Brussels and my wife and my other son Victor have recently left to visit him and confer with my publishers. I am deserted!' He waved his arms theatrically, as if in despair, but having seen him with M'dame Drouet, I thought it unlikely he missed his wife.

I nodded in sympathy and picked up the bundled paper and pens and he led the way back to the hall. Suzanne was standing near the impressive portal, eyeing the carvings. As we approached she dropped a curtsy to M'sieur Hugo and took hold of half of the papers from me. As we left he inclined his head towards me, saying he looked forward to seeing me again soon. I managed a smile and followed Suzanne down the steps, turning left to go up the road towards La Fallue. Neither of us spoke as we walked, my own head full of what I'd seen and heard that morning. I dearly wanted to explore that house some more and hoped to do so in the future. My eyes had been opened to another world and I wanted to be a part of it.

❧ CHAPTER 12 ❧

Tess – April 2012

Tess emailed her CV to Jonathan the next day before leaving for work. It was more or less up to date as she had planned to approach local GP practices shortly, wanting a new position before she was due to finish at the hospital. The extra training she had undergone in order to become a GP was nearly at an end and she couldn't wait. Now all she had to do was tell her parents. Tess phoned them that evening and was pleased when her father answered.

'I'm trying for a job in Guernsey, Dad…' She told him about her friend's husband and the vacancy and that she was sure about returning to the island.

'Whatever you decide, I'll back you, Tess. You know that, love. I've always been so proud of you becoming a doctor and you've earned the right to make your own choices.' She heard him sigh. 'Coming here was great for my career, no question, but I miss the old place and our friends. To be honest, I was wondering about going back now I'm retired, but your mother isn't keen. Says she would miss city life and her friends. But if you're there, perhaps we could come and visit, eh?'

Tess had never heard her father say he missed Guernsey and was taken by surprise.

'Of course you could, Dad. But don't book your flights yet as there's a lot of work to be done on the house first.' She laughed, imagining her mother's face if she saw the place now!

'Don't worry, I can guess. I suppose you want to talk to your mother, but she's out at some ladies' supper and won't be back till late. In fact, she's hardly ever at home these days. I'm beginning to wonder if she's got a lover on the side,' he laughed. Tess heard a falseness in his laugh and was shocked.

'You don't mean that, do you, Dad?'

'I don't know, love. It's just…your mother seems more distant these days and we hardly ever go anywhere together anymore. She hasn't said anything to you, has she? If she's unhappy about something?'

'No, but I don't think Mum would share anything that personal with me. Don't worry, Dad, I'm sure she's just making the most of retirement. Why don't you suggest you two go away for a weekend? Get some quality time together.'

'Good idea, will do. Anyway, I'll tell her you called and to ring you tomorrow. Night, love.'

Tess switched off her phone and poured a glass of wine. Surely her father had got it all wrong? Women in their late sixties didn't have affairs, did they? She cast her mind over anything her friends said about their parents' relationships and came up with nothing. Thinking about it, her mother had changed a bit lately. New, younger hairstyle – often a giveaway – new wardrobe and a change of make-up. She had put it down to a belated midlife crisis and saw it as something positive. But what if it was because of a new man in her life? Tess prayed her father was wrong as she didn't want him hurt. But if it was true, she wouldn't speak to her mother again.

One evening two days later Tess received an email from Jonathan to say his partners had all agreed to invite her in for an informal interview on her next visit. She punched the air in excitement. Looking good, girl, looking good. Curled up on the sofa, she had been flicking through the TV channels trying to find something light to watch as an antidote to the grimness of a day in A & E. She had narrowed the choice on iPlayer between *Mrs Brown's Boys*, *Have I Got News For You* and *Doc Martin*. The email made the decision for her. *Doc Martin* would get her in training for life as a GP, she thought, grinning. When it had finished she heaved a contented sigh, imagining herself in beautiful Guernsey, not that dissimilar to Cornwall, and spending her days ministering to her patients with a rather better bedside manner than that of Doc Martin. Then having fun with friends on the beach. Idyllic! Tess made a cup of coffee and was about to reply to Jonathan's email when her phone rang. Glancing at the screen, her happy mood subsided. Her mother.

'Hi, Mum. Dad gave you the message I rang, then?' Her tone sarcastic.

'Yes, but I've been busy and this is the first evening I've had free.' Elaine sounded abrupt, as if Tess was lucky to be phoned at all.

'Dad mentioned you're out a lot these days. Have you made some new friends?' Tess tried to keep her voice light, but talking to her mother always set her teeth on edge.

'As it happens, I have. A couple of women I met at a talk recently. They...they ask me to go to the cinema with them and, oh, various talks and things. Nothing that would interest you,' Elaine said quickly. Too quickly, Tess, thought, her heart sinking. Maybe Dad was right...

'What did you want to tell me, Tess? Your father didn't say what it was.'

She told her mother about the chance of a job in Guernsey which had confirmed her decision to move back. There was silence on the line.

'Mum, you still there?'

'Yes. For what it's worth, I think you're making a big mistake. Guernsey's a backwater and you'll be bored to tears within months, if not weeks. And as for that house! I told you it's unlucky and old Doris used to mention odd things happening. Like it was haunted. Why don't you sell it and buy a nice house in Exeter? No mortgage, you'd be laughing.'

Tess gritted her teeth. Stay calm, she admonished herself.

'I'm sorry, Mum, I've made up my mind. Dad was happy for me, says he's been missing Guernsey and would love to visit me once I've settled in.'

A sharp intake of breath echoed down the line.

'Your father's getting maudlin in his old age. Only remembers what he wants to remember about what he refers to as "the good old days". Pah! They weren't that good or we wouldn't have left, would we? Still, it's your choice, my girl. Don't say I didn't warn you. Now, I must get on, promised to call a friend before it gets late. Goodnight.'

Tess was left trying to make sense of her mother's attitude. Something wasn't adding up, as why would she be so against her living in Guernsey? It wasn't as if they were close, far from it. Elaine had always favoured her brother and had been devastated when he moved to Canada. And she had been dismissive of her father's view on the move. It didn't sound as if they were getting on, which confirmed what he had said. Knowing there was probably little she could do, Tess switched on her laptop and sent an email to Jonathan. At least that was positive.

A week later Tess received an email from Andy, attaching the final List of Works they had agreed, and informing her he had two builders lined up to visit the house prior to tendering quotes. He explained no-one else was available in the foreseeable future, but thought two would be enough. One was Premium Builders, a large company Andy had worked with on several projects and the other was Jack Renouf. Tess was surprised he'd agreed to quote after her terse dismissal of his offer to buy. Reading the email she wasn't sure how she felt about him being her builder. It would be more awkward for him than her, given that he was primarily a developer not a builder. A question of swallowing some of the abundant male pride. Ah well, she'd have to wait and see. Maybe the other firm would win the contract. Andy had arranged for Premium to come on the Friday afternoon and Jack on the Saturday morning. And with the meeting at the surgery planned for early Friday evening, it promised to be quite a weekend.

As the plane taxied on the runway in Guernsey, Tess couldn't help thinking about how different this trip was compared to her first only two weeks before. With a potential job and builder on the horizon, her life was moving forward at a fast pace. And she no longer felt as a stranger in her homeland. Colette had invited her to stay, but she had declined for two reasons. Her friend was only two weeks from her due date and secondly, Tess was concerned there might be awkwardness between her and Jonathan if the interview at the surgery didn't go well. Much as she would have loved staying with them, they also lived quite a way from Hauteville and it suited her to have a short walk from the hotel. As it happened, Andy had invited them all for Sunday lunch and it promised to be great fun. Tess found herself smiling broadly as she left the terminal and headed towards the taxi rank.

An hour later and she was walking down Hauteville towards *St Michel* ready for a morning of sifting and boxing. Soft clouds scudded across the pale blue sky, propelled by a sea breeze carrying the familiar salty tang. May was around the corner and Tess promised herself that if she made good progress this weekend, she would take time out for a cliff walk to admire the spring flowers. And it would provide much needed exercise.

Tess took a cautious sniff as she unlocked the front door. Not too bad. Stale, but not as unsavoury as last time. Again she opened windows everywhere before carrying empty boxes and black sacks upstairs. At least the bedrooms were not full of stuff like downstairs. She packed the boxes with books from the overflowing shelves on the landing before going through drawers and cupboards for items to throw away or keep. She struck lucky in one drawer, finding a handwritten family tree, presumably drawn up by Doris. It started with Eugénie and ended with Clive and herself. It detailed the marriages and births down the five generations and what struck Tess was how few children were born and that not many had lived beyond late middle-age. Perhaps her mother was right about the house being unlucky, she thought, putting it in her bag for safe keeping. By the time she had finished it was lunch-time and Tess, after piling up more rubbish bags outside, locked up and returned to Pandora for a shower and change. A leisurely bar meal sitting outside on the terrace and she was ready to return to meet the first builder.

The chap who turned up was pleasant and professional and they went round the house together as he scribbled notes on his clipboard. As he left he said he would email his quote to both Andy and herself, probably within the week. Andy had already told her the reports from the damp and rot firm were okay, only unimportant issues having been found. The roofer had listed some minor repairs to the roof and pointed out the lack of adequate felting. So far, so good. All she had to do now was find storage for the many boxes and start a thorough search of the masses of papers left by Doris. The big disappointment had been the lack of anything directly connected to Eugénie. No diaries or letters. Nothing. Feeling too tired after her exertions and the early start, Tess decided to finish for the day and went next door to see if Heather was in. She was and it wasn't long before tea and cake were spread before them as Tess brought her up to date.

'Sounds as if everything's moving along well, especially if you get the job at the surgery. We'll have you over here before you know it,' Heather smiled, topping up her tea.

'Yes, I'll have a lot of decisions to make. A bit scary, really. I'm not used to making such big changes and apart from my time at university in Plymouth, I've spent the past twenty years in Exeter.' It was beginning to hit home what a big change she was making.

Heather nodded.

'I can relate to that. As you know, we came here for Neil's work, and although I was looking forward to it, I was also apprehensive. A born and bred Londoner, it was a bit out of my comfort zone.' She laughed. 'But you have the advantage of having been born here, spent your early childhood here. Surely it will feel like you're just coming home?'

'Yes, you're right, but when I think of all I have to do…' Tess spread her hands wide and grimaced. What she didn't want to say was that she was worried her parents were heading for a split and maybe she shouldn't be moving away. For her father's sake.

'You'll be fine. I had you down as a very competent and self-assured young woman and I'm never wrong.' Heather tilted her head to one side and Tess had to smile.

'Okay, you've convinced me.' She chased some cake crumbs around her plate and licked them off her finger. 'I tell you what I was hoping to discover among Doris's papers was something either about or personal to Eugénie and Hugo. Did Doris ever tell you she had anything like that?'

Heather frowned.

'I don't think so. To be honest, I never asked if she'd found proof of the supposed liaison with Hugo. I assumed the family had something to back up the story. Couldn't it still be there? You said there was an awful lot of stuff piled up.'

'Possible, I guess. I think Doris may have started out trying to keep to a kind of filing system, and then it all got out of control and she ran out of room as she was becoming more frail.' Tess frowned, adding, 'But I'm determined to find whatever is there, no matter how long it takes. Family honour is at stake.'

This made them both laugh and Tess declared she'd better leave and prepare herself for the meeting at the surgery. Heather gave her a hug as they said goodbye, and wished her luck. As Tess walked back to the hotel and passed Hauteville House, she couldn't help whispering, 'Are you my great-great-great-grandfather, Victor? Or is it all a silly family fantasy?'

CHAPTER 13

Tess – April 2012

Tess pulled nervously at her jacket as she sat in the waiting room in the surgery. Normally this would have been full of anxious patients, but now it was just her, sitting in eerie silence before being called into the practice manager's office for her interview. A bit like a patient, she felt as if her life depended on the outcome of this appointment. Not physically, of course, but her mental and emotional wellbeing. She had chosen a confidence-boosting red jacket partnered with a navy skirt and cream blouse, acknowledging her usual outfit of jeans and plain cotton top would not have the right impact. Hospital doctors weren't known for their sartorial excellence, but Tess reckoned GPs had a certain standard to maintain.

'Doctor Le Prevost, we're ready for you now.' The practice manager, who had shown her around the surgery earlier, appeared at the door. Tess, taking a deep, calming breath, smiled brightly and followed her into the proverbial lions' den.

An hour later she emerged, still smiling. What a nice bunch they were! Friendly, but professional, and apparently impressed with her qualifications and training. Their questions had been searching but asked in a manner designed to put her at ease. Jonathan had taken a back seat, throwing her an occasional encouraging smile. They ended the interview with the senior, retiring partner saying they would be in touch within the week.

'Well, that wasn't too bad, was it?' Jonathan said, as he followed her out. He was taking her home to have supper with them.

'No, much better than I'd expected, thanks. For what it's worth, I'd really enjoy working here and I'm impressed with your facilities.'

'Good, I've certainly been happy here anyway. Now, let's get home for supper and agree on no more shop talk so we can relax. Okay?' he grinned.

'Okay,' she said, looking forward to catching up with Colette.

Tess woke early the next morning, keen to go for a walk round Havelet Bay to build up an appetite before breakfast. Colette had produced a delicious three-course meal the night before, in spite of being about to 'pop', as she put it. A south-westerly breeze soon cleared any sluggishness Tess felt as she walked briskly down the steep, winding road to the bay. A scattering of cloud masked the sun, but she could see it was going to be a warm, dry day. Perfect for a walk on the cliffs later. Slipping onto the sandy beach, Tess stood and looked up towards Hauteville. She picked out Hugo's house, easily distinguished by its size, the glass extension on the roof and the white spiral staircase leading down to the first floor. Using this as a marker, she was able to pinpoint her own house. Not too difficult as the granite stood out from the neighbouring white houses. A surge of pride flowed through her body as she squinted at what looked like a doll's house from below. Grinning, she began the ascent up the hill to the hotel, ready for breakfast and then it was off to *St Michel* to meet the other builder, Jack Renouf.

He was late. Tess fumed as she paced around the limited free floor space in the sitting room. If there was one thing she hated with a vengeance, it was being kept waiting. Boyfriends had been given their marching orders at their first late arrival and tradesmen were given short shrift. She looked at her watch again. Ten minutes now. If he didn't turn up in the next five…

The strident ring of the doorbell echoed in the hall. Hmm, he'd need a good excuse if she were to let him in.

'*Doctor* Le Prevost, my apologies, but I had a call from a client with a flooded kitchen and as my plumber's away for the weekend I went round to sort it. Rather than waste time phoning you I came as soon as I could.' He didn't look at all sorry, she thought, unimpressed by the emphasis on 'doctor', but his jeans did look damp.

'I see. You'd better come in, as long as you're not going to drip everywhere,' she said coolly, not keen on the idea of wet footprints through the house.

Jack grinned.

'No worries, I've changed my shoes.'

She waved him into the hall and proceeded to show him around at a steady pace, not wanting to get drawn into unnecessary conversation, focusing solely on the list of works they were both carrying. He seemed to pick up her mood as he made few comments along the way, jotting down notes on his list. By the time they had been in every room, including the attics, Jack looked both puzzled and annoyed.

'Do you have a problem with me, Doctor? I'm here at Andy's request, to provide a quote for your building work, but it seems to me you can't wait to get rid of me. Why?' He stood in front of her, his arms crossed and head tilted in an intimidating fashion.

Tess took a deep breath. How the hell was she going to answer? Pretend he was wrong? But he wasn't, was he? She had resented him door-stepping her that first time with his offer to buy *her* house. Could she trust him not to try to make her change her mind? By coming in with a high quote or telling her the house had a lot of problems?

'To be honest, Jack, I didn't appreciate you turning up the day after my aunt's funeral, trying to buy the house. I thought it was…ill-mannered.' She looked him squarely in the face. If he didn't like it and left, fine.

His expression softened.

'You're right. I'm sorry, I see that now. You must have been upset and I barged in.' He ruffled his hair, looking thoughtful. 'Can we start again? It was crass of me, and I have no excuse, other than I wasn't expecting you to be so…young and keen to keep the house.' He smiled and Tess found herself letting go of her annoyance with him.

'I guess. As long as you think you can be unbiased about what needs doing…' she trailed off.

'You mean I might try to put you off renovating in order to persuade you to sell?'

She nodded.

'Well, I can hardly blame you for thinking that, can I? But, as Andy would tell you, I've a good reputation on the island and if I were to play dirty with you, the way news spreads around here, I'd lose it pretty damn quickly.' He spread his hands in a conciliatory gesture and Tess realised, with a jolt, how attractive he was. Muscular, with thick dark hair and a strong jaw. She had been so focused on being angry with his behaviour that she hadn't really seen him as a *man*.

Clearing her throat, she replied, 'Okay, let's agree to forget the earlier…misconceptions and I'm happy for you to draw up a quotation. As long as you agree with Andy's suggestions about retaining the original features wherever possible.'

'Absolutely. One of the reasons I was drawn to buying this house was because I knew it hadn't been modernised and ruined in the process.' He gazed around what had once been the dining room before looking out of the window. 'This will be a beautiful home for you when it's finished and with views to die for.' He turned to face her, adding, 'I envy you, but I promise I'll be straight with you if I'm given the job.'

For some reason, Tess felt flustered and dropped her gaze, as his dark brown eyes seemed to bore into hers. God, surely she didn't fancy him? That would be too much to deal with!

'Right. I'll wait for your quote, Jack. I do have other builders tendering, of course. What would be your lead time if I were to choose you?'

He frowned as he checked his list.

'About three or four weeks, giving me time to order materials from the mainland and get my team on board.'

'Fair enough, thanks. I look forward to hearing from you.' Tess led the way to the front door and Jack proffered his hand as he stepped outside. As she took it she was aware of the warmth and strength of his fingers as they enclosed hers. He seemed to maintain his grip longer than was necessary and Tess had to pull her hand away, catching his quizzical glance. Jack murmured, 'Bye for now, *Doctor* Le Prevost,' and turned away before she could reply.

On her own again, Tess was left wondering what had happened. Something had shifted between them. A spark of attraction? Well, it would have to be quenched as the last thing she needed at the moment was a man in her life. Unless his sole purpose was to help her create a beautiful home before disappearing into the distance. With that thought she locked up and walked into Town for some window shopping and lunch.

Tess looked eagerly out of the car window as Jonathan drove them to Andy's house on Sunday. Poor Colette shifted uncomfortably in the front passenger seat and Tess hoped her friend would survive the lunch intact. She certainly looked ready to burst and Jonathan's face was creased in concern when he picked Tess up earlier. At least Colette would have two doctors on hand if she went into labour, Tess thought, looking out for familiar landmarks as they headed towards the west coast. She smiled as memories of her time with the family on Cobo beach filtered into her mind, wishing it was hot enough for a spot of sunbathing. It was a little early for that, but warm April was about to give way to May and summer was around the corner. Light, fluffy clouds drifted overhead as they passed Saumarez Park, just inland from Cobo, and again Tess remembered happy times spent there as a child, particularly at the colourful North Show.

Minutes later Jonathan swung the car left towards the lanes running up towards Le Guet, a wooded area above Cobo bay and where Andy and Charlotte lived. This was another area Tess knew as a child, enjoying fun times with her brother as they make-believed being spies hunting each other, James Bond style. Thinking of him made her realise how much she missed him since he had emigrated and hoped he would fly over soon. He had done well in Canada, something techie, which she didn't fully understand, but had made him wealthy and he was now engaged to a stunning-looking girl. Although Tess was happy for him, she felt like an underachiever in comparison.

'Here we are, Tess. Have you been daydreaming in the back there,' called Jonathan, eyeing her through the rear mirror.

She smiled at his grinning face and nodded.

'Yes, old memories.' She looked around her as the car entered a drive leading to an impressive Victorian house. 'My! This is some place. If Andy can afford a place like this, I might not be able to afford his fees!' she said, laughing.

'Oh, don't worry, he's had a bit of an inheritance and his wife Charlotte has a bob or two. In spite of that, they're a lovely couple,' Colette said, as Jonathan brought the car to a halt at the side of the house.

Tess helped Colette out of the car as Jonathan rang the doorbell.

'You okay, no pains?' she asked as her friend struggled to stand.

'I'm fine, just a bit clumsy thanks to the bump.' Colette eased herself upright with a sigh.

A small figure hurled themselves out through the door and flung their arms around Colette's legs, nearly unbalancing her again. Tess looked on bemused as Colette finally extricated herself, laughing.

'James, lovely to see you, but careful or I'll fall over.'

A tall woman, with glossy long brown hair and an enviable cream complexion, grabbed the toddler, saying, 'Sorry, Colette, he's been so excited knowing you were coming, wanting to know if your baby has arrived yet. I think he expects the postman to deliver it,' she laughed, a deep, throaty laugh. Turning, she smiled at Tess. 'Hello, I'm Charlotte and you must be Tess, who Andy's told me so much about. And this,' she added, struggling to hold onto the wriggling child, 'is James. Say hello to the lady, darling.'

The little boy stared at Tess with large brown eyes, his fist in his mouth. She smiled back. 'Hello, James, I'm Tess. How do you do?' She reached out as if to shake his hand and, after a moment's hesitation, he took it from his mouth and let it sit in her hers. It felt sticky.

''Ello, Tess.' She gently removed his hand and grinned at Charlotte.

'What a lovely little boy. Isn't he the image of his father?'

'Well it's good to know there's no doubt on that score,' said Andy, newly arrived at the door. He gave Tess and Colette pecks on the cheek before relieving Charlotte of James. 'Come in, everyone, and let's have a drink before lunch.' He led the way through an elegant hallway, set off by a central mahogany staircase and Tess couldn't help comparing it to her own.

'How beautiful! I'm quite envious,' she said to Charlotte as they followed Andy and the others.

'I can assure you it wasn't like this when we bought it. In fact it was almost derelict. It's all down to my clever husband that it looks gorgeous now. And I'm sure he'll make sure your house is lovely, too. He's passionate about restoring the original beauty of a house and he tells me yours has great potential.'

'It's good to see he practises what he preaches. I can't wait to see what my house will look like.' By now they were walking through a graceful drawing room with marble fireplaces and high, corniced ceilings and Tess looked around, wide-eyed. They followed the others through a double-door in the far wall leading into a conservatory.

'Wow! This is amazing and so...unexpected.' The Victorian conservatory was not only large, but it was furnished in Moroccan style with colourful divans and chairs, onto which Colette had already eased herself.

'Now this I am fully responsible for, and I absolutely love it. Fun, isn't it?'

'It certainly is. And what a view! Almost as good as mine.' Tess laughed, gazing over the lush gardens sloping away towards the wood of Le Guet and Cobo bay.

Charlotte opened her mouth to reply when Andy came over to offer her and Tess a glass of Prosecco. 'Thanks, darling. Shall we sit down, Tess? Lunch will be about thirty minutes.' Tess plumped for the divan next to Colette's chair and Charlotte joined her. Colette nursed a small glass of fizz.

'My doctor's given me permission, seeing as it can hardly hurt baby now, can it?' Colette grinned, nodding towards Jonathan, building bricks with James on the floor.

'Quite right. It might even spur the little one on. The last few weeks do drag, don't they?' said Charlotte, with a fond gaze at her son. 'Right, everyone, let's drink to new babies and new homes!'

They raised their glasses and took a sip of wine. Tess settled back on the divan with a sigh. It was good to be so welcomed into people's homes and she hoped they would become firm friends once she moved. And Colette had mentioned others in their circle, including her brother Nick and his wife, Jeanne. She couldn't wait to meet them all.

'I gather you're not local, Charlotte,' she said, turning towards her hostess.

'No, I'm English, but absolutely love it here and can understand you wanting to move back. It's an idyllic place to bring up children, isn't it?' Charlotte's smile was warm.

Tess nodded.

'My brother and I had a great childhood, for sure. We'd go off for hours without our parents worrying where we were or what we were up to. Just as well!' she giggled. 'I don't think it's quite as safe to let children do that now, but if they love the outdoors they'll have a whale of a time.'

'James loves being outside and adores trips to the beach and Andy will take him fishing when he's older.'

Colette butted in.

'I agree with Tess, it'll be great for James.' She patted her belly. 'And for this one. If it's a boy he might become best mates with James and go off adventuring together. Or is that a scary thought?' she added, laughing. Tess and Charlotte joined in until Colette gave a gasp.

Jonathan looked up from the floor, his face creased in anxiety. 'You okay?'

Colette gritted her teeth. 'Not really. Bad stomach cramp.' She clutched her stomach and Tess rescued her glass while Jonathan settled by her side, saying, 'Take deep breaths and it might pass. Could be another Braxton Hicks.' He turned to Tess, 'She's been having them on and off the past couple of days and I don't think she's going into labour just yet.'

Tess nodded, aware the cramps could happen before labour truly sets in. 'Any easier?' she asked Colette, who was looking calmer.

'Yes, thanks. Bloney uncomfortable, but the pain's gone. Do you think junior was objecting to the bubbly?' she managed a grin.

'I shouldn't think they've even got a sniff of it yet, so don't worry. Are you happy to stay? We could go home if...' Jonathan said, holding her hand.

'Let's stay. At least you guys offer a distraction for me. At home I'm more aware of what my body's up to.' Colette reached for her glass and took a sip. 'Ah! That's better.'

Andy, who had been trying to stop James from flinging himself at Colette, chimed in. 'I think we should have lunch, just in case Colette has to, er, leave suddenly,' he smiled at her.

Charlotte stood, saying, 'Excellent idea. I for one am starving. Into the dining room, folks.' She waved her arms in a shooing movement and Tess followed behind Jonathan and Colette, concerned her friend was all right. Andy led the way across the hall to another elegant room set with a round modern dining table surrounded by upholstered chairs with arms which looked eminently comfortable, even for a heavily pregnant woman. Between them was a high chair for James.

'Please, sit down everyone. I'd like you to sit by me, Tess, if you don't mind, so we can get to know each other,' Charlotte said, guiding Tess to her seat. The places were set with starters of what appeared to be a scrummy salad with duck, melon and herbs. As Tess sat down Charlotte settled James in his high chair next to Andy and Colette and Jonathan sat together.

'This all looks wonderful, Charlotte. Do you enjoy cooking?' Tess asked.

Muffled giggles came from Colette and Andy grinned.

'Let's say she was a late-starter in the cooking department, but she's doing really well, aren't you, darling?' He gave his wife a fond look.

Charlotte explained to Tess that she had never had to cook in her life before she met Andy, being brought up in a wealthy household with a cook, and that she had made a conscious effort to learn when they started dating. 'And now I do my fair share and quite enjoy it. Although I'll never be as good or as keen a cook as dear Colette.'

Colette added, 'She's being modest, Tess. We've enjoyed many a good meal here and I take my hat off to her for achieving so much in only a few years.'

Wine was poured and they started eating and Tess enjoyed herself, chatting to Charlotte between mouthfuls. By the time the main course of roast lamb was served, she felt as if they had been friends for ages.

'We have something in common, Tess, which is one of the reasons I was so glad to meet you. I've recently finished writing an account of Victor Hugo's time on the island and I believe you're linked to him through an ancestor. Is that right?' Charlotte's eyes were bright with interest.

Tess was so surprised she let her fork, speared with meat, drop back on the plate.

'So I understand, but I haven't seen any concrete proof yet. But fancy you writing about him! Colette told me you were a writer but I didn't know you wrote books. Small world, isn't it?' She took a gulp of wine. 'You must have done a deal of research on Hugo. Did you come across the name Eugénie Sarchet?' She held her breath.

Charlotte smiled.

'Yes, only a brief mention of her as being employed as a copyist for Hugo from 1862, and there's no date for when she left. I assume she's your ancestor?'

'Yes. My great-great-great-grandmother.' Tess was pleased to learn of further confirmation of Eugénie's story. She drank more wine before continuing, 'It's her house I've inherited.'

Charlotte clapped her hands.

'That's what I'd guessed. Isn't it exciting? Not that I've mentioned her in my book, I hasten to add,' she said, 'in case you were worried.'

Andy must have heard the conversation, as he said to Tess, 'Colette mentioned there was a story behind your house to do with Hugo and I'd wondered if it had been owned by someone Charlotte had found. Did your aunt leave you any papers from that time?'

Four pairs of eyes turned towards her expectantly and Tess wished she could satisfy their curiosity.

'Not that I've found. But there's a humungus amount of papers, as you probably noticed, Andy, and I can't really go through them properly yet. I hope to find somewhere to store them with good access and lighting which I can visit once I've moved here. All my aunt ever told me was that Eugénie had been widowed young, inheriting her husband's house and worked for Hugo.' Not quite the truth, but Tess didn't want to spread the story that Eugénie had borne Hugo a child, from whom she was supposedly descended, without proof. She could end up looking idiotic if it wasn't true.

'Well, we have rooms in the attic which we don't use. You'd be welcome to store what you need there, wouldn't she, Andy?' Charlotte gazed at her husband, who was trying to persuade James to eat more vegetables.

'Yes, sure,' he said, spearing carrots on James's fork. Once they had disappeared into his son's mouth, he turned to face Tess. 'Where do you plan to live when you move? The house will be uninhabitable once the builder starts work.'

'Thanks for the offer of storage, I'd be happy to take you up on it. With regard to where I'll live, I hadn't given it a lot of thought. It will partly depend on whether or not I have a job,' she smiled at Jonathan, whose face gave nothing away. 'Perhaps rent a room in a house. I don't need much as I'll have no furniture, only clothes and basic stuff.'

Tess caught Charlotte raising an eyebrow at Andy, who nodded.

'Would you consider staying in one of our spare rooms? You could be as independent as you want and have ready access to your papers. And we'd love to have you, I can tell we're going to be firm friends,' Charlotte said, with a warm smile.

Tess was touched at the generous offer. Colette had been right about what a lovely couple they were.

'That's so kind of you both, particularly as you hardly know me. I'll have to wait and see how things pan out over the next few weeks and let you know. I admit it's a very tempting offer,' she smiled at her hosts.

'Well I think it's a super idea! So let's hope my lovely husband and his cronies offer you the job and we have you here permanently as soon as poss,' Colette cried, raising her glass. The others joined in and they all drank to Tess, who was feeling overwhelmed by the warmth surrounding her. As long as she had a job – even as a locum, if necessary – she knew life in Guernsey would be a turning point for her. The only proverbial fly in the ointment being her parents. Something she had to address back in Exeter.

CHAPTER 14

Eugénie's Diary – March/April 1862

Today was the first day working with M'dame Drouet and it was hard work. I made only a few errors, but the level of concentration made my head ache and my eyes itch. She assured me my eyes and head would become accustomed to the work and made sure I rested my eyes for a few minutes every hour. I became engrossed in the story I was copying in my neatest hand. I understood the first volumes of the work had already been sent to the publisher in Belgium and these latest pages were Volume Four, Book Second, *Eponine*. I wished I had read the earlier volumes, but managed to make some sense of what I was copying after m'dame explained the outline of the novel.

'It is a work dedicated to those unfortunate to be born poor in this century, and describes, in m'sieur's own words, *"the degradation of man through pauperism, the corruption of woman through hunger, the crippling of children through lack of light"*, set against the background of the wars of the early part of the century and the political unrests some years later. The central character, Jean Valjean, experiences poverty, imprisonment, a rise to wealth and respectability and helps many poor unfortunates, *les misérables*, becoming eventually the guardian of a poor orphan, Cosette.' She sighed, rubbing her eyes. 'Parts are so moving I am brought to tears, as you, *ma chère*, may be also.'

I hung upon her words, proud to be playing a small, but nevertheless, important part in bringing this work into the world. I was to work in the mornings only as m'dame would often accompany M'sieur Hugo in the afternoons for either a ride in the hired carriage or a walk towards Fermain. I learned that he would usually join her for dinner in the evenings while M'dame Hugo was away.

My own life was more solitary. I went home and enjoyed Sophie's excellent cooking which was encouraging my appetite to return. I needed to regain the weight I'd lost and to feel stronger. After a short rest I returned to devouring *Les Contemplations* like someone dying of hunger. Not being in a position to continuously buy more books, I am resolved to join the lending library, and will take out books in both French and English. My father taught me English, for which I am eternally grateful. The educated islanders speak both languages, with French being the official language and there is also a local *patois*, but English is creeping more and more into general use. An English newspaper, *The Star*, is published alongside the Guernsey French paper, *La Gazette*. From now on I shall buy copies of both in order to stay in touch with what is happening both locally and in England.

It occurs to me that spending time in the company of such worldly people as M'sieur Hugo and M'dame Drouet is pushing me to become more knowledgeable about the happenings of the world and to be a more interesting conversationalist. Arnaud had always come home with new stories to tell and as I listened was only too conscious I'd never see the places he described so vividly. It is hard for women to do anything a little adventurous unless they are wealthy, and I will never be that.

Today the warm spring-like sun has tempted me to go for a walk towards Fermain, where I was headed that fateful day I lost my child. It will be invigorating after a morning spent concentrating on my copying. I want to stroll through the woods where bluebells will shortly be in abundance and follow the cliff paths above Fermain Bay. The birds are in fine form, chirruping to each other as if to say spring is on its way and it is good to be alive. And it is. I find myself smiling and greeting those I meet, where once I would have averted my eyes, not wishing to be acknowledged. Even my widow's black fails to dampen my humour as I stand on one of the paths and gaze down towards the bay. The golden sand gleams under the sun and I am reminded of my home in France. Cherbourg has similar cliffs and sandy beaches and in the school holidays my parents took us for picnics and paddling in the sea. My heart clenches at the memories of the days gone by and my beloved family, but I am determined not to become maudlin. They are gone, but I am still alive and have much to look forward to.

'Oh, Papa, you would be amazed to learn that your little girl is now a scribe for none other than M'sieur Victor Hugo himself! Who would have expected that?' I whisper to the swaying leaves of the tree I am propped against, imagining my father's delight. I hear a deep chuckle behind me and turn to see a smiling M'sieur Hugo not two feet away, his back to a tree. I want the ground to open up and swallow me. Dropping a curtsy, all I can do is stand there, bereft of speech. He doffs his hat.

'Don't upset yourself, *ma petite*, I often talk to the trees when I'm alone. And you were talking to your late papa, *non*?' I nodded. 'Then I do hope he heard you and is proud of what you are doing. My own father, a general, was disappointed in me as I preferred poetry and politics to following him into the army.'

'I cannot imagine such a life would have suited you, m'sieur, and the world of literature would have been the poorer.'

He lifted my hand and kissed it. I feel heat rise to my cheeks.

'You are right, of course, and thank you for your kind words. I'll leave you to enjoy your walk as I continue my own.' With a nod, he continues on the path leading towards the bay. I am about to enquire after M'dame Drouet, but perhaps it is as well he has turned away. I don't want to appear too nosy. Deciding it's better not to follow him, I turn onto a different path which winds its way back towards the top road, breathing in the scent of wild garlic and primroses scattered along the verges. Another twenty minutes and I am beginning to tire, my body not yet accustomed to such exertion. Fortunately, I'm a matter of a few hundred yards from home, where I arrive with legs like jelly and a fast-beating heart.

'Oh, m'dame! What have you been doing? Off to bed with you now, for a nice lie down. I'll be up later with a cup of tea.'

I hardly need Sophie's exhortations and am soon lying down fully clothed apart from my boots. It has been an eventful, and tiring, afternoon.

The Inheritance

It was the first day of April and I sensed the nearness of spring as I made my way to *La Fallue*. I was at my usual place copying the latest pages of *Les Misérables* when m'dame motions me to stop a moment.

'We have noticed how proficient you have become, *ma chère*, and think it's time for you to work alone. You write so much more quickly than I, and will achieve more if m'sieur can send completed pages directly to you at his house. He will expect you there at nine o'clock tomorrow morning.' Her face bore a strained expression, as if she was not quite in agreement with this decision.

'Oh, m'dame, I'm grateful to be so trusted, but I shall miss your company in the mornings. I...I've grown to look forward to our time together.' It was true, apart from Sophie, she is my only companion and has become like a mother to me.

She smiled and patted my arm.

'And I shall miss you. But it doesn't mean we cannot spend time together on other occasions. We could meet up for tea in the afternoons when I'm back from my constitutionals and at other times when I'm alone. As you probably realise, I don't go out socially as it's a little *délicat*,' she coughed, 'for someone in my...position.' She gazed into the distance, no longer seeing me. 'I have few real friends here, as is to be expected, I suppose. These islanders view things differently to us French and are quick to condemn women such as I, even without knowing all the circumstances.' She turned back to face me, her expression dreamy. 'I fell in love with m'sieur when I was twenty-seven and now, at fifty-six, am as much in love as I was then. As is he. His marriage is...' she shrugged, 'as it is.'

For the first time I felt sorry for her. Until now, I have almost envied her lifestyle. To be at the side of such a man for so many years. But she wasn't truly at his side, was she?

'Of course we shall still meet up, m'dame, whenever you wish. I also don't have any friends here and...and miss my husband and my family. I wouldn't have made such a good recovery without your care.' We ended by giving each other a hug before continuing with our work. As I leave I can only look forward with joy to working more closely with M'sieur Hugo.

CHAPTER 15

Tess – May 2012

During her lunch break at the hospital on Tuesday Tess received a message from Jonathan announcing the arrival of baby Rosie, weighing in at 7lbs 4oz. A fuzzy photo accompanied the text, with the message saying mother and daughter were both well. Tess immediately replied offering her congratulations to all and spent the rest of the day smiling at everyone, even the grumpy old boy who insisted he should be admitted although his only problem seemed to be poor hygiene. Tess suspected he was probably homeless and referred him to a local charity for help. When her shift finished she bought a card and present from the hospital shop to send to Colette.

Once home Tess prepared a quick supper and poured a much-needed glass of wine. The good news about the baby had taken her mind off her own problems for a while, but now they herded back into full view. The chief one was what, if anything, to do about her parents. Sipping the wine, she came to the conclusion the only thing to do was confront her mother. And not on the phone this time. It would have to be face to face so she could see her mum's reaction. She was on an early shift the next day so sent Elaine a text to say she would like to meet for a drink at five o'clock as she had something to discuss, suggesting a wine bar handy for both of them. A reply came back an hour later – just one word, 'OK'. Tess spent the rest of the evening absorbed in another episode of *Doc Martin* to take her mind off the meeting to come.

The bar was nearly empty, waiting for the regulars who popped in after work for a quick one or two before going home. Her mother hadn't arrived and Tess ordered two glasses of white wine before settling at a table near the back which would, hopefully, remain quiet. Five minutes later, Elaine came in and she waved her over. She noticed her mother was dressed particularly smartly for a casual drink; a leather jacket she hadn't seen before, a silky blouse and figure hugging trousers. Her heart sank. Not a good sign.

'Hi, Mum, I've got you a drink. Pinot Grigio, okay?' She forced a smile as Elaine sat down, nodded and picked up her glass.

'So, what did you want to discuss that you couldn't say on the phone or at home?' she said, with a scowl.

Tess cleared her throat, wishing too late she hadn't suggested the meeting. The phone would have been easier...

'It's about you...and Dad. You don't seem to be getting on these days and, to be honest, I'm wondering if there's a...a problem.' Tess took a gulp of wine and hoped her mother would offer an angry response.

'If there was a problem, what business would it be of yours?' Elaine shot back.

'I'm your daughter, so of course it's my business if you and Dad don't get on. You...you've changed, Mum. Dad says you're never in and it's hard to get hold of you.' She bit her lips. 'You're not seeing someone else, are you?'

Silence sat heavy between them for what seemed like hours but was probably a couple of minutes.

'Yes.'

'Mum!' Tess found a lump in her throat. Her poor father...

Elaine looked up from her glass, a look of defiance on her face.

'Nothing's happened yet, not that that's any of your business, but I'm not saying it won't.'

'How long have you known him?'

Elaine tossed her hair back, in the manner of a young girl, Tess thought.

'A few months. We met at a mutual friend's birthday party and we just seemed to click.' She dropped her eyes, perhaps not wanting to see the condemnation in her daughter's face.

'I see. So he knows you're married?'

Elaine nodded.

'Yes, your father was at the party, too. The...man's a widower, has been for five years. Hasn't been out with anyone since his wife died.' Elaine twiddled her glass, still avoiding Tess's eyes.

What could she say to her mother? At least she wasn't having an affair *yet*.

'But what about Dad? Don't you love him anymore?'

Elaine finally raised her eyes.

'To be honest I don't know. As I said the other week, we don't want the same things anymore. He's changed since he retired, lost the drive he used to have. I'm not ready to settle for carpet and slippers yet. I want to enjoy life, go places, have fun.' Her face took on an animated look as she said this.

Tess groaned inwardly. It was getting worse.

'Have you considered counselling, Mum? You and Dad. Talk through your feelings and what you want from life. It might help, before it's…it's too late.'

Her mother shook her head.

'I doubt if that'd help, but I understand why you're suggesting it. You want everything to carry on as normal, don't you? Then you can forget about us and swan off to Guernsey with a clear conscience,' Elaine said, her face flushed with anger.

Taken aback by her mother's vehemence, Tess sat mute. Was she only interested in how her parents splitting up would impact on her? Or did she care about the effect on *them*? It didn't take her long to come to a conclusion.

'Mum, whatever you may think, I do care about both of you and would hate to see you split up. And if it was because you found someone else, then I admit I'd be on Dad's side. But whatever happens, I have to live my life as I see fit and it looks like that means moving back to Guernsey.' She stared hard at her mother, who returned her stare, defiance in her eyes. 'I think you should give your marriage a chance before taking up with someone else that's all. But,' she sighed, 'I expect you'll do just what you want.'

Elaine swallowed the rest of the wine and stood, her face pinched with anger.

'Thanks for the drink.' She turned and marched to the exit.

Tess was left wondering if she'd made the situation worse and put her head in her hands. Her eyes blurred with tears. Should she or shouldn't she tell her father?

Work kept her preoccupied the next day and by the time Tess arrived home she was in no mood to dwell on her parents' marriage. She switched on her laptop to check her emails and saw one had arrived from the practice manager in Guernsey. Taking a deep breath she clicked on it and scanned it quickly. Relief flooded through her as she read 'pleased to offer…probationary period six months…on completion contract…could lead to a partnership'. The tension of the last couple of days floated away and she punched the air as she poured herself a glass of wine to celebrate. Reading the email again, Tess noted they had mentioned a start date of 1st July, subject to references. This fitted perfectly with the end of her current contract which ended in six weeks, giving her a couple of weeks to settle into life in Guernsey before starting work.

After firing off her acceptance of the offer, including details of her referee, Tess phoned Jonathan to talk jobs and babies. After that, her rumbling stomach insisted on being fed and she cooked some pasta, serving it with a readymade sauce for ease. She told herself that once settled in her Guernsey home, she would make more of an effort with cooking. After all, there would no longer be the excuse of extra-long shifts and unsocial hours.

The next day Tess saw her boss who was happy to supply a reference and wished her well with her new job. That evening she phoned her father on his mobile to tell him.

'That's wonderful news, love. I couldn't be more pleased for you and I know it's what you want. When do you start?'

She told him, then said, 'And how are things with you, Dad? You sounded a bit down when we last spoke.'

She heard him sigh.

'I'm okay, but something's not right with your mother. She's out more than she's in and when I offered to take her away for a weekend she flatly refused to go. Said she had a lot of social events coming up and didn't want to miss any. So I'm back to square one.' He coughed. 'Still, I'm sure it will sort itself out.

The important thing is you've got a new job and a new house back in Guernsey and that makes me very happy. As long as you'll have us over when the house is ready, mind,' he said, laughing.

'Oh, for sure. No worries. I'll ring soon, Dad. Take care.' She had come to the conclusion it wasn't her place to tell him about her mother, much as it hurt her to think how he was being deceived. Tess then sent a text to Elaine telling her about the job. Best to avoid further confrontation.

After making further calls to local friends and Charlotte and Andy in Guernsey with her news, Tess sent an email to her brother suggesting they talk via Skype soon. It occurred to her she needed to put the flat on the market. The equity wasn't great but would help towards the cost of renovating *St Michel*. Sighing, she started writing a To Do list, not looking forward to the upheaval that lay ahead. Still, it would be worth it in the end.

The next few days were filled with work, arranging for valuations of the flat and writing lists of what she wanted to keep and what could be sold or given to charity shops. Early the following week the quote came in from Premium Builders and it was higher than Andy's ballpark figure. Tess could only hope Jack's figure would be lower, even though that meant she would have to have regular contact with him. The thought was unsettling and she wasn't sure if this was because he had seemed too sure of himself or because she found him attractive. Pushing it to the back of her mind, Tess whipped around the flat making it presentable for the estate agents arriving the next day.

As Tess closed the door on the third agent she heaved a sigh of relief. All their valuations were better than she had hoped and within ten thousand pounds of each other. It appeared the market was picking up after the crash a few years before and the agents were confident the flat would be easy to sell. One firm appealed to her above the others for their enthusiasm and professional approach and she phoned to confirm them as sole agents. Another tick against the ever-present To Do list.

The quote from Jack Renouf popped into her inbox the next day and Tess held her breath as she opened the attachment. Phew! It was close to Andy's figure and Jack had confirmed a start date of three weeks from the quote being accepted and a build time of about three months, meaning Tess would be able to take up residence by late August, if all went to plan. She'd just have to learn to get along with Jack for the short time they would spend together. No problem. Tingling with excitement now the last jigsaw piece was slotted into place, Tess emailed Jack to accept his quote and then phoned Andy.

'Hi, I've accepted a quote from Jack…' she went on to give Andy the details and to ask if he and Charlotte were still happy to have her as a lodger.

'We'll be happy to have you. The guest suite is self-contained as we designed it with Charlotte's mother in mind.' He chuckled, adding, 'We both felt we'd cope better with her visits if there were some space between us. And I'm glad you've gone with Jack. He takes pride in his work and any developments he's completed have been first rate. What are you going to do about the contents of the house?'

'There's very little worth keeping so I thought recycling or the tip. I need to come over for a day or two and organise that and getting the boxes to your place, if you can recommend a man with a van?'

'Sure, I'll email you some contact details. It might be worthwhile asking Jack's advice on the furniture as he's got a nose for what's good and what isn't.'

After a quick chat with Charlotte, Tess was reassured she was also happy to have her stay and in fact was looking forward to female company. And now it was time to start the clear-out in the flat.

The next few weeks sped by as Tess counted down the days to her departure to Guernsey. She saw little of her parents but kept in touch by phone. Ken made no comment about Elaine's behaviour so Tess hoped her mother was reconsidering her new 'friendship'. Viewings on the flat were encouraging and nearly three weeks after accepting Jack's quote, Tess flew over to Guernsey on her day off to arrange removal of the contents of the house. The boxes had already been collected and were now stored in Andy's attic and when Tess walked into *St Michel* it looked so much bigger then she remembered. The house had a different feel to it now only the furniture remained. Tess thought of Eugénie. Would she learn more of her story? She wanted to. But where was the evidence? Was there anything left in the house from that time? Apart from the bed and a couple of other pieces of furniture, nothing. Surely there must be something, somewhere, she thought, stroking a table.

She wandered around the house waiting for Jack to arrive at nine o'clock, somewhat unsure of how they would react after their last meeting. At least the air had been cleared, and he obviously was keen to work for her so she only needed to be the polite but firm client and all would be well. So why did she feel more like a schoolgirl about to meet her latest crush? Jack was coming round to help her decide what furniture was worth selling, keeping or recycling so the house could be emptied ready for the work to begin the following week.

He surprised her by arriving dead on time.

'Morning, Doctor,' he said, as she opened the door.

'Morning, Jack. And for heaven's sake drop the "doctor". You've made your point,' she said, exasperated. 'Tess will do.'

He inclined his head in acknowledgement and followed her into the hall, a clipboard under his arm.

'Before we start, I'd like to say thanks for entrusting the work to me and my team. I promise you won't be disappointed.' His dark eyes crinkled at the corners as he smiled and Tess felt heat rising up her neck. She turned away to hide it and muttered an innocuous reply before moving swiftly into the sitting room. He followed behind.

'I suspect some of this stuff is as old as the house. Certainly looks early Victorian. Are there any pieces you particularly want to keep?' he said, his voice neutral, as they stood in the sitting room. She glanced at her list.

'The bookcases and the dining table downstairs. Nothing in the kitchen and perhaps the four-poster in the main bedroom and the bookshelves upstairs.'

He nodded.

'Good choice. You could sell any of them for decent money but they'll mix well with any modern furniture you buy. And it's nice to have a few family heirlooms to pass down. I'll make a list as we go round and if you only plan to keep a few items they can probably be stored in one room out of harm's way as we work through the house.'

'Great.' That would save paying storage, she thought, as they made a start downstairs.

By the time they had finished, the list for sending to recycling or the tip was far longer than what she wanted to keep. Jack pointed out that some of the better furniture, ornaments and paintings which she didn't want were worth sending to auction, with the auctioneers conveniently situated in Cornet Street.

'Why not give them a call? There's a good chance someone could pop round today and if they agree to sell anything for you see if they can collect as soon as possible. The rest,' he scanned the long list, 'I can organise to go to the recycling at Bulwer Avenue or the tip at Chouet. And if you've time today, it'd help if you could remove all the old curtains and bag them up with any small items going to the tip.'

Tess readily agreed and they then spent time confirming the timetable for the agreed works. Andy would project manage until Tess arrived and would remain on hand as needed.

'Right, I'll be off. See you in a few weeks. Good luck with your new job.' Jack reached out to shake her hand and she took it, thanking him. After he left she experienced the odd sensation of being abandoned. Weird. Trying to shake it off, she phoned Martel Maides, the auctioneers, and they agreed to send someone round at twelve. She kept busy by bagging up the curtains which almost fell off the old brass rails, leaving rust stains from the hooks on the material. More light flooded the rooms as the curtains came down, exposing the dingy paintwork and peeling wallpaper. Tess double-checked for anything else to bin before piling up the black sacks outside. She just had time to wash her hands before the valuer arrived from the auctioneers. He agreed with Jack's assessment of their having value and said all the items could be added to their next general sale in two weeks and offered to collect them the day the builders were due to start. Tess signed a form to this effect and breathed a sigh of relief. Mission accomplished! With a few hours clear before her return flight, she phoned Colette and asked if she could come round to admire the baby. Permission duly granted she called a taxi before popping next door to say a quick hello to Heather with the news of her job and the start of the building work.

'Brilliant news, Tess. So pleased for you and I look forward to you being our new neighbour eventually. Just pop in whenever you're round at the house, won't you?' Heather hugged her goodbye and Tess promised to do so, as the taxi arrived to take her to Bordeaux. Now for some fun time.

The trip to Guernsey, short as it was, had been enough to make Tess impatient to leave Exeter for good. The time spent with Colette and baby Rosie had reminded her how much she was looking forward to being able to see them regularly and to building up a network of new friends. Possibly even embark on a proper, meaningful relationship. Unlike the short-term relationships based mainly on lust which had been the feature of the last few years. Not that she was looking for a forever-after partner, but she was ready for more than a quick fling.

Tess had only been home an hour when her phone rang.

'Hi, Dad, good timing. I was going to ring later. Everything all right?' For a moment the line remained silent and then she heard her father's voice say, heavy with despair, 'I'm so glad you're back, love. Your...your mother's left me.'

❧ CHAPTER 16 ❧

Tess May/June 2012

Tess drove to her parents' house as fast as the traffic allowed, her hands gripping the steering wheel hard. The pain in her father's voice still echoed in her head as she weaved through the evening traffic, anxious to be there for him as he had always been there for her whenever she had been upset as a girl. From the time, at age eight, she was bullied by a gang of girls at school to the time at the age of fifteen, her first proper boyfriend, had callously announced he'd found someone else at her birthday party. Her father had reassured her of how much he loved her and that the actions of such people said more about them than her. Now she had a chance to redress the balance.

'Oh, Dad!' She flung her arms around him as he opened the door and they stood in a silent embrace for a few moments before he pulled back and led the way to the sitting room. He looked to have aged ten years since she saw him only a couple of weeks ago and his eyes were dull, devoid of their usual twinkle.

'I'll put the kettle on, shall I? Tea or coffee?'

'Tea, love. Thanks.' He slumped into his usual chair while Tess went into the kitchen to make the tea. Judging by the mess, her father had eaten and left the plates and pots in the sink. While waiting for the kettle, she stacked the dishwasher and cleaned the worktops. The tea made, she took the mugs back into the sitting room.

'Right, now tell me exactly what's happened, Dad,' she said, handing him his mug and sitting opposite him.

'I went off as normal this morning about ten to play golf and left your mother getting ready to go out for coffee, so she said, with her friends. Nothing out the ordinary.' He rubbed his face with his free hand and drew a deep breath before continuing. 'I came back at two, expecting to see her car in the drive, but it wasn't there. I just assumed she'd decided to stay out for lunch, as she does sometimes, but when I went into the kitchen there was this…this note on the side.' A flash of pain swept his face and Tess reached over and squeezed his arm. 'She said she'd met someone else and…and wanted some space while she made up her mind what to do. Staying with a friend, she said, but didn't say where or who.'

Tess sipped her tea, anger at her mother's cowardly behaviour making her hands shake. She hadn't even had the guts to talk to her father face to face.

'Anything else in the note, Dad?'

He shook his head.

'Have you tried ringing her?'

'Oh, yes. Goes straight to voicemail. Tried a few times so I assume she's avoiding talking to me.'

As they drank their tea Tess decided to tell her father about her meeting with her mother a few weeks before.

'I didn't tell you at the time as I hoped it would blow over and Mum assured me nothing had happened between them. I'm so sorry, Dad.'

'Not your fault, love. I did say I thought something was up with her, but was too scared to say anything. Talk about having my head in the sand, eh?' He gave her a half-hearted smile and her heart lurched. He didn't deserve to be cast aside like a worn-out coat, but then her mother had always been selfish.

'Have you told Clive?'

'No, thought I'd wait and see if we could sort it. No need to involve the lad, as what can he do thousands of miles away?' His face took on a faraway look, as if he was trying to see her brother. They'd been close, doing manly things together, like fishing and making odd-looking objects in the shed, but Ken had given his blessing when Clive said he wanted to move to Canada, even though it must have been hard for him. Her father had never been one for showing a lot of emotion, unlike her mother, who was prone to let everyone know when she was upset or angry.

'You're right. Let's keep it between ourselves for the moment and you can tell anyone who asks that Mum's gone to visit a sick friend. Do you think you can pretend nothing's wrong, Dad? For the moment, anyway.'

'I suppose so. It'd be better than being the object of pity,' he said, with a deep sigh.

'Good. In the meantime I'll try and get hold of Mum and encourage her to talk to you. She owes you that, at least.' She glanced at her watch. 'Are you going to be okay if I leave you? I'm on an early shift tomorrow and need to get to bed soon.'

He nodded.

'Yes, you get off, love, and thanks for coming round. Don't worry about me, you've got enough on your plate at the moment.' He stood as Tess went to hug him and clung to her for longer than normal. She felt bad about leaving him but they were so short-staffed at work, she had no choice.

Tess didn't get a chance to phone her mother until late the next morning when she was on a break. To her surprise, Elaine answered.

'I've been expecting you to call, Tess. Did your father put you up to it?'

'No, he didn't, I offered to contact you as you've ignored his calls. Does you moving out mean you and this…this other man have got more serious?' Tess could barely get the words out, cringing at the thought of her mother having sex with someone other than her father.

'Maybe. But moving out has more to do with wanting time and space to decide whether or not I want to stay with your father.' Elaine's voice was brittle and Tess fought to hold back her anger.

'I see. As it's all come as a shock to Dad, do you think you could meet him to talk about how you feel? He's terribly upset and would like a chance to discuss it with you. Not too much to ask, is it?'

A heavy silence echoed down the line.

'I'll think about it. Tell him not to keep phoning and I'll ring him when I'm ready.' After a pause, Elaine asked, 'How are your plans for your move going?'

'Fine, the builders start work next week and I'm staying with friends until I can move in.'

'Hmm. Well, I must go now. Bye.' The line went dead.

Tess was left feeling as cast aside as her father and if she hadn't been in the staff canteen would have vented her anger by throwing something. As it was all she could do was grit her teeth and return to the chaos of A & E.

Viewings of the flat were steady and a couple of weeks later two people had made offers, both a little low. The agent discussed this with Tess and they agreed both parties would be told of the other offer and within hours one had upped theirs to the asking price. First time buyers, Tess was delighted to agree completion mid-July and even happier when the young couple wanted to buy some of the furniture. Being a one-bedroom flat there was little furniture anyway and Tess advertised the remainder on Gumtree. The days were taking her nearer to her leaving and as yet her mother had still not phoned her father, leaving him looking more drawn every time she saw him. Tess invited him round for meals when she could, determined to make sure he ate proper meals sometimes. She sent Elaine texts, urging her to phone Ken, but these were ignored. Worried her father was slipping into a deep depression, she could only hope her mother would get in touch, even if it was to say their marriage was over. At least he would know where he stood.

Tess was in constant contact with Andy and Jack as they kept her updated with progress on *St Michel*. Old, crumbling plaster was hacked off the walls and floorboards lifted so joists could be inspected. Tess gasped at the photos of the inside now looking somewhat worse than when she inherited it. She had agreed to the removal of the chimney breast in the dining room and the bedroom above to make the rooms bigger and this had made the rooms look like war zones. Steel joists provided appropriate support. She took a deep breath, reminding herself this was temporary and focused on planning her new kitchen, bathrooms and a new downstairs cloakroom. This was the fun part and, whenever she had a spare moment on her own, would pore over the drawings Andy had sent, envisaging herself in what promised to be an elegant and beautiful home with shed-loads of original charm.

May morphed into June and Tess was up to her eyes in packing, planning and working long shifts in the A & E. She arrived home one evening and had just put the kettle on when her father phoned.

'Hi, Dad, how are things?'

'Okay. I've had a call from your mother and she wants us to meet for a talk. Wouldn't say if she was coming back.' Tess heard the catch in his voice and her stomach twisted. 'We're meeting tomorrow afternoon so I guess I'll find out then what she wants.'

'Let's hope it's good news, Dad. I'll be rooting for you.' Ken then asked how things were progressing with the house before finishing the call. For a moment Tess was tempted to phone her mother, but thought better of it. She would know soon enough what her mother had decided.

A serious multi-car crash on the M5 the next day meant Tess and all the hospital medical staff were run off their feet, with no-one stopping for a break. By the time she arrived home all Tess wanted to do was grab some food and fall into bed. She checked her phone to find four missed calls from her father and remembered he was meeting her mother. Deciding she had to eat before calling him, she made some toast, slathered it with butter and jam and made a cup of coffee. Feeling more human, she dialled his number.

'Hi, Dad, sorry I haven't got back before, nightmare at work today. How'd it go with Mum?' She crossed her fingers.

'Bad, love. She...she says she wants a divorce.' Heavy sobs echoed down the line.

❧❧ CHAPTER 17 ❧❧

Eugénie's Diary – April 1862

I arrived promptly at Hauteville House, my palms clammy from nerves. The thought of copying the manuscript unsupervised and within m'sieur's own walls suddenly seemed quite frightening. The maid led me to the staircase on the left of the hall, quite narrow dark wood which twisted upwards towards a skylight some floors above. The walls are covered in fabric and carpet covers the stair treads. She turned through a doorway on the left and I followed her into a room even more flamboyant than the tapestried room I'd seen on my first visit. Hung with red damask and embroideries of glass beads and gilt and copper thread on the walls and ceiling. Red and gold curtains hung at the full-height windows. My jaw dropped.

'Takes your breath away, doesn't it? Only finished a few months ago, it was, like the blue drawing room through there,' the girl nodded to an archway separating this room from the next. A softer, cooler-looking room lined with blue damask and pearl and silver tapestries. Together the rooms must have been around twelve metres long. I felt even more insignificant and out of place.

'The master says you're to work at this table,' she continued, going over to the large carved table in the middle of the room, where paper, ink and pages of handwritten manuscript were waiting for me. An armchair was already placed, facing out to the window to the garden below.

'Thank you, it all looks splendid.'

'I'll bring you a carafe of water, m'dame, and would you like some coffee now or later?'

'Later would be fine, thank you.'

She nodded and left, closing the door behind her. Before setting to work I couldn't resist the opportunity to explore a little. Tiptoeing across the brightly-coloured carpets, I took a turn about both rooms, noticing a door on the left leading to a conservatory furnished with ottomans and a carpet. New shoots from plant pots curled up the windows. Everything smelled fresh and newly painted. After a quick look out of the window I took my place at the table and began to work, becoming absorbed once more in the story of Cosette and Valjean taking shape as I transcribed the scribblings of M'sieur Hugo.

The time passed quickly and it was only a rumble in my stomach that alerted me to the approach of lunchtime. I knew that m'sieur always broke off at one o'clock for lunch and that was the time for me to stop work. An elegant clock on the mantelpiece showed the time as fifteen minutes to the hour. I put my pen in the tray and flexed my fingers before running my eyes over the last paragraph I'd written.

At nightfall, Jean Valjean re-entered Paris, and got into a cabriolet which conveyed him to the Esplanade of the Observatory. Here he got down, and the pair proceeded in the darkness toward Boulevard de 'Hôpital. The day had been strange and full of emotions for Cosette: she felt tired, and Jean Valjean perceived it by her hand, which dragged more and more...

The door opened and, turning, I saw M'sieur Hugo enter the room. He looked dishevelled, his hair springing up from his head and his hands blotted with ink stains. Standing, I bobbed a curtsy.

'You are finishing for the day, *ma petite?*' he said, his face creased with tiredness. I knew he started work early in the morning and felt guilty I was only required to work for four hours.

'Yes, m'sieur. That is the arrangement as I understand it, but I'm happy to work longer—'

He shook his head and smiled.

'No, no we must not wear you out also, *n'est ce pas?* Let me see how many pages you have copied.' He stood by me at the desk and checked the pile of freshly written pages. 'Why, this is excellent work. You write quickly, *ma petite*, and at this rate you will be able to keep pace with me and we'll be ready to send another volume to the publishers quite soon.' He rubbed his hands together, his tiredness seemingly dissolved. 'Come, I have something to show you before luncheon is ready.'

He led the way up the stairs and two flights later we stood on the narrow landing with the skylight ahead. He beckoned me through a narrow doorway on the left and we entered a low-ceilinged, narrow room with little decoration and not much furniture. I was puzzled. What was so interesting about this small room? Then I turned to face the window and understood.

'Oh! It's like a miniature conservatory!' I cried, gazing at a fully glazed room perched as it was on the roof, and reached through a glazed door which once must have led onto a terrace.

'Isn't it marvellous? Today is the first time I've been able to work in here even though it's not finished. I call it my "crystal room". Come,' he added, inviting me to join him, 'see what I look out onto when I'm in here.'

I picked my way carefully through piles of violet, blue and white faience tiles waiting to be mounted on the far wall where the outlines of structures had been partly tiled. Some rubble lay on the bare floor and an unfinished tiered seating area took up space on the right-hand side. Joining him at the furthest glazed wall I stared at the view spread out before me.

'See, *ma petite*, I am in the clouds up here, at the centre of my universe: overlooking not only Castle Cornet and St Peter Port, but all the islands and when it is clear, as it is today, the coast of our beloved France.' His eyes sparkled with enthusiasm, as well they might. It was a wondrous sight. A veritable eyrie in the sky.

I touched the dark window frame, surprised to find it cold.

'The frame is of steel, to give it strength and survive against the onslaught of the sun. I am installing a fireplace and the seating will be carpeted, but there is little else I shall need, other than my writing table,' he said, pointing to a wooden flapped table against the inside wall.

'It is indeed a wonderful construction, m'sieur. I've never seen anything like it.'

He threw his arms wide.

'It is a miniature version of England's Crystal Palace is it not? I shall be working in here instead of my old lookout.' He waved to the small room behind us. 'As you see, exile has not only detached me from France, it has almost detached me from the Earth.' He laughed. 'But now I must hurry or I'll be late for lunch and you must be off home. Let's go down.'

I collected my belongings from the salon below and arrived in the hallway in time to see m'sieur greet a young woman about to enter the dining room at the bottom of the stairs.

'Papa, I must speak with you...' she stopped when she saw me, her eyes wide with surprise.

'Adèle, my dear, this is M'dame Sarchet, who has begun work as my copyist and will be here in the mornings.'

'M'amselle,' I said bobbing a curtsy. She inclined her head. I saw the resemblance between her and the dead Léopoldine, only this woman had a wildness about her eyes. They travelled over me, taking in my mourning garb but she made no comment, only grabbing hold of her father's arm and forcing him into the dining room. I caught a hurried nod from him before they were out of sight. The maid, who'd been hovering in the background now came forward to see me out.

'Don't worry, m'dame, she's an odd one, that one. Doesn't like other young women around her father and spends most of her time at the blessed piano, driving everyone mad.'

'Oh, I wasn't upset, just thought...well, it doesn't matter. What's your name? I feel I should know it if I'm to be a regular visitor here.' I smiled at the girl, not more than about fourteen years old, I thought, with an open, friendly face.

'Henriette Morvan, m'dame. I've only been here a few weeks myself, and still getting used to the ways of the household.' She opened the door for me and I stepped out into the hazy sunshine.

'Thank you, Henriette. I'll see you tomorrow.'

She nodded and the door closed behind me. As I walked the few yards to my home my head was full of the events of the morning and my first sight of Adèle Hugo. With a shock, it came to me that the expression on her face was of jealousy. I would need to take care around her.

Friday 11th April
I have seen the young woman again today. I had been working as normal upstairs in the drawing room and was collecting up the copied pages of manuscript when M'sieur Hugo rushed in. I

had only caught brief glimpses of him in the previous days and my little friend, Henriette, had told me how busy he was and hardly stopped even to eat. Certainly the piles of the manuscript had been growing at an alarming rate and I was struggling to keep up.

'Ah, *ma petite*, I need your help. With my wife and sons away, we need more hands to help with the dinner for the poor. Are you able to stay? Naturally you will be able to eat with us.'

My face must have shown my puzzlement as he explained that for some weeks, every Friday, he had opened his house to poor children and their mothers and they were fed a simple meal before being encouraged to play in the garden. This week there were ten children and they were served by himself, his family and the servants.

'I would be honoured to help, m'sieur. What a wonderful gesture! Not unlike something Jean Valjean would do,' I replied with a smile.

He clapped his hands in delight.

'Well said! You are enjoying my book, then?' I nodded, somewhat unsure whether I had been too bold. 'Good, but we must hurry as the children and their mothers are gathering in the kitchen to wash their hands before adjourning to the dining room. My daughter Adèle will be helping, too.'

As I followed him downstairs my initial pleasure at being of service evaporated at the thought of how his daughter had behaved towards me the first time we met. I sighed inwardly, hoping she would pay me no heed and concentrate on the poor children.

We arrived in the hall as the children and their mothers filed up from the kitchen, escorted by Henriette and Marie Sixty the cook. The faces of the 'guests' were pinched with hunger and their clothes little more than rags and my heart went out to them as they shyly shook the host's hands before entering the dining room where the table was already set for the meal. I noticed Mam'selle Adèle waiting at the end of the table as she directed the children to their seats. There was no warmth in her actions and I gained the impression she felt this mingling with the poor was beneath her and she made sure not to touch them. Very different from her father, who gaily welcomed them all as if they were honoured guests and not from the slums of St Peter Port. It was as we were taking our seats that Adèle saw me and her face became even more closed in, if that were possible. I made sure to stay as far away as possible, standing behind two mothers who looked as if they hadn't eaten since last they were here.

M'sieur said a simple prayer, offering thanks to God, and then we started serving the food. I was amazed to see plates of meat and vegetables and carafes of wine, for both the mothers and their offspring, though served with water to the children. It was a common practice in France, but I'd not seen it in Guernsey, where sobriety was much admired. The diners were silent as they ate, the children pushing food into their mouths as if this were likely to be their last meal for some time. Marie and Henriette returned to the kitchen for more food and I busied myself with cutting up food for a small child who struggled with the cutlery.

A voice hissed in my ear, 'What do you think you're doing here? At my mother's dining table while she is away?'

I jumped with shock and turned to see Adèle behind me, her face close to mine and her eyes dark with fury. Glancing across the room I saw m'sieur deep in conversation with a young lad at the other end of the table. He didn't seem aware of where his daughter was.

'I do not know what you suspect me of, mam'selle, but I assure you I'm a respectable widow who is grateful to your father for offering me honest employment after my recent loss. He asked me to help today as you have so many guests.' I met her glare with forced calm, determined she would not see how I shook inside. Her insinuation was hurtful and without any basis, except perhaps in her fevered imagination.

She opened her mouth to respond when M'sieur Hugo called out, 'Is something amiss, Adèle?' Turning to face him I saw he was frowning, tapping the table as if annoyed. His daughter arranged her features into a smile, replying that all was well. She left my side but not before pinching my arm hard enough to bring tears to my eyes. I bent down as if to retrieve something from the floor and wiped the tears with my handkerchief. The child gaped at me open-mouthed but said nothing. Marie and Henriette arrived with more food and the meal continued without further incident. At the end m'sieur again offered a short prayer before suggesting the children go into the garden to play and their mothers could go with them to enjoy the sunshine. Marie led them out and Henriette began to clear away their plates and glasses, placing them on trays set on side-tables. I moved to help her but m'sieur came up to me and said I was to take a seat and Marie would bring us our food.

I was uncomfortable at the thought of sitting down with Adèle after her outburst, but realised she was nowhere to be seen.

'Please, sit. You have earned your meal and I'd like to talk to you.' He pulled out a chair for me and I sat, wondering if he believed I had done something to anger his daughter. My stomach lurched at the thought. I dearly wanted to keep my place as his copyist. The maid left with a full tray and we were alone.

'It seems my daughter doesn't share my good opinion of you, *ma petite*.' He sighed, drumming his fingers on the table, his gaze on my face. I swallowed. Was he going to dismiss me? Shifting in his chair, he went on, 'Adèle is a little…difficult. She is prone to melancholia and the doctors have tried their best with her and she is, I know, lonely since we left Paris, missing the excitement of the social whirl we enjoyed. And now she is without her mother and brothers and feels I should devote all my attention to her, when I'm not working. You understand?'

'Of course, m'sieur.'

He patted my arm.

'Good. Please make allowances for her if she is less than polite towards you. I don't want her to scare you away.'

I breathed a sigh of relief and further conversation was interrupted by Marie and Henriette bringing in our food.

'Where's Mam'selle Adèle, m'sieur?' Marie asked as she deposited a tray on the table. I noted we were to dine on the same fare as the poor mites before us and was impressed by the egalitarianism of this.

He waved his hands in exasperation.

'Oh, she has gone to her room in a sulk, Marie. Please take a tray up to her, if you would be so kind.'

Marie rolled her eyes, as if to say this was not a new occurrence and bustled away, followed by the maid, who winked at me as she left. M'sieur poured us both a glass of wine and I filled my plate, aware of how hungry I was after a good morning's work. Between mouthfuls, he regaled me with stories of his time in Paris, of the salons and theatres and the glittering crowd of artists, actors and writers. I was spellbound. His descriptions were so vivid I could imagine myself there, discoursing with the likes of Balzac, Gautier and Flaubert. And as a Senator, he'd been active in government, fighting for the rights of the poor. My admiration for him rose the more I learned. I left for home almost dizzy with the visions he had laid before me, flattered that I was deemed worthy of such conversation. And relieved that Mam'selle Adèle had not turned him against me.

CHAPTER 18

Tess – June/July 2012

Tess's vision blurred as anger shot through her and she had to take a number of deep breaths before saying she would be right round. She drove on auto-pilot; fortunately there was little traffic and she pulled up in the drive fifteen minutes later. Tess sat in the car until she felt calmer and then rang the bell. Her father, his eyes dull and red-rimmed, opened the door.

'Hello, love. Come in.'

Tess threw her arms around him, and could feel his bones where once was flesh. Smelling whisky fumes on his breath, she bit her lip, let go and gently pushed him to the kitchen. She saw an open bottle of whisky and a glass on the table but no sign of any food. Not good.

'I'll make you some coffee and then order a takeaway. Do you prefer Chinese or Indian?'

'I'm not hungry, Tess. Really.' Ken slumped into a chair and Tess returned the whisky to the cupboard before filling the kettle.

'Dad, you have to eat. Doesn't matter if you can't manage much, but you have to eat something. So, Chinese or Indian?' She pulled out the takeaway menus from a drawer and placed them in front of him.

He looked up with a wry grin.

'Always were bossy, weren't you? Okay, let's go for Indian. You choose.'

Tess knew his favourites and rang through an order for both of them, hungry after missing lunch. They sat drinking coffee while they waited for the food and Ken told her more about Elaine's visit.

'She reckons she and this guy love each other and want to be together. And…and she says she no longer loves me and won't change her mind.'

By the time they had talked through the implications, including selling the family home, they were both in tears. The arrival of the food proved a welcome relief. Before she left, Tess suggested her father see his doctor for help with depression, worried about his lack of appetite and poor sleep. With her leaving in less than two weeks, the timing couldn't be worse. Driving home, Tess wondered if Elaine had deliberately chosen this time to drop her bombshell. Could she have hoped Tess would change her mind about leaving and stay for her father? And it also occurred to Tess that perhaps the reason her mother had been so upset about not inheriting the house was because she had seen it as a way to fund a new life. Well, in that she would be disappointed, Tess thought, grimly. *St Michel* was destined to provide a new start for *her* in Guernsey, which she had been forced to leave by her parents. From what her father had said recently, that decision had been led by Elaine and now, thanks to Doris, she was able to return. A sign of good karma, perhaps?

A couple of days before she was due to finish work, Tess was invited by a colleague to go for a farewell drink the following evening. She was happy to accept as they had become pals over the year she had been working in A & E. And it would be a welcome relief after having to cope with her father's low spirits. He had finally agreed to see his doctor and was now on antidepressants.

As Tess pushed through the doors to the pub favoured by the hospital staff, a cheer went up and she was taken aback to see a room full of medical colleagues waiting for her, including her boss. She caught a glimpse of a table laden with party food before being enveloped in hugs and having a glass of something chilled thrust into her hand. Afraid she was about to burst into tears Tess took a large swallow of wine before she could risk talking to anyone. Showered with questions about her move to Guernsey, it was a while before she managed to make a break for the food. She found a relatively quiet spot and tucked into a plate of chicken drumsticks, mini pizzas, rice salad and quiche. Music played in the background and the combination of wine, food and buzzy company encouraged her to relax and enjoy herself. Wisely, she had taken the bus to work that morning, anticipating a fairly heavy drinking session with her friend. The intensity of working in hospitals, particularly in A & E, could lead to staff engaging in stress-releasing drinking sessions after work. Tess had been to a number over the years and now hoped being a GP would be less stressful, for the sake of her liver if nothing else. Later, her boss called for silence as he gave a short speech, thanking Tess for her 'hard work, compassion and devotion to the patients' and wishing her well in her new life. When the clapping subsided, there were cries of 'speech, speech' and Tess was pushed towards the bar and her smiling boss.

'All I can say is thanks, boss, for saying such nice things about me and the cheque's in the post,' she said, with a grin. Once the laughter died down, she continued, 'You've been a great team and I've learnt a lot from you all this past year. The most impressive being the ability to down the equivalent of a week's recommended alcohol allowance in one evening and be able to turn up for an early shift the next day ready to save lives.' More laughter and a few claps. 'Seriously, although it's been tough, and there have been times when I just wanted to go home and cry, I stuck it out because I couldn't let you down. I'll miss you, but not the long, unsocial hours and I'm looking forward to my new life as a GP with time to hit the beach whenever I want. Not that I want to make you jealous, or anything.' She smiled as a few groans broke out. 'Thanks for arranging this evening and I wish you all the best in the future. Here's to you all,' she finished, raising her glass. Everyone joined in with the toast and Tess went in search of any remaining food. The party continued until closing time and taxis were called to deliver everyone home safely. Tess fell into bed in a happier mood than she had been for weeks.

At work the next day, Tess wasn't surprised to see a few bleary-eyed colleagues who gave her a cheery wave before rushing off to deal with the latest emergency. By the end of the busy day, she was both sad and excited about leaving and walked to her car dragging her feet. She was going out for a farewell dinner with her father and wasn't sure how he'd be.

Her mother had not suggested they meet, sending a text to wish her good luck. It promised to be a great evening. Not.

As it turned out, her father made a huge effort to be cheerful, even laughing when she told him about her leaving do. He said he thought the combination of antidepressants and a mild sleeping pill were helping.

'I'm still unhappy about your mother, love, but I'm trying to get on with my life. I joined that Facebook thingy you've told me about and connected with old Guernsey friends. Might go over soon and meet up with them. Stay in a B & B and have a little holiday. What do you reckon?'

'Brilliant idea, Dad. I could show you my house and we could have a meal or two together. It'll be fun.' Tess smiled at him, genuinely pleased he was making an effort. And it would ease her guilt about leaving him on his own if he made a trip to Guernsey. She enjoyed the evening and hugged him goodbye, with a promise to phone as soon as she arrived in Guernsey.

The next day Tess was up early and after loading her cases and a few boxes in the car, dropped off the flat keys at the estate agents. The ferry from Weymouth was leaving late morning and it was an hour and a half's drive from Exeter. The journey to her new life was about to begin.

The ferry crossing was smooth and much quicker than the old ferry Tess and her family had sailed in years before. The ship bustled with early summer tourists and locals returning from the mainland and Tess was relieved she didn't succumb to the seasickness that had plagued her on the previous journey. On her last flying visit Tess had bought a copy of Perry's guide showing all the Guernsey roads, indispensable for tourists and locals alike, thanks to the many unmarked lanes and small roads for such a small island. She had tried to memorise the route to Andy and Charlotte's house and set off up St Julian's Avenue heading towards the Rohais and the road to the west coast. Tess relaxed, taking in unremembered roads as the early summer sun bathed the island in warmth, filling her with a sense of optimism. Charlotte's warm welcome reinforced the feeling.

'Welcome, Tess. How was the crossing?' Charlotte said, flinging her arms around her. As Tess answered, Charlotte led her indoors, insisting on making her a drink before they unloaded the car. Tess was shown to what would be her home for at least a couple of months, a mini self-contained apartment on the top floor, which even boasted a tiny kitchen. Charlotte said she was welcome to share meals with them or be independent as she wished. Tess, once on her own and surrounded by unpacked cases and bags, couldn't help thinking how lucky she was, sending up a silent thank you to Jonathan and Colette for their introduction. She then phoned her father to tell him of her safe arrival. He sounded a bit flat, but said he was coping. Tess hated knowing there was nothing she could do to help and hoped her mother would see sense and go back home.

The following day Andy joined Tess to check on the progress at *St Michel*. Although she had been receiving updates, Tess was nervous about seeing the reality. And, she had to admit, of seeing Jack again in 'her' space. As she entered the hall the sound of drilling and banging filled her ears and she immediately thought of her neighbours and what they had to put up with. Andy steered her into the sitting room and she gasped. Since the last update the wall between this room and the dining room had been knocked out, creating a large, light room drawing the eyes to the view of the sea and Castle Cornet.

'Wow! This is better than I'd imagined. I'm going to have so much space,' she said waving her arms around.

'Glad you're pleased. I think you'll find the whole house will seem a lot bigger by the time it's finished,' Andy said, with a smile.

Tess took in the patches on the walls where crumbling plaster had been hacked off, exposing the old wiring, now to be replaced. The original floorboards looked to be in good condition, which was a bonus, although some had been uplifted. As Andy was explaining that so far any joists checked seemed sound, Jack walked in, dust turning his dark hair grey.

'Hi, Tess. Andy. Didn't hear you come in, I was upstairs checking the lads. So, what do you think?'

She was surprised to find the sight of Jack somewhat unsettling. Apart from the dusty hair, he was immaculate in a suit and tie. Hardly the normal attire of a builder. And very sexy. She cleared her throat.

'I've only seen this room but think it's great.'

He must have noticed her staring at his suit.

'Oh, I only called round to check how the work's going and to see you, of course. I don't usually get hands-on unless one of the men is sick and we have a deadline.' He grinned and went on, 'I have a meeting with my bank manager later so I spruced up a bit.'

'Right. Then you'd better shake off the dust in your hair,' Tess said, feeling stupid. Why would the owner of a successful property development company dirty his hands with his men? Somewhat tartly she added, 'Do you have time to show me around before your appointment?'

'Sure, that's why I'm here. Why don't we start downstairs? Too much of a racket upstairs at the moment,' he replied, running his hands through his hair.

Tess caught Andy giving her a quizzical look, but simply shrugged and followed Jack down to the basement. It had been completely gutted, the only sign it had ever been a kitchen the old pipes for the sink leaning awkwardly against the wall. Again, Tess found the space bigger than it had seemed, and what had been the old pantry and loo, an early twentieth century addition, now formed what would be a utility area. The original small kitchen window had been replaced with a French window bringing in more light. At the moment this led into the garden but would form the entrance to a conservatory when she could afford to add one.

Andy produced his 3D drawing of the proposed new kitchen and they spent some minutes discussing the choice of finish for the units and worktops. Tess liked the idea of a mix of contemporary with a touch of traditional and it was left that she would visit a showroom to finalise her choice. She also had to choose the bathroom and cloakroom fittings and promised to do it all within the week.

'Good. Let's go upstairs and see what you think. We've done most of the first floor and a guy's just started in the attic rooms. You'll have to watch your step as some of the floorboards are up.' Jack led the way up to the hall, pausing to show Tess how they proposed to fit a tiny cloakroom under the stairs. She had to admire the thought that was going into the work and it looked as if he and Andy made a good team.

Upstairs the floors were covered in a grey powder and bags of old plaster waited to be cleared. Like downstairs, the floorboards still in place looked to be in good condition and would only need a sand and polish, she thought. A couple of men were hacking away at the walls in the main bedroom and, judging by the noise, the same was happening in the attic. Tess was with Andy and Jack in the bathroom, now cleared of tiles and sanitaryware, visualising Andy's design, when there was a shout from above.

'Hey, boss, think you should come and see this.'

'Coming up,' Jack shouted back and started for the stairs, followed by Tess and Andy. The mess was even worse up here, with large pieces of plaster littering the floor, leaving little of the original in situ. Tess wasn't surprised as Jack had previously explained the attic walls were in poor condition thanks to damp under the windows and poor ventilation. They arrived in the larger of the two rooms to find a labourer, covered in so much dust only his eyes were clear in his face, standing by the middle of one wall which he had partly cleared of plaster. There seemed to be a large crack down the wall.

'What is it, Larry?' Jack said as they crowded in.

Larry grinned, revealing white teeth in the grey mask.

'Think I've found something interesting, boss. Look!' He slipped his fingers into the crack and pulled. Tess gasped as she realised it was a door and as Larry opened it wider, behind was what looked like a large walk-in cupboard. She moved forward to get a closer look in the dim light and Larry produced a torch, shining it over the contents. There was an antique looking desk, various cardboard boxes and, on the wall above the desk, several unmistakeable images of Victor Hugo.

CHAPTER 19

Tess – June 2012

'So this is where she kept everything!' Tess said quietly, her heart thumping with excitement. She stroked the desk, releasing more dust motes into the already dusty air.

Andy peered over her shoulder and whispered, 'Is this what I think it is? Does it belong to the woman you told us about?'

'Yes, I think so. I don't know why it had to be hidden like this, but hopefully the answer lies in here somewhere.' She pulled out a drawer revealing an assortment of personal items – handkerchiefs, pens, scraps of paper, an old-fashioned man's neck tie. Hugo's? Closing the drawer, Tess then removed the lid of one of the boxes. Inside was a stack of red cloth-bound books, each labelled 'Journal'. She pulled one out and flicked to the first page. It was beautifully written – in French. Of course it was! French was the language in the islands back in Victorian times, Tess knew that from school. Fortunately it had been one of her best subjects. She was about to read a bit when a cough reminded her she wasn't alone.

'I take it this is something important for you?' Jack asked with raised eyebrows.

'It is, yes. My ancestor Eugénie worked for Victor Hugo and it looks as if she kept her diaries hidden for some reason. Can we keep this cupboard as it is as I want to examine everything in more detail? How long has it been sealed in under the plaster?'

'Sure. We can have a handle and a lock on the door if you wish.' Jack examined the wall more closely. 'I'd say this was plastered over a hundred years ago as it's the lime plaster used at the time. Certainly not recent.'

'Thanks, I would like a lock and I'd rather no-one said anything about it,' she added, nodding towards Larry who had walked over to the door to chat with a mate.

'No problem. I'll ask the men to keep quiet, saying it's personal.'

'Thanks. Shall we continue our tour now? I'll come back later to have a closer look in the cupboard.'

Jack asked Larry to fit a door handle and lock before going back downstairs to finish looking around the first floor. Tess struggled to focus on what was being said, her mind buzzing with thoughts about their find. Her first impression had been it was a kind of shrine. A shrine to Victor Hugo by Eugénie Sarchet, her three-times great-grandmother, and who had kept items once belonging to her famous employer. She couldn't wait to examine everything in more detail but now was not the time. And to think this treasure trove had been here all along and Doris had never known! All that searching in the library and newspapers and it was under her own roof. Tess felt sad for her aunt, who had been so obsessed by Eugénie and Hugo.

When they had finished their discussions, Jack left for his appointment and Andy returned to his office, leaving Tess at a loose end. The sound of drilling reminded her about Heather and she popped next door.

'Tess! Good to see you, come on in and I'll make some coffee.'

Heather ushered her inside.

'Shall we go downstairs and sit outside? It's too nice to be stuck indoors.'

Tess agreed, conscious of the sounds coming through the adjoining wall and wondering if Heather was being tactful. She followed her friend down to the kitchen who signalled her to continue through the conservatory to the garden. Outside, Tess sat at a table on the patio and turned her face to the sun. As soon as Heather came out with a tray of coffee and cake Tess burst out with the news of the hidden cupboard.

Heather's eyes widened.

'Oooh! I thought you looked excited about something. Do tell me more.'

As they drank their coffee Tess told her the little she knew so far and that she would be undertaking a more thorough search later.

'Fortunately, my French is pretty good, thanks to an exchange visit I did in my teens. I can hardly wait to take the diaries home and start reading them. Find out what, if anything, happened between Eugénie and Hugo.' Tess tapped her fingers on the table as she imagined the possible tales hidden in those volumes. 'Of course, I've no idea how many diaries there are and what period they cover, but I did notice "1862" on a page in the diary I glanced at.'

'What a shame your aunt didn't know about this secret cupboard. She used to say she'd been sure there must be some record of Eugénie in the house, but never found anything. Odd, isn't it, that it was sealed away? Why the secrecy?' Heather's face screwed up in puzzlement.

'Exactly. Perhaps it will become clearer when I've gone through everything. All I can say now is that Eugénie must have had some crush on Hugo to squirrel away stuff like that. Almost creepy, like someone a bit unbalanced.' She chewed on her cake, wondering if Eugénie had been mentally unstable, and it had passed down the generations, as her mother had suggested about Doris.

'That's a bit dark, Tess. She was only young wasn't she? Lost her first husband tragically, Doris told me, so may have seen Hugo as a father figure. Who knows? But I look forward to you finding out more, to add a bit of excitement to my life,' Heather said, licking crumbs off her fingers.

'I'll keep you posted, don't worry. Oh, and before I forget, I'm so sorry about the noise, I hadn't appreciated how bad it would be.'

Heather shook her head.

'It's okay. That rather attractive builder of yours, Jack, came round to explain it would be worse initially while they're ripping stuff out, but it should improve soon. I've been spending time working in the garden, making the most of the lovely weather and going out for walks. Luckily, your other neighbour,' she waved her arm to her right, 'is away on a cruise and won't be back for ages. And it's good for us all to see your house renovated; property values and all that.'

Tess nodded, her mouth full of cake and her head noting Heather's description of Jack. She had to admit he was attractive, in spite of her reservations about him. At least if he wasn't around all the time, she might hardly see him. Which was good, wasn't it? He unsettled her, but she didn't want to look too much into why he did. Her life was complicated enough at the moment.

She stayed chatting with Heather for a while longer, enjoying the chance to sit in the sun and do nothing after the frenetic last few weeks. The thought of the mysteries lying in wait next door finally propelled her to her feet saying she should be going. As they reached the upper hall the silence told her the men were probably taking a lunch break and, after saying goodbye to her friend, Tess went back to *St Michel* for another look in the cupboard.

Larry was with the others, squatted on the stairs eating sandwiches and drinking from flasks. He proffered the keys for the new cupboard lock and Tess skipped upstairs with mounting excitement. While she had been next door the rest of the loose plaster had been removed and cleared and she undid the lock and pulled on the newly fitted handle. Everything was just as it had been. Using the spotlight on her phone, she examined the walls in more detail. Not only were there photos and drawings of Victor Hugo, but there were some small framed paintings and drawings of unusual landscapes, including what could be a stylised drawing of Castle Cornet and a couple of seascapes of rough seas and storms. They weren't signed but looked, to her untrained eye, to be by a competent hand. Then another picture caught her eye. The tones were sepia, of two women, in Victorian dress, sitting on a rug in the midst of a picnic, one young woman in a dark grey dress and the other late middle age, wearing a light coloured dress. The women were laughing and looking towards each other. As Tess shone the light more closely, she saw an inscription underneath, in French.

'*À ma chère Mme Eugénie Sarchet, en mémoire de notre pique-nique avec Mme Juliette Drouet*
Victor Hugo

The hand holding the phone shook as it dawned on her what she saw. A picture by Victor Hugo of her long-dead ancestor, Eugénie, having a picnic with his mistress. Wow! Tess was frozen for a moment while she let it sink in. Shining the light back on the other pictures, she realised they were probably by the same hand. Hugo's. What to do with such a find? For the moment she could leave everything locked away, but decided to take the boxes of diaries and the picture of Eugénie and Juliette. She needed Charlotte's help. After locking the cupboard Tess carefully carried the boxes downstairs until she came on the men finishing their lunch. Larry jumped up and offered to carry them to her car. Minutes later she was on her way to Charlotte's house.

Charlotte was nearly as excited as she was when Tess carried in the boxes and explained their provenance.

'What a find! And if the pictures you mention are also by Hugo, then they'd be worth a pretty penny,' Charlotte said as she studied the picture of Eugénie.

'That's not what interests me as much as the diaries. I'm hoping to learn more about Eugénie's relationship to Hugo which, from what I've seen so far, was at least very friendly,' Tess said, spreading out the diaries on the dining table. She checked the dates and set them in chronological order, beginning in 1861 and ending in 1888.

'It looks as if she started the journals when she married Arnaud Sarchet – see, it's here as the first entry.' She pointed it out to Charlotte, with the date 16th Mars (March).

'From my research, it appeared Eugénie began working as a copyist for Hugo about a year later, in 1862.' Charlotte flicked through the pages. 'I can see why he chose her, what beautiful writing. Easy to read, too, unlike some of the original writing by Hugo himself. Look,' she pointed, 'March 1862, Eugénie describes meeting Hugo and Juliette Drouet – oh!' She looked at Tess, frowning. 'I think you should read this yourself, it's quite…quite sad.'

Tess started reading, translating the French as she went. Her earlier excitement faded as she read what had happened to the poor girl.

'How awful. Not only to be widowed so young, but to have lost her unborn child in such circumstances. And Hugo and Juliette virtually witnessing it. No wonder they all became so close and Juliette seems to have taken on the role of surrogate mother.'

'It explains so much. And did you note that Eugénie was the image of Hugo's dead daughter, Léopoldine? It's not surprising seeing her had such an impact on Hugo. Well, this is extraordinary.' Charlotte sat back in her chair, lost in thought and Tess's head was filled with the image of a young woman in widow's weeds suffering a late-term miscarriage in front of strangers. If it hadn't been for their help, it was possible Eugénie might have died.

'I wasn't expecting any of this. Not that I knew what to expect, exactly, but these,' she said, pointing to the journals, 'are bringing that poor girl to life. Making her flesh and bones, not simply an abstract ancestor, who may or may not have slept with one of the most famous writers in history.' Tess stood and paced around the room, vaguely registering the distant view of trees framing the deep blue sea and golden beach.

'You don't have to rush through these, Tess. It may even be that the diaries become a bit mundane later. The usual "Got up, went to work, came home, went to bed".' Charlotte stopped her pacing with a hug. 'I bet you haven't had any lunch yet, have you?' She shook her head. 'Nor have I, so how about I rustle up something and we can wash it down with a glass of fizz? To celebrate a wonderful find that is probably making your poor aunt turn in her grave!' she said, laughing.

Tess had to smile. Charlotte was right; food and a glass of fizz were just what she needed.

During the afternoon Tess studied the diary entries for the next few months of 1862. It was slow and laborious translating as she read and she had to take regular breaks to clear her head. Charlotte was right, there was no rush. It was possible the diaries had lain hidden for over a hundred and twenty years, so what was a few weeks now? Tess could feel Eugénie's grief as she buried her child and continued to mourn her lost husband. Then her slow recovery and pleasure when offered work by Hugo. The pattern of her new life emerging over the weeks, taken up with spending some time with Juliette Drouet and then working at Hauteville House. What an opportunity and honour that must have been. Tess had visited Hauteville on a school trip and remembered thinking how flamboyant and slightly weird it was. Totally unlike anything else in Guernsey, for sure. Exotic, foreign and unique, yes. Eugénie's descriptions of the rooms matched her own memory and made her shiver as she read them. Talk about bringing history to life! Reading about Eugénie's response to copying out chapters from *Les Misérables* also reminded her of her own emotions when she watched the stage musical. She had cried at various points, particularly towards the highly emotional end when so many lives were lost. Tess decided she must read the book when her life had settled down, having such a familial involvement in its production. In English, though, to stop her brain becoming completely frazzled.

'Well, that was quite a surprise today, wasn't it?' Andy said, walking into the kitchen where Tess and Charlotte were having a cup of tea while supervising James feeding himself. Charlotte gave him a kiss and offered to make him some tea.

'It sure was. If I hadn't agreed to your suggestion to upgrade the attic bedrooms, we might never have found that cupboard. So thanks for twisting my arm,' Tess said, grinning.

'You're welcome. And apart from this fantastic discovery, you'll be increasing the value of the house by more than the cost. A win-win. Now, I'm sure you're bursting to tell me what you found, so fire away.' He patted Tess's arm and joined them at the table with his tea. Tess described what she thought were drawings and paintings by Hugo, and showed him the inscribed picture of Eugénie and Juliette. Andy's eyes opened wide as he listened while examining the painting.

Charlotte, who had been focusing on James, spoke up.

'It's an incredible find, and I could wish Tess had found it before I wrote my book on Hugo. The thought of all that first-hand knowledge of the man is enough to make any writer's heart beat faster with anticipation.' She sighed, a touch dramatically, Tess thought, until she saw the laughter in Charlotte's eyes and smiled.

'Sorry about that. You might find enough material for another book here,' she said waving at the diaries.

'Perhaps, but I've decided to try my hand at something contemporary. But our friend Jeanne might be interested; she writes both fiction and non-fiction historical books about Guernsey and is gaining quite a reputation for herself.'

'She's married to Nick, Colette's brother, isn't she?' Charlotte nodded. 'Then I expect I'll meet her soon, Colette's mentioned getting together.'

'What are you going to do about the other stuff in the attic? Anything to do with Hugo will be valuable so it needs to be somewhere secure,' Andy said, flicking through a diary.

'You're right. I'll pack everything up and bring it here, all except the desk. Which reminds me, I took a photo of how it was when we found it, Charlotte. Here,' Tess said, tapping her phone and passing it to her friend.

'Oooh! I see what you mean; it does look like a shrine, or memorial. I do hope you find out why it was sealed up as at the moment it makes no sense.' Charlotte studied the photo, zooming in for a closer look.

Andy cleared his throat.

'I know this is incredibly exciting and I understand your enthusiasm, but have you given any thought to dinner tonight? Or do you want me to cook it?'

Charlotte dropped a kiss on his cheek and smiled.

'It's under control, darling. Steaks are marinating in red wine and I've made a salad to go with some new potatoes. Will be ready in less than half an hour if you'd like to bathe your son?'

'Great, will do.'

Tess watched entranced as Andy wiped James's hands and face before lifting him from the high chair. He was a natural with James, she thought, making him laugh as they left to go upstairs for the bath. Charlotte had confided in her that she wasn't sure if she could get pregnant when they married as she was approaching forty, but Andy wanted to marry regardless. Thinking about their relationship brought home to Tess her own single state. Not that she was having to watch the biological clock at thirty-one, but she did like the idea of having a partner to share things with. For some reason, Jack's face popped into her head. She let out a stifled laugh and Charlotte, busy cleaning the high chair, looked up.

'Come on, share the joke.'

'Oh, it was nothing. I was only thinking that upstairs are all those boxes of stuff my aunt had accumulated and I spent ages sifting through and probably won't need any of it now,' Tess improvised, feeling her face flush at the lie.

'Maybe not, but there's no harm in hanging onto them. They're not in our way,' Charlotte said, removing the steaks and salad from the fridge before putting the potatoes on to boil.

'Anything I can do to help?'

'No, all under control, thanks.' Charlotte turned to face her. 'Would you mind if I came with you tomorrow when you pack up what's in the cupboard? I'd love to see it first-hand and I've always adored poking round old houses. Mrs B will be here to look after James.'

'Sure, you'd be welcome. And I can pick your brains about possible final finishes. I love what you've achieved here.'

The two of them chatted for a few minutes about paint colours and the merits of different brands before Andy returned, bearing a pyjama-clad James for a good-night kiss. He then went off to put his son to bed. By the time he came down again the dinner was ready.

The conversation turned inevitably towards Tess's house and the hidden cupboard and the progress of the work.

'Are you happy with what they've done so far?' Andy asked, leaning back in his chair and nursing a glass of wine.

'Yes, I think so. I've never been involved in house renovation before, so it's hard to know what to expect.' Tess pursed her lips as she mentally reviewed what she had seen that morning. 'With the excitement of finding the cupboard, I forgot to ask Jack if he's on track for finishing in the three months he quoted.'

'Should be, according to the schedule we drew up initially...' He was interrupted by a wail coming through the baby monitor and Charlotte left to check on James. Andy seemed to hesitate before continuing, 'Are you okay with Jack? I sensed a bit of an atmosphere between you and couldn't help wondering if you've not seen eye to eye about something.' His gaze fixed on her face.

Tess waved her hand.

'It's nothing. We got off on the wrong foot when we first met, but we're okay now. And anyway, I don't expect we'll see much of each other as he's not working there.'

'Perhaps not, but as I recommended him I'd feel responsible if you weren't happy with his work.'

'No worries, Andy, it seems fine so far and I'm looking forward to keeping up with the progress more often now I'm here. Ah, Charlotte, is James okay?' Tess was relieved to change the subject as Charlotte returned, feeling uncomfortable talking about Jack. He had got under her skin, for sure, but at the moment she couldn't say whether it was in a good or bad way. Time would tell.

CHAPTER 20

Eugénie's Diary – April 1862

This morning M'dame Drouet sent round an invitation for me to join her for lunch and I went after leaving Hauteville House. It had been another busy morning of copying and I was glad of a diversion.

'I hear you helped serve at the dinner for the poor yesterday. I would love to know if it was a success,' m'dame asked, as we took our seats at the dining table. She looked tired, I thought, and had a persistent cough.

'Are you unwell, m'dame? That cough...'

She waved her hand.

'It's nothing. This house is prone to dampness and I am prone to cough as a result. It will pass. Now, about the lunch?'

I was happy to describe it in almost complete detail, omitting only the interaction between myself and Mam'selle Adèle. She listened intently, nodding approvingly when I told her we all ate the same food.

'M'sieur wants to set an example to others of his class that treating the poor more as equals is the way to providing an escape from poverty. We have had many discussions on the subject.' She smiled. 'These dinners are already attracting comments here in Guernsey. Perhaps others will follow suit, which would be wonderful, would it not?'

Nodding my assent, we continued our talk and the colour returned to her cheeks. I realised I missed the times we had spent together while I was an invalid in her house and she had told me what it was like to be a part of Parisian society. She had many tales to tell and I provided an entranced audience. I could see why she and m'sieur were such a devoted couple, albeit not one universally acknowledged or accepted. She confided how much she missed Paris and found Guernsey somewhat stultifying, with limited cultural activities. Or, at least, ones she could be seen to attend.

'At least I am able to see more of m'sieur here, which is a great comfort. As you have realised, his wife now spends more and more time in Paris or Brussels and this allows us ample opportunity to spend time together. I am happy to be his helpmate in producing his great works.' She sighed and I sensed the undeclared desire to have been more than a 'helpmate'. But he had married his wife when young, only twenty, and was already a father when he met M'dame Drouet. Marriage was never a possibility, she told me.

Before I left, we arranged to meet again in two days' time. M'sieur Hugo had told her he was too busy with his writing to spend as much time with her and I think I'm to be used as a substitute and keep her up to date with what happens at Hauteville House. I don't mind as I enjoy her company and am equally lonely. At least she has lived, I told myself as I walked down Hauteville to my home, whereas I have done so little and ended up completely alone at the age of nineteen. I have to force myself not to become maudlin and be grateful for what I have, but there are times when it is difficult.

I am as keen as anyone to learn what is to become of Cosette, Marius and Jean Valjean. The first part – *Fantine* – was published on 3rd April, the day m'sieur had worked for the first time in his new glass lookout. As I was sitting at the table in the red salon, he told me what a success it was and how people were clamouring for the next part and the publisher was sending him letters almost daily urging him on. It was being hailed as *'the social and historical drama of the nineteenth century'*. M'sieur strutted around the room, pushing out his chest like a peacock as he told me this. I could not blame him for being a little arrogant as I know how many years he had devoted to writing it and I have never read anything so poignantly detailed about how life was for the poor in France. Some passages, I confess, are a little long and not quite to my taste, such as the chapters about Waterloo. The newspapers quoted the less generous remarks from literary critics, but m'sieur seems unconcerned. He has created a mass market for his work few contemporaries had achieved, he said, handing me the latest pages to be copied. I am working longer hours than normal to keep up, but this is no hardship now I am once more in good health. And I am paid handsomely for this extra work and able to add to my meagre savings.

20th May

'Sales have surpassed all expectations,' M'sieur Hugo said, waving a letter in his hand as he strode into the salon. I was finishing off that day's copying, my eyes itching after hours of concentration. The second and third parts of *Les Misérables* had just been published.

'I am so pleased, m'sieur, but not surprised. How could anyone not want to read your work?' I pointed to the stack of paper on the table.

'You are too kind, *ma petite*, and it seems many agree with you. The English translations are selling well also and my publisher, Monsieur Lacroix, is promising the public the final two parts will be ready by the end of June.' He moved to my side, placing his hand lightly on my shoulder. 'We will both have to continue working long hours, *ma petite*, but will it not be worth it to know this long voyage, which for me was started in 1845 is soon to be at an end?'

My stomach clenched. Would this mean I might lose my employment?

Taking a deep breath, I said, 'Of course, m'sieur, it will be a proud moment for me when you send off the final proofs to M'sieur Lacroix.' Pausing, I went on, 'But I would be sad to feel I was no longer of any use to you.' I lowered my gaze, not daring to see his reaction.

'But of course I will still need you! I have many further works planned and will continue to require such an excellent copyist as yourself.'

I looked up and saw his eyes twinkling at me and smiled back.

'Thank you, m'sieur, you have made me so happy. I…I was worried you would manage without me in future and I have come to…take pleasure in working for you these past months.'

'And I enjoy your company, *ma petite*, as well as your admirable work. You will, however, be having a respite from your endeavours in the near future as I have arranged to travel to the Rhineland with Madame Drouet in July. It's something we do each year to ensure my health is renewed after working so hard.'

My earlier happiness dissipated. They were leaving and I would be alone. How would I cope? The sadness I felt must have shown in my face as, squeezing my shoulder, he went on, 'Don't worry, I shall pay you a retainer while we are away. I can't expect you to have no income for three months and there are some works still to be copied at your leisure.'

Three months! I forced a smile and thanked him, while inwardly I was bereft. It is kind of him to pay me, for which I am truly grateful, but the thought of the three lonely months looming ahead brought me close to tears. Stupid, I know, having only known them for a few months, but they have been my salvation since I lost poor Arnaud and our son. It is my own fault; I rely too heavily on them and must find other companions. It will not be easy as a widow in early mourning is not encouraged to socialise and is meant to stay shut away indoors instead of reminding others of the spectre of death.

Today the manuscript was finished and ready to be sent to Brussels by tomorrow's mailboat and an air of excitement fills Hauteville House. M'sieur insists I share a glass of wine before I leave for home and I am happy to accept. Collecting my shawl and bag, I follow him down to the dining room where Marie has laid out a tray with a carafe of red wine and two glasses.

'Your daughter is not joining us, m'sieur?'

Passing me a glass, he shook his head.

'No, can you not hear that awful noise? She is playing that mournful music on the piano again and refuses to leave the room.' He frowned and I felt sorry for him, who seemed so unlucky with his daughters. I had seen little of Adèle of late and was glad our paths did not cross that often. Sometimes she has turned up to help with the dinners for the poor children but simply ignores me as I serve the food. It was as if we had an unspoken agreement not to notice each other.

'Come,' he added, brightening. 'Let us toast the conclusion of the final parts of my work and may it receive the same reception as the earlier parts.'

We raised our glasses and I took a sip of the excellent wine, far superior in quality to that offered at the meals for the poor, I noticed. Gesturing for me to sit, he paced around the room as he drank, appearing preoccupied.

'Is there something troubling you, m'sieur?' I asked, hesitantly.

He stopped and stared at me, as if he had forgotten my presence.

'My apologies, *ma petite*, my mind was elsewhere. I wish to thank you for all your hard work over the past months. You have proved to be a great asset to us and wondered if you would care to join us this afternoon for a little carriage ride? I know you are in mourning but we both think you would benefit from such a ride into the country. You are still a trifle pale.'

'I…I would be honoured, m'sieur.' A lump forms in my throat at this sign of our friendship. For this is what it is. I am not just an employee, but someone they both care for and are happy to acknowledge in public.

He smiled.

'Good, we were afraid you would be concerned about any impropriety, but you are a woman of spirit, *n'est ce pas?* These islanders gave us the cold shoulder when we first arrived, and I was vilified for my morals and politics, but now I am considered something of an asset to them and the newspapers write of my dinners for the poor in glowing terms.' He puffed out his chest in an exaggerated manner and laughing, went on, 'And as my fame grows with this latest work, well, then they will be beating a path to my door, begging to be my friend, will they not?'

Carried along by his good humour, I joined in and we were both still laughing when a cold voice cut in, 'What is so amusing, Papa?'

I turned to see Adèle standing in the doorway, her hair in disarray and a wild look in her eyes as she glared first at her father and then at me.

'A little joke, Adèle, nothing more. Do you wish to join us in toasting the despatch of the final parts to the publishers?' He offered his glass to her but she shook her head.

'No, I do not. I have a headache and will go and lie down.' She turned on her heel and was about to leave when her father called out, 'I have received a letter from your mother, Adèle. She and your brother will arrive the day after tomorrow and she hopes to find you in good spirits. I trust you will not disappoint her.' His voice was stern and she stopped, twisting round to face him. She was smiling.

'Mama and Victor will be here in two days? Oh, that's wonderful news! Thank you, Papa.' She rushed out of the room a completely different woman to the one who had entered only minutes ago.

M'sieur shrugged his shoulders.

'You see? My daughter is like a dual personality and we never know which one we will see. But at least she will be happier when her mother is here.'

It occurs to me that I have yet to meet M'dame Hugo and wonder if she would dislike me as her daughter did. With m'sieur going away for a few months, that could prove difficult for me. My earlier happiness drains away.

'Come, *ma petite*, it's time you went home and we will see you at two o'clock for our drive. Don't be late,' he said, patting my arm.

I finish my wine and leave as Marie arrives with his lunch. Sophie will have a cold repast ready for me and there is enough time for me to eat and change. With the arrival of summer I have purchased a dark grey dress in a lighter material and a small widow's cap to replace my heavy black crepe dress and hat and decide this is a good time to wear it. It may raise a few eyebrows but I need to be comfortable. I'm sure Arnaud would have agreed with me, he was never one for stuffy tradition. The thought of my beloved brings the familiar lump to my throat and tears creep out of my eyes. Instinctively, my hands settle on my stomach and more tears appear. Forcing myself to think of happier things like the forthcoming carriage ride, I change into my new clothes. Immediately, I feel lighter, less restricted. I know I will never stop loving and missing my husband, but I am young and in sore need of a little pleasure.

The small open carriage was pulled up outside Hauteville House as I approached and the coachman was standing by the horse's head feeding him a carrot. He touched his cap but remained silent. I recognised him as the fellow who was driving the carriage the day I began miscarrying my child and felt myself grow hot with embarrassment. I was debating whether or not to ring the bell when M'sieur Hugo appeared at the door, his hat in his hand.

'Ah, good, you are punctual, *ma petite*. Let us go and collect Madame Drouet.'

The coachman assisted me into the carriage and m'sieur sat opposite and a minute later we stopped as M'dame Drouet emerged from the lane. In her hands were two parasols, one cream silk and the other dark grey. M'sieur helped her into the carriage and she took her place beside me, proffering me the dark grey parasol as she dropped a kiss on my cheek.

'I thought you might be glad of this, it will shade you from both the sun and prying eyes, *ma chère*. And I am pleased to see you have changed your dress. That other one was too heavy for you, don't you agree, m'sieur?'

'I confess I hadn't noticed, but you are, as ever, right, m'dame.' He smiled at us both and I opened my parasol to hide my blushes. Suddenly the carriage seemed such an intimate space and I was conscious of knees only inches apart from each other. Perspiration formed on my forehead before the horse broke into a trot and a breeze brought me some relief. It was decided we would drive along the lanes to Jerbourg and then stop for a picnic, provided by Marie and packed in a hamper behind our seats.

M'sieur Hugo was in jovial mood and as the carriage rattled along up George Road and then onto Fort Road, past the barracks on our left, he kept us amused with tales of his latter months in Jersey when he upset the local dignitaries with his impolite references to Queen Victoria. None of this can have been new to m'dame, of course, who was also in Jersey, but she smiled and laughed as if hearing the stories for the first time. I noticed how pale and tired she looked and wondered if their forthcoming trip was as much for her sake as for his own. Selfishly, I didn't want them to go, but no-one of his years could keep up the punishing pace of work he had set himself without affecting his health. My only consolation was thinking they would both return much refreshed and ready to continue with more wonderful projects.

The hedgerows and trees were in full leaf and formed quite a contrast to the grey warren of houses and shops in the centre of Town. It was another world, with open spaces and only an occasional house as a reminder people lived here, too. A country girl at heart, it lifted my spirits to be in such excellent company and to see so much greenery as we headed out further towards Route de Saumarez. As we approached the imposing gates of Saumarez Manor on our right, I asked m'sieur if he had ever visited the house.

'Pah! I am not a particular friend of the de Saumarezes and they consider me an outlaw, not fit for genteel society.' He threw his hands up in the air and scowled. 'What do these so-called society people know? They are narrow-minded and believe the church is omnipotent. Do they not realise I am a peer of the French realm? A count! No, I would not set foot inside such a house, even if I were to be asked. I prefer to mix with those who earn an honest living and are open to modern ideas such as equality and social reform.'

I was mortified. To have made him so angry! As I was about to apologise, m'dame tapped my arm.

'Do not worry, *ma chère*, he is not angry with you, but with the way society is organised here. Is that not so, m'sieur?'

To my relief, he smiled.

'Of course. You asked an innocent question and I lost my temper, not with you, but with men such as those who live there,' he waved in the direction of the manor, now behind us as we turned into the lane leading to Jerbourg. M'dame steered the conversation away from anything controversial by asking if he planned to spend more time painting or drawing now the great work was completed. It had been a revelation to me that he was a talented artist, several works of his were displayed in Hauteville House. They tended to be somewhat sombre and even macabre, like the image of a hanged man I had seen in his study. However, he was also fond of painting the local scenery and I particularly liked his colour washes of stormy seas, all blues and greys.

'Yes, I plan to sketch while you ladies amuse yourselves. It will help to clear my head now the pressure has lifted,' he said, his humour restored.

Concerned I might say the wrong thing again, I only half-listened to their conversation while taking a keen interest in the vista of fields and the occasional run-down farm cottages. We were now in the parish of St Martin, an area given over to farming, with the cows producing the rich creamy Guernsey milk and where an abundance of vegetables are grown. Rutted tracks lead off the lane towards the farms and I caught a glimpse of cows being led by a young lad with a large stick from their field to a distant barn for the afternoon milking. I breathed deeply, allowing a feeling of contentment to wash over me. As we passed an elderly woman laden with baskets of green vegetables, M'sieur Hugo doffed his hat and called a greeting, being rewarded with a gap-toothed smile.

Moments later we arrived at Jerbourg Point, known for the clear views of all the other islands when the sky was clear, as it was today. Atop a cliff, there was an area of open scrubland popular for al fresco picnics. Today, it was quiet and we were the only ones to take up residence on a patch of grass near the edge of the cliff while our driver, after unhitching the carriage, guided the horse to the opposite side to graze at his leisure. M'dame and I set out the picnic rug and hamper while m'sieur sat with his sketchbook a few feet away. I was so engrossed in laying out the contents of the hamper that I did not notice that instead of facing towards the islands of Herm and Sark, he was facing us and was already busy drawing.

'We appear to be the subjects this afternoon,' m'dame said, with a laugh. 'Is this the first time m'sieur has drawn you?'

'It is and I feel quite unworthy to be chosen.' This was true. No-one had ever considered me a suitable subject before, although Arnaud had insisted we have out photograph taken when we married.

Once the picnic of pies, cold meats and salads was laid out m'sieur joined us, pouring the wine and helping to pass around the food. He then read to us from one of his poems and, to our amusement, a cow in the nearby field came up to the hedge and leaned over, as if it were listening to his words. When he stopped reading, the cow moved away, but returned once he resumed. It made us all laugh. Once we had cleared away, m'dame and I went for a stroll along the cliff while m'sieur returned to his sketching, this time focusing on the islands. We were not allowed to see his earlier picture as he wanted to finish it off later, he said, waving us away. M'dame graciously offered me her arm as we walked and it was as if I was taking the air with my own dear mother again. She was as warm to me as any mother could be and I think she had taken on that role almost from our first meeting. The thought that I was soon to be without her took away some of the joy of this special time together. How was I going to bear it?

❧ CHAPTER 21 ❧

Tess – June 2012

Before Tess left the house the following morning she phoned Colette for a brief chat and arranged to call around that afternoon, dying to tell her friend about the discovery at her house. She also had to call in at the surgery soon but thought it could wait another day. At the moment the priority was safeguarding Eugénie's legacy. Once James was handed over to Mrs B, the live-out housekeeper, Tess and Charlotte headed off to Town with several empty boxes in the boot ready to fill with what remained in the cupboard.

As Charlotte drove her eyes sparkled with excitement and Tess couldn't resist teasing her.

'Anyone would think this find belonged to you instead of me,' she said, with a laugh.

'I know, I can't help it. Ever since I finished my last book life has been a little, dare I say, flat? It had absorbed so much of my time, living and breathing my work over many months, only surfacing for Andy and James. So after publication I was at a loss with little to drive me on.' She sighed. 'Don't get me wrong, I adore James but small children aren't that great at intellectual stimulus are they?'

Tess grinned.

'No, they do have limitations. Can't you start another book?'

'In theory, yes, but at the moment I feel I should spend more time with James after being glued to the computer for months. I grew up with nannies, hardly ever seeing my parents, but Andy's mum was a full-time mother before he went to school and he often says how much he enjoyed that time with her. It's difficult to find the right balance, which is why you coming to stay and all that's happening at your house are proving a godsend. I shall have to live vicariously through you for a while,' Charlotte said, flashing her a smile.

'Happy to be of use! And I'm glad of your input with regard to anything to do with Hugo, so it's not entirely one-sided.'

They arrived in Hauteville and carried the boxes into *St Michel* accompanied by the sound of hammers and drills. Dumping the boxes in the hall, Tess offered to show Charlotte round before heading to the attic, starting with the sitting room. Charlotte was immediately drawn to the far window.

'What a marvellous view!' she cried. 'You'll be able to watch all the comings and goings of the harbour just as Hugo did from his look-out at Hauteville House. What fun!' She spun round and Tess watched as her friend gazed at the empty space.

'This will be a lovely room when it's finished. I could tell from Andy's plans the whole house has such potential. Can't wait to see the rest of it.'

'Come on, then.'

By the time they had seen everywhere but the attic rooms, Charlotte had made it clear how much she approved of the house and what Tess proposed to do to it, throwing in occasional comments about possible paint colours. The builders looked on bemused as the women navigated uplifted floorboards and drums of electric cables waiting to be buried under floors and in the walls. Finally they arrived on the attic floor and Tess led the way into the room with the now not so hidden cupboard. The last of the plaster had been removed, exposing the panelled wooden door set in the alcove wall.

Charlotte rubbed her hands as Tess unlocked the door, swinging it wide open.

'What a pretty desk, definitely a woman's and probably French,' Charlotte said, as Tess aimed a proper torch over it. Her friend was right, it was pretty, something she hadn't noticed before, too excited by the pictures and then finding the diaries. Walnut, heavily inlaid with marquetry and boasting bow-front drawers and cabriole legs. Definitely not something to be hidden away but put on show and admired.

'Expensive, too, I'd guess. My mother has something similar in our Somerset home and I was never allowed to touch it as a girl. So, how did a poor widow manage to buy something like this?' Charlotte ran her fingers over the dusty surface, peering at the elaborate inlay.

Tess was taken by a thought.

'I wonder if it was a gift from her employer? For services rendered?' she said, smiling.

Charlotte laughed. 'Hugo wasn't known for extravagant gestures, but he was quite generous when it suited him. Perhaps the answer lies in those diaries. This gets more intriguing, doesn't it?'

'Sure does. I can't wait to read them but for the moment let's box up everything,' she waved her arm to include the pictures on the walls and the desk drawers, 'as I want to keep it safe.' They lifted the pictures from their hooks and placed them carefully in a box before opening the drawers. Tess had only taken a brief look before and was surprised to find some leather-bound books and ribbon-tied sheets of handwritten paper in a large drawer. It was frustrating to have to wait to examine them properly, but a building site was hardly appropriate. She continued to fill another box with the miscellany of items that appeared to include items once belonging to Hugo, like his handkerchief.

'Right, I think that's everything. We can have a good snoop later when we have better lighting. A bit like Christmas, isn't it?' she said, closing the flaps on the box.

'Even better! We might be touching items that Hugo touched or used and no-one has seen for over a hundred years.' Charlotte lifted up a box, saying, 'What are you going to do about the desk?'

Tess frowned. 'It should be safe locked up for now, but I don't like the idea of leaving it here long-term. I'll certainly keep it, although it's not my usual style, which has been Ikea until now, but it's lovely and…and has history.'

'Quite right. We could always take it to my house before the builders start working in here–'

'Someone mention the builders?'

'Oh, hello, Jack. I didn't hear you come in.' Tess turned to see him standing in the doorway, casually dressed in jeans and T-shirt and smiling broadly. She cleared her throat, 'Charlotte, meet Jack, my builder. Jack meet Charlotte, Andy's wife.'

'Hello, Jack, I've heard so much about you. Good to meet you at last,' Charlotte said, balancing a box under one arm and offering a hand.

Jack duly shook it, saying, 'Pleased to meet you, too.' His gaze returned to Tess who had picked up a box, ready to leave. 'I'm guessing you've emptied the cupboard. Would you like a hand with the boxes? Wouldn't want either of you having an accident on the stairs,' he said, straight-faced.

Tess was torn. On the one hand she knew the stairs were hazardous, particularly if you couldn't see where you were going; on the other hand, she hated being perceived as a vulnerable woman. She was debating what to say when Charlotte, with her sweetest smile, said, 'How kind, Jack, thank you,' and passed him her box. Tess had no choice but to hand him hers, accompanied by a quick nod. Jack went off saying he would see them downstairs.

Charlotte giggled.

'Your face! I could see you were determined not to give him your box for some reason, but didn't see why we should risk twisting our ankles, or worse. You fancy him, don't you?'

Tess's jaw dropped.

'No, I don't. It's just that he's…patronising. And…and he wanted to buy my house, turning up the day after my aunt's funeral.' The words tumbled out and Tess felt her face flush under her friend's cool stare.

'I was right, you do fancy him. And why not? He's rather sexy, all dark and brooding. Is he single?'

'I…I don't know. Look, we should go down, he might be waiting to take the boxes to the car.' Tess was annoyed with herself; if her friend could read her face, could Jack?

'Okay. But I wonder if I should invite him round for dinner sometime. After all, Andy likes him, and I can ask other friends, too.'

Tess didn't know what to say, shrugged and started down the stairs with Charlotte following. Jack was talking to one of the builders in the hall when they arrived.

'I was just asking Larry if he'd carry your boxes to your car as I have to dash. Only popped in for a quick recce. Unless you have any queries, Tess?' he asked, heading for the door.

145

'No, I'm good, thanks.'

'Right, bye then, ladies. Give my regards to Andy, Charlotte.' He nodded and was gone.

Tess was left feeling as if she'd been snubbed, and had to force down her annoyance. Meanwhile Charlotte was giving her car keys to Larry so he could load up the boot. Once he had gone, she turned to Tess, her eyes gleaming.

'I've had a marvellous idea. It would be wonderful to have confirmation of the provenance of the items you've found, including the desk. Agreed?'

'Agreed.'

'Good. When I was researching Hugo for my book I became friendly with the staff running Hauteville House, who were incredibly helpful. Stéphanie Duluc, in particular, was lovely. Now, we could show her a photo of the desk and see if she has any record of Hugo ever buying anything like it. They have tons of material archived as he kept everything, no matter how trivial. And we could show her the items Eugénie stowed away and see if they can be verified as genuine. What do you think?'

'I think it's a brilliant idea. We'll need to examine what's in the boxes more thoroughly first, but I'm happy for her to see them.' A thought struck her. 'They wouldn't try and lay claim to them, would they? If they had belonged to Hugo?'

'I doubt it. He was known to give small gifts to people around him so it's not likely Eugénie actually stole anything. Certainly nothing of real value.' Charlotte grabbed her arm. 'Come on, we've things to do.'

Once settled at Charlotte's house, Tess carefully spread out the items found in the drawers while Charlotte spent a few minutes with James. She was immediately drawn to a leather-bound copy of *Les Misérables* and on opening it was thrilled to see the handwritten dedication to *'Eugénie Sarchet'* signed *'Victor Hugo'* and dated July 1862. A first edition and signed by the author! Her heart raced as she turned the thin pages slowly, anxious not to cause any damage. The book was in pristine condition and Tess wondered if Eugénie had ever read it. But she hadn't needed to, had she? She would have known the story well from copying it for publication. Tess picked up the be-ribboned handwritten pages and, untying the ribbon, saw they looked like some original pages of *Les Misérables* written by Hugo with various crossings-out and scribbles making them difficult to decipher. Unless you were his copyist, she thought, gleefully.

Charlotte arrived, bearing two cups of coffee and before she could put them down, Tess shot up, saying, 'Careful! We can't drink those here,' she gestured to the part of the table covered in the scattered pages, 'let's sit over there and I'll explain.'

Settled at the opposite end of the dining table Tess told her what she had found. Charlotte nearly spilled her coffee.

'Oh, my God! This is incredible. What a find! That Eugénie must have been really important to Hugo for him to sign that book, which was most likely a gift. And it's known he was careful not to let copies of original manuscripts get out, so she must have secreted pages without his knowledge. I wonder why?' Charlotte's face was animated as she drank her coffee.

'I think she must have been in love with him, or at least in thrall. Hopefully the diaries will tell us. But for now, there's still more to look at.' Tess waved towards a pile not yet studied. She finished her drink and returned to her original place. Charlotte joined her. After her friend had examined the book and the manuscript, together they looked through the other items. Another bound volume, also signed, was of *Les Travailleurs de la Mer*, dated 1866.

'I learnt about that book in school but left before we were due to study it. As it was Hugo's homage to the island it was more important to us than *Les Mis*. And now I have a signed, dedicated first edition!' Tess grinned at Charlotte.

'Lucky you! What other gems are there?'

Tess found another single handwritten page, which proved to be even more personal than the dedicated books. As she started to read it, she gasped.

'Hugo wrote her a poem!'

❧ CHAPTER 22 ❧

Tess – June 2012

'What!' Charlotte looked over Tess's shoulder, seeing neatly written French lines of poetry, she translated the first few:

> *Oh, why not be happy this bright summer day,*
> *'Mid perfume of roses and newly-mown hay?*
> *Great Nature is smiling—the birds in the air*
> *Sing love-lays together, and all is most fair.*
> *Then why not be happy*
> *This bright summer day,*
> *'Mid perfume of roses*
> *And newly-mown hay?*

There were two more verses and it was titled *Oh, why not be happy, Eugénie?* and signed, with a flourish, *Victor Hugo*.

They looked at each other and laughed.

'It gets better and better! I can hardly wait to see what their reaction is at Hauteville House. And there's still the diaries,' Charlotte said, shaking her head in bemusement.

'Yes, I'm planning to read some each day and make notes of the more important entries. It'll take ages, though, having to translate it as I read.' Tess knew she had to be patient, but it was hard after the excitement of the wonderful finds. In a way, it no longer mattered to her whether or not Eugénie and Hugo had been lovers and she was descended from their union. She now had ample proof that they had been close and she could be proud of that connection. As she began returning the precious items to the boxes, Charlotte interrupted her thoughts.

'With your permission, I'd be happy to help with the diaries. I could do what you suggest and write notes of relevant entries to save you time. And I hope you know you could trust me implicitly not to tell anyone what I read.'

Tess jumped at the idea.

'That's kind of you, and it would save so much time. As long as you're sure? Could be a bit tedious reading of Victorian day to day occupations, particularly in French.'

'You forget I'm a writer and used to research in French. I can fit it in around James's naps and it will be good to keep my brain from atrophying. Really, you'd be doing *me* a favour,' Charlotte said, laughing.

'On that happy note, I'm due to have lunch at Colette's and must be off. If you want to make a start on the diaries, feel free. Although I began reading the 1862 entries I didn't make notes so that might be a good place to start. Or earlier if you like.' Tess gave her friend a hug and left, a spring in her step from the morning's discoveries. Time now to catch up with her old school friend and her baby.

Two hours later Tess left Colette's house full of delicious homemade soup and memories of time spent cuddling baby Rosie. Colette looked to have settled into motherhood well, in spite of lack of sleep, and Rosie, she said, was a contented baby. Tess was inclined to put that down to Colette's obvious contentment and joy in her baby and was showing signs of becoming a true earth mother, happy to be surrounded by children while preparing nourishing meals in the kitchen.

Tess detoured to the surgery, thinking it politic to check in with the practice manager now she had arrived. The meeting went well and, seeing the surgery again, brought back to Tess how much she was looking forward to taking up her role as a GP. There was no rush or melodrama, simply patients waiting quietly for their appointment. Tess knew there would be heartache and pain beneath the surface for some, but felt well qualified to cope. For a brief moment the image of a deadly pale Gary laid out on a trolley flashed into her head and she had to bite her lip, praying she wouldn't have to deal with something like that again. Back in her car, Tess drove down towards the Halfway junction and right into Vale Road, planning to drive towards L'Islet and the road along the west coast, keen to have some sea air blow through the windows. As she reached Le Grande Havre bay and caught sight of the kiosk she had a sudden desire for an ice cream and pulled in to the car park. Minutes later she was perched on the sand, licking the ice cream and gazing out to sea. Yes, this was the life she wanted. This was home.

'Hi, Tess, did you enjoy your lunch?' Charlotte greeted her as she walked into the conservatory, to find her friend on the floor playing with a giggling James.

'Yes, it was lovely, thanks. And little Rosie is absolutely adorable. Colette sends her love and invites us all round for lunch on Sunday, together with Nick and Jeanne. Should be fun,' Tess said, flopping onto the floor beside James. He offered her a bright red brick to place on the tower he was building and as she did so it promptly collapsed, and James dissolved into laughter.

'Gosh, that's brave of her to have us all round so soon. I could barely rouse myself to make a slice of toast three weeks after this little imp was born.' She tickled her son who laughed so much he began hiccupping.

Tess didn't voice her thought that Colette being ten years younger than Charlotte may play a part, instead saying how much she looked forward to meeting more of the gang of friends.

'You'll like them and their children, Harry and Freya. Jeanne will be absolutely fascinated to hear about your family history and what you've found. Unless you want to keep it a secret?' Charlotte said, trying to soothe James's hiccups.

'I'm sure I can trust them to be discreet and I've already told Colette, who always knew about the family connection to Hugo. Have you had a chance to look at the diaries?'

Charlotte nodded, releasing James to wander off in search of a new toy.

'I began at the beginning and it's so sad to read how happy the couple were, all sorts of plans for the future when Arnaud finally left the sea...' Tess listened intently as Charlotte recounted what she had read. Images of the young married couple filled her head and made her sad.

'How far did you get?'

'I read most of the first volume and, to be honest, much was not that interesting and have made notes of the more important parts. Women had no lives outside the home, particularly with absent husbands. I would have gone spare, wouldn't you?'

'Absolutely. The more I learn about life for nineteenth-century women the more I thank heaven I was born in the twentieth. It's possible poor Eugénie may not have lost her baby if that had happened now. And she was lucky to pull through herself.' Tess sat back on her heels, watching James as he presented his mother with a toy car. They were both glowing with health, the picture contrasting painfully with the image Eugénie had conjured up in her diary of her miscarriage and slow recovery. The two women glanced at each other, sharing a common thought.

'In the diary Eugénie says she will never consider having another child. But she must have, or I wouldn't be here. I can't wait to find out what happened to change her mind, assuming she *did* have a choice. Oh, there's so much I don't know!'

'Don't worry, all will be revealed I'm certain. Although the diaries and the other items were hidden, something tells me Eugénie wanted someone to know her story. Otherwise why write the diaries, or if having written them, why not destroy them? And, before I forget, I spoke to Stéphanie Duluc this afternoon and she's happy to meet tomorrow morning before the house is open to the public. She sounded suitably excited at the mention of Hugo artefacts. I'd love to come along, too, if that's all right?'

'Of course. We can take a box of the most important items. Did you do all your research at Hauteville House?'

'No, I spent a lot of time at Priaulx library initially, they have a fantastic collection of books about Hugo and his family. The librarians, like many islanders, are terribly proud of the Hugo connection and are extremely knowledgeable. It was one of them, Dinah Bott, who gave me the tip about talking to Stéphanie. I wouldn't be surprised if your aunt spent a lot of time at the library over the years.'

'I think she did, judging by some of the papers I found. I hope she isn't turning in her grave at missing out on what's been found.' Tess frowned, knowing how obsessed Doris had been.

'Maybe, in the great scheme of things, you were the descendant meant to find what Eugénie locked away. Who knows? I'm a great believer in nothing happening without a reason and inheriting the house has enabled you to make a fresh start in Guernsey, hasn't it?' Charlotte smiled at her.

'You're right; I might never have considered coming back otherwise.' She stood and stretched her legs. 'I'll leave you to play while I go upstairs and read some more of the diary for 1862. Thought I'd make my own supper this evening, give you and Andy time together.'

'You don't have to, but thanks for the thought. See you later.'

Tess waved at a smiling James, who waved back, and collected the diary to take upstairs. It was no hardship to spend time in her guest suite and she was conscious of intruding on family life. And much as she enjoyed their company, she did like her own space. Tess settled into a comfy chair with the diary, a mug of tea and a notebook and pad. Time to revisit the past.

A couple of hours later, Tess put the diary to one side and went into the tiny kitchen to make her planned supper of warm chicken salad accompanied with a glass of white wine. The tremendous concentration needed to translate from the French had left her wanting nothing more than to chill out in front of the television. It dawned on her that once she started work, the last thing she would want to do once she was home would be to read the diaries. It was great that Charlotte had offered to help and she might need her to do most of the reading. Finding the desk and the diaries had brought home to her how much she wanted – needed – to learn all about Eugénie and her life. Her other priority was to see the building work finished as soon as so she could move in and fully embrace her new life. Coming to that conclusion felt good. Then she remembered her father and picked up her mobile.

'Hi, Dad, it's me. How are you?'

'Not too bad, love. I looked into coming over for a break, like I'd said. An old pal recommended a B & B and they had a vacancy next week for three nights, so I took it and booked my flights,' he said, sounding cheerful.

'That's great, Dad, I look forward to showing you my house. Talking of which...' she went on to tell him about the find in the attic and he sounded impressed and excited for her.

'Your mother will be pig sick, though. Although she was sniffy about the family connection with old Hugo, she always expected to inherit the house, as you probably gathered. But I think Doris made the right choice in leaving it to you, love. She knew how much you loved Guernsey and that Elaine didn't. Have you spoken to her lately?'

'No, and I don't plan to. Not yet, anyway. Has she phoned you?'

'No. Probably just as well as it would only upset me and I'd rather have something nice to look forward to, like coming over to see you and my old mates.'

Tess made a note of his flight the following week and said she'd pick him up before signing off. It had been great to hear him sound more like his old self and she wondered if coming for a break would get him thinking about moving back. Something she would love.

James was once more left with Mrs B and Tess and Charlotte set off to Town, their appointment with Stéphanie Duluc arranged for nine o'clock. The traffic at that time of the morning was the usual nightmare and they arrived with only minutes to spare. The meeting went well and Hugo's archived handwriting was compared to items Tess had brought along and declared a match.

'And here's a photo of the desk belonging to Eugénie. We were wondering if it may have been a gift from Monsieur Hugo.' Tess handed it to Stéphanie who agreed to check the records for the 1860s, commenting it looked French and from the right era. The painting of Eugénie and Juliette was also declared to be genuine.

Goodbyes were shared and they left, Tess smiling broadly.

'Well that went well. I was half afraid she would say they were fakes and I was the victim of a hoax,' Tess said, clutching the box of precious items as they walked down the road towards *St Michel.*

'I always believed they were genuine, but that's because I had access to Hugo's work at Hauteville. Do you want to check on the building work while we're here?'

Tess nodded, locked the box in the boot of the car and led the way into her house. They had barely stepped in the door when a loud crash, followed by a resounding yell of pain, came from upstairs. A white face peered over the bannisters, shouting, 'Please help, there's been an accident.'

🐾 CHAPTER 23 🐾

Eugénie's Diary – June 1862

Today I met M'dame Hugo, who has just returned. M'sieur will be leaving shortly and I couldn't help but think it odd he was departing so soon afterwards.

M'sieur and I were in the red salon and he was explaining what he required of me when I heard a noise at the door and, turning, saw a woman I hadn't seen before.

'Ah, my dear, let me introduce you to my new copyist, Madame Sarchet, who has been an invaluable help these past few months.'

I dropped a curtsy and, without raising my eyes, felt the power of her stare.

'There is something familiar about her...' She stopped and I lifted my head, afraid of her reaction.

'She has a strong resemblance to our dear Léopoldine, does she not? I noticed it the first time we met.' He smiled at his wife and then at me.

M'dame paled but remained calm. A matronly figure, with a large, square forehead and greying hair parted in the middle and set in ringlets, the dark shadows under her eyes indicating a woman not in the best of health. I forced a smile to my lips, with the hope of winning her over. Otherwise, the next few months could be somewhat unpleasant.

She advanced towards me and I felt my legs tremble.

'You do indeed remind me of my poor daughter, m'dame, and are about the same age as she was when...when she died. Too young.' She shook her head, a hint of sorrow in her eyes. 'And you are in mourning, I see. A parent?'

I explained about my husband and that I had recently lost our child and her face, which had been somewhat stern, softened.

'You poor girl. Then I hope that working for my husband has given you some diversion from your sorrows.'

M'sieur Hugo explained I was to continue my copying work while he was away and would be using his study upstairs to avoid any inconvenience to her.

'Oh, and Madame Sarchet has been a great help with the dinners for the poor children and would be pleased to continue, is that not right, *ma petite?*'

I nodded my agreement, willing to keep in everyone's good books.

M'dame Hugo smiled.

'That's most kind of you. I intend to welcome even more children over the coming weeks as there are so many here in great need. I expect my son, Victor, to be on hand also, when he is not busy with his translations.'

M'sieur Hugo added, looking pleased, 'My son has enjoyed success as a translator of Shakespeare's works from English to French and my wife,' he said, waving his hand toward her, 'is writing my biography. So you see why this house is sometimes referred to as "a veritable writing factory".'

'Indeed,' I murmured, conscious of my own small part in the 'factory'.

M'dame said something about needing to talk to the housekeeper and left, offering a quick nod towards us. We returned to the scattered papers on the table and m'sieur pulled out a thick sheet of art paper and handed it to me.

'I finished this yesterday and thought you might like it,' he said.

It was his sketch of M'dame Drouet and me on our picnic and the bold strokes caught our likenesses exactly. I must have been laughing at something m'dame had said as my head was thrown back a little and my mouth open. We were facing each other and she also looked to be laughing. He had lightly colour-washed the picture and it was a delightful portrayal of what had been a happy afternoon. Underneath I read the words

'À ma chère Mme Eugénie Sarchet, en mémoire de notre pique-nique avec Mme Juliette Drouet'
Victor Hugo

I stammered my thanks, overcome with gratitude.

He waved his hands.

'It was my pleasure to draw such a one as you. Young, beautiful and so natural. And both of you enjoying yourselves! It may serve to remind you of us while we are away and on our return we must have more such jolly outings.'

As I left for home later, I clutched the precious picture to my chest and planned to visit the art shop in Town after lunch. I wanted something so prized to be properly framed and be on view to all who visited my home.

It was with a heavy heart that I said farewell to M'dame Drouet at her house today. Her trunk was standing in the hall and she was busy giving instructions to the cook who was to be in charge of the house while she was away. Suzanne was to accompany her and looked harassed as she darted about fetching items her mistress declared she had to take with her.

'My dear, come, let's take tea in the garden away from this upheaval.'

I had to smile as she was the one causing everyone to rush around. We made ourselves comfortable at the table set on the terrace while poor Suzanne, rolling her eyes, went to the kitchen for our tea.

'You have met M'dame Hugo, I believe?' she said, her lips pursed.

'Yes, and I found her quite pleasant, if a little taken aback by my likeness to her daughter. She seemed happy I will be continuing to help with the dinners for the poor.'

'Good, I was a little concerned she would not be very, shall I say, accepting of you. And I realise it will be lonely for you when we are abroad. I do wish you had some friends to turn to.' She frowned, her concern touching my heart.

'I have resolved to make an effort, m'dame, and will invite a neighbour around for tea one day. She has been quite solicitous of me when we meet in the street and I think we could be friends.' It was true, Mrs Rabey, my immediate neighbour, had continued to be most civil to me and I felt guilty that I hadn't pursued a friendship. I had been too taken up with m'sieur and m'dame and it was time to spread my wings a little.

Her brow cleared.

'That is good to hear, my dear. And while we are away, do feel free to borrow any books you wish from my collection. Cook will let you browse whenever you wish.'

'Thank you, that's most kind. I shall certainly avail myself of the opportunity.' I was touched by her continuing generosity towards me and couldn't wait to explore her collection. The lending library had a limited choice and I had borrowed those I considered the most interesting. Suzanne arrived with the tea and the conversation turned to the forthcoming trip and where they hoped to visit. I tried hard not to feel envious, but would have given anything to be accompanying them and had to accept that I was unlikely to leave Guernsey for the rest of my life. Arnaud had always promised he would take me travelling one day and we had had such fun poring over his battered atlas to choose likely destinations.

My face must have betrayed my sad thoughts as she took my hand, saying, 'Don't be sad, my dear. The weeks will soon pass and we will come back with many tales to entertain you, never fear. And now, we must say goodbye as I must depart soon. Come, embrace me and wish me well.'

I did as she asked and it was if I was saying goodbye to my own mother. Managing to keep the tears at bay, I hurried away before I disgraced myself, wishing September would come quickly.

❧ CHAPTER 24 ❧

Tess – June 2012

Tess shot up the stairs and followed the lad into the main bedroom to be met with a scene reminiscent of A & E. Larry was stretched out on the floor with blood gushing out of a deep gash in his leg. Beside him was a cordless drill covered in blood and a knocked over stepladder.

'Call an ambulance, say it's urgent, a severed femoral artery.' She knelt beside Larry whose face was pale and beaded with sweat. 'It's okay, Larry, I'm going to try and stop the bleeding.' Charlotte appeared beside her, handing over a long silk scarf. 'Will this help?'

'Thanks. Can you put pressure on the wound while I make a tourniquet?' Tess pulled off her cotton jacket and gave it to Charlotte who pressed down on the gash in Larry's lower thigh while Tess tied the scarf tightly above it in an effort to stop the blood flow. She looked around and spotted a large tool box and pulled it under Larry's leg to further reduce the blood flow. The jacket was soon soaked with blood but within a minute or two the flow slowed. Tess checked Larry's pulse. Faint. His skin was glassy, but at least he was breathing.

'What happened?' she asked the lad, a teenager whose name she couldn't remember but had seen before. He was shaking, wiping sweaty palms down his jeans.

'Larry...was up the ladder, fixing battens...he was reaching out to drill a screw...leaned too far and the ladder...fell and the drill caught his leg. All happened so...quick. Nothing I...could do.'

'It's okay, I understand. Sounds like he misjudged it.' The wail of the ambulance pierced the air and moments later the other workmen, who had crowded onto the landing, moved back to allow two paramedics through.

Tess explained what had happened and that she was a doctor while they checked his vital signs.

'Lucky you were here, Doctor. He's stable for the moment but we'll get him to the PEH and warn them he'll need surgery and a possible transfusion. How long's the tourniquet been on?'

'Ten minutes.'

'Okay. I'll need his details.' The lad gave him Larry's full name and address and Charlotte's scarf was replaced by a medical tourniquet before the paramedics strapped him onto a stretcher. Once he was secure they carefully manoeuvred it through the door and down the stairs.

Tess and Charlotte were about to follow them when a breathless Jack bounded up the stairs into the room and stared, wide-eyed at the blood soaked floor.

'What the hell happened?' he shouted at the trembling lad who, Tess could see, was close to meltdown. She put her hand on his arm and squeezed. 'It's okay, I'll tell Jack. You go and grab a hot drink, with plenty of sugar.' The lad nodded and ran off. Tess took a deep breath and faced Jack, telling him what had happened. 'An ambulance was called while we worked to stem the blood loss. I...I think he'll be okay.' She looked down at her blood-soaked jacket on the floor, idly wondering if she'd be able to wash the blood out.

'My God! And you're both covered in blood! I saw the ambulance leaving as I arrived and was told there'd been an accident. Look, you two need to clean up but the only tap's down in the kitchen. Why don't you wash your hands and I'll send someone out to get coffees.' Jack barked orders at a workman and led the way downstairs, Tess looking forward to sitting down with a strong coffee.

'You okay?' she asked Charlotte as they arrived in the hall, impressed with her friend's calmness and prompt action earlier.

'Fine. I was brought up in farming country and there was always someone falling foul of dangerous equipment. I must say, I thought you were brilliant, Tess, and you probably saved that man's life,' she added, quietly.

'You didn't do so badly yourself. Let's sit outside for some fresh air once we've washed our hands.'

The tap in the kitchen was a makeshift job but they managed to clean themselves and Jack provided a fairly clean towel for drying.

'Sorry, it's a bit basic, but that's the nature of a building site,' he said, waving his hands at the stripped out kitchen area. 'I'll check the chairs are clean for you,' he added, going outside. The women followed and found him wiping down the two chairs and small table left by Doris.

'Thank you, Jack. What a relief to sit down after all the drama,' said Charlotte, with a sigh.

Jack disappeared inside and they were left to their thoughts. Tess was just glad to sit and breathe clean air. Ten minutes later Jack reappeared.

'Any update from the hospital?' Tess asked.

'He's headed for theatre to be stitched up and should make a full recovery. No nerve damage, thank goodness,' Jack said, perching on a pile of rubble. He stared at his feet, looking lost in thought and Tess was about to say something when a workman arrived with three coffees. Jack handed them round and Tess took a grateful sip. Although used to dealing with trauma at work, it was a whole different ball game to be confronted with a life or death situation without warning and without the back-up of a trained team, and she was feeling the after-effect.

'On behalf of Larry and myself, I can only say thank you for what you did today, Tess. Seems like your prompt action saved his life and it was just so fortunate you happened to be here at the right time. Both of you,' he said, nodding towards Charlotte. He looked drained, Tess thought, and she had the bizarre notion of wanting to stroke his hair and tell him all would be okay. She gave herself a mental shake. Where on earth did that come from?

'I'm glad I was able to help. A few minutes later and it might have been a different story.' She avoided his eyes, hoping her face didn't reflect her inner, crazy thoughts.

'How's the young lad? He looked to be in shock,' Charlotte said, gripping her coffee.

'Pete? Yes, poor kid. He's only been with us a week and is pretty shaken up. I've sent him home for the day and he'll be okay tomorrow. Talk about a baptism of fire, eh? And I've had a word with all the lads about being more safety-aware when on ladders and using power tools. Even though I have insurance, they need to be careful. Larry should have known better, but,' he shrugged, 'they think they're invincible.'

'I know, I've seen the result in A & E often enough.' Tess stood, draining her coffee. 'We'd better get off, we need to shower and change, I think.' She looked at the blood splatters on her jeans and T-shirt and Charlotte's clothes were as bad.

'Look, let me pay for anything you can't get clean. It's the least I can do.' Jack stood and moved back to let them through.

'Thanks, but I'm hoping they'll be fine. Oh, my jacket! It must be upstairs.' Tess rushed inside and up the stairs. In the bedroom someone had cleaned the floor, only a faint pink stain testament to what had happened. She found her jacket screwed in a red ball in the corner. Lifting it gingerly she realised it was beyond saving and dropped it.

'That's your jacket? Oh, God. Then please buy a new one and I'll pay for it,' Jack said, coming up behind her.

'I don't know…'

'I insist. And I was also going to ask if you'd let me buy you dinner, as a thank you.' He was close enough to touch and Tess, surprised, stepped back.

'Well, that's not necessary, but thank you. I…'

'Please say yes. I owe you big time and I hate being in debt to anyone,' he said, his eyes boring into hers. How could she refuse? She'd look churlish. And it might actually be fun.

'Okay, if you insist,' she said, with a smile.

'Good. How about tomorrow night? I'll pick you up at seven thirty from Andy's. Okay?'

Blimey, he was sure of himself. But she didn't have anything else on, even though it was Saturday night.

'Yes, okay. Now I must go or Charlotte will wonder what's kept me.' With a quick nod, she moved past him and down the stairs to the entrance hall where her friend was looking bemused. Tess grabbed her arm and pushed her out the front door before muttering, 'Jack's invited me out to dinner tomorrow night. Says he owes me for what I did for Larry.'

'Oh!' Charlotte said, her mouth open in surprise. 'Come on, let's get in the car and you can tell me all about it.'

By the next morning Tess was having doubts about having dinner with Jack and said as much to Charlotte.

'Honestly, Tess, don't be a wimp! He's a perfectly decent man and I'm sure will buy you a nice meal in a smart restaurant and may even prove to be a good conversationalist. What's not to like? As I said to you yesterday, I think it's a lovely gesture and if he does fancy you, well, it can lead to something else if you want it to. If not, you've had a pleasant evening.' Charlotte stood in the kitchen, her arms crossed, the embodiment of an older sister, Tess thought, with a reluctant grin.

'Okay, you win. I just think it could be awkward if we don't hit it off and have to see each other while he works on my house.'

'If that were the case I'd say it was more likely to be a problem for him, not you. You're the client; you're the boss. Now, what are you going to wear?' Charlotte busied herself with the coffee machine while Tess collected the mugs. She hadn't given clothes any thought. When she'd gone out in Exeter, whether with a boyfriend or girlfriends, she had generally plumped for jeans and a smart top. Comfort was more important than glamour.

'I expect you're going to say I can't wear jeans?' she said as Charlotte poured the coffee.

'That's hardly making an effort, is it? Jack's only seen you in jeans so far and people usually dress up a bit on a Saturday night. At least, those without a toddler do,' Charlotte said, wistfully.

'I'm happy to babysit anytime if you and Andy want to go out—'

'Thanks, I might hold you to that. But not tonight,' her friend laughed, 'tonight you're Cinderella off to the ball and you must dress accordingly. Do you possess anything suitable?'

Tess mentally reviewed her wardrobe.

'I do have a couple of dresses that might do, I suppose. But I'll be pretty annoyed if Jack doesn't make an effort.'

Charlotte nodded, sagely.

'Oh, he will, don't worry.'

After a day spent mainly outside, enjoying a bracing walk on Cobo beach and exploring the wooded area of the Guet, Tess was surprised to find herself looking forward to going out to dinner. Something normal and civilised after the events of the past weeks. After showering and washing her hair, she chose a short, slim-fitting dress in green which emphasised the green of her eyes. She styled her hair loose around her shoulders and applied a touch of make-up, accentuating her full mouth with lip gloss. To complete the outfit Tess chose nude high heels and matching bag. Studying her reflection in the full-length mirror she decided Charlotte would approve. As for Jack, well…

The doorbell rang on the dot at seven-thirty and Tess, who had been hovering in the drawing room, smoothed down her dress and went to answer it.

Jack stood with his hands in his pockets, looking relaxed but smart in a crisp white shirt, tailored jacket and slacks. A faint aroma of something woody drifted towards her. She took a deep breath.

'Hi, you found us all right.' Banal, but she didn't know what to say. It wasn't a date and it wasn't business, either. She really would have to chill out or the evening would be a disaster.

'Yes, no problem. Are you ready?' Jack smiled, giving her an appraising look.

Feeling more confident, she said, 'I'll get my bag,' and popped into the hall, catching a glimpse of Charlotte, peering round a door and giving her the thumbs up sign. Grinning, she waved and left.

'I've booked a table at Fleur Du Jardin in Kings Mills. Do you know it?' Jack said, opening the door of the Range Rover for her.

'I don't think so. I was too young for pubs when I left the island.'

He climbed into the driving seat and started the engine.

'It's more of a hotel with a damn good restaurant and bar and not far from here.' He swung the car around and drove through the gates at the bottom of the drive and then turned right towards Rue D'Albecq. 'Nice house they've got,' he said, glancing towards her.

'It's beautiful, but what you'd expect for someone with Charlotte's background and Andy's experience as an architect. And I'm so grateful to them for putting me up.'

'I've known Andy some years, but purely professionally. Always thought he was a decent bloke and Charlotte's quite something, isn't she?'

'Yes, she is.'

They lapsed into silence as Jack negotiated the numerous bends and Tess enjoyed the chance to take in the scenery. It was a lovely evening, warm for June, and still light although the sun was hanging low on the horizon over Cobo bay.

'I saw Larry today and he's recovering well, going home tomorrow. He said to pass on his thanks to you both, although he doesn't remember what happened after the fall. I told him you saved his life and he's suitably grateful,' Jack said, keeping his eyes on the road.

'Oh, I'm so glad he's better. I don't expect he'll be back at work yet; his wound will need time to heal.'

'No, he's been signed off and I've another guy coming in next week, hopefully a bit more sensible on ladders!' he said, with a wry grin.

She smiled.

'Ditto that!'

Again there was silence between them as Tess, for one, felt a tad uncomfortable in the intimate confines of the, admittedly large, car. It would be easier in the restaurant, she reasoned; more people, more space, food to focus on. Was Jack finding it awkward, too? He usually came across as uber confident, but that may be for work. Women might be a whole different scenario. She had asked Andy if he knew anything about Jack's personal life and the only thing he could tell her was, to the best of his knowledge, Jack had never been married and had no kids. Which was something, she supposed, but not entirely reassuring. Tess gave herself a mental shake. Why did it matter? It was a 'thank you' meal, not a date. She spent the rest of the drive staring out of the window to avoid eye contact.

Jack slowed down as they came abreast of a lovely old farmhouse-style building and turned right into the car park. Tess had vague memories of passing this way as a girl, but didn't think she'd ever been inside. Tables and chairs were set out on a terrace; some occupied with people enjoying a drink, others with plates of bar snacks.

The car park was busy but Jack found a space at the end of a row and pulled in.

'We're booked in the restaurant as it tends to get cool once the sun goes down, but I thought we could have a drink on the terrace first, if you'd like?' he said, switching off the engine.

'Lovely, thanks.'

She went to open her door, and before she could step down, Jack was there to help her.

'Allow me.' He smiled, offering her his hand.

His fingers were warm and strong and his touch sent a tingle through her veins. With a muttered, 'thank you', she stood on the gravel while he shut the door and locked the car. Jack led the way to the terrace to find a table. A waitress appeared and showed them to a table for two at the back before asking what they would like to drink.

'Do you like cocktails?' Jack asked, pulling her chair out.

'Yes, I'd love a mojito, please.'

'Good choice. We'll have two mojitos, please,' he said to the waitress.

'This looks very nice. Is it a favourite of yours, Jack?' she asked, gazing around her. The evening air was suffused with the aroma of garlic, fried fish and French fries from nearby tables and her mouth watered.

'One of them. I live near the reservoir, just down the road. So, how long is it since you left Guernsey?'

She told him a little of her background and what a wrench it had been to leave, and how fortuitous it was to inherit her aunt's house at this time.

'Naturally I was sorry Doris died, but it sounds like she had severe health problems at the end and was struggling to cope. She didn't let on or I'd have come over to see her. Makes me feel guilty about her leaving me the house.' Tess bit her lip.

'Old people can be very stubborn. My grandfather was too independent for his own good, living on his own in a cottage in Torteval and telling us he was managing fine. Then one day my mother went round without warning and found him passed out in his chair, drunk, an empty bottle of whisky on the floor.' Jack paused as the waitress arrived with their drinks and copies of the menu.

As they picked up their mojitos, Jack said, 'Santé!' as he touched her glass with his.

'Santé!' she replied, and took a sip. 'Delicious, thanks. What happened to your grandfather?'

'My parents thought it was best if he went into a home as they were still working full-time and couldn't look after him. He died a few months later. Nice old boy, taught me to fish when I was a kid. But life goes on, eh?' He twirled his glass, looking thoughtful.

'Are your parents still around?'

Jack looked up.

'They're alive, for sure, but moved to Australia when they retired about five years ago. My dad's brother married my mum's sister, they actually had a double wedding, and my aunt and uncle emigrated soon after. So when my parents retired they went over to join them in the sun. Can't say as I blame them.'

'Are you the only one here? No siblings or cousins?'

'All alone, I'm an only child. But it's fine, I've loads of friends and in such a small place you're never really alone, are you?'

'Suppose not.' Tess felt a pang of sympathy for him, knowing how much she missed her brother.

Jack handed her a menu.

'We'll need to order soon, I can see the waitress watching us. And I can recommend everything; I've never had a duff meal here.'

Tess studied the choice. It all looked so good.

'If you like tapas, I'm happy to share,' Jack said, nodding towards the choice of starters.

They agreed on tapas to start and Tess chose slow braised lamb shank while Jack plumped for the fish pie. He ordered a glass of red wine for Tess and mineral water for himself. While they waited to be called to their table in the restaurant Jack asked Tess about her family. She told him about her brother in Canada and her parents in Exeter, not mentioning they were heading for divorce. Much too personal.

'In a way, you're in a similar position to me. On your own on the Rock, except your parents are a short flight away.'

'I guess. My father's coming over for a few days next week and he's keen to see the house. He misses Guernsey much more than my mum does.' Tess drained her glass as the waitress came to lead them inside. Jack had been right, the air was cooling and few tables remained occupied. They passed through a traditional, cosy beamed bar set with tables for diners, mostly occupied, into the large, light-filled restaurant with a pale painted ceiling and wooden floor. The girl took them to their table near a window and Jack helped Tess into her chair.

A waiter arrived with the drinks and a moment later the tapas, on a large board, were placed in the centre of the table.

'This looks incredible,' Tess said, admiring the choice, including chicken liver parfait, baked Camembert, smoked salmon, and garlic bread and dips.

'Tuck in, before I beat you to it.' Jack grinned as he spooned Camembert onto his plate.

The food, and the wine, helped Tess to unwind and she was pleasantly surprised to find Jack good company. When he asked a question, he actually listened to her answer, and was more interested in letting her talk than he was in talking himself. Made a nice change from some of the blokes she'd dated recently. Not that this was a date, but still, a man and a woman having a cosy dinner together wasn't exactly business, was it?

'What made you choose a place near the reservoir? I'd imagined you in one of those swish new apartments going up in Town,' she said later, as they waited for the main course to arrive.

'I may be a developer, but I prefer old properties to new. A run-down cottage in a quiet lane came up for sale a few years ago and I bought it as a personal project. I spent most weekends working on it over many months, wanting to do virtually everything myself.' He scratched his chin, adding, 'To be honest, I was trying to impress someone with how clever I was, but it didn't work. On the plus side I ended up with a home I'm proud of, built almost entirely by my own not-so-fair hands.'

'That's impressive. A true Jack of all trades, then?' she teased him.

He laughed.

'You could say that. But in my case, a master of many. Perhaps I'll show you sometime, get your opinion on my workmanship.'

Tess was taken aback. Was he thinking they might see each other again? Like a date? Did it mean this dinner was an excuse to see if they clicked? It put a whole new take on things and Tess was both flattered and wary. She was saved from answering with the arrival of the main courses, served by two waiters. The lamb shank oozed a heady bouquet of red wine and herbs and Tess couldn't wait to tuck in, glad of the excuse not to talk.

After a few minutes of them both focusing on their food, Jack asked her how much she thought Guernsey had changed since she left. Feeling less sure of revealing her thoughts on anything now, she admitted for one thing she wasn't impressed with the modernisation of the market area.

Jack agreed with her and then went on to explain some of the concerns of islanders, particularly in regard to locals being priced out of affordable housing, and how he would like the opportunity to build low-cost houses for those on lower incomes. Tess could only applaud his ideas and they became drawn into a discussion of what should change. By the time they finished the meal, she was surprised how quickly the time had passed and, in spite of her mixed feelings about Jack, how much she had enjoyed herself. And how extremely attractive he was. Drinking her coffee, she cast a sly glance at him as he settled the bill. He smiled at the waitress as he said how much they'd enjoyed the food. Then he turned his warm brown eyes on her.

'Ready?'

She nodded and he came round to pull her chair out before gently resting his hand under her elbow as they threaded their way out. Jack nodded to a few other diners on the way, but didn't stop to talk to anyone. Tess was glad, not sure how he would have introduced her. A client? A friend? The woman who saved his workman's life? Outside, she shivered as the cool air encircled her.

'Cold? Here, let me.' Jack removed his jacket and placed it around her shoulders. 'Better?'

'Yes, thanks.'

He steered her to the car, saying, 'You should buy yourself a jacket, and I'll reimburse you, like I said.' Opening the door, his hand rested on her back as she stepped in.

'I will.' She settled into her seat, hugging the jacket around her as she breathed in Jack's scent embedded in the material. Something woody, masculine, with a hint of lime. Nice. Her stomach fluttered.

He climbed into the driver's seat and started the engine before pressing some buttons on the elaborate dashboard.

'Right, heating and music's on. Let's go.' He reversed out of the space as the sound of Coldplay's 'Paradise' filled the air. Tess tapped her feet to the music as Jack drove onto the road. 'You approve of my choice?' he asked, glancing at her.

'Yes, it's one of my favourites.'

'Good, we have something in common.'

Tess merely nodded, enjoying the sensation of being snuggled up in his jacket a mere inches away from him. A very different sensation than when he picked her up.

It seemed only a matter of minutes before Jack pulled into Charlotte's drive and parked near the front door. Lights glimmered through the curtains downstairs, and glancing at her watch, Tess was amazed to see it was only ten o'clock. Jack came round to open the door and help her out. She removed his jacket and handed it to him.

'Thanks for a lovely evening, Jack. I…I really enjoyed it.'

He shrugged into his jacket and moved closer to her.

'You're very welcome. And I enjoyed your company. Perhaps we could do it again sometime?' He put his hands on her arms and brought his face close to hers. Her heart hammered.

'Yes, I'd...like that, thank you.'

'Well, no doubt we'll be seeing each other soon, we'll arrange something then. Goodnight, Tess.' He dropped a kiss on each cheek and pulled back, smiling.

'Goodnight, Jack.' Tess returned the smile and hurried to the front door, shivering from the cool air or...what? She wasn't sure.

❧ CHAPTER 25 ❧

Tess – June 2012

Tess hesitated by the drawing room door. They were bound to have heard Jack's car and she guessed Charlotte would be eager to know how the evening had gone, but part of her would have liked to slink upstairs to her room and an early night. She was about to turn away when the door opened and Charlotte called her in, offering a glass of wine as an inducement. Tess walked in to see Andy asleep on the sofa and the television on low.

'Bless him, he's worn out. All that fresh air today, and running around after James. Come on, let's go into the kitchen and we can chat.' Charlotte held a bottle of red wine and two glasses and led the way to the kitchen where they perched on stools while Charlotte poured the wine.

'I can tell from your flushed cheeks and the sparkle in your eyes you had a good time. So...?'

Tess grinned.

'Yes, I did. Jack was...lovely. Interesting to talk to and an attentive host and the restaurant and food were great.' She took a sip of her wine, trying to avoid Charlotte's probing gaze. 'Have you been to the Fleur? I can recommend it.'

Charlotte waved a hand.

'Several times. It's not the food I'm interested in, and you know it. Did he say anything about going out again?' She leaned forward over the counter.

'Yes, and earlier mentioned he might show me his house sometime.'

'And?'

'And what?'

'Are you interested in "dating"?' Charlotte asked, signing quotation marks in the air with her fingers.

Tess swallowed more wine while she thought about it. Did she want a relationship as she was about to start a new job and while in the middle of a major house renovation, being carried out by the said possible boyfriend? It wasn't great timing, no, and what happened if they fell out? Tess looked up to see Charlotte staring at her, her lips twitching in amusement.

'What's funny?'

'You. I can read your face like a book and you're weighing up what to do, all the while knowing full well you want to go on seeing Jack and can hardly wait to get into bed with him.'

Tess spluttered, drops of wine dripping down her chin.

'You're impossible, Charlotte!' she managed to say, dabbing at her face with a tissue thoughtfully handed to her by Charlotte.

'I'm also right, and there's no point denying it. But I'll stop teasing you and go and wake up my husband so we can all go to bed. Sweet dreams,' she said, blowing her a laughing kiss as she left.

Tess couldn't help smiling. Her friend was right so she might as well admit it and go upstairs and hope for 'sweet dreams'.

She woke the next morning after a somewhat restless night, with no recall of particular dreams, only a feeling of lack of sleep. Struggling to wake, the memory of Jack kissing her goodnight made her smile. Okay, it wasn't a proper kiss, but it had felt good to have him hold her for a moment. And if they did go out again, then the next kiss might be more thrilling. Hugging the thought to herself, Tess shuffled into the shower to start the day.

'Morning. Enjoy yourself last night?' Andy asked, looking up from the Sunday newspaper spread over the kitchen table.

'Yes, I did, thanks. Lovely meal. You were conked out on the sofa when I came home,' Tess said, grinning.

Andy rolled his eyes.

'God, I'm already turning into my father, falling asleep in front of the television. Makes me feel old and Charlotte's offered to buy me a pipe and slippers!' A look of mock horror crossed his face, followed by a grin.

'And where is your loving wife?' Tess filled a mug with coffee and sat down beside him.

'She's taken James out for a walk, hoping to wear him out a bit before we go to Colette's for lunch. He becomes over-excited when he's with other children and seems to have a bit of a crush on Freya, Jeanne's little girl.'

'I'm looking forward to meeting everyone. I have vague memories of Nick, though he was so much older than Colette and me and probably thought we were a real nuisance. How old are Freya and Harry?' She took a swallow of coffee, waiting for the caffeine to kick in.

Andy frowned.

'I think Harry's five and Freya must be three, I guess. Harry's at school and considers himself quite grown-up compared to his baby sister, but he's a nice kid, if a bit boisterous. Freya's a sweet little thing and more like her mother.'

'Sounds like it'll be fun and the weather looks great,' she said, looking at the sun streaming through the window. Andy nodded and went back to his newspaper, leaving Tess with her thoughts. Their peace didn't last long as the kitchen door swung open and James rushed in, hurling himself at his father, who swung him, giggling, up in the air. Charlotte followed more sedately, her cheeks pink from their walk. After a fresh cup of coffee, she announced it was time to get ready for lunch at Colette's and Tess returned to her room to freshen up. Downstairs again, Andy loaded up the car with what he referred to as The Toddler Essentials and Charlotte grabbed wine and a home-made dessert from the fridge.

'We can hardly go empty-handed, can we? Thought we could pick up some flowers from a stall on the way to Bordeaux.' Charlotte handed Tess the bag with the wine and dessert and managed to gather up James who had been running up and down the hall. Tess sat in the back with James, safely strapped in to his car seat and Andy drove. James kept chanting, 'goin' to see Freya', as he gazed out of the window, his little hands tapping his legs. After a few minutes Andy turned up the sound on the car stereo, catching Tess's eye in the rear window and winking. She grinned, preferring the melodic tones of Adele to James's chanting.

As they drove along La Route de L'Ancresse, Charlotte asked Andy to pull in to a lane on the right. Attached to the wall were wooden shelves holding beautifully presented bunches of flowers and Charlotte bought a couple, dropping the money in the honesty box.

The scent of sweet peas and freesias accompanied her back in the car.

'Gorgeous, aren't they? I usually buy from this lady if I'm around here. I hope Colette likes them.'

'Bound to. I'd almost forgotten the Guernsey tradition of selling home-grown produce by the wayside. Beats supermarket buys any time,' Tess replied, sniffing the heady scent.

Andy rejoined the main road and carried on towards Bordeaux and five minutes later they drew up in their hosts' drive, alongside a battered Land Rover.

'Freya 'ere! Freya 'ere!' James cried, struggling to get out of his seat.

Tess leaned across and undid his straps, pulling him into her arms.

'Come on, James, I can't wait to meet your friend, Freya.' She waited for Andy to open the door and passed him the wriggling child before getting out of the car and helping Charlotte to unload the boot. James ran to the front door, opened by Colette who was holding the hand of a little girl, who promptly let go and flung her arms around James.

'That's the famous Freya, I presume?' Tess grinned at Charlotte.

'Yes, and she's adorable. Isn't young love sweet?' she said, with arched brows.

Tess, laughing at the insinuation, followed her friend to join Colette and the others. After various hugs and kisses they all made it inside the house, with Colette ushering them to go straight through to the garden. Tess would have recognised Nick, he and Colette had similar dark blue eyes and shared a certain kind of 'look'. He was laughing next to a dark-haired woman who could only be Jeanne, with a wide, open smile. Jonathan was running after a little boy who was a miniature version of Nick.

'Hello, Tess, good to see you after all these years. Colette was so excited when you got in touch,' Nick said, giving her a kiss on each cheek. Up close she saw the deeper lines in his tanned face and flecks of grey in his hair. 'And this is my wife, Jeanne.' He put his arm around Jeanne, pulling her closer.

'Hi, Jeanne, nice to meet you at last. I've heard so much about you from Colette. And your gorgeous children.' The women exchanged kisses and then they were joined by a red-faced Jonathan and Andy and Charlotte. As more greetings were swapped the noise level increased, made worse by the excited children running around the lawn.

'I think we all need a drink, don't you?' called Jonathan, pushing his glasses up his nose.

He was answered by a chorus of 'yes, we do' and headed to a make-shift bar set up on the terrace. Tess joined the queue and chose a gin and tonic. It was likely to be a lively and long lunch. Realising Colette wasn't outside she went in search of her, finding her, as she might have guessed, in the kitchen finishing off the preparations for lunch.

'Hi, do you need a hand? You shouldn't have to manage alone.'

Colette looked up from the salad she was preparing and smiled.

'To be honest, while Rosie's enjoying her nap, I love nothing better than messing around with food. So calming and...and grounding when you've had little sleep. Anyway, there's not much needs doing. You should be mingling, getting to know people; that's why I invited you all round. Have you spoken to Jeanne yet?' She carried on slicing avocados and tomatoes like the pro she was, leaving Tess with knife envy.

'Only briefly, it was becoming a little noisy with the children screaming their mutual delight at being together. She seems nice and they make a great couple, don't they?'

'Yes, and they've been so generous to me. Did I tell you Nick as good as financed my restaurant?' Tess shook her head and Colette went on to tell her how, after Nick and Jeanne became a couple, he let his sister have the proceeds from the sale of his cottage to start her business.

'What a wonderful gesture! No wonder you're all so close.' Tess sipped her drink, wistful as she thought of Clive in Canada. They'd been such good mates and as they'd grown older, he'd been the one to look out for her, as Nick did with Colette.

'Hey! You're looking sad, not allowed under my roof. What's the problem?' Colette asked, touching her arm.

'Nothing really, just missing Clive. Canada's so far away and I envy you having Nick so close.'

Colette pulled a face, saying, 'I am lucky, I know. My family's not spread their wings like other local families. But hey, Clive's doing well you told me, so he might come over for a holiday sometime. Now,' she added briskly, 'cheer up and go and chat to Jeanne. She's dying to know all about your house and what you've found. I scent a new book idea for our favourite local author.' Colette grinned, shooing Tess away with her hands.

Back outside she found Jeanne and Charlotte huddled together, their heads close, while their menfolk played with the children at the bottom of the garden. Tess smiled. A bit of peace.

'Ah, there you are! Come on, I've been telling Jeanne about your wonderful inheritance and she's been all ears.' Charlotte beamed at her and Jeanne moved to make room for her on the garden bench.

Tess was happy to answer Jeanne's questions, catching the gleam of interest in her blue eyes. The world of writers was new to her, but it was clear Jeanne and Charlotte were dedicated inhabitants, with Jeanne having now published several books, both fiction and non-fiction.

'I've always focused on the German Occupation in my historical books, but Charlotte sparked an interest in me about Victorian Guernsey when she wrote her latest. And what you're telling me about Eugénie and Hugo is absolutely fascinating. Definitely cue for a book,' Jeanne said, leaning forward

'See? I said she would be interested, didn't I?' Charlotte said, tapping her aristocratic nose.

'We don't know the whole story yet so it might turn out to be less exciting than we think. But I'm happy to fill you in once we've read the diaries, which won't be that soon as it's hard going translating from the French.'

'Thank you, depending on what you find, it might form the basis of either a novel or non-fiction. Hugo's such a popular figure, either way it's got legs.' Jeanne twisted her hair round a finger, looking thoughtful.

Their conversation was interrupted by Colette calling out that lunch was ready and could they come into the dining room. The men rounded up the children, while the women went indoors clutching their glasses.

'I thought the children could sit together at their own little table if you're happy with that?' Colette said, pointing out a small table set for three.

'Great idea, James has come along really well with his eating and being with the older two might make him feel more grown-up.' Charlotte watched as her son proved eager to sit next to Freya and the mothers grinned at each other. The adults sat at the table to enjoy their starters and Colette positioned a baby-monitor nearby to listen out for Rosie. Tess and her friends tucked in to *insalata tricolore* served with crusty bread and the conversation around the table became animated. By the time they had finished the main course of coq au vin Tess felt as if she'd known them all her life. Colette, walking past her to check on Rosie, whispered in her ear, 'All right? Are you enjoying yourself?'

Tess turned and whispered back, 'Absolutely. They're a great bunch.'

'Good, another time you must bring Jack, I'm eager to meet him. Charlotte says he's a dish and I'm surprised you didn't tell me about your date last night.' Colette's eyebrows rose in enquiry.

She felt her face flush. 'I didn't want you reading too much into it. He took me out to dinner to thank me for what I'd done for Larry. Wasn't a date as such.' She sounded unconvincing to her own ears and by the look on Colette's face, she didn't believe it either. Grinning, she squeezed her arm before going up to Rosie's room. Tess was left wondering why it was women were so keen to see their girlfriends hooked up with men. Perhaps it had something to do with the overdose of domestic harmony surrounding her. Catching sight of the three children squealing with delight at each other's company, she thought they may have a point.

❧ CHAPTER 26 ❧

Eugénie's Diary – Late September 1862

Oh, I am in heaven! I have received word of the return of my friends M'dame Drouet and M'sieur Hugo and she has invited me to have lunch with her today. I am not due to work at Hauteville House until tomorrow and although I knew of their imminent arrival from M'dame Hugo, it is still heartening to know they are safely returned from their travels. It is hard to contain my patience knowing I shall see him tomorrow and we will be working closely together once more. How I have missed those times! To know I am needed and appreciated is balm to my soul. M'dame Hugo has indicated she expects to remain in Guernsey for the rest of the year so it's possible my time alone with m'sieur will be limited, but it will be better than not seeing him at all.

I dressed carefully in a new dark grey summer dress, no longer wearing a widow's cap and only my jet beads proclaiming my recent loss. I then made my way to M'dame Drouet's house, taking me past Hauteville House. It looks exactly the same, no hint that the master has returned and reclaimed his eyrie. There is a skip in my step as I walk down the few yards to *La Fallue*.

Suzanne opened the door and embraced me like an old friend.

'My, you are looking so much bonnier than when I last saw you. Come, m'dame is anxious to see you and lunch will be served *toute de suite*.' She beamed at me before leading the way to the dining room where m'dame was gazing out at the sea. She turned as I entered and her face lit up and her arms reached out to me as I moved towards her. Tears of happiness slid down my cheeks as we embraced.

'My dear, you look wonderful! There is a colour in your cheeks that was missing and your eyes are bright. Indeed, it looks as if you haven't missed me at all!' She laughed, holding me at arm's length to study me properly.

'Oh, I have missed you, but I have been taking long walks, enjoying the summer air, and my appetite has been much improved. But you also look well, m'dame. I trust you are restored to health? Your eyes are improved?' There was a flush to her cheeks, showing that she had been taking the air in Austria, air that is known to be of great benefit to the sick, so I believe.

She smiled and indicated we sit at the table.

'Thank you, I am in much better health and my eyes have benefited from not having to read endless manuscripts. M'sieur is adamant I am no longer to overtax myself and we will be relying on you to take on more of the work. If that suits you, my dear?' She cocked her head on one side, as if not quite sure of my response.

'Indeed it does, I am keen to work harder than ever now I feel fully recovered.' My hand went automatically to my flat stomach and for a moment I felt an ache inside and knew I would probably never completely recover from my double loss.

She nodded, patting my hand as if she understood. Which, no doubt she did, having lost her own child. Any maudlin thoughts were chased away by the entrance of a grinning Suzanne with a laden tray and we were soon helping ourselves to the food, accompanied by glasses of red wine. After describing some of the sights of Austria and the other travellers they had met, she insisted I tell her of how I had spent my summer.

'I have made a friend in my neighbour, Mrs Rabey, and we have gone shopping in Town together and in fact she helped me choose this dress,' I said, smoothing the crisp cotton folds. 'We have entertained each other for afternoon tea and she and her husband invited me to supper one evening. It was most pleasant and once I am out of mourning she has promised to introduce me to other acquaintances. Her husband travels a lot for his business and she is glad of some company, as am I.'

Juliette pursed her lips, and I wondered if she was slightly jealous of my having a new friend. But no-one would replace her in my heart. She undoubtedly saved my life with her quick actions and has proved a sincere friend to me over these past months.

The conversation moved onto the continuing success of *Les Misérables* and how M'sieur Hugo had invited her to be his guest at a banquet in Brussels, organised by his publishers and attended by authors, statesmen, scientists and journalists from around the world. It was the first time she had been by his side at such a public event and her eyes shone as she described it to me. M'sieur has returned keen to return to his writing and it seems he has a number of projects in mind. By the end of our lunch I returned home much cheered at the prospect.

'*Ma petite*! How well you look! And wearing such a stylish dress, I see.' M'sieur Hugo took my hands in his as he studied me, a smile lifting his moustache. I had been awaiting him in the red drawing room since nine o'clock and it was now near to nine thirty when he burst through the door and advanced towards me, arms outstretched. I just managed to drop a curtsy before he took my hands, my heart hammering in my breast.

'M'sieur, it's good to see you, and looking so well. I understand your trip was a success?'

'Indeed it was and now I'm happy to be back on this rock of hospitality and freedom, this isle of Guernsey. And you, *ma petite*, you are happy to continue with your work here with me?'

'Indeed I am, and I believe you have ideas for your next works?'

After dropping a kiss on my hand, he began his usual pacing around, arms waving as he exclaimed about the first project, to be entitled *William Shakespeare* but was to be dedicated to various men of genius. As I listened I was able to observe him without fear of being noted. His thick hair was neatly trimmed, but his attire was the usual careless mix of well-worn trousers and jacket over a crumpled shirt and floppy tie. To me he appeared the opposite of what you would expect from such a wealthy and successful man, although I knew he could be pompous and demanding at times.

'You have met my son, Victor?' he said, coming to a stop. I nodded. His full name was François-Victor, but the family called him Victor. I had seen him flitting to and fro along with the various fellow exiles invited by m'sieur as guests. Also at the dinners for the poor where we had exchanged courteous greetings, but never held a full conversation. His furrowed brow left me with the impression he was too busy for idle chat and I knew he was responsible for translating his father's foreign correspondence.

'I am to write the preface for his translations of the works of Shakespeare, which I consider an honour. We will be a busy household for some time to come, *ma petite*, will we not?' He rubbed his hands gleefully.

'Yes, m'sieur, we will.' My heart was bursting with excitement and something deeper, something I am afraid to acknowledge.

CHAPTER 27

Tess – Late June 2012

Sunday lunch had extended through to the evening and everyone agreed it had been great fun. Left-overs from lunch had provided supper, making for a relaxed time even for the hostess. Tess hadn't enjoyed herself as much for a while and was happy to think this was a sample of what her new social life would be like. Together with some dating, perhaps?

When she woke on Monday morning her first thought was about Jack and how he had spent Sunday. Somehow she doubted if it would have been with young families even though she put him at about late thirties, likely to have some married friends. As she showered and dressed, his image kept popping into her head and she forced herself to think of other things. Like, what was she going to do today? She planned to nip round to the house, to make sure all was back to normal after the trauma of Friday, and then return to read the diaries for an hour or two. Any longer and her brain would explode. After a simple breakfast of cereals, juice and coffee, Tess went downstairs to find her hosts.

'Morning. Do you have any plans today?' Charlotte asked when Tess found her in the conservatory playing with James. He came over, arms outstretched, and she gave him a hug and a kiss. Satisfied, he wriggled until she set him down again.

'Only a quick trip to my house. Thought I might do some more reading later. What about you?'

'Supermarket shopping's the main item.' Charlotte pulled a face. 'And at some point a walk with this young man or possibly a trip to the play area in Saumarez Park. Which, I promise you, is eminently more enjoyable.'

'I bet! Well, I'll catch you later. Bye for now.'

It was mid-morning and the roads to Town were relatively quiet and it struck Tess that the following Monday would be her first day at work and she would be joining most of the adult population driving across the island early in the morning. One of the downsides of living in a small space with a high per capita number of cars, her friends had told her. After parking near *St Michel* she went in hoping to see Jack, but was told he wasn't expected until later. All the men were busy at work and the atmosphere had returned to normal. She saw a new face and assumed he was Larry's stand-in. After a quick look around and checking the desk was still safely locked in the cupboard, Tess left to see Heather, who invited her in for a coffee, keen to know why an ambulance had been there on Friday. She explained about the accident and how it had been lucky she was on the spot.

Heather was round-eyed when she finished.

'How awful for you, having to deal with such an emergency in your own house. Is everything else going well?'

Tess said it was and she would be starting work the following week and wouldn't be able to come round as often, but she trusted Jack to keep a keen eye on progress.

'I'm still hoping to be in by the end of August. And I can't wait to invite you and other friends round for the house-warming.'

Heather smiled, offering her a piece of homemade cake.

'I look forward to it and I'll bring some cake as my contribution.'

Tess took a bite.

'Delicious, as always. Have you never considered baking professionally? I'm sure there must be shops and cafés keen to buy such lovely cakes as yours.'

'No, I haven't. I'm not sure I'd have the confidence to approach anyone to buy from me.'

'If I could find someone interested in buying them, would you be up for baking to order? It would mean a proper commitment.' Tess was thinking of Colette, who if she didn't want them herself might know of other outlets. Heather had admitted to being a bored housewife so…

Heather chewed her lip.

'I do have time on my hands, yes, and it'd be nice to have more of a sense of purpose. But are you really sure my cakes would be up to scratch? I've only ever considered myself a competent amateur, not like those in the *Bake Off* competition on TV.'

'Honestly, your cakes are as good as any I've tasted from professional bakers. And I think it would be wonderful to give others a chance to eat them. But it's up to you.'

'In that case, I'm happy to have a go. More coffee? Or cake?' she laughed.

Tess grinned. 'No thanks, I'm full. I'll talk to my friend and let you know. And now I'd better get off.' She stood and Heather showed her out, giving her a quick hug.

'Thanks. Even if no-one is interested in my cakes, you've boosted my confidence.'

Tess could only hope she'd find a buyer, keen to help her new friend find an outlet for her talent. As she walked down the path, a voice called her name and she turned to see Jack getting out of his car. She found herself breaking into a broad smile.

'Hi, Jack. How are you? Did you have a good weekend?'

He came up to her and kissed her cheek. Her pulse quickened.

'I'm good, thanks and enjoyed my weekend. Particularly Saturday evening,' he said, grinning. 'And you?'

'Yes, the same.'

'Have you been in the house this morning?' He moved as if to go towards the front door.

She nodded. 'Earlier. Everything seems to be fine and I'm about to go home.'

'Right. In that case, are you free for dinner this week? Tomorrow night?' He touched her arm.

'Ah, not tomorrow, as my father arrives for a few days and we're having dinner together. He leaves on Friday, so I'm free then.'

'Okay, Friday it is. If I don't see you before then, I'll give you a ring.'

'Great, I look forward to it.' She hesitated. Would he kiss her goodbye?

He leaned closer. 'Bye for now,' he said, and kissed her cheek.

'Bye.' Her smile was broad as she walked towards her car.

Charlotte's car was missing when Tess arrived home so she went up to her room and phoned Colette about Heather and her cakes.

'That's interesting. I don't serve cake in the restaurant, only the usual desserts, but I've been toying with the idea of opening earlier in the day to offer coffee and snacks. There's not much competition around The Bridge and think we could do well.'

'Sounds good. And everyone loves a slice of home-made cake with their tea or coffee, don't they?'

Colette chuckled.

'Islanders do, anyway. Tell Heather to contact me and we'll take it from there. No promises, but I'm always happy to talk to anyone who can bake or cook.'

They spent a few minutes chatting before Colette had to go and feed Rosie. Tess rang Heather who was delighted to have the chance to speak to Colette. Pleased with her good deed for the day, Tess dug out the diaries to catch up with Eugénie and Victor Hugo. A couple of hours later she took a break for lunch and then went downstairs to see if Charlotte was back. She found her having a cup of tea in the kitchen.

'I've just put James down for his nap. Want to join me for a cup?'

'Thanks. I've been reading more of the 1862 diary, but not much is happening as Hugo goes away with Juliette for three months, leaving Eugénie a tad sad, by the sound of it. I'm sure her feelings for him are growing.' She sat down, accepting the proffered cup.

'He was a rascal, wasn't he? Taking his mistress off for a trip abroad just as his wife returns to Guernsey. But Adèle must have gone along with it, she was too strong minded a woman to be walked over.' Charlotte sipped her tea. 'I found the whole *ménage à trois* fascinating. He must have had something about him to be the object of such strong devotion from *two* women. Although Adèle's love waned earlier in the marriage and she took a lover, before Hugo fell for Juliette. And then, when he's well past his prime, a *third*, if Eugénie proves to have fallen under his spell.' She laughed, the deep throaty laugh that Tess found so infectious.

'There's no sign of anything happening between them yet, but Eugénie misses him while he's away. Absence makes the heart grow fonder, so they say.' Tess's thoughts slipped to Jack and their forthcoming date. She cleared her throat, 'By the way, I bumped into Jack this morning and he's taking me out to dinner again. He suggested tomorrow but Dad's arriving in the morning so we settled on Friday.'

Charlotte's eyebrows rose.

'Ooh, he does sound keen. But I think it's good you can't see him when he wants, you mustn't sound too keen yourself. Keep it cool.'

Tess giggled. 'Is that what you did with Andy? Played it cool?'

'Ah, that was different. I was helping research his family's history so we had to meet quite a lot to discuss my progress.' Charlotte tried to look serious, but failed.

'Not that different to Jack and me, then. Only I'm checking on his progress with my house.' Tess started laughing and Charlotte joined in.

'Touché! Whatever, I wish you well. If it goes all right on Friday, I'll invite him round next time we have friends for a meal. I now owe Colette and we went to Jeanne's a few weeks ago so the pressure's on.'

Tess stood and stretched.

'I'll leave you to your plans and go for a long walk. See you later.' She left, striking out through the nearby woods, planning to end up with a walk on the beach. A chance to clear her head.

At eight the next morning Tess was parked outside the airport on the look-out for her father. The early arrivals through the doors were clearly business passengers, there for the day, clutching briefcases or odd-looking boxes holding goodness knew what. Then those with luggage trickled through and she spotted her father, looking perplexed like someone in a strange land rather than his birthplace.

'Hi, Dad. Had a good flight?' His eyes lit up as he saw her and they shared a hug.

'Yes, it was fine. But what have they done to the airport? I hardly recognised it.' He looked back at the tall glazed building behind him.

'It's called progress, Dad. You'll see lots of changes, some good some not so much. But, hey, you're here and I'm sure you'll enjoy yourself.' She stowed his case in the boot and they jumped into the car.

'Right, I'm guessing you've not had breakfast?' He shook his head. 'Nor have I so I suggest we go to the café in Waitrose at Admiral Park as it's open early and on the way to your guest house. Okay?'

'Guernsey's got a Waitrose? Well, I'm blowed!' he said, chuckling.

'Actually, there are two, one's in the Rohais. I did tell you there have been a lot of changes, but I think the supermarkets have been popular. Now, what are your plans so far?' He told her about meeting up with friends for lunch in Town when they'd make further arrangements for the rest of his stay. Tess suggested she took him round her house after checking into the B & B and then going into Town for a coffee and a mooch around. Ken was happy with the idea and as Tess negotiated the traffic he stared out of the window, making the odd comment about anything new.

A couple of hours later Tess and her father stood outside *St Michel* while he studied the façade.

'I'd forgotten what the old place looked like, only remembering the houses here looked a bit shabby. But they don't now, do they?' He waved towards the neighbouring properties, showing off the result of serious investment in renovations. 'Those chaps knew how to build in the nineteenth century, didn't they? And your house looks as solid as the rest.' He put his arm round her shoulders, saying, 'I'm so pleased for you, love. Now let's have the grand tour.' Tess grinned, happy to see her father showing such an interest after his weeks of depression. The medication seemed to be working.

The workmen were busy preparing the walls for plaster boarding and the installation of the new electrics and they had to tread carefully where floorboards were missing, but Ken was unfazed by the upheaval. By the time they reached the attic rooms he was as keen as Tess on the proposed renovations.

'And what views you'll have! I do miss being close to the sea.' Ken sighed, looking out of the attic window.

'Come and see the cupboard, Dad. And the desk, which is lovely.' She unlocked the door and stood back to let Ken take a good look, opening the drawers and fingering the inlay.

'Nice piece of furniture, all right, and fancy locking everything up like that. Still, if they hadn't you'd have been the loser, as God knows what would have happened to it over the years.'

'True. Have you seen enough? We can go and grab a coffee now.' She locked the cupboard and they returned downstairs. She heard Jack's voice as they arrived in the entrance hall and she felt butterflies in her stomach as he turned round. His broad smile said it all.

'Hi, Tess. And you must be her father, Mr Le Prevost? Jack Renouf, I'm the building contractor.' He shook Ken's hand.

'Nice to meet you, Jack. Looks like you're doing a grand job and it'll be good to see the old place smartened up,' Ken said, giving him a keen look.

Tess noticed Jack had been talking to an official looking man with a clipboard and decided they ought to leave.

'We were just going for a coffee, Jack. Catch you later.' She flashed him a smile and took her father's arm to leave.

'I think that guy's from building control or something and needed to talk to Jack,' she told Ken once they were outside, hoping it wasn't about Larry's accident.

'Well, I think you're in safe hands with that Jack, for sure. I was worried you'd end up with a cowboy, but they look like a professional outfit.'

Linking arms they walked down the hill towards the town centre and Tess tried not to worry about the man with the clipboard.

The next few days sped by, with Tess spending as much time as she could with Ken when he wasn't with his friends. They had meals together and she introduced him to Charlotte and Andy when she made supper for him one evening. It was years since she had spent so much time with her father and they discovered how much they had in common, particularly their love of Guernsey. The subject of the impending divorce didn't come up until Thursday evening when they were enjoying a last meal together at Crabby Jack's at Vazon.

'You know, love, coming here has made me see things differently. I'm still angry and upset about what your mother's done but, looking back, I now see that things hadn't been right between us for years. I'd been blinkered, not wanting to see what was really happening. Not wanting to make changes, I suppose.' Ken raked his hand through his greying hair and grimaced.

Tess squeezed his hand, her heart breaking for him.

'So, what do you plan to do now, Dad?'

'I want to move here, for sure. There's not much to keep me in Exeter now, what with you and Clive having left. House prices here are bloody high, though, and I won't get much for my half of our house. A small apartment, maybe. As long as Elaine isn't too greedy, I could just about manage to live here on my pension,' he sighed, fiddling with his glass of wine. 'But I'd rather be some place where I'm happy than carry on living on old memories and have money in the bank.'

Tess toyed with the idea of suggesting he lived with her and was about to say something when her father went on, 'And no, I'm not asking you to let me move in. That wouldn't be fair on you and I want to keep my independence. But at least we could choose to spend time with each other, rather than be forced to. Agreed?' He patted her hand.

'Agreed.'

Tess – Late June 2012

Tess dropped her father off at the airport the next morning feeling more positive than when he arrived. She still hadn't talked to her mother and decided to wait a little longer. Elaine could phone her if she wanted to. With Ken planning to put the marital house on the market, it might not be too long before he was able to formalise their separation and buy a place in Guernsey. As she drove into Town Tess reflected on how much had changed in the three months since Aunt Doris had died. Humming to herself, she thought of her coming night out with Jack. Another change in her life: but would it last? Well, that remained to be seen, but it was better than the casual flings of the past few years. It was time to grow up and have a grown-up relationship. And she sensed it might be what Jack wanted, too. She parked the car and saw his Range Rover was already there. Her stomach fluttered in anticipation as she went in.

The place was a hive of activity with men in the hall and sitting room and she asked one where Jack was and he pointed downstairs. She found him studying the drawings with the electrician known as Sparks.

'Morning. Everything all right?'

Jack looked up and smiled.

'Hi, yes it's been a good week. Sparks has started first fixing in some of the rooms and we were just going over the plans for the kitchen. As it needs a lot of electrics we were double-checking everything. In fact, it's good you're here because you can confirm what you want.'

Tess pored over the plans and they discussed sockets, under-cabinet lighting, ceiling lights and switches. Jack said the kitchen units were due in about a month and he wanted to ensure Sparks and the plumber had completed their initial fixes.

After Sparks left them alone, Jack gave her a kiss on the cheek.

'I don't think it's a good idea for the men to know we're seeing each other, do you? Thought it better to be professional when we're not alone.' His eyes crinkled up as he smiled.

'Absolutely, that's fine. And it's still on for tonight?' She took a step back, her senses on full alert so close to him.

'Sure. I've booked a table at Village East in Town for eight o'clock, and thought we could have a drink somewhere first. Should be at yours about seven, if that's okay?'

'Great. I–' the jingle on her mobile pierced the air and with a muttered, 'Sorry,' she answered it, listening carefully. By the time the caller rang off, Tess was tingling with excitement. 'That was Stéphanie Duluc, from Hauteville House. She kindly agreed to check if there was an invoice in Hugo's name for the desk we found in the attic. And there was! Dated 1865 and marked with the initials "E.S." My ancestor.' She hopped from foot to foot in delight.

'Hey, that's wonderful news. A real piece of history, attached to such a famous name as his.' He paused. 'I wonder if we should leave it up there? I'd hate for anything to happen to it and we already know accidents can happen.'

'You're right. As I've got so much stuff at Charlotte's one more piece might not make much difference. Let me ring her.' Tess tapped in the number and her friend was only too happy to oblige, sounding as excited as she was at the news. Ending the call, she turned to Jack, saying, 'It's too big to go in my car, though.'

'It should fit in mine. I'll get one of the men to help me put it in the back and will bring it round later this afternoon. I've booked a taxi for us for dinner.'

'Thank you. While I'm here, is there anything else we need to discuss? What was that man wanting the other day?'

'He's my quantity surveyor and we were going over our costings. Nothing important.'

Jack then told her the arrival dates of goods ordered from the mainland were on schedule, and Tess was relieved there were no issues relating to Larry's accident. One of the men came in search of Jack and she left them talking about insulation and plasterboard and went next door to see Heather.

'Tess, I'm so glad to see you. Come in, come in.' She was ushered into the sitting room and Tess could tell by the sparkle in her eyes that she had good news. Colette had loved the cakes she had tasted and placed an order on a trial basis.

'Thanks so much for suggesting this, Tess, it's not the money that interests me, it's the being of use. Doing something creative. And Colette thinks I should offer my cakes to shops if I can keep up with demand. She's even letting me use the restaurant kitchen in order to comply with food regulations.'

'That's brilliant news and I'm sure you'll be rushed off your feet. Are we celebrating with a coffee and a piece of cake?' Tess said, laughing.

'Of course, hang on while I go and make it. The coffee, I mean, not the cake!' Heather rushed off leaving Tess sending a silent prayer of thanks to Colette for her endorsement.

The desk was delivered late in the afternoon and squeezed into a space in the guest suite, as Charlotte was concerned to keep it out of reach of James. Jack didn't stop to chat, only saying he would see Tess later. Charlotte left her son downstairs with Andy and joined Tess to admire the desk in its new light-filled setting.

'There's hardly a mark on it. It's difficult to believe it's about one hundred and fifty years old,' Tess said, running her fingers over the intricate wood.

'Not surprising if it's been locked away most of that time. And I'm sure young Eugénie would have cherished it as the fabulous gift it was,' Charlotte said, pulling the writing flap down. 'Will you keep it? Must be worth a fortune, thanks to its provenance.'

'For sure. But I don't think I'd actually use it as a working desk, too decorative, and not big enough for a PC. Perhaps pride of place in my new sitting room?' She tried to picture where Eugénie had sat at the desk before locking it away. Her bedroom? Sitting room? Living on her own, apart from her maid who presumably slept in the attic, she had ample choice. Suddenly, the image of a young woman in a pale grey Victorian dress sitting at the desk and writing with a pen appeared in front of her. It was so vivid, so real. Tess blinked. It disappeared. What on earth was that?

'Are you all right? You look distracted.' Charlotte squeezed her arm.

'Yes, just an odd thought, that's all.' She glanced at her watch. 'I'd better go and have a shower and get ready for my date, he'll be here in less than an hour.'

Charlotte nodded and left her alone. Tess was still shaken by what she'd 'seen'. Instead of the room here, the woman had been sitting at the desk in what Tess recognised as the front room of *St Michel*, the windows onto the street clearly visible. Telling herself her imagination was running away with her, she headed into the bathroom for the hottest shower she could stand.

Later, dressed in a short skirt and silk blouse, Tess went downstairs to wait for Jack. Five minutes later a taxi pulled into the drive and she went out as Jack slid out and held the door for her. A quick exchange of kisses on the cheek and they slipped into the back seat. Conscious of the lack of privacy, little was said other than Jack saying how lovely she looked. The taxi dropped them off in the Lower Pollet and he suggested they had a drink in Christies, a few yards away.

'Do you remember Christies from when you lived here?' he asked, reaching for her hand. She loved the feel of his fingers around hers, experiencing a frisson of electricity.

'I do, not that I was a regular, an occasional coffee or milkshake with friends. We felt very sophisticated sitting in the window on a Saturday morning, watching the world go by.' Tonight people were streaming past, on the way to the various bars and restaurants of Town, laughing and light-hearted on a beautiful evening. Tess caught their mood and trotted along beside Jack feeling little older than her twelve-year-old self when she last enjoyed a coffee there with Colette.

'My mates and I went there to eye the girls walking past and, I'm ashamed to say, when the windows were open, we'd call out or wolf whistle. Needless to say, they ignored us and I've gained a lot of respect for the female sex.' He grinned, guiding her through the door. The bar was busy and Jack had to search for a table, eventually finding one tucked away towards the back. Tess studied the drinks menu and chose a gin and tonic. A waiter turned up to take the order and Jack settled on a local cider.

'It tends to be a bit noisy to talk in here, but it'll be quieter in Village East. And I like this place to chill, get the weekend started. Okay?'

'Sure. The pubs and bars in Exeter were great for chilling in, as well. We'd sometimes get hammered to help us forget the traumas we'd dealt with at work. I don't have that excuse, or need, these days.' She had to lean in close to be heard over the sound of music, talking and laughter and breathed in Jack's aftershave. She felt a bit light-headed.

'I honestly don't know how you coped with the horrors you must have seen, day after day. Which reminds me, Larry's home and doing well and should be back at work in another week.'

The waiter arrived with their drinks before Tess could respond. After a clink of their glasses, she said, 'It was tough in A & E but also rewarding when we managed to save lives. Not so good when we failed, and those were the bad days when we needed to let go and forget for a while.' She sipped her drink as the unbidden image of young Gary surfaced. Would she ever be free of the memory? With a mental shake, Tess continued, 'I'm really pleased about Larry, he was one of the success stories.' She managed a smile which Jack returned.

For a moment they lapsed into silence; Tess, for one, aware of the beat of the background music as she took swallows of her drink. She found herself tapping her foot in time to the music as she embraced the Friday night mood. Glancing at Jack she noticed he was tapping his fingers on his leg and as he caught her glance, they both laughed.

'Good beat, isn't it? Great for dancing.'

'Do you dance, Jack?'

'Sure, if the music's good and I'm with someone I'd like to dance with. I'm not one of those guys who gets on the floor and does his own thing in a show-off kind of way. What about you?'

'I love to dance, but I've probably danced more with my girlfriends than a bloke. A bit crazy style when we're having a great night out.' She grinned, taking another sip of her drink.

'I'd like to see that, you going a bit crazy on the dancefloor,' he said, his eyes narrowing.

Tess looked down at her glass, feeling self-conscious at the idea. Squashed close on a dancefloor was too intimate a thought when they were still getting to know each other. Perhaps Jack picked up on her hesitation as he suggested they should head to the restaurant, literally around the corner on the North Plantation, opposite the harbour.

Once outside he reached for her hand and she was happy to let him as they had to push through a crowd to reach Village East, the bistro spilling outside with tables set on the pavement. It was in one of the old Georgian buildings, narrow but tall spread over several floors. Jack led her inside and was welcomed by a cheerful Portuguese man he introduced as the boss, Nobby.

'I come here at least once a month and Nobby and I have become friends. Right, Nobby?'

'Right, Senhor. Your usual table is ready if you'll follow me, please, Senhorita.'

Tess followed Nobby upstairs and he led them to a table set for two in the window, with an uninterrupted view over the harbour entrance and the islands of Herm and Sark. He left them with menus and went to take an order from another table.

'This is lovely, Jack. You must be popular to get the best table like this.' Tess picked up the menu.

'I've known Nobby since he ran Crabby Jacks at Vazon so he tends to look after me. And the food's good, particularly the fish, which I'm going for. How about a bottle of white wine?'

Tess was happy with that and a bottle was ordered while they perused the menus. She decided on seared scallops followed by sea bass and Jack chose crab cakes and Dover sole. The wine arrived and was duly poured. Lights started to twinkle around the harbour as the sky darkened and Tess sighed, entranced.

'You look happy, enjoying yourself?' Jack stroked her fingers and she felt a tingle of electricity.

'Yes, thanks. It's a nice way to end a good week. What about you?'

'I'm happy, thanks to the delightful company.' He smiled and Tess felt her stomach lurch. He really was sexy. Was she going to be able to resist him? And why should she? She took a deep breath.

'There's quite a lot I don't know about you, Jack. How about filling in the gaps?'

'Sure. Where shall I start?' He took a swallow of wine and went on, 'How about after I left school?' She nodded. 'I didn't go straight to uni but took time out and went with a couple of mates to the Far East, spending time in Vietnam, Cambodia and Japan. Mind blowing!' He spread his hands. 'We had a great time, but were pretty broke as it was hard to get jobs except in bars catering for English speakers. We survived, just, and then came back to go off to uni.'

'Sounds quite brave. I managed Australia and New Zealand, but I was on my own and had to play it safe. Had a lot of fun, though, and got pretty good at surfing.'

His eyes lit up.

'That's great, I love the water. Perhaps we could surf together sometime?'

'Sure, that would be good.' Umm, he definitely wanted them to spend more time together. 'So, which uni did you go to?'

'Bristol, for a degree in civil engineering. At the time I wasn't that keen on returning to Guernsey, thought it too insular after my time abroad. I figured an engineering degree would guarantee me a good career in the UK or abroad.'

'What happened to change your mind?'

'By the time I graduated I realised I actually missed home and the slower pace of life. My degree studies increased my respect for building construction and, with my father's help, I started my own business. And the rest, as they say, is history.'

A waiter arrived with their starters and Tess waited until after he'd left before replying.

'I'm impressed. I hadn't realised you had such a technical background. Must help when you're deciding on potential projects. Any regrets about not staying in the UK?'

He gave her a long, slow look.

'Not from where I'm sitting, no.'

She felt the heat rise to her face and lifted her glass to her lips as a foil.

'Now it's your turn. Tell me about your time since school.'

'After my gap year I went to Plymouth medical school and it was during clinical practice that I decided to train as a GP. And here I am, ready to start on Monday.'

Jack raised his glass.

'Well, here's to your first day in your new job. I'm sure you'll nail it, no problem.' Tess smiled as she raised her own. She certainly hoped so, or coming home could prove her worst decision yet.

The rest of the meal was a pleasurable combination of good food, wine and animated conversation. It was as if their original business relationship had segued into one much more personal and Tess, though still somewhat nervous, looked forward to seeing how it developed. Jack was easy to talk to and they had more in common than she'd realised. The arrival of coffee and small glasses of port marked the imminent end of an evening she had thoroughly enjoyed.

Jack's eyes appeared to mirror her own feelings as they gazed at each other over the port. He stroked her palm with a light touch.

'I'd better order the taxi. We, er, have two choices. I can ask them to drop you off first or we could go to my place and have another drink and I'll arrange another taxi for later.'

'Let's go to yours. I'd love to see it.' There, she'd said it. They both knew she wasn't just wanting to see his house. She wanted to see more of *him*.

CHAPTER 29

Eugénie's Diary – June/July 1863

The Hugo household is in turmoil! I arrived to find M'sieur
Hugo in furious discussion with Victor, holding a letter aloft as
if it would burn his hand. I quickly made my way upstairs out
of earshot, not wanting to be a party to their obvious upset. I
heard the word 'Adèle' and that was enough. As I settled down
to my task that day, my mind went over what I knew
concerning the young woman. Not really that young, either, at
thirty-two she was considered to be headed for spinsterhood,
having, according to her father, already spurned five suitors.
Personally, I was surprised anyone would have offered for her,
as her moods were becoming more and more strange and
unpredictable. I kept my distance as much as possible as she
made it clear my presence was abhorrent to her. Over the
months I have learnt of her obsession with an English soldier,
Lieutenant Pinson, whom she had met in Jersey and has
corresponded with since. Adèle left Guernsey yesterday, 18th
June, to join her mother in Paris and I surmised the letter in
m'sieur's hand concerned this event.

I was fully engaged in my work when he appeared in the
salon a few hours later. He barely acknowledged my curtsy,
pacing around the table picking up and putting down my
copied pages.

'Are you well, m'sieur?' I ventured to ask, curiosity giving
me confidence.

At last he stood still, running his hand through his hair with
a dramatic sigh.

'Yes, I am, thank you, but I have an ingrate for a daughter.
Instead of going to join her mother, she has instead gone to
England to stay with a friend which we think is a subterfuge
and she is actually on her way to join the soldier, Pinson, in
Canada. We do not know if she is to marry him or not. As if we
would have hindered her had we but known. In fact she has

our blessing if he was to ask for her hand and we are sending our consent if a marriage is to take place. Although it is not clear if it will, as I suspect her feelings for him outmatch any he might have for her.' He paced around the table again as I tried to think of what to say.

'It's not the way it should have happened, I agree, but if she does marry this man, would you not be pleased? Is it not what all fathers want for their daughters?'

He stared at me and not for the first time I wondered if he saw me or Léopoldine.

'You are right, of course. I'd be pleased, and so would her mother. Although she could have chosen someone so much better to join a family such as ours. At least she would become his problem now,' he added, under his breath. He gave my arm a pat and left. My thoughts spun around my head as I took in the enormity of Adèle's actions. Her reputation would be ruined if the marriage did not take place and it would reflect badly on her parents. No wonder m'sieur was angry.

30th June

Another letter arrived on 30th June from Adèle's friend in London confirming she had indeed left for Halifax, Nova Scotia. M'sieur confided in me that M'dame Hugo and Charles were returning to Guernsey while they decide what to do. M'sieur and Victor spent much time together as they waited for M'dame Hugo to arrive and when she did raised voices could be heard through the house. It is not a happy place to work in and I try to keep out of the way. I only catch the odd glimpse of M'dame Hugo and Charles and they are to leave soon.

12th July

M'dame Hugo and Charles left today and the atmosphere has improved in Hauteville House. M'sieur looked slightly less harassed when I saw him this afternoon.

'I am sending her an allowance, but there's no word of a marriage as yet and this troubles me,' he said, pulling at his beard. I murmured some words of comfort, but it was clear how much he was affected by Adèle's erratic behaviour. M'sieur has thrown himself into his writing, which promises to be an epic critique of Shakespeare and his works as well as others such as Homer, Juvenal and Dante. I am engrossed as I work, my mind opened to new ideas and literature I'd never dreamt of studying. I copied out his words, '*Each new genius is an abyss. Yet there is such a thing as tradition. A tradition which passes from one chasm to the next*'. I could not help but wonder what part he himself played in this gathering of geniuses, for surely he was one. My admiration grows unchecked as I listen to and read his words. And I realise it is more than admiration, but something that can never be acknowledged. For him, I am a somewhat poor substitute for his beloved Léopoldine, and he continually shows me kindness and generosity, including gifts that I will always treasure. It was merely a trick of fate that I should resemble the poor girl so nearly, but one for which I will be eternally grateful as it had brought me to him. Alas, that I shall never be more than his copyist and friend!

August 1863
In spite of only receiving an occasional letter from Adèle, addressed to her brother Victor, and not knowing exactly what was happening with her, M'sieur Hugo and M'dame Drouet left for Brussels today, 15th August for their summer break. I am missing them already and the time drags as I work in the now silent house.

October 1863
I'm thankful my friends have returned! Our routine will soon be re-established and I cannot wait.

Today I was in the red salon working as usual when m'sieur burst in, crying, 'Adèle is married!' The deep lines of his forehead looked less pronounced as he flourished a letter in his hand. I offered my congratulations before he rushed off, presumably to write to his wife. There was an immediate lift in the atmosphere and I happily continued working.

Oh, no, a letter has been received by Victor from Adèle, asking for money. M'sieur was in a fury as he relayed the events to me, saying her landlady was about to throw her out and that the marriage hadn't taken place.

'I shall shame the man into marrying her! No-one makes sport with the daughter of the Viscount and Viscountess Hugo of France!'

He stormed out and the tension in the household was palpable for the rest of the day.

Today an announcement of m'sieur's daughter's engagement to the lieutenant appeared in the local paper, and I understand on the mainland. Presumably this was to shame the soldier into marrying, as m'sieur had threatened. But it proved a failure.

There has been no marriage and Adèle continues to stay in Halifax, much to her father's despair.

Late 1863–1864

I went for lunch today to M'dame Drouet's and found her in a state of much excitement.

'*Ma chère*, see what I have received in the post today,' she said, handing me a leather-bound volume. It was M'dame Hugo's biography of M'sieur Hugo and at the front was a signed dedication to M'dame Drouet.

'Do you not think this is most charitable of M'dame Hugo? I shall treasure it as much as any of her husband's books.' ·

'I think it a gracious gesture and I'm truly pleased for you. Perhaps her sons have told her how kind you are to them when they are here without her.' It was true, when in Guernsey Charles and Victor dined at her home with their father and other guests. They had known her since they were children and she has told me how fond she has become of them. I gather they had all felt a little unsure when M'sieur Hugo first suggested it, but it has been a great success. I admit to being somewhat envious of these soirees, but apart from m'dame, only gentlemen are permitted and the conversation can be a little embarrassing to the hostess, she has said.

'There is something else which I must share with you. M'sieur and his sons have been saying for some time that this house is too damp for me and I confess I think it has affected my health, particularly in the winter months. And so a new house is to be found for me as near as possible to his. I don't like the thought of moving, but I must consider my health.'

I was pleased to hear this as I had thought the same about the house for some time.

Spring 1864

M'sieur Hugo's work, *William Shakespeare*, is published, selling in the anticipated large numbers. However, the critics are harsh and m'sieur is scathing of them. His humour isn't helped by the continued absence of his daughter Adèle and her constant need for funds. The household is not the most cheerful at this time but m'sieur keeps busy with his writing which means I am also much occupied. I would like to think he finds my company uplifting and he often holds me in conversation when he has more time and I am happy to join him. My life outside my work is still limited to visits with m'dame, occasional trips out with her and m'sieur, and my friendship with Mrs Rabey. It is now two years since I had lost Arnaud and the baby and I am out of mourning, but my life remains that of a widow.

April

Today, m'sieur joined m'dame and me for lunch at *La Fallue*, which has occurred more often with the continued absence of M'dame Hugo.

'I have found you a house, *ma chère*,' he announced to m'dame, who tried to look pleased. 'And you will be surprised to learn it is No 20, where I was housed when we first arrived here. I've been trying to get Thomas Domaille to sell it to me for a while and he's finally agreed. So what do you think?' He beamed at her.

'Oh, that's wonderful! Still near to you, m'sieur. Will it need much work done?'

'A certain amount, but I expect to have you in there by June. And just think, we shall have the pleasure of designing the rooms to your taste and buying whatever you need to make you comfortable. Is that not good news?' He spread his arms and Juliette clapped her hands in agreement. I was even more pleased as the house was a mere three doors away from mine, which she was quick to point out. We raised a toast in celebration and spent a most pleasant lunch together.

June

M'dame has duly moved in to what is now called *Hauteville Faerie*, the work deemed essential by m'sieur being completed. They spend a deal of time visiting antique shops looking for furniture and furnishings. I gathered from her that m'sieur wants to create a miniature Hauteville House and the décor does begin to resemble the style of the mansion, but on a much smaller scale. One of the rooms designed by him is already known as the Chinese room and will be used for soirees. Other rooms are adorned with damask hangings, antique mirrors and wonderful collections of odd items collected from flea markets. M'dame's theatrical dresses from her days as an actress have been transformed into coverings for chairs and sofas by m'sieur, whose artistic creations continue to surprise and amaze me. M'dame, unable to spend as much time writing thanks to poor eyesight, has given herself up to fashioning a new home and seems much happier than she's been for a while. M'sieur Hugo also appears to have shaken off some of the strains of the past months and both households enjoy the benefit.

The work on the house does not mean the writing has slowed down and after the publication of *William Shakespeare* m'sieur started on a new novel and also began collating poems, some written a few years previously, to form the collection, *Les Chansons des Rues et des Bois*. I have found them quite a contrast to other works I have copied, being of a lighter nature and with certain undertones which bring a flush to my cheeks as I write. If he is in the room I have to avoid my master's eye although I am sure he knows full well the effect his words would have on me. It is well that he cannot read my heart, for I have surely lost it to the man I can never have. I am in a worse position then my dear M'dame Drouet, for at least she is loved in return and can enjoy her love in her own home. There are times when it feels too much of a burden and the tears fall unheeded when

I retire to bed. However, it would be far worse to never see my beloved again!

The younger Victor has become engaged to a charming local girl, Emily de Putron, of good family, who he met soon after arriving in Guernsey. She has helped him with his translation of Shakespeare's works and I have seen her on several occasions and it was clear theirs was a love match. M'sieur Hugo is delighted as it will keep his son in Guernsey. Charles, I understand, had grown restless and left in 1861, before I met the family, only returning on occasion.

December

I was at m'dame's for lunch, an established routine now M'dame Hugo has returned, and after Suzanne left us, m'dame brought up the subject of marriage.

'Is it not wonderful that Victor is soon to be married? Something joyful to look forward to for a change.' She gave me a sly look as she poured the wine.

'Indeed, it is. They make a good match and now we must hope Charles finds a partner before he is much older. It's unusual for a man of thirty-eight to be unmarried, especially from such a family as his.'

She waved her hand.

'Oh, Charles will find a bride in his own time. But it is not the Hugo menfolk I'm concerned about, *ma chère*, it is *you*. It's nearly three years since you lost your husband and are you not considering your own future?'

'My future? Why, I'm perfectly happy working for M'sieur Hugo and see no need to make any changes, unless he wants me to leave?' My chest grew tight with the fear of such a thing happening. I couldn't leave him, I couldn't!

'No, of course he doesn't want you to leave. But we are both aware that you are still young and with your looks and intelligence, could be considered a suitable wife for any man.' She smiled as if I should be pleased to hear such a thing. But in truth, it was the very last thing I wished to consider. I never wanted to stop working for m'sieur and would have to if I married. And I had vowed never to have another child and so for those two reasons I could never marry again.

❧ CHAPTER 30 ❧

Eugénie's Diary – January 1865

This year has not started well and the Hugo family is in mourning for poor Emily de Putron who has succumbed to the tuberculosis. Young Victor is devastated and plans to leave Guernsey for good, so he has told his father. M'sieur is to give the oration at the funeral and I and other members of the household will attend at the Cimetière des Indépendants in Town.

> ...*She was like a joyful flower strewn in the house. From the cradle she was surrounded by every tenderness; she grew up happily and, receiving happiness, returned it; loved, she loved...*
> *She has left, youth journeying to eternity; beauty to perfection; hope to certainty...*

As I listened to these beautiful words I wondered if M'sieur Hugo also thought then of his own lost daughter, Léopoldine. He looked so sad, and no wonder. His family have suffered many blows. His son took ship yesterday and missed the funeral, heading for Brussels and plans to stay abroad for some time, I believe. His mother is shortly to follow him. M'sieur Hugo has responded to his loss by closing the billiard room.

M'dame Drouet has taken on the role of de facto housekeeper at Hauteville House now that m'sieur has been left alone. She returns to her own house each evening and I spend time with her as before. He has thrown himself into work and the poems are now published while he continues writing what I consider to be his most extraordinary book to date. He calls it *Les Traveilleurs de la Mer* (Toilers of the Sea) and is full of giant creatures and super-human beings like a fairy tale, but is set here in Guernsey.

Today I asked him about his inspiration for the story as he produced more pages to copy.

'Coming by ship in exile to these islands was the first time I had been at sea and it had, and continues to have, a profound effect on me. You will have noticed, *ma petite*, how much time I spend gazing out from my lookout, observing the sea in all its many variations. Also, I have spent many hours talking to the good fishermen and sailors at the harbour and have listened mesmerised to their tales of life at sea.' He paced about, stroking his beard, his eyes bright with passion. 'I have wanted to dedicate a volume to these brave men and to the islanders who have given me such refuge over these many years and this work is my homage to them all.' He stopped, pointing at the papers on the table, and said, 'And what is your opinion, *ma petite*? Do you think I have done them justice?'

'Oh, indeed you have. The poor, brave Gilliatt, undertaking so much for the young woman, Déruchette, is a fine example of the local fishermen who brave the dangerous waters to provide us with fish. And from your detailed descriptions of what it's like to sail a boat in these waters, no-one would guess you had never done this yourself.'

He beamed at me.

'You are most kind, and I am particularly pleased with those passages. It remains to be seen what the public's views will be.'

'Will you include your illustrations, m'sieur? They are quite some of your best, I feel.' He had the habit of including little drawings in the margins of the manuscripts and also sketching larger versions, such as that of the *pieuvre*, a sea monster like an octopus.

'I will consider it, yes. Now, I must return to my desk – ah, that reminds me. Do you have a desk for your correspondence at home?'

'No, m'sieur, I use my dining table.'

'Ah, that is what M'dame Drouet thought. We were inspecting the latest items in Mr Symes's shop in Mansell Street when we saw the most splendid French ladies desk. I immediately thought of you and asked her if she thought you might like it and she said yes. So, I have reserved it and it is yours if you so desire,' he said, smiling broadly.

I was so astonished my mouth fell open. He had given me numerous small presents over the years, but a *desk*!

'I...I do not know what to say. What have I done to deserve such a gift, m'sieur?'

He took my hand and looked earnestly at me.

'You have worked tirelessly for me for more than three years, *ma petite*, and have become a friend to us both. Your presence has helped me to deal with the sad loss of my daughters, as even Adèle is lost to me these past two years.' He sighed, and I saw the sadness in his eyes and wished I could comfort him. He continued, 'It would give me pleasure if you were to accept this desk as a token of my affection and gratitude.'

A lump formed in my throat and I struggled to reply.

'In that case, m'sieur, I would be honoured to accept, however unworthy I am to receive such a gift.'

'Splendid! I will have it sent to you directly. But now we both have work to do, *n'est ce pas*?' He released my hand and strode off, leaving me trembling with shock and...what? Feelings I could not admit to, made even more powerful by his generosity. I had to pace around the salon a few times, emulating m'sieur's habit, before I was able to focus on my work. By the time I finished some hours later I was calmer and hurried home wondering when the desk would arrive.

'Oh, m'dame! You'll never guess what's been delivered barely ten minutes ago!' Sophie was wringing her hands with excitement as she met me at the door. Striving to appear more serene than I felt I allowed her to drag me into the parlour where m'sieur's gift now had pride of place near the window.

'Isn't it beautiful, m'dame? I don't think I've ever seen anything like it afore. Is it a present? Looks very expensive.' Sophie gabbled on while I examined the exquisite inlaid desk with a drop-down top hiding drawers and cubbyholes. Unmistakably French, and as Sophie said, expensive. Even my beloved Arnaud had never spent so much on a gift for me and I was quite overcome. Telling her I was ready for my lunch, I shooed her downstairs to the kitchen while I stood admiring the workmanship a little longer, tears sliding down my cheeks. The first letter I would write would be one of thanks to M'sieur

Hugo and Sophie can deliver it after lunch. I will treasure this desk to my dying day.

October 1865

At last M'sieur Hugo and M'dame Drouet have returned! They have also brought the welcome news that Charles has married a young French woman, Alice Lehaene, with good connections. This talk of a marriage has prompted M'dame Drouet to again raise the question of my remarrying, but, as I told her previously, I am not interested in finding a husband. I could not tell her the true reason, and she must have thought me odd to be so stubborn.

March 1866

At last *Les Travailleurs de la Mer* is published, shortly after m'sieur's birthday. He has written a dedication which I find quite moving –

I dedicate this book to the rock of hospitality and liberty,
That corner of old Norman soil where dwells that noble little people of
the sea;
To the island of Guernsey,
Austere and yet gentle,
My present asylum, my probable tomb.

It is a time of celebration and he is particularly pleased that no less than the writer Alexandre Dumas, whose work I also admire, held a party to celebrate the publication. The novel is selling in even greater numbers than *Les Misérables*, m'sieur informs me, rubbing his hands together when he sought me out in the red salon.

'I am not surprised it is proving so popular, I admired it greatly. Do you have another work in mind, m'sieur?' Each time he finished a great work I was afraid he would decide to take a long break from writing and leave me unemployed.

'Indeed, I have an idea for another novel and also some other projects. Don't worry, I still need you,' he said, smiling. Just then, Henriette burst into the room saying that Sénat, his beautiful greyhound, had run off again.

'That dog is costing me a fortune!' he shouted, and Henriette and I shared a smile. M'sieur was referring to the dog's collar, engraved in a verse written by him, and considered a valuable trinket by those lucky enough to find him.

In French, it reads: *'Je voudrais qu'au logis quelqu'un me ramenât Mon état? Chien   Mon maitre? Hugo   Mon nom? Sénat'*
In English: 'I would like someone to take me home
My profession? Dog   My master? Hugo   My name? Sénat'

Later on M'sieur returned, in a calmer mood, and presented me with a beautifully bound and signed copy of *Les Travailleurs de la Mer*. I thanked him profusely, honoured again by his continuing generosity towards me.

April 1866
M'sieur has heard from his daughter Adèle's landlady that she has left Halifax and followed the regiment to Barbados. I feel sorry for him as he paces about, hands thrust in his pockets, as he considers what, if anything, he could do. The whispers among the servants are that the family has a history of madness and that Adèle is possibly afflicted. It does fit with her odd behaviour but is no comfort to her father, alone in Guernsey while his other children and his wife stay in Brussels or Paris. At least M'dame Drouet stays by his side, ever his stalwart companion. And I like to think I play my own small part in keeping him from melancholy.

1868 – August
The most distressing news. M'dme Hugo has died in Brussels while the whole family – apart from Adèle, who was still away – was there. M'sieur had gone with M'dame Drouet for their usual summer trip and they were staying with Victor. When M'dame Hugo was last in Guernsey, early last year, she had seemed to be unwell and was in pain with her eyes, she told me. She and M'dame Drouet spent some time together and they became friends. For the moment m'sieur and m'dame are to remain abroad but in her letter to me, she says she will try to persuade him to return soon. His own health is suffering and

he has lost weight, she says. The tragedy not only reduces me to tears but brings home to me my vulnerability and I barely leave the house now, feeling lost and alone even though I do have some friends and my faithful Sophie.

1868 October/November
M'sieur Hugo and M'dame Drouet are returned! Seeing them again in Hauteville House lifts my spirits but m'sieur has aged. He complains of rheumatic pains and heavy nose-bleeds and I know m'dame is concerned for him, as am I. The wet, cold winter weather makes it hard for anyone to shake off the doldrums, but the one ray of light at this time is the child, Georges, born to Alice and Charles some months before and adored by both his grandfather and M'dame Drouet, who, I think, sees herself as a surrogate grandmother. I am happy for them both, after all they have endured, they deserve some joy. I know it must seem contrary that I wish m'dame joy with M'sieur Hugo, given my own feelings for him, but she has been his rock, his muse, and his faithful lover for so long that she surely has the greater claim. My love pales in comparison, though is no less real and causes me some pain, knowing it will never be returned. This I must endure if it means I can remain by his side.

This adored grandchild did, however, put m'dame in mind of my own situation as she has again raised the subject of my future.

'You know how much we both care for you, my dear, you are as a daughter to us. We wish to be assured you are settled now there is a chance we will be returning to France in the not too distant future.' She poured the coffee as we sat in her drawing room and I felt the fear clutch at my heart. I had known, since the change in the political atmosphere in Paris, that the way might open for them to return, but had tried not to dwell on it.

She passed me my coffee, and I noted the dark shadows around her eyes as she attempted a smile.

'I am aware of your aversion to marriage, but if there was a gentleman who is known to and approved of by M'sieur Hugo and myself, would you not at least consider meeting him to see if you found him agreeable?'

I took a sip of my coffee to give myself time to think. Now twenty-five years of age, I had matured from the young and naïve girl of nineteen and was aware life could be very difficult for a woman on her own. I owned my house, but my income was solely from my work as m'sieur's copyist. If he were to leave the island, then I would lose my income as well as enduring a broken-heart. The spectre of Adèle, made mad with unrequited love living in a strange country alone, loomed large in my mind and gave me cause to consider my choices. If I was going to lose m'sieur anyway, and, in truth, he had never been mine, then would it be so awful to contemplate someone who might be a companion and provider? If I were to fall pregnant, then was there any reason I would lose the child as before? The thoughts tumbled through my mind while m'dame sat in silence, as if knowing I had much to consider. I took a deep breath.

'I'm grateful for your affection for me and concern for my happiness. Is…is there a particular gentleman you have in mind?' My hand shook as I gripped the cup.

She smiled and reached out to pat my hand.

'Yes, my dear, there is. You have met the French teacher, Paul Stapfer, at Hauteville House, have you not?' I nodded, he was a regular visitor and lived in upper Hauteville. 'Well, he has a friend, a fellow teacher at Elizabeth College, to whom we were introduced some months ago, Pierre Blondel, a widower. Paul has intimated that his friend wishes to remarry and, having seen you and knowing a little of your circumstances, Paul asked if his friend could meet you. M'sieur Hugo is quite taken with the man, finding him a gentleman and excellent company and is happy to arrange such a meeting if you are willing to consider it.' Tilting her head to one side, she added, 'We only have your best interests at heart, my dear, and you are free to say no.'

It seemed churlish to refuse as I have free will and if I do not like the look of the man, then that is the end of the matter.

'Then I agree to meet him if this will be in company.'

'We thought a little supper at Hauteville House, with both M'sieur Stapfer and M'sieur Blondel invited. Oh, I do hope you like each other, as I find him quite charming and he is very personable.'

I admit I was intrigued and m'dame said she would advise me when a date and time were arranged.

When I went to work today, m'sieur arrived with pages of his new project; his novel, *L'Homme qui rit* finished yesterday and off to the publishers. He made no mention of Pierre Blondel and I understood that he wanted it to appear, for the sake of propriety, as if any arrangements were made by m'dame and not himself.

I have received a note from m'dame asking if I am free to attend a supper party on the following Friday evening and I duly replied that I was. To my surprise I felt some excitement at the prospect of meeting this 'charming' man at last.

Friday

I have taken great care over my toilette this evening. My choice of gowns used to be limited, but m'dame has been kind enough to give me, some weeks ago, one of her beautiful silk gowns which no longer fitted and which she asked her dressmaker to alter for me. She has expensive taste, both in clothes and jewellery, and is fortunate that M'sieur Hugo is happy to indulge her. The dress is deep blue with exquisite embroidery around the neckline and on the sleeves and I have never possessed anything as lovely. As I stood in front of the bedroom mirror I hardly recognised myself in the elegant young woman staring back at me. Sophie has styled my hair in soft ringlets instead of my usual neat bun. Unbidden, an image of myself in my widow's garb came into my mind and I gasped. 'Forgive me, Arnaud, please forgive me.' I brushed away an errant tear before picking up my cloak and going downstairs.

'You look ever so lovely, m'dame. That blue suits you, it does. I'm sure the gentleman will be smitten,' Sophie grinned as she helped me on with my cloak. I felt my face redden and mumbled something about not needing to wait up for me. The night was fine, though crisp, and I pulled my cloak around me as I walked the few yards to Hauteville House. It was strange to be dressed in finery and to be arriving as a guest rather than an employee and I had to take deep breaths to steady my nerves. I had barely knocked when the door was opened by the maid, Henriette.

'Ooh, m'dame, you look beautiful. Let me take your cloak. They're gathered in the lower drawing room, if you'll follow me.' She led the way to what I thought of as the tapestries room, beyond the billiard room, and announced me, giggling, before leaving with my cloak.

M'dame Drouet, who had been talking to a man I didn't recognise, turned and came to me arms outstretched and kissed my cheek, whispering in my ear, '*Vous êtes belle.*'

'*Ma chère*! I'm so glad you could join us. Come and meet our other guests.' She took my arm and led me to two men, M'sieur Stapfer and the stranger. M'sieur Hugo, sitting in an armchair, rose and came to greet me, a broad smile lifting the corners of his moustache.

'Messieurs, may I present our dear friend, M'dame Sarchet. M'sieur Stapfer, you have met, and this is M'sieur Blondel, a fellow teacher at the College.' The gentlemen bowed and I dropped a curtsy. M'sieur Blondel was of medium height and build, with dark, waved hair and small dark eyes and was clean-shaven. I thought I detected an approving glint in his eyes as he kissed my hand.

'*Enchanté*, m'dame,' he murmured, his voice deep and warm.

'M'sieur,' I nodded.

'Would you like some wine, my dear?' M'dame asked, steering me to the side table where various bottles and glasses were arranged. I chose red wine and she filled my glass, whispering, 'What do you think? He is handsome, is he not?' I nodded, not daring to speak, and took a swallow of wine to calm myself.

M'sieur Hugo then began a conversation about the social inequality in the island and what he felt should be done about it. It was one of his favourite topics and no doubt the gentlemen had heard it before, and soon they were joining in with their thoughts. I was asked my opinion and, somewhat shyly, agreed with M'sieur Hugo's views. We were then called to dine by young Henriette and M'sieur Blondel offered his arm to lead me down the hall to the dining room. I had not been in such close proximity to a man since my dear Arnaud was alive and felt unsure how to respond. He made idle conversation as we found our seats at the dining table; he was on one side of me and M'sieur Hugo on the other and opposite were M'dame Drouet and M'sieur Stapfer. Marie Sixty and Henriette began bringing in the food and conversation slowed. I recognised the soup of yellow peas and sausages as being one of m'dame's own recipes and it was delicious, served with fresh baked bread.

'You are a widow, m'dame, I understand?' M'sieur Blondel said, after we had all been served.

'Yes, it's been nearly seven years since my husband drowned. And you, m'sieur? How long since you lost your wife?'

He paused, his spoon poised over the bowl.

'Not quite two years. Sadly, she died giving birth to our child, who also died.' His face was sombre and I was touched by his double loss.

'I'm sorry to hear that. I also lost our child soon after my husband's death so we have that in common.'

'Indeed we do. Let us hope we have more pleasant things in common, also. Would you mind telling me a little of your background? I know you are French, but not how you came to be here.'

I told him about my family and why I came to Guernsey and met my husband while we continued eating our soup. We talked over the courses, which seemed to go on forever and included fish, roasted chicken with vegetables, followed by an English dish, beef Wellington, which was beef encased in pastry and served with gravy. I was astonished by the amount of food, and the copious bottles of wine being served and could only eat small amounts from each course, unlike M'sieur Hugo who ate like a true gourmet and gourmand. M'dame ate and drank in moderation while the two gentlemen guests vied with their host. After a salad, a dessert of chocolate mousse with brandy sauce was served and I ate only a token spoonful.

My fellow diners kept up a conversation, with m'dame dividing her time between m'sieur and Paul Stapfer. It seemed to me that they deliberately left the way clear for M'sieur

Blondel and me to converse as few questions came our way. I learnt that he, like me, was an orphan, and his father had been a shopkeeper but realising his son had intelligence and ambition, saved to send him to university to become a teacher. His mother had died when he was a child and it sounded as if his life had been hard, as it is for many.

When the meal was finished and the table cleared, bottles of port and brandy were placed on the table and the conversation became more animated, focusing on the situation in France and whether or not Napoleon III would stay in power much longer. M'sieur Hugo had always said he wouldn't return to France until there was real freedom under a new republic. The combination of an excess of food and wine made me drowsy and I had to hide the occasional yawn. M'dame must have noticed and whispered to me, 'Do you wish to leave?' I nodded.

'*Messieurs*, our young friend requests your permission to leave us. Would you be kind enough to escort her home, M'sieur Blondel? You're welcome to return and continue your evening, if you wish,' she said, smiling at him.

'Of course, I will be honoured, m'dame.' M'sieur Blondel rose and bowed to me, offering me his hand. I thanked my hosts for their hospitality and Messrs Hugo and Stapfer stood and bowed as I curtsied and left. Henriette, sleepy-headed, handed me my cloak and M'sieur Blondel settled it around my shoulders as she opened the door. The night air was keen and I shivered.

'You are cold? Would you like my coat?' He went to take it off, but I shook my head.

'It's only a short walk, thank you.' We walked in silence down the street and all I could think of was how I longed for my bed instead of what I thought about my escort. My head swam from too much wine and the mix of emotions brought on by being seated between the man I loved, who could soon be out of my life, and this man who had wanted to meet me with a view to marriage. Despair, loss, fatigue, grief and fear mixed with anticipation all sought to take precedence and I was overwhelmed.

We arrived at my door and M'sieur Blondel kissed my gloved hand as we said our goodnights. I unlocked the door and slipped inside as he turned to leave and I walked upstairs in a daze. Once undressed and in bed I was soon asleep.

CHAPTER 31

Tess – Late June 2012

Tess opened her eyes and for a moment wondered where she was. The sound of steady breathing next to her acted as a reminder. She was in Jack's bed and her toes curled up at the memory of their passionate love-making the previous night. They hadn't even bothered with the nightcap he'd suggested, or the tour of his cottage, delightful though it looked as he led the way upstairs to his bedroom. Tess bit her lips as she recalled how quickly they'd pulled off their clothes and jumped into bed. Wanton hussy! She grinned, thinking Jack had been no better. Turning slowly onto her side so as not to wake him, she watched the rhythm of his chest's rise and fall and admired his unfairly long eyelashes curled on his cheeks. She had to fight a strong desire to stroke the outline of his lips with a finger, longing for more of his kisses.

'I know you're watching me. Hoping for a repeat performance?'

Tess giggled as, still with his eyes closed, Jack reached out and pulled her close.

'That's better. Now, what was it you wanted?'

An hour later they sat in the kitchen, the table covered with the paraphernalia needed for a substantial breakfast, including coffee. Jack had cooked a full English breakfast and Tess, now tucking into toast and marmalade, couldn't believe how hungry she had been. As he filled a second cafetière she studied the kitchen Jack had built himself using recycled units and a glorious selection of tiles someone had thrown out, he'd told her.

'Honestly there's so much waste on the island. When anyone with loads of money, particularly Open Market, buys a place and they don't like the kitchen, even if it's brand new, they rip it out, chuck it in a skip or send it to be recycled, and buy a new one. Friends of mine have renovated their whole house with stuff that's been thrown out. I've used a fair bit here, too, but there's still a lot I had to buy.'

He set the pot of coffee on the table and sat down facing her.

'Everything all right? You look thoughtful.'

'I'm fine, just admiring your kitchen. Will you show me the rest of the cottage before I go? I might pick up ideas for my house.'

'Sure.' He lifted her hand, kissing her palm. 'When are we seeing each other again? If you're free tomorrow we could go to the beach for some surfing and take a picnic.' Another kiss. Tess found her insides melting.

'Sounds lovely, thanks. I...I hadn't any plans.'

His smile lit up his eyes.

'Great. Now that's sorted I'll show you round the cottage, and perhaps we could finish in the bedroom?'

Charlotte's eyebrows rose to what must have been their highest point.

'I assume the evening was a success?' she drawled, her eyes gleaming as Tess entered the kitchen. She was relieved to find her friend alone, although she still felt a bit like a teenager returning home after spending the night with a boyfriend.

'You could say that,' Tess replied, yawning. 'Sorry, I need to catch up on my sleep. I had a great night and Jack's invited me to spend the day with him tomorrow.' She pushed her hair out of her eyes, aware she looked as hungover as she felt.

'I'm glad you had fun and you can tell me more about it later. Off you go and get some beauty sleep.' Charlotte gave her a hug. Tess ran up the stairs with a huge smile on her face, glad there was nothing she had to do today, other than recover from the previous night.

On Sunday the combination of a cloudless blue sky and face-warming sun provided a stunning opener for July and Tess took a deep breath as she opened the bedroom window. After a relaxing Saturday, which had included some reading of Eugénie's diary and a stroll on the beach, she was looking forward to spending time with Jack. He was due to pick her up at twelve, leaving her free to spend time with her hosts in the morning. Once dressed in T-shirt and shorts she went downstairs to look for them, and following the sound of James's giggling found them in the garden where the toddler was splashing in a paddling pool.

'Morning. You all look like you're having fun,' she called as she joined them on the lawn.

Charlotte swivelled round to say hi and that it was too nice to be indoors, while Andy raised a hand in greeting. A large jug of lemonade and several glasses sat on the nearby table and Charlotte told her to help herself. Tess did so before sitting cross-legged on the grass next to her friend.

'What are you guys up to today?'

'We're going round to Andy's parents for lunch and probably off for a walk afterwards to work it off. Yvette's a typical Frenchwoman who assumes us Brits don't eat properly and prepares a mini banquet to compensate.' Charlotte grinned at Andy and he laughed.

'True. And you're out for the day, I hear? Great weather for surfing, judging by the waves,' he nodded towards the clearly visible white-capped waves hitting the sands of Cobo bay. Tess was glad, intensive exercise was just what she needed after yesterday's lethargy.

Dead on twelve the crunch of tyres on the gravel announced Jack's arrival and Tess, after an exchange of goodbyes, went back into the house to collect her beach bag. She met Jack at the front door, looking suitably beach ready with his bermuda shorts and T-shirt showing off his tan.

'Hi, you look good enough to eat,' he said, before kissing her firmly on the mouth. She wrapped her arms around his neck and breathed in his woody scent.

Coming up for air, she laughed. 'I think we'd better leave before we have an audience.'

'Right, let's go and have some fun. It promises to be a great day.' Jack kissed the tip of her nose before opening the car door and placing her bag on the back seat. They were soon driving out of the gate and heading for the sand and surf of Vazon.

Five hours later, tired but happy, Tess was being driven to Jack's cottage. The afternoon had been full of swimming, surfing and a spot of sunbathing after a surprisingly good picnic lunch. Jack had invited her to have supper with him at home and she had agreed, with the proviso that he take her home no later than ten. She wanted to be fresh for her first day at work on Monday. Right now, though, the thought of spending more time with Jack was heady. Once in the cottage they both voiced the need for a shower and as it was a large walk-in unit, they took one together. This inevitably led to time in the bedroom before finally going downstairs for the promised supper. Jack rustled up a chicken stir-fry and they sat on his small terrace to eat it, unwilling to spend more time indoors than necessary.

'How lovely it is here. So peaceful you could imagine yourself the only person on the island,' Tess said, breathing in the stock-scented air. The detached cottage's garden was compact, but surrounded by trees, with an air of isolation that she found comforting after the built-up-ness of her flat in Exeter.

'It suited my mood of wanting to get away from it all when I bought it. I don't need that as much nowadays, but I still enjoy being close to water and trees.' He poured her a glass of wine and opened a can of lager for himself.

'I shall appreciate having somewhere peaceful to relax when I'm working again. I've been spoilt the past couple of weeks, with no work and a lovely house to spend time in. It's back to reality tomorrow and I'll need to focus all my energy on the job until I've learned the ropes.' She sipped her wine, dwelling on the impact on their time together.

'Message received and understood. I guessed you'd probably not be free during the week and I wouldn't want to distract you from your work. Tempting though it is,' he said, grinning. 'But if you could keep Friday evenings and the weekends free, that would be fine.'

She laughed.

'You mean to monopolise me? But what about my other admirers? What chance do they get of enjoying my charms?'

He shook his head.

'None at all, that's the idea. Any objections?' He leant forward and kissed her mouth.

After a few seconds, Tess pulled back slightly, whispering, 'No, none at all.'

At eight o'clock the next morning Tess, dressed in a smart skirt suit and blouse, paced nervously around Linda, the practice manager's office. She had gone to find out if the partner Tess was to shadow for the day was ready for her. Coming back a few minutes later she escorted Tess to his consulting room. Geoffrey was the senior partner retiring in a matter of weeks and the plan was for Tess to slowly take over his patients as he reduced his hours accordingly. They had met at her interview and he soon put her at ease, inviting her to sit alongside him during the appointments. Geoffrey told his patients Tess was to replace him and no-one seemed to mind her presence. She took notes and by the end of the morning felt more confident about the way the practice operated. At lunchtime Jonathan sought her out.

'Hi, how's it been?'

'Better than I expected. Everyone's been so nice and I'm actually looking forward to having my own patients tomorrow.'

'Good. Now Colette insisted I took you home for lunch as she wants to hear all about it. I usually pop back to check she and Rosie are okay. You happy with that?'

Tess was delighted and minutes later she was being embraced by her friend and offered a quiche salad while at the same time being bombarded with questions. Jonathan rolled his eyes, grabbed his plate and left them to it.

The afternoon passed quickly and Tess left the surgery just after six and arrived home to find Charlotte insisting she ate with them and again she was happy to join her friends, wanting to share what had been an important day for her. After a cheerful meal she retired to her room and phoned her father for a catch-up. He told her the house was on the market and he'd been in touch with Elaine to let her know.

'What was her reaction, Dad?'

'Didn't say much, just said to make sure I got the best price. The agent says the market's quite good for family homes such as ours, so quite hopeful. But there's no rush, I'm not giving it away, that's for sure.' There was a short silence before he asked, 'And how did the job go, love?'

She said it went well and then told him her other news.

'I'm seeing someone, Dad. In fact you've met him. Jack the builder. We've been out a few times now and I really like him.'

Her father chuckled.

'I thought there was something between you two. It was the way you looked at each other. I hope it works out for you; he seemed a nice enough chap. At least you'd never have to pay for any jobs around the house.' His chuckle deepened.

Relieved he approved, if for perhaps the wrong reasons, Tess chatted a bit longer before saying goodnight. Making a cup of tea, she wondered what it would be like having Ken living in Guernsey. On one level it would be great; she'd be able to keep an eye on him and make sure he didn't slip back into depression; on another level she hoped he wouldn't become dependent on her for his social life. She had her own plans for that.

The next few days sped by as Tess settled into life as a GP, enjoying the interaction with both patients and other members of the practice. House calls were strange at first, partly because she had to refresh her memory about the various lanes and roads from her childhood, but also because she felt at a disadvantage in someone's home, as opposed to the surgery. House-bound patients were mainly elderly or incapacitated in some way and all were grateful for her visit. As patients had to pay more for home visits than seeing a doctor in the surgery, at least there were no time-wasters. On Friday Tess was puzzled by one request for a home visit. It was to a Mrs Sally Le Page, who from her notes was only in her thirties, with a young baby. She had phoned to say her baby was unwell but she had had a fall and wasn't able to drive to the surgery. Tess would have expected the woman's husband to help, but went along as requested. From the notes, it did seem she was accident prone, having made several visits to the surgery over the previous months.

The house surprised her. It was an enormous detached property set back from the road and surrounded by extensive gardens near L'Ancresse. Pulling into the drive, Tess noted an upmarket SUV in front of the garage. Everything shouted money. Grabbing her medical bag, she headed for the front door, but before she could ring the bell, it opened. A pale woman stood there, or rather appeared to be leaning heavily on the door.

'Mrs Le Page? I'm Doctor Le Prevost, I believe you're expecting me?'

'Yes, Doctor, please come in.' Her voice was well modulated, but Tess heard the underlying pain and wondered if she had two patients on her hands.

'The baby's through here,' she pointed to a door on the left and began hobbling towards it.

'Are you all right? You seem to be in some pain.' Tess laid her hand on the woman's arm and she flinched. Tess's concern grew.

'It's nothing, I…I tripped over a step in the garden and bruised my leg and hip. I'll be fine,' she smiled faintly, and Tess saw the whiteness around her lips. Alarm bells rang, but she knew not to force anything. Not yet anyway. She followed her into a large, open-plan kitchen and dining room and was astonished to see a travel cot set up near the dining table. Mrs Le Page hobbled towards it and Tess caught up with her and looked down at the red-faced baby thrashing their arms and grizzling. She picked the baby up and laid him on the table for a closer examination.

'Has he got a fever? He's been like this since last night.' Sally hovered nearby wringing her hands.

'Does Rupert have any teeth yet?'

'No, of course not, he's only four months old.' She looked surprised.

'Babies can start teething at almost any age, and I think your baby's just starting.' Tess pulled on a latex glove and inserted her finger into his mouth and he immediately clamped onto it. She felt a slight bump on the gum. 'Yes, there's a tooth coming and that's why he's upset. There's no fever and he'll be fine. You can use a teething gel or a teething ring to ease his discomfort.' She smiled at Sally and handed her Rupert to cuddle. She took him and Tess noticed her wince as she moved her left arm. Something wasn't right, but what could she do? In spite of the hot day, the woman was wearing a long-sleeved blouse and as she tried to settle Rupert in her arms, the sleeve rucked up and Tess saw vivid bruising on her arm. Sally must have seen her staring and pulled the sleeve down.

'I hurt my arm when I...I tripped. I've always been a bit clumsy and seem to have got worse since having Rupert. I put it down to lack of sleep. I'll be better when he sleeps through the night.' She smiled, but Tess noticed it didn't reach the pain-filled eyes.

'Why's the cot downstairs, Mrs Le Page?'

'Well, I find the stairs a bit difficult since my fall, so my husband set up the travel cot down here, to make it easier for me. The big cot's still upstairs in the nursery.'

'I see. And where are you sleeping?'

The woman shifted awkwardly.

'The past couple of nights I've slept down here with Rupert, on a blow-up mattress.'

'Mrs Le Page, you're obviously in some pain. Could I take a look at you, please? I might be able to help.' Tess locked eyes with the woman, an unspoken message passing between them.

'Thank you, Doctor, but there's no need. It's only bruising and...I'll be better soon. While I'm breast feeding I can't take painkillers, anyway.' A flush crept up the woman's cheeks and Tess felt a surge of anger...and pity. Anger towards the man who had done this and pity for the woman who stood by him.

'Well, as long as you're sure. But if you have any more...accidents, please feel free to phone me at the surgery. I'd be happy to help, any time.' She forced a smile, hating to leave her like this.

'I appreciate the offer, Doctor. And I'm sorry to have troubled you over Rupert's teething. You must think me a complete ninny for not recognising it was only teething.'

'Not at all. It's not easy being a new mother and I'd rather you phoned us if you're worried.'

They headed towards the front door and exchanged goodbyes. Tess drove back to the surgery with her hands clenched on the steering wheel. She had seen too many victims of domestic assault in A & E not to recognise the signs. And she determined to do all in her power to protect the young mother from serious, possibly fatal, harm.

❧ CHAPTER 32 ❧

Tess – July 2012

As soon as her last patient left that day, Tess sought out Jonathan to tell him of her concerns about Mrs Le Page and her husband. As he listened his expression grew more serious.

'You won't know this, but the husband is a well-known, successful businessman who also happens to be a States Deputy with friends in high places. Anyone would have to tread carefully with accusations of abuse.'

Her heart sank.

'I see. No wonder she isn't letting on. Poor woman! She must wonder if anyone would believe her if she admitted what's happening. Do you know him, Jonathan?'

'Not as such, I've met him at a couple of social dos, and he came across as quite charming. To be honest, I've not heard a whisper against him. I remember the wife, too, and that she hardly said a word, letting him do all the talking. I didn't think anything of it at the time, but if what you say is true, then it would fit with him being a controlling person, which abusers generally are. It's a power thing.'

'I went through her notes and any injuries have been on the body and nothing on the face. So he's calculated enough to ensure when he hurts her, no-one can see the result.' Tess had to force herself to push down rising anger towards the man. 'Is there anything I can do? Surely I can't simply ignore it?'

'Flag it up in her notes in case another doctor treats her in the future, but apart from that just be vigilant when she or her baby need treatment. If you're seriously concerned for her safety then we'll consider the next step. There's a local organisation for sufferers of domestic abuse, called Options, and you could suggest she contacts them. Unfortunately, I think it's unlikely she'd do that because of who her husband is.' He patted her shoulder. 'It's frustrating, I know, but we can't force her to take action. And at least you're now on the alert, so well done for that.'

'What about the police?'

'They can only act if she presses charges, which seems doubtful, I'm afraid.'

Tess reluctantly agreed to take his advice and left the office, not exactly in the right mood for her date with Jack. In the past she'd learnt to leave work behind when she finished for the day, and it was time to do that now. Taking a deep, calming breath, she drove home. By the time she had showered and changed she had managed to let go her frustration and was looking forward to the evening. Jack had offered to cook dinner and she was driving to his cottage on the understanding she would spend the night with him. Although they had spoken on the phone most days, she had missed seeing him.

After gathering a few toiletries and change of clothes into a holdall, she popped in to see the family gathered in the kitchen with James in his high chair. Charlotte gave her a hug, scrutinising her face.

'You look as if you've had a rough day. Fancy a small glass of vino before you leave?'

'Yes, please. It was a bit stressful. What about you two?' She looked at Andy who was sitting by James watching him eat while nursing a glass of wine.

'My day was good, thanks. Finally got the planning permission for a job that's taken forever and now have one happy client. I take it you're off to Jack's this evening?' he said, eyeing her bag.

She nodded as Charlotte handed her a glass of wine.

'Yes, he's cooking so will be a quiet night in. But we're out tomorrow, I think. What did you get up to today, Charlotte?'

'Not a lot, but I did manage to get back to the diaries and it's getting interesting. I'm up to 1863 and Hugo's daughter Adèle is causing problems, I've made some notes and we can chat about it when you, um, have time.' She winked.

'Great, thanks, I look forward to it. Perhaps tomorrow afternoon?' For Tess, the desire to know more about what did or didn't happen between Hugo and Eugénie was still important but had been overtaken by her new job, boyfriend and the incredible finds at the house. Charlotte helping with the diaries would be a godsend. After chatting for a few minutes Tess left, saying she would be back late morning.

Jack opened the front door as she drove into his less than generous drive. She was about to get out of the car when he opened the door, pulling her to her feet and into a close embrace.

'Missed me, have you?' she murmured, surrendering to his touch.

'You bet. Here, let me take your bag,' he said, reaching into the car, 'and I thought we might eat outside as it's still warm.' Flinging one arm around her shoulder he steered her inside the cottage. A wonderful aroma of garlic and herbs filled the air and Tess's mouth watered as she followed him into the kitchen.

'Something smells delicious but I'm not sure what it is.' She looked around but whatever was giving off the inviting scent wasn't visible.

'Ah, that's because it's my own special recipe and it's keeping warm in the oven while we have a drink first. Wine or gin?' He waved his hand towards a selection of bottles on the side.

'Gin and tonic, please.'

'Right, you go through and I'll bring the drinks and some nibbles out in a moment.' Jack gave her a quick kiss and pushed her gently towards the door opening onto the garden. She found the table set for dinner and sat on one of the cushioned chairs, breathing in the heady scent of stock and jasmine, competing with the smell of whatever was hidden in the oven. The restful air of the garden was a balm to her spirits after the first week at work. And being pampered by a gorgeous man was an added bonus.

Jack brought out a tray with the drinks and a bowl of olives and, after depositing them on the table, sat next to her. They touched glasses in a toast before taking a sip.

'What's the verdict on the job? Are you going to be happy there?' He put his arm around her and she moved closer, enjoying his warmth.

'Yes, it's been good, thanks. Feel a bit like the new girl at school, but it's early days.'

'Good, so you'll stay in Guernsey?' He squeezed her arm.

'Oh, for sure. No worries there! I have my soon to be gorgeous house to keep me here for a start,' she said, a hint of teasing in her voice.

'Well, there is that, of course. And I hope not to keep you waiting much longer. Anything else keeping you here?' She felt his grip tighten and twisted her head to see his face. There was a look in his eyes…

'My friends, of course, both old and new. And now Dad's planning to move here–' she was stopped by his mouth pressing on hers and the kiss seemed to go on forever.

'And?' he said, pulling back, his head tilted to the side.

'There's someone I'm seeing who I quite like–' another kiss interrupted her and, after a moment enjoying it, she pulled back, laughing. 'Okay, you win. Though I don't know what your intentions are, Jack. Could you be serious about us?' She searched his face and his eyes gave the game away.

'Oh, yes, I could be serious, if that's what you want. Is it?'

'Yes, I…I think so.'

The next morning Jack suggested they visit her house and then do any shopping in Town before returning to the cottage. Tess was dying to see what work had been done and they set off soon after nine. What struck her as soon as they entered the hall were the walls lined with plasterboard with wires poking through in strategic places.

'What progress! It looks so much more…more normal,' she said, no longer faced with bare brick walls.

'The guys have done well this week. Come on, I'll show you.' He took her hand and they explored the rooms, one by one, some still needing a lot more work, but definitely a big improvement on the previous week. Tess's thoughts kept turning to Eugénie, and when they were in the front room, imagined her sitting at the desk near the window. Why, oh why, did she hide the desk away? Hopefully, the answer would be in the diaries.

'You okay? You look miles away.'

'Sorry, just…thinking.'

'Right. We're on schedule to finish in about four to six weeks, so you should be able to move in by mid-August. Have you got any furniture to bring over?'

Tess shook her head.

'None. I'll need to buy a suite for the sitting room for starters and a mattress for the bed and…'

'Hey! I think you'd better make a list and I can point you in the direction of appropriate shops. Now let's go grab some coffee.'

By the time Tess arrived back at Charlotte's her head was buzzing with thoughts about what she needed for her house. And the fact that Jack saw them as having a future as a couple. She had been afraid to acknowledge the depth of her feelings for him until now, but since last night could admit she was falling in love with him. It was a strange sensation as she had deliberately kept her heart to herself since uni, not wanting to risk anything getting in the way of qualifying as a doctor. Oh, she'd been happy to have casual flings, some even lasting several weeks, but nothing serious. Now, it was different. Now, she was a grown-up thirtysomething, a practising GP and the owner of what would soon be a beautiful family home. It only needed the family. Not immediately, of course, the biological clock had a few years to go before Doomsday beckoned. Charlotte was a great example of a woman becoming a mother at forty and Tess had met others over the years. Not that she would deliberately wait quite so long. And if it did work out with Jack…

The family were out when she reached the house and Tess made some lunch before sitting down with Eugénie's diaries. She picked up where Charlotte had left off and was soon lost in the Victorian world of the Hugo family and her ancestor. After more than a year of working for Victor, Eugénie's life seemed to revolve around him and Juliette. Tess could see she was obsessed with him, taking the place of both her father and husband. Not healthy, but understandable in such times. There was no hint of Hugo having similar feelings toward Eugénie, although he continued to express his fondness for her with little gifts and joint outings with Juliette. Never just the two of them. Tess wondered how she would have behaved if she had been in Eugénie's shoes. Would she have fallen for such an iconic figure? Hmm, not sure. With a sigh, she packed up the diaries and placed them in the desk, their rightful home. She was about to close it when a powerful image of the woman she had seen before flashed in front of her eyes, like a hologram. Again, she was sitting at the desk and writing, her head bent in concentration as the pen flew over the page. A page of her diary. She looked about twenty, slim and dark, wearing a plain grey dress. Tess stood rigid with shock. The image faded and she collapsed onto the sofa. The woman was so *real*. She could have touched her. Staring at the desk, Tess wondered if she was going to be forever haunted by Eugénie. For she knew without any doubt, it was her.

That evening Jack collected her to have dinner at The Rockmount at Cobo, from where the views of the sunset were the best on the island. Tess appreciated the laid-back pub atmosphere and they settled for battered fish and chips with a glass of lager each.

'Another of your favourites, Jack?' she asked, after they had ordered.

'It's got everything; fantastic view of the bay, good food and local beers. What more could a man ask for?' he grinned, taking her hand in his.

'Depends on his priorities, I guess. When I came with my parents, it was for a bottle of Coke and a packet of crisps, sitting on a bench outside.' She nodded towards the window, where the wooden tables outside were all occupied. 'It was considered a treat to come here and stay until sunset. Ah, memories, eh?' Their eyes locked and a flick of desire swept through her. She saw the answering desire in his eyes and dropped her gaze as she imagined the night ahead. Weekends hadn't been such fun since forever.

The following week seemed to speed by for Tess. Her workload increased with more patients transferring from Geoffrey as he approached retirement. This suited her as the variety of problems presented kept her on her toes. There was no sign of Mrs Le Page and Tess began to hope that any abuse had been a one-off. Work on the house progressed well and she called in on Saturday morning to see the work for herself. She had a sneaking suspicion that since they had become lovers, Jack had pressured his team to work even harder as a way of impressing her. Not that she minded, being keen to have her own place as soon as possible. It would mean she could invite Jack to hers, for a change. Essential furniture and furnishings had been ordered and the kitchen would be arriving soon. Whenever she had some free time, Tess read more of the diaries, and between her and Charlotte they had covered 1863 and were now reading the entries for 1864. Eugénie wrote about Juliette being bought a new house by Hugo, only three doors from her own and Tess smiled as she knew the house, *Le Faerie*, bearing a plaque mentioning Juliette's residence. And Hugo published a new work called *William Shakespeare*.

Charlotte organised a barbecue for friends on the Sunday, and Jack had been invited. This would be their first group social event as a couple and Tess was keen for her friends to meet him.

Sunday dawned with a cloudless blue sky and the promise of high temperatures for the afternoon. Tess had spent the night at Jack's, squirreling in a few toiletries and spare clothes now it was becoming routine. He had cooked supper and this again was part of the pattern, alternating going to restaurants with home cooking. This Sunday, she had woken first and tiptoed downstairs to make their tea before returning with a tray to the bedroom. He was lying on his stomach, arms spread out and looking so peaceful she hesitated to wake him. She carefully placed the tray on the bedside table and took up her mug, moving to the seat by the window.

'I am awake, you know. Just waiting to see if I'm offered the tea before it goes cold.'

She laughed, turning to see Jack's eyes open and a huge grin on his face. Handing him a mug, she perched on the bed as they shared a brief kiss.

'I'll make breakfast after my shower, and then I must be off as I promised Charlotte I'd help prepare for the barbecue this afternoon. Will you be able to amuse yourself in my absence?' She gave him a teasing kiss on the cheek.

'I'm sure I'll think of something. Now be off with you, woman, and make my breakfast!' Jack's attempt at fierceness had them both giggling like youngsters and it was a while before Tess managed to head for the shower.

Charlotte was in the kitchen when she arrived back, a huge amount of food spread across the worktops waiting to be transformed into delicious salads, dips, finger foods and puddings.

'You haven't invited the entire population of Guernsey, have you?' Tess asked, laughing.

Her friend, busy checking a list, grinned.

'I was brought up with the maxim that it's better to have too much food for a party than not enough. Andy and I will be living off any leftovers for as long as it takes.' She gave Tess a searching look. 'Are you ready to give me a hand or do you need a strong coffee to wake up properly?'

'I'm ready; just tell me what to do.'

An hour later the prepared food was stored in containers in the enormous American fridge and the women took a chance to have a coffee before the guests arrived. Andy wandered in and out with bits of the barbecue kit for a final clean in the utility room.

'Well, I think we're ready and if we've forgotten anything it's too bad. It's time to have some fun,' Charlotte said, waving her arm in the air.

The first of the guests to arrive were a married couple Tess hadn't met, Louisa and Paul. Louisa was a slim woman with freckles and a wide smile and Paul was tall, blond haired and with the most amazing blue eyes Tess had ever seen. Charlotte introduced them.

'Louisa's a physio at La Folie health centre where we met and Paul's the manager. I also met Andy there so it's a special place for all of us, isn't Louisa?'

Louisa, shaking Tess's hand, nodded.

'Sure is, not to mention it's where Paul and I met and it happens to be owned by my father who I met for the first time there!' She laughed and Tess smiled, noting how Louisa positively glowed.

'Wow, this place, La Folie, certainly has a story to tell. I must visit it sometime. I'm always interested in places offering different forms of healing.'

The conversation between the three of them became lively and Charlotte moved off to welcome Jeanne and Nick. Tess soon realised she and Louisa had enough in common to become good friends and admired Paul's zen-like calmness. Perhaps she should take up yoga, something he taught to all their guests, apparently. Their chat was interrupted by Jack's arrival, apologising for being late and giving Tess a kiss before being introduced to Louisa and Paul. Then they all went over to say hi to Jeanne and her family and Tess introduced Jack. The last ones to arrive were Colette and Jonathan, bearing a sleeping Rosie in a baby carrier.

'Colette and Jonathan, this is Jack. I've told him all about you both,' Tess said.

'Hope it was all good,' Colette replied, accepting a kiss on the cheek from Jack.

'Oh, yes. It's great to finally meet you, and you, too, Jonathan. Tess has told me she loves working at the surgery.'

'We're glad to have her.' The men shook hands. 'Now I'd better find somewhere quiet to leave this little one as from experience I know things are going to get rather noisy,' Jonathan said, pushing his glasses up with a smile. Charlotte went inside with him and Rosie and Andy came round offering drinks to everyone. Freya and Harry, watched by Nick, began running around the garden and James staggered after them, squealing in delight. Jonathan and Charlotte emerged and grabbed some drinks before joining the others near the barbecue where Andy was keeping an eye on the food.

'Well, it's lovely to see you all here; it seems like forever since we've all been together like this. And our little gang is growing, with the addition of Tess and Jack, and I hope we'll see a lot more of them. Cheers all!' Charlotte cried, lifting her glass.

'Cheers!' rang out from the others and Tess noticed Louisa and Paul share a hug before Paul pulled away, calling out, 'Attention, please!' Everyone turned to face him and a now blushing Louisa.

'Charlotte mentioned our gang growing bigger, well it's going to get bigger still as Louisa and I are expecting a baby!'

Whoops and cheers went up from everyone and Louisa and Paul were engulfed in hugs and kisses. Charlotte whispered to Tess, 'They've been trying for ages, so it's wonderful news.' Tess nodded, happy for her new friends and noticing that Louisa was holding a glass of orange juice. That and the glow should have been a giveaway.

Andy had just started handing out the hot food when a heartrending cry split the air. Tess instinctively ran towards the sound, further down the garden, closely followed by Jeanne. They found a sobbing Freya on her knees, her face and hands covered in earth and leaves. A sullen faced Harry stood nearby.

'It was an accident! Didn't mean to knock her over,' he said to his mother, who had picked up Freya. She and Tess carefully wiped away the dirt and found only a scratch on one small hand.

'Harry...push me, Mummy. Fell...in the flowers.' Freya, still sniffing, pointed to the nearest bed, where flowers had been squashed flat.

Tess, satisfied no real harm had been done, left Jeanne to give Harry a telling off, joined now by a cross-faced Nick. Back at the barbecue she explained what had happened, telling Charlotte her flower bed had suffered the most.

'Oh, thank goodness it's only flowers. Young Harry will have to learn to be more gentle with his sister, won't he, James?' But her son had already trotted off to see Freya and everyone stood grinning as they watched him give her a cuddle. Drama over, the party carried on.

The afternoon, as Jonathan predicted, was full of noise; laughter, music, lots of talking and the excited shouts of the children. Tess felt particularly blessed to be part of such a group of friends and Jack had soon mingled with everyone, chatting easily with people who had been strangers only a few hours before. She took a deep breath, drawing in the soft smells of summer – roses mingled with the sea air wafting up from Cobo. It wouldn't be long before she would be able to stand in her own garden and breathe similar air and the thought made her smile. Then the image of Eugénie flashed into her mind and she wondered if she'd found happiness after losing her first husband and child. Frowning, she realised it was important for her to know and decided to find more time to read the diaries.

CHAPTER 33

Eugénie's Diary – 1869

March

Although I still feel wary of forming a new attachment, I have allowed M'sieur Blondel – Pierre – to pay court to me. He lives in rooms provided by the College and are not suitable for me to visit so we are limited in where we can meet. I invited him to lunch here today, being Sunday, and he greatly admired my house. He is indeed personable and seems anxious to win my affection although I confess I find him a little too serious. I can't help thinking of the fun Arnaud and I had in our short time together; we found much to laugh about, whereas Pierre is less frivolous, wanting to discuss such matters as the work on the harbour or the state of the roads out of Town.

I have discovered that we have in common a love of books and he has introduced me to new authors, in particular Edgar Allan Poe and his short stories and poems. I have previously concentrated on French literature, but Pierre, being a Guernseyman, has read more English and American books. He teaches literature at the College so is well qualified to advise me on what books to read.

April

Last night we attended a supper at Hauteville House and it passed pleasantly enough. However, I have to admit to enjoying listening to M'sieur Hugo's words more than Pierre's. He is such a man of the world! I do not think there is any subject m'sieur cannot discourse on. I am aware that he and m'dame take a keen interest in how the courtship is progressing and today she asked me outright about my feelings.

'I can't yet say I love him, and perhaps I never will. Not all marriages are based on love, I know, but mine to Arnaud was and has created an…an expectation in me.' I twisted my hands together in my lap as we sat in her drawing room.

'Would you consider a marriage based on affection, companionship and shared interests, my dear? Which is what many do choose, is it not?' She peered at me with her ailing eyes and again I felt for her and the sacrifices she had made to remain by m'sieur's side. Although now widowed, he has no intention of marrying her and my friend asserts she understands and is content. But I do wonder.

'Yes, I think so. I have begun to realise how insular my life has been and if – when – you and M'sieur Hugo return to France, I shall have few friends around me. Perhaps it's time I considered my future.'

'Life can be hard for us women, *n'est ce pas*? I do truly wish for your happiness and in time you may find M'sieur Blondel takes a place in your heart. Now, I have had Suzanne go through my wardrobe and there are several outfits which are no longer any use to me and I wish you to have them. Naturally, I'll arrange for them to be altered for you so you can look your best when on the arm of your suitor.' She smiled, and sought my hand.

I was overcome by her continued generosity and thanked her with all my heart. When I left a lump had lodged in my throat from the suppressed emotion. How would I manage without her friendship and love when the time came for her to leave? And m'sieur? It was with heavy heart that I walked the short distance to my own house and spent the afternoon gazing into the fire in the parlour, as if the flames could tell me what the future held.

May 1869

M'sieur Hugo's latest novel, *L'Homme Que Rit*, is now published and the reception from readers is not greatly favourable, I heard. To be honest, I had not enjoyed it as I had his other works, finding it quite a puzzle to follow. M'sieur explained to me that it represented his view of the English aristocracy in the seventeenth century, and, to my mind, it was not very complimentary. Sales are lower than for his previous books but France is in the middle of elections, with Republicans gaining seats and weakening Napoleon III's hold on power. Thus bringing closer the opportunity for m'sieur to return to his beloved France. My own feelings are not as strong for my birth country, not being a famous giant of literature and a peer of the realm, with much to gain on their return. M'sieur is still writing, which is like air to him. He needs to write and I am happy for it gives me not only a reason to be near him but to earn a living.

Today I met with Pierre for a walk. The spring sun has encouraged us to take exercise and our favourite is to walk to Fermain Bay and stroll on the beach. Today we arrived to find M'sieur Hugo sitting on a large rock as if it was an armchair, gazing out to sea, deep in thought. Not wishing to disturb him, we retraced our steps up the lane.

Lectures are held at Clifton Hall in Town and we attended one today on what changes are needed in Guernsey in order to keep up with the new technological world. Not very romantic, but it allowed us to spend time together. Afterwards, Pierre surprised me with a box of confectionery, delivered with a bow and a smile. I was a little embarrassed to receive such a gift, but accepted it with a smile. It is pleasant to be admired as an attractive woman and indulged. He is not one for flowery speeches or grand gestures, but he appears sincere in his affection for me. I could wish he laughed more and at times his smile does not quite reach his eyes, but he would be a steady companion, I feel. The subject of children arose as we made our way home and he made his feelings clear.

'I was naturally grieved at losing my dear wife, but also mourned the loss of our child. I have always wanted to have a family and, for the moment, the boys under my care at the College are my substitute family. But it's not the same as nurturing a child of your blood from infancy, is it?'

I took a deep breath, my own loss still painful to contemplate.

'No…it is not.'

He drew me closer to him as we walked and I'm sure he assumed I wanted more children, as all women were supposed to. In one way I would love to have another child, someone to love and take care of; it is only fear that holds me back.

June 1869

What I have been both expecting and dreading has happened – Pierre has asked for my hand in marriage. It was not a romantic proposal, like Arnaud's, accompanied by expressions of undying love. We were sitting on a bench in Cambridge Park listening to the militia band playing as they do on two evenings a week. The walk around the park is very pleasant on a warm evening, with an avenue of elms offering shade in the heat. As we sat and applauded the band, Pierre pulled out a small box from his pocket, saying, 'Will you do me the honour of becoming my wife, Eugénie?' His serious expression caused me to wonder if I had heard him correctly, but then he opened the box to reveal a small garnet ring. I must have looked startled, for he said, 'I understand you might wish to think about it and I'm happy to wait a few days for your answer.'

'Oh! It...it's, I mean, you've taken me by surprise, Pierre. We haven't talked much about the future...' This was true, there had been no talk of love, or spending our lives together, only the type of conversations friends have. Apart from his desire for children.

'I'm not one for fanciful declarations, Eugénie, such as M'sieur Hugo and his fellow poets would offer you. We've both been married and sadly lost our partners, and now we are looking for friendship, and a companion, are we not?' He smiled, patting my hand.

I could only nod my head, not sure enough of my own feelings to say anything. I knew I did not love him, although I have become fond of him, but in a contrary way, I wanted him to *love me*. Not just see me as a companion.

'May I give you my answer at the end of the week? It's such a big decision to make in a rush.' It was now Thursday so I would not keep him waiting long.

His smile slipped for a moment, but was quickly replaced.

'Of course, my dear.'

Today I confided in m'dame and she was delighted for me, but understood my hesitation.

'I know you wanted love, *ma chère*, as do we all, but it might grow, on both sides. But I think there is something else troubling you, yes?' She gently touched my face.

'This might sound terrible, but sometimes I wonder if he is only interested in my house, as he has none of his own and no chance of owning one. Each time he's been around he walks about the rooms, stroking the mantelpieces, the furniture, the staircase. And he has only ever kissed my hand, nothing more.' Since the proposal, I have thought of these things until they have filled my mind to the exclusion of all else.

She frowned.

'I see. It's usually the other way around, is it not? We women are accused of wanting a husband for what he can provide – a home, security, children – and not necessarily for love. But I think M'sieur Blondel does have feelings for you, he simply does not find it easy to express them. He has told M'sieur Hugo how much he admires you and how much he enjoys your company. Your lovely house is indeed an asset, but I feel it's not your only one, *ma chère*. Not by a long way.'

Her words cheered me and I began to think it was my own fear which had conjured these concerns. And as both m'dame and m'sieur considered Pierre an excellent choice for me, then perhaps I was simply exaggerating my concerns. I still was not *happy* at the thought of marrying Pierre, it was more a feeling of having little choice but to marry again and he was quite agreeable.

Sunday

Pierre and I met today and I accepted his proposal. This time his smile was broad and he flung his arms around me before kissing my cheek. Encouraged by his response I laughed and he joined in! He suggested we called on M'sieur Hugo to tell him the news, seeing him in the role of my surrogate father as well as employer. I was a little hesitant to call uninvited, but he assured me m'sieur would want to be the first to hear our news. In truth who else was there to tell?

'*Ma petite*! I am overjoyed for you. This is cause for celebration, is it not, m'dame?'

We were in the garden where we had found them relaxing after their lunch. I was hugged and kissed by them both and Pierre's hand was shaken before M'sieur Hugo sent for wine. Although pleased with m'sieur's obvious delight, I was contrarily wishing he forbade me to marry anyone so I could stay at his side. A foolish notion indeed and I immediately pushed the thought away as Pierre put his arm around my waist and squeezed me. His face shone with happiness and I was caught up in celebratory mood. The wine arrived and we sat and drank with them for most of the afternoon.

The subject of the wedding date was raised and M'sieur Hugo suggested the following month of July and Pierre agreed, seeing no need to delay. I had expected a longer engagement but M'sieur Hugo explained, 'We shall be away from August for some months and we cannot miss your wedding, *ma petite*, and indeed, see ourselves *in loco parentis* and wish to be the hosts. You can have a party here after the service in church. What do you say?' Taking my hand he beamed at me and tears sprang to my eyes at his loving words. I mumbled a thank you while Pierre offered a fulsome speech of thanks, something about 'overwhelmed by the honour and generosity'. It was undeniably a great honour and while Pierre discussed details with M'sieur Hugo, I sat with m'dame, who explained they had previously agreed to be my 'family' in the event of my marrying.

'We see you as our daughter, *ma chère*, one dear to both our hearts. And I insist on providing you with a wedding dress, to be made by my dressmaker. Oh, I'm so excited!' she clapped her hands. 'A wedding! They have been a rarity in our lives, as you are aware, and it's good to have something to celebrate. You will marry at the Town church? Pierre's a Protestant, is he not?'

'Yes, and it's where I married Arnaud, also a Protestant. I don't see myself as a Catholic these days so it makes little difference which church we choose. Any…children are to be brought up as Protestants, as required by Pierre.'

We spent some time discussing who to invite to our wedding before we took our leave. More hugs and kisses before a giggling Henriette escorted us to the front door. Pierre walked me home and then left to return to College, promising he would contact the rector the next day about a date for the wedding and to arrange the banns.

M'dame took me to Agnew's drapers in the High Street to choose the material for my wedding dress and we settled on an embroidered cream silk from India. We then purchased cream leather boots from Beghins before visiting M'dame Aubert in Commercial Arcade for the final item, my hat, also in cream with soft feathers. M'dame usually has her dresses made in Paris but has been using a local woman for alterations and she was charged with producing a dress that would not look out of place in London or Paris.

24th July 1869

My wedding day! I am writing this quickly before I depart from the house. I awoke after a restless night with my stomach knotted and my nerves in shreds. Any dreams I remembered had been dark and unsettling; in one the sea monster from m'sieur's *Les Travailleurs de la Mer* lured me from a boat into the sea and wrapped its tentacles around me until I was near drowning, and then, thankfully, I woke up. In another, I was being chased by a baying mob. Not dreams to expect on the eve of one's wedding! Even though I have reservations about the marriage, I have come to terms with the *idea* of it and that it is the right path for me. Pierre is a good man and I hope to love him in time.

My dress is beautiful. I am delighted with it. Today is the first time I have worn the complete outfit and Sophie has helped me dress.

She wiped away a tear as I stood in front of the mirror in my finery.

'You do look such a beautiful bride, m'dame. And the groom is such a handsome man, too.

'Thank you, Sophie. And I'm so happy you've agreed to stay on with us. If funds allow, I hope to take on a scullery maid to help you as the work will increase now.' I smiled at her, one of the few people I could rely on, now wearing her Sunday best for the wedding.

We left the house and made our way to Hauteville House where a carriage waited to take me, M'sieur Hugo and m'dame to the Town church. Although it was a short walk down the hill, M'sieur insists we arrive in style. Of course, all eyes will be on him, not me, but I am content. Peter the driver doffed his hat as I arrived and wished me a good day. Inside the house, maids are rushing about with the last of the preparations for the wedding breakfast and I found my hosts in the tapestries room.

I was immediately fussed over by m'dame, resplendent in a wine silk dress, while m'sieur kissed my cheek as he exclaimed I had never looked more beautiful. The heat rose to my cheeks and m'dame commented on 'the blushing bride'. M'sieur Hugo looked dapper for someone who was usually more careless with his attire. His jacket and trousers were freshly pressed and he wore a neat bow tie with a cream silk shirt. He suggested a small glass of Calvados to fortify us before we left and I was glad of it as my nerves were in shreds. The fiery liquid brought a sense of calm and I felt more composed as we took our places in the carriage, cheered on by the staff.

I felt like a person of importance as we arrived at the Town church, thanks to the crowd waiting to see M'sieur Hugo. A brief cheer went up, and some kind folk shouted 'Bless the bride!' I entered the dimness of the church on M'sieur Hugo's arm and walked down the aisle, my head held high as we passed the waiting guests. My eyes were focused on the men standing in front of the priest, Pierre and his groomsman, a fellow teacher named John Martel. Unfortunately, Paul Stapfer had recently left the island or he would have been asked. When Pierre turned round, he smiled as he saw me while m'sieur moved away. For a moment the memory of my dear Arnaud, standing in the same place, with his face filled with love for me, quite unnerved me. I faltered and m'sieur came back to place a steadying hand on my back. I smiled my thanks and took a deep breath.

The service was short, as becoming the wedding of those widowed, and it wasn't long before we were climbing into the carriage for the short drive up the hill to Hauteville House. Another carriage had been hired to take M'sieur Hugo and M'dame Drouet home first. We waved at the well-wishers, including a group of College boys, who raised their hats as we passed.

'Well, that went smoothly, did it not? And how do you feel to be M'dame Blondel?' Pierre said, with a kiss. This was only the second time he had kissed my mouth, the first being moments before in the church and it felt strange. Not unpleasant, but not as I would wish; it lacked enthusiasm. And my body did not respond as it had to Arnaud's kisses. I must stop comparing them, I know, but it's to be expected, surely?

'I don't feel much different, as yet, M'sieur Blondel. But I expect that will change.' I managed to smile at him.

He nodded, saying, 'By tomorrow you will be truly my wife, and for now we have the pleasure of the celebrations at Hauteville House.'

The reminder of the night ahead did little to cheer me, but the sight of the waving staff on the steps was uplifting and as Pierre came round to assist me from the carriage, he circled my waist with his hands, lifting me high in the air to the delight of the maids. I joined in the laughter and he dropped a kiss on my cheek as he set me on the ground. Monsieur Hugo and m'dame appeared in the doorway and Pierre escorted me towards them. She was quite overcome and kept hugging me, tears seeping out of her eyes. We all waited in line to welcome the guests before moving out to the garden where a large table, decorated with sprays of roses, was set ready for the wedding breakfast.

I only have jumbled memories of the celebrations, but I do recall M'sieur Hugo delivering a speech extoling my supposed virtues which made me blush and an answering speech, much shorter and less fulsome, by my husband. The wine flowed and the food, as bountiful as ever, was served by the maids for what seemed like the whole day but was nearer three hours. I was unused to being the focus of attention at such a meal, and with such hosts, and nervousness led me to drink more wine than I was used to. By the time the guests began to disperse, I was overcome with fatigue and had to stifle a yawn. M'dame must have noticed for she suggested I return home for a rest before the evening's excursion to the theatre, a treat planned for me by Pierre.

My husband agreed and escorted me to my – our – house. I expected him to stay, but he said he would leave me to sleep and returned to Hauteville House. This was a relief, as having slept so little the night before I was exhausted. Sophie helped me undress and I slipped into bed and fell asleep almost immediately. I was awakened by Sophie at five o'clock with a cup of tea and I felt refreshed and ready for the trip to the theatre. As she helped me into my blue silk gown, Sophie chatted about how beautiful the wedding had been and what a handsome couple we made.

After the theatre, Pierre and I returned to *St Michel*. I had told Sophie not to wait up and now I was alone with my husband I felt unsure of myself. He suggested a nightcap and I accepted, glad to delay retiring upstairs. We sat awkwardly on the sofa in the parlour with our drinks, almost the first time we had been totally alone that day. Strewn around the room were boxes of his belongings, mainly books, delivered from the College. His clothes were already in the wardrobe in one of the bedrooms, now designated his dressing room.

Pierre loosened his tie and stretched out his legs.

'The day went very well, do you not agree? And I think you should write a letter to M'sieur Hugo, expressing our thanks for his generous hospitality.'

I had already planned to write such a letter and it irked me that he should suggest it. Taking a sip of my port, I agreed with him. Pierre talked at some length about the advantages to be enjoyed by being seen to be close to M'sieur Hugo and it occurred to me what a snob he must be. I wondered how I had not noticed it before.

'Come, you must be tired after such a long and eventful day. Let's go to bed.' He led the way upstairs like the master of the house he now was, and left me to undress alone while he went into his dressing room. Anxious as I was, I fumbled over the fastenings and had only just changed into my nightdress when he returned, picked me up and threw me onto the bed.

(The above description of my wedding day I wrote early the following morning.)

CHAPTER 34

Eugénie's Diary – October 1869

I am *enceinte*! Pierre is delighted and hoping for a son. Naturally I am pleased but also frightened, but I cannot acknowledge this. Although the pregnancy has just been confirmed, I have had my suspicions for some weeks, having missed my monthlies soon after my wedding. Then I was sick the last few mornings, as I was with baby Arnaud. I can only hope that my child, if it survives, will bring me the love I long for. The doctor calculates the birth will take place next April. I am still not in love with my husband, and I suspect he does not love me, but we rub along well enough. Pierre is an indifferent lover, and I do not enjoy our lovemaking. At least I can now say we should desist until after the baby is born and he can sleep in his dressing room. My marriage has not yet brought me the contentment and the companionship I crave and does not compensate for the loss of the work I so enjoyed, with the chance to spend time with M'sieur Hugo.

Today I spent time with Florence Rabey and we took one of our favourite walks along to the top of Hauteville and then, turning right, continuing uphill until we reached the leafy lanes leading to Millmount, the home of the artist Paul Naftel. It is a peaceful area and fit only for pedestrians, a perfect choice for two women on their own. I do admit to finding the company of women to be more comfortable than that of men. There is an ease to our conversations and we have so much more in common.

November 1869–February 1870
I am so happy! My friends are returned! And they are overjoyed to hear I am to have a child. M'dame is particularly concerned about my health, which touches me deeply. Charles and Alice

are here and I find her delightful, and their two children Georges and Jeanne.

We went to supper last night, joining with the émigrés who have yet to return to France. From the talk around the table it may not be long now before the last of them return and I dread that time. I think even Pierre will regret it when M'sieur Hugo leaves as he makes much of our association with him. He says things like, 'M'sieur Hugo said this to me the other day' or 'when I was at Hauteville House for supper' when talking to friends or acquaintances, leaving me embarrassed for us both. I feel it is a sign of ill manners and I'm beginning to see a different, darker side to Pierre. It seems he had hoped for advancement at the College and it hasn't materialised, meaning our income remains modest while he loves to spend. Possessing a fine house has made him act as if we are the equals of our superiors and he spends accordingly, particularly on good wine. We had an argument about this when we returned from Hauteville House last night and, although he was not violent towards *me*, he threw a glass on the floor and shouted abuse at me. I am becoming more fearful about the future.

March 1870

I am safely delivered of a beautiful son! I can hardly believe it is true. A miracle! He was born yesterday, a few weeks early so it was unexpected and I was afraid I would lose him as I did poor little Arnaud. Doctor Corbin and the midwife were on hand and kept assuring me all was well through the long, painful labour. I lost much blood and at one time wondered if I would live, but I have and am truly grateful. My son is healthy and a good weight considering he came early and I delight in stroking his soft, dark hair and holding his tiny hands. I can gaze at him for hours while he lies in his cot beside me. The only sadness is that Doctor Corbin has said I will not be able to conceive another child. But perhaps that is as well and I can devote all my love and time to this child. The doctor has told my husband this and Pierre, overjoyed to have a son, has not yet remarked on this. We have agreed to name him Victor, in honour of M'sieur Hugo.

I have received word from M'sieur Hugo, congratulating me on the birth, and he has offered to be his godfather, in spite of his views on religion. M'dame Drouet has also sent round a letter, expressing her felicitations over my safe delivery, accompanied by a basket of fresh fruit for my enjoyment. Sophie is looking after me well and insists I stay in bed until I am fully recovered. I am only too happy to agree. Victor's christening will be held at the Town church.

April 1870
Poor m'sieur is in mourning for his friend Hennett de Kesler, who has died (6th April) and is to be buried at Cimetière des Indépendants, where poor Emily is buried, and M'sieur Hugo will offer the oration. Those in exile are either dying or returning to France and I grow more fearful of the time when my friends decide to leave.

My son thrives as my marriage falters. In order to protect my privacy and the writing of this journal, I have had my desk moved up to Sophie's room where Pierre would not care to go. She I can trust implicitly. My strength is returning and I was well enough for our son's christening yesterday. Pierre makes much of baby Victor but spends as little time as possible with me, for which I'm glad. He seems bitter and he is out in the evenings, coming back smelling of liqueur.

July 1870
I am spending time with m'dame this morning, who loves to fuss over my son, and this afternoon I am invited to join the family at Hauteville House. These days M'sieur Hugo seems to like nothing better than to play with his grandchildren. He quite dotes on them and I've never seen him like this before, no longer the genius of words, but the grandfather happily on his knees with the children in the garden. He's as attentive to little Victor, for which I am grateful and treasure spending time with him even though I am no longer his copyist.

19th July 1870

I was at Hauteville House this morning when news arrived saying France has declared war on Prussia. M'sieur commented, sadly, 'It has pleased certain men to condemn a part of the human race to death.' It is assumed the war will soon be over, thanks to France's superior military, and troops will be marching on Berlin in a matter of days.

Late July 1870

The war is going badly for France and m'sieur has published a letter in our local paper, then taken up on the English mainland, addressed 'To the Women of Guernsey' and asking for bandages to be distributed equally between the French and German casualties. Some may wonder at this apparent lack of patriotism, but I feel it shows how much he cares for all humanity.

August 1870

France has lost Alsace and Lorraine and Louis Napoleon has proved to be a poor leader. I was at Hauteville House today and the family talked of leaving Guernsey and travelling to Brussels, with no mention of coming back. I am heartbroken, for both the fate of France and the imminent parting with M'sieur Hugo, his family and M'dame Drouet. Everyone is rushing around, packing trunks and M'sieur has packed away all his manuscripts in a large trunk to be deposited in the strong room of the Old Bank in the High Street. They are to leave on the 15th and it takes all my strength to act as if we are parting for a matter of months only. I cannot allow Pierre to know how deep are my feelings of grief at the prospect.

15th August

They are gone! They took the evening ship to Southampton and Pierre and I went to the harbour to see them off. I had already visited Hauteville House earlier, alone, to make my farewells to M'sieur Hugo and M'dame Drouet in private and tears flowed on all sides. We agreed to write to each other, the war permitting, and m'sieur generously gave me 1000 francs for my son, which I will keep safe for him.

'Ah, *ma petite*! What a journey we have shared, *n'est ce pas*? You have been one of the bright joys of my exile and I'm sure we'll meet again. Even if I do take up my old life in Paris, remember I have a home here and will want to visit it when I can.'

'I look forward to that day, m'sieur.'

If it were not for my son I would be in a deep depression. In previous years I've always known they would return after their vacation, but now...All I can do is hug the memories to myself, replaying the precious times I've spent with M'sieur Hugo over the past eight years. Pierre is on the summer break from College and at the moment is in a good humour, suggesting we go to the beach tomorrow and take a picnic. I must learn to enjoy any good days I'm offered.

December 1870

I am in despair and afraid for the future. My husband's moods have been gradually becoming darker and last night he punched and kicked me after drinking heavily during the evening. All I had said was perhaps he had had enough to drink when he went to open another bottle of wine and he lost his temper. Shocked and in pain I crawled up to bed and locked the door. He came up later and tried to come in but I told him to sleep in his dressing room. This morning he was all apologies and begged my forgiveness. My face is bruised and there are other bruises on my body. I am in no mood to forgive him. I told Sophie I had hit my head on the dressing table, but by the look on her face I don't think she believed me. I feel I can no longer trust Pierre but I'm trapped, as are all married women. My hope is this won't happen again, as he has promised.

March 1871

Terrible news from France! Poor Charles Hugo has died of a heart attack, brought about by his excessive eating and drinking. How sad for M'sieur Hugo! M'dame has written to me with the news, saying they were in Bordeaux when tragedy struck and the funeral was held in Paris, with a large turnout in respect for the father, not the son. She wrote:

'*We left Paris with some speed as it's not safe there for us and journeyed to Brussels in order to settle Charles's estate. What a shock for M'sieur Hugo! Charles had been living in expectation of his inheritance and had built up huge debts which have to be settled for the sake of Alice and the children. As you can imagine, ma chère, this has only added to his grief. We intend to stay here some months while Paris is still under siege…*'

My thoughts are with the Hugo family in Brussels, particularly poor Alice and her children. I never had a high opinion of Charles, who seemed to rely too heavily on his father for an income rather than earn his own, unlike his brother Victor. M'dame didn't mention a possible visit to Guernsey this year so I will have to be patient.

Pierre has been violent towards me again and has expressed remorse. But it means nothing. It is no way to live, but what choice do I have? As a married woman I have even forfeited the ownership of my own house.

February 1872

M'sieur Hugo writes to say that his daughter Adèle has arrived in Paris from Barbados, in the company of a Barbadian, Mme Baa. It was quite a shock for him as there had been no word from her for some time. She apparently turned up on the doorstep of the family doctor who then alerted her father. I was so pleased as I read this, hoping they would now be united as a father and child should be. Alas, he went on to say Adèle was confused and agitated and did not recognise him and is to be sent to an expensive nursing home situated near the cemetery where M'dame Drouet's daughter Claire is buried. So sad! He keeps busy with his writing and is preparing a new volume of poetry. Oh, what would I give to be by his side, copying the beautiful words that burst forth from his imagination! There isn't a day goes by that I don't think back to those happy days at Hauteville House. Each time I pass by while taking my son for an airing in the perambulator, I recall the first time I arrived to start my work. The house looks so sad shut up and with only a few staff in residence. My life now revolves around Victor, who will soon be two years old. A sturdy little chap, he always has a smile on his face and can brighten my gloomiest mood. As for Pierre – well, he does not improve in his behaviour towards me and I have learnt to keep out of his way when he has been drinking. Before he left Guernsey, Paul Stapfer had hinted to me that Pierre's lack of advancement at the College was due to his heavy drinking, so he only has himself to blame. But it would be foolhardy to tell him so.

August 1872
Oh, joy! My friends have arrived from France! There is a full house as the party includes Alice and the children and Victor. A message was sent to me to call round and I took my son to see his godfather. I found both M'dame Drouet and M'sieur Hugo looking old and tired and his son Victor seemed quite ill. It appears they all hope the wonderful sea air will revive them. However, m'sieur was unhappy about the state of his house.

'It's a hovel. Everything is in tatters, the hangings are drooping, the gilt is falling off, the room I inhabit is a garret,' he said, pacing around in the garden where we sat watching the children, including my son, running around squealing in delight. I had to agree the house did look in poor repair.

'Will you be staying long this time, m'sieur?' I asked, offering a piece of cake to my son who watched round-eyed as I cut a slice.

'I think we will stay until next summer, though the family may return sooner. I've missed the ocean air and the peacefulness of the island compared to Paris, where there are too many demands on my time. I have a novel in mind and being back here will, I believe, offer both a chance to improve my health and many quiet hours in which to write.'

'How wonderful. If you have the time, I would look forward to seeing more of you and m'dame while you're here.' My heart lifted at the thought of having my friends close again for so long.

He sat down beside me and picked up my hand.

'*Ma petite*, I will always find time to be with you and little Victor. You are as a daughter to me and one of the delights of returning here is to see you again.' His eyes bored into mine and he frowned. 'I sense something's not right with you. The light has gone from your eyes. Are you ill?'

I felt myself blush under his scrutiny.

'No, I am well, thank you. Perhaps a little tired.' How could I tell him the truth? That my husband beat me and was a drunkard? And we were constantly short of money. I would be too ashamed.

'Hmm, well we must try to bring back the colour to your cheeks and the twinkle in your eyes. You can join us on our excursions and it will be like it used to be, yes?' He patted my hand, smiling.

'I would enjoy that, thank you.' I raised a smile and our conversation was interrupted by Jeanne and Georges as they begged to be lifted onto his lap. He is such a devoted grandfather and I can see how much joy the children bring him. They will be the light of his old age, sorely needed after the heavy losses he has endured. As I hug my own Victor I wonder if I will be fortunate to experience the delights of being a grandmother. Although not yet thirty, I feel my body has aged beyond my years and am doubtful.

CHAPTER 35

Tess – July 2012

Over the next few days Tess settled into the work routine and continued to look out for any calls from Mrs Le Page. There were none. In the evenings she took out the diaries and by Tuesday between her and Charlotte they had progressed to the years 1866 and 1867. Charlotte had been excited to announce when she arrived home from work that 'the desk' had definitely been bought as a gift by Hugo and showed Tess the entry in 1865.

'This proves it's worth the effort of reading the diaries. Just wish they were in English, we'd have read them all by now.'

Later that evening Charlotte joined her for a glass of wine and to ask how she was getting on.

'I've just read about Hugo writing *Les Travailleurs de la Mer* and it brought back memories of reading it at school. It gave me goosebumps to read about my ancestor copying out the same words over a hundred years ago. Quite spooky, in a way.' The thought prompted her to share something. 'Talking of spooky, I think I've seen the ghost of Eugénie sitting at her desk,' she nodded towards the desk behind her.

Charlotte's lips formed an O shape.

'No! Really? Why didn't you say anything?' She leaned forward, her eyes shining.

'I felt stupid. I'm a scientist and not supposed to believe in such things as ghosts, but…but reading these diaries is bringing Eugénie alive for me and the image of this woman sitting at the desk, looked so *real*. As if there's a connection between us.'

'Which there is, of course. What did she look like?'

'Like the picture Hugo drew, but wearing a light grey dress and her hair was styled in a bun at her neck. I've seen her twice, now, but the vision only lasts a few seconds. So, you don't think I'm mad to think I've seen a ghost?' Tess asked, sipping her wine.

'Goodness, no. We had one in our country house, though I was never lucky enough to see it. I did feel the presence of my father after he died, though. My friends Nicole and Fiona have seen ghosts here in Guernsey, but they're away at the moment. Must introduce you sometime. I say, this is exciting! A ghost in my house!' Charlotte stared at the desk, as if willing Eugénie's ghost to appear.

Charlotte finished her wine.

'I'll crack on with the diaries tomorrow when I can grab any free moments.' Charlotte stood and stretched, giving the desk another searching look.

Tess laughed. 'I don't think we can force Eugénie to appear, you know.'

Charlotte grinned. 'I know, but one can hope. Night night, thanks for the wine.'

After a quick hug she left and Tess was alone with her thoughts. What other revelations were hidden in those pages? She'd have to be patient, and with so much going on in her life at the moment, she had enough to think about.

Her father phoned the following evening.

'I've sold the house, Tess, and will be coming over to look at apartments next week. There's a couple I'm interested in.'

'Oh, Dad, that's great! I'm pleased for you. And if you don't find what you want my house will be ready in two or three weeks and you can stay with me. Any news from Mum?' Tess had sent her mother a couple of emails a few weeks ago but had not heard back. Still upset by what her mother had done, she didn't feel inclined to chase her. It was up to her mother now.

'Only through the solicitors.' She heard him sigh and her heart ached for him. 'She knows someone was interested in the house and has sent a list of the stuff she wants. Furniture and suchlike. She can have what she wants as far as I'm concerned. I want a fresh start and that goes for furniture too. I was never that keen on the suite she chose, anyhow.'

'So, where's she going to live?'

'I don't know for sure, but I think they'll be going abroad. Probably France. She's mentioned it before and now she'll have a decent sum to buy what she wants. I don't have an address for her, everything goes through the solicitor. Do you want me to ask her to let you have it?'

'Only if she wants to, Dad. We've not spoken in ages and perhaps that's the way she wants it.' Tess wasn't sure how she felt about not seeing her mother again, but the longer it went on, the harder it would be.

Her father then asked how things were with her and she spent a few minutes bringing him up to date. They finished by agreeing she and Jack would see him when he came over for the viewings. Tess then went back to the diaries. Charlotte had filled her in with the main points of 1868, including the death of M'dame Hugo and the return to Guernsey of a rather depressed Hugo and Juliette. Tess read about Juliette's attempt to marry Eugénie off, suggesting a man called Pierre Blondel. The name rang a bell and she remembered that, according to Doris's family history, Eugénie married him in 1869. Reading on, she was sad to see that Eugénie doesn't fall in love with him and that Pierre wasn't exactly the romantic type. But could anyone have matched Hugo in Eugénie's eyes?

The next day Tess was kept busy at work all morning and it wasn't until she showed the last patient out that her secretary managed to catch her.

'Sorry not to give you much notice, Doctor, but Mrs Sally Le Page has rung in, asking if you can do a home visit as soon as possible. She sounded extremely distressed.'

❧ CHAPTER 36 ❧

Tess – July 2012

Tess drew up by the front door, noticing the SUV as before. Grabbing her bag she strode to the front door and rang the bell. When there was no reply she tried the door and found it opened.

'Mrs Le Page? Sally? It's Doctor Le Prevost.'

A faint voice called back, 'Up here, in the bedroom. Door's open.'

Tess took the stairs two at a time, her heart beating fast. A door along the landing stood partly open and she went towards it, pushing the door open wider. The room was dominated by a huge four-poster bed and for a moment she couldn't see her patient. 'Sally? Where are you?'

'Here.' A muffled voice came from the bed and as Tess walked closer she saw a figure under the heaped up bedclothes. Pulling them back gently, Sally's head appeared. She had a bruise on her forehead and her eyes were puffy and red.

'Okay, Sally. Tell me what happened. The truth, please.' She kept her voice gentle.

'We...we were at a social event last night and Don, my husband, had a lot to drink. Not that it showed, he's...very careful like that. When we got home, he started yelling at me that I'd been flirting with another man on the same table, but I hadn't. It was...the other way round. He started punching me...body...then...banged my head on the post. Called me names. I must have passed out. He slept in the spare room. Before he left this morning...he looked in and said something...can't remember what, but I must have answered. Then he went. I've been sleeping on and...off all morning. Head hurts. Body hurts.' Tears trickled down her face.

Tess took a deep breath.

'Okay, Sally. I need to examine you, but first, where's Rupert?'

'At my mother's. She had him last night...I phoned her to keep him today. Said not well.'

'I see, that's good. Now let me have a look at you.' Gently she helped Sally turn, easing off her clothes to see where she was injured. Livid bruises covered her torso and arms. Tess sucked in her breath. The poor woman had been used as a punch-bag. The bastard!

'Sally, we have to get you checked out in the hospital...'

'No, please! I can't. Don will kill me!'

'I understand, but we might be able to keep it hushed up for the moment. I'm prepared to back you up if you say you fell down the stairs, but we need X-rays to check if there's anything broken and I'm concerned about your head. If there are no fractures or breaks, I might be able to find somewhere for you to go–'

'I can't go to the refuge! I'm too well known–'

'I realise that. I was going to suggest somewhere else. More private. Have you heard of La Folie? The health centre?'

Sally sniffed.

'Yes.'

'And, forgive my asking, but would you be able to afford to pay for a few days stay, if there's a vacancy? And would your mother hang onto Rupert? Are you still breast-feeding?'

'I have my own money. I stopped breast-feeding last week...becoming difficult. Can ask Mum...should be okay.' Sally winced with pain and Tess knew she had to act quickly.

'Good. I'll call an ambulance and while we're waiting I'll pack a bag for you if you tell me what you need.'

By the time the ambulance arrived a bag was packed and Tess had helped Sally dress in loose yoga pants and a long-sleeve T-shirt. While the ambulance left for the Princess Elizabeth Hospital, Tess called the surgery to say she was escorting her patient to hospital and then rang Paul at La Folie. She explained the situation and he said they could find a room if needed. She then set off to the hospital.

She arrived to find Sally had been sent off for X-rays and a brain scan and managed to talk to the A & E doctor. He was puzzled, saying it didn't look like a fall down stairs to him, and Tess explained who Sally was and that they were trying to keep the assault quiet for the moment for her sake. He agreed to play along, as long as she received the right care. While she waited for the results, Tess phoned Jonathan, who fortunately was on his lunch break. He listened in shocked silence while she explained what had happened and what she was planning to do with Sally.

'What a bastard! It's hard to take in but…With regard to booking Sally into La Folie, although it's unorthodox, if it keeps her safe, then it shouldn't be a problem. Are you going to try and persuade Mrs Le Page to report him to the police?'

'Not necessarily me, but I'm hoping Paul or a counsellor might be able to convince her. But if he wasn't taken into custody, I'd be afraid what he'd do.'

'And me. Let's see what happens with the X-rays. You've done well, Tess, and you've obviously gained her trust which is good. What's happening about your afternoon surgery?'

'My secretary's rescheduling non-urgent appointments and the others are being shared among the partners.'

'Okay. Keep me posted. Bye.'

Tess slumped back in the chair, praying Sally hadn't suffered any permanent damage. Fifteen minutes later the A & E doctor came through to find her.

'The scan and X-rays are clear, and there's no obvious damage to any organs, but there are signs of old hairline fractures.' He frowned. 'This isn't the first time, then?'

'No, although Sally hasn't said as such. Are you okay for her to go to La Folie? They have a doctor on the staff and I'm happy to visit if necessary. Just until she has a chance to heal and make some decisions.'

He nodded.

'Sure, we certainly wouldn't send her home. Normally I'd be flagging this as assault, but I'll hold back for now. And unless Mrs Le Page wants to press charges, there's no point involving the police. Are you taking her to La Folie in your car?'

'Yes, I suppose so. I just have to confirm we're coming.'

'Good. I'll see a nurse gets her ready. Good luck, Doctor.' He shook her hand and left.

Tess breathed a sigh of relief. Right, time to book Sally a room.

Thirty minutes later, Tess was relaxing in a squishy chair in the grand reception hall of La Folie while Paul arranged for Sally to be shown to her room. The atmosphere was one of peace and calm and the scent of aromatic oils wafted through the air. The white uniformed staff had treated Sally with the utmost concern and gentleness. Tess was not only impressed, she was wishing she could spend a few days here herself, being pampered the way Charlotte had once described to her. On the drive here, she had asked a pale Sally what she would tell her husband.

'My mother's going to tell him I've gone away for a few days and she's looking after Rupert. She suspects that Don…hits me, but I haven't admitted it. Yet. I…I still love him, crazy as that might sound, and we have a baby. I don't know what to do.'

'I understand. There's a counsellor at the centre so perhaps you can talk to her and work out how to go on from here. All I'll say is, it was a vicious assault, Sally, and you're lucky it wasn't fatal.'

Sally nodded, her expression bleak.

'Right, Tess, Sally's settled in her room and thank you for thinking of us. We don't normally get asked to take in victims of assault, but I'm only too glad to be of help. Poor woman,' Paul said, shaking his head. 'She'll be well looked after, I promise you. We've told staff Sally's here to recover from a serious accident and needs time on her own.'

'Thanks, Paul. Give me a call if you've any concerns. Oh, and I suggested to Sally she might want to talk to a counsellor and I think she might be willing to do that.'

'Good, it's something I'll encourage. Go and relax, I can see you've had a stressful day.'

She gazed into his hypnotic blue eyes and smiled. Yes, Sally was in good hands.

By the time Tess arrived home she was famished as well as drained. Charlotte took one look at her and insisted she joined them for supper, about to be served. Andy was putting James to bed and would be down shortly.

'I know you can't give details, but you've clearly had a bad day. I'm happy to listen if you want to talk.' Charlotte pushed a glass of wine towards her as she took a seat.

'Thanks. It's a nasty case of domestic abuse and the poor woman still loves her husband and doesn't know which way to turn. I've found her a safe place for the moment but...' she shrugged, before taking a swallow of wine.

'Oh, that's horrid. Poor her and poor you. No wonder you look done in.' Charlotte began setting the food on the table and Tess helped herself to some chilli con carne and crusty bread. Just what she needed after missing lunch. Andy came in and said hello before taking his seat.

'Tess has had to deal with a domestic abuse today, and is shattered, so I asked her to join us,' she said, squeezing Andy's shoulder.

'Oh, right. Tough one. Must be hard not to become emotionally involved with something like that,' Andy said, filling his plate.

'It is. It makes me so angry I see red. Have to really work at staying calm. I find it hard to imagine why a woman would stay with a violent man these days, when we have much more independence than our forebears.' Tess took a mouthful of food to try and take her mind off Sally's reluctance to leave her husband.

The conversation then shifted to the progress on Tess's house and how pleased she was with the work.

'I should be able to move in three or four weeks and I can't begin to say how grateful I am to you both for putting up with me all this time. You've been the best hosts.' Tess would miss them, but hey, they lived on a small island.

'You're more than welcome. I've enjoyed having another woman around for a good gossip and our door's always open.' Charlotte started clearing away the plates and Tess suspected she was trying to hide her real feelings and gave her a hug.

'Can we be sisters? I love my brother but have always wanted a sister.'

Charlotte grinned.

'As an only child I missed out big time. Louisa and I have declared ourselves sisters and I'm happy to gain another. What fun!'

'I'm beginning to feel quite left out. Can't I be something?' Andy asked in a sorrowful voice.

'You're my husband, my best friend and lover. What more do you want?' Charlotte said, planting a kiss on his forehead.

'Guess that'll have to do, then,' he said, with a grin.

At a partners' meeting at the surgery the next day, one of the items up for discussion was the case of Mrs Sally Le Page. Tess had been warned by Jonathan that this would happen, but assured her it was normal procedure. Not totally reassured she spent an anxious time waiting to be asked to give her report. Once she had done so, the matter was discussed between the partners on their own. She was then called back to be told they found her actions, although not strictly in keeping with normal procedure, to have been in the best interests of the patient and her safety. It was decided if the husband were to ask questions, he would be told nothing. Tess, relieved, carried on working that day, feeling she had undergone a baptism of fire. The white face of young Gary as he lay stretched out on the hospital trolley still occasionally haunted her. She didn't want another unnecessary death on her hands.

It was Friday and Tess was looking forward to seeing Jack and she was due to spend the weekend with him. After throwing a few clothes and necessities into a bag she popped into the kitchen to say she was off and Charlotte asked how she was.

'Much better, thanks. And I had a good day at work. What about you?'

'Read a bit more of the diaries, including Eugénie's wedding. Hugo's obviously very fond of her isn't he? But definitely no hanky-panky between Victor and Eugénie, so you can't be descended from him, I'm afraid.' Charlotte pulled a face.

'Fine by me. I'm more than happy with knowing what good friends they were. He must have loved her like a daughter; rather sweet, don't you think?'

'Definitely. Much more wholesome. Which is more than can be said for your activities this weekend, I expect.' Charlotte winked at her.

Tess laughed.

'I certainly hope so. Have a good weekend and see you on Sunday.'

'Bye.'

By the time Tess arrived at Jack's cottage she was in thoughtful mood and less sure of what she felt about her relationship with Jack. Jonathan's description of Don Le Page as a 'charming man' juxtaposed with the image of Sally's battered face had made her check him out online. He looked the archetypical successful businessman; smooth good looks and oozing charm. It occurred to Tess that she hardly knew Jack and yet she was allowing herself to fall for him, bigtime. Should she hold back a bit? Not that she thought he might be violent, but…

They spent most of the weekend at the beach and she felt like a new woman, sporting a healthy glow from the sun's rays and full of endorphins from the swimming and surfing. Tess knew she'd been a bit detached over the weekend and when they were saying goodbye Jack had asked her if there was anything wrong.

'Oh, it's just work. I've had a bit of a shitty week.'

He seemed to accept it and gave her a big hug.

When Tess arrived home early Sunday evening she phoned Paul to ask after Sally.

'She's doing quite well, Tess. Louisa has given her a private session of physio in the pool, which has eased her stiffness and we'll repeat it. She's also agreed to see our counsellor, Molly, tomorrow which is encouraging. So, all good so far.'

'Great, thanks, Paul. I'll phone tomorrow for an update. Bye.'

Relieved to hear her patient was making progress, Tess went in search of Charlotte, finding her in the kitchen studying a cookery book with a glass of wine.

'Hi. Trying something new?' Tess plonked down beside her.

'Just looking for inspiration. Salads can be so boring, can't they? As it's too hot to spend hours over a hot stove I've invested in a book specialising in unusual salads and some look absolutely scrumptious.' She closed the book. 'Andy's reading James a bedtime story and we're going to have an omelette for supper later. Care to join us?' Charlotte topped up her glass of white wine and poured Tess a glass.

'Thanks, I'd like that. Cheers!'

They shared what they'd done over the weekend, Charlotte saying they'd taken James to the beach and been to see Andy's parents.

'And I found time to do a little more reading.' She explained about Eugénie's pregnancy and the slightly premature birth of a son in March 1870. Called Victor after Victor Hugo, who became his godfather.

'Ah, I wonder if that's what fed the rumour about Hugo being the father?'

'That's what I thought, too. There's no sign that Pierre doubted he was the father, so the rumours must have started later.'

'I guess. I'll carry on from where you left off later this evening. Eugénie's really getting under my skin. I want to know everything about her.'

After supper Tess went to her room with the diary Charlotte had been reading. She settled down on the sofa and found the place her friend had marked and started reading. It always took her a few minutes to get to grips with the French. She was near the end of the entries for 1870 when she cried out, 'No! Oh, no!' and re-read the words *last night he punched and kicked me after drinking heavily during the evening*'. Reading on, Tess saw how trapped she felt and was angry on her behalf. Glancing up, she saw Eugénie weeping at her desk.

CHAPTER 37

Eugénie's Diary – Autumn 1872

I was sad to say goodbye to Alice, the children and Victor as they left to return to France. Victor had regained some of his strength since being on the island, but still looked unwell. My son misses Jeanne and Georges having spent so much time playing with them during the summer. I am thankful m'sieur and m'dame are staying on for some months, so that we may continue to enjoy our walks and trips in the carriage. I believe Pierre is a little jealous of the time I spend with my friends, but he can hardly complain as he must attend to his duties at the College.

Pierre and I attended a soiree at Hauteville House last night and he embarrassed me by his loud behaviour. I caught M'dame Drouet and M'sieur Hugo exchanging glances and wonder if they will stop inviting us. I do hope not.

This morning m'dame sent a message to ask if she might call round and I replied immediately that I'd be happy to receive her. Together Sophie and I made sure the parlour was clean and tidy and I changed into one of my better dresses. Some are now a little threadbare and only worn about the house. I have to watch every franc and cannot afford to buy new clothes for myself, but make sure Victor is always well turned out.

'My dear, how are you today? I thought you looked a little peaky last night,' she greeted me as Sophie showed her into the room.

'I am well, thank you. Would you care for some coffee?' I had already asked Sophie if we had any left and she said there was enough for two cups. It has become a treat since the need to economise.

'Thank you, I would.' We made ourselves comfortable on the sofa while Sophie went to prepare the coffee and m'dame asked after Victor.

'He's well and having his nap.'

'Such an engaging child, he's a credit to you. And your husband, of course.' She touched my arm and smiled. All I could do was nod, sensing that she had not come here for a casual conversation and was afraid she was going to say I was no longer welcome thanks to Pierre's behaviour.

Sophie arrived with the coffee and after pouring it for us, left.

I took a sip and then m'dame, after placing her cup on the table, turned to face me.

'We have known each other a long time, have we not? It must be more than ten years and I like to think we have become close friends. Would you agree?'

'Indeed, yes. You and m'sieur are very dear to me…' Fear clutched at my heart.

'As you are to us. And that's why I want you to tell me what has happened to change you while we've been in France. You told M'sieur Hugo you're not ill, but something is wrong and I wish to know what it is.'

It was as if a dam burst inside me. All the pain and worry I had bottled up inside me came to the surface and the tears flowed as I told her the truth about my marriage. Her eyes widened in shock and she held me tight in her arms as I wept. At last I managed to stop and, pulling out my handkerchief, wiped my eyes and blew my nose. Part of me was relieved to admit the truth, but another part was filled with shame.

'*Ma chère*, this is awful! If only we'd known, we would never have encouraged you to marry this man. I'm so sorry you've had to suffer at his hands. M'sieur will be so angry and will no doubt tell your husband what he thinks of him.'

'Oh, please, don't let M'sieur Hugo say anything to Pierre. It would only make things worse for me once you leave Guernsey. I…I will manage.' I wasn't sure how, but knew I hadn't much choice, for the sake of my son.

M'dame squeezed my hand.

'You're right, we cannot confront him, much as we might want to.' She was thoughtful for a moment, then went on, 'At least we may be able to help you financially. I cannot bear the thought of you being kept short of money after managing so well on your own all those years. I'll talk to M'sieur Hugo and see what can be done. I assume your maid knows what's happening?'

'Yes, she's seen my bruises enough times though nothing is said, and is aware there is sometimes little money. We did have a scullery maid for a short time but had to let her go. Sophie's made it clear she wishes to stay with me even when she's late being paid.'

'Good, I'm pleased you have such a loyal girl by your side.' She lowered her voice, even though we were alone. 'Has your husband been violent towards you lately?'

'Not since you arrived back on the island. He knows we are close and I think he fears me confiding in you.'

'Then you may be safe while we are here, which is some consolation.' She finished her coffee and stood. 'I must be away but will be in touch shortly. Take care, *ma chère*, and remember we are here for you.'

We embraced then m'dame kissed my cheek before leaving. Not wanting to face Sophie I made for my bedroom, quickly checking Victor was still asleep. Slipping off my shoes, I lay on the bed going over what m'dame had said. Although I knew there was little she or even M'sieur Hugo could do, it cheered me to know they might help in some way.

Today I received a note inviting me to call at Hauteville House for lunch at twelve o'clock. Would m'dame have spoken to m'sieur all ready? My stomach fluttered with nerves as I forced myself to take Victor for an airing, even though I wished to avoid seeing anyone. Fortunately, I met no-one who engaged me in no more conversation than a 'Good morning'.

Leaving Sophie giving Victor his lunch, I made my way to Hauteville House and was shown through to the dining room where my friends were waiting.

M'sieur Hugo rushed towards me, arms outstretched.

'*Ma petite*! M'dame Drouet has told me all. *Je suis désolé*! To think what you have been going through with that...that man.' He threw his arms around me and I breathed in the familiar smell of ink and soap I always associated with him. It was good to be in his arms, even for a short while.

'Come and sit down and we will discuss what's to be done after lunch.' It was just the three of us and I sat in the middle while he poured the wine. Mary Sixty came in with a tray laden with pâté and bread. From experience I knew there would be several more courses to come and that M'sieur Hugo preferred to focus on eating rather than talk of anything unpleasant at luncheon. That would come later. By the time we had eaten the main course of roast lamb with potatoes and vegetables, I was anxious to know his thoughts on my plight, but grateful for the substantial meal, having little in the larder at home. Once the cheese had been eaten m'sieur filled our wine glasses and turned his attention to me.

'I have given much thought to what options, if any, you may have and there appears to be few. Are you able to obtain a divorce under Guernsey law? It's been banned in France for years since that poor excuse of an Emperor came to power.'

'I…I don't think so and wouldn't consider anything so drastic even if it were possible. I'm resigned to staying married for the sake of my son, who I'm determined will inherit the house one day.'

He nodded, stroking his beard.

'It's what I expected you to say. The issue then is money, and there I can help. For the time being, while I'm in Guernsey, you could take up your old post of copyist and I can pay you a wage as before.'

'Oh, m'sieur, there's nothing I'd like better, but there's no way Pierre would allow it to be known I had to work. He would be belittled in his colleagues' eyes.'

'In that case, we say you can spare a few hours a day and are only too pleased to help me for nothing while I'm here. Obviously, I would pay you and the money would be for your own use. What do you think?' He leaned forward to grasp my hand.

'What an excellent idea, m'sieur! Surely your husband can have no objection to such an arrangement?' said m'dame.

'I…I suppose not. And I would be glad of the extra money if you truly do need my services.'

'As M'dame Drouet will tell you, I'm progressing well with my latest project covering the Revolution and there is plenty of work for you both. It will not be charity.'

'Then I'd be happy to accept, as long as Pierre raises no objection.'

M'dame clapped her hands in delight.

'Wonderful. I'm sure Sophie will look after young Victor while you're here and your husband should not be put out in any way.'

'I'll write a letter to him, requesting permission for you to help me for the next few months. He should be honoured I value his wife so highly and can hardly say no.' M'sieur Hugo sat back, beaming.

I looked from one to the other and my throat tightened with emotion as they again showed their love for me. Even though I still had to live with my violent husband, for a while at least I could earn my own money and vowed to save as much as possible.

Early July 1873

My friends are to return to France later this month and I am already dreading the day. It is wonderful to work alongside m'sieur again as he writes *Quatrevingt-treize*, his novel set during the Revolution of the last century. Again I admire his prose and the characters he portrays so clearly that I feel I know them. It is almost finished and staying here has, he says, helped him make more progress than if he had remained in Paris. His strength has returned, the only setback being when a thorn lodged in his foot, making it painful to stand at his desk to write. Today I noticed some tension between him and m'dame and the cause appears to be her new young maid, Blanche, who has caught his eye. I've long been aware of his attraction for the maids and felt pain both for myself and for M'dame Drouet, who deserves better. But then, great geniuses must be allowed their weaknesses, *n'est ce pas*?

I am saving from my earnings, which have been more generous than previously, and Pierre has no idea of the arrangement. He continues to behave more properly towards me and even reduced his drinking a little, but I know as soon as my friends depart he will relapse.

Late July 1873

They have gone! And this time I don't know if or when they will return. We had an emotional goodbye, the three of us, in the red salon this afternoon. The past few months had drawn us closer together and none of us were dry-eyed.

'*Ma petite*, I only wish you could come with us, and bring little Victor, but you will be in our hearts and thoughts even while apart. I have arranged for you to receive a pension from me, to be collected monthly from my housekeeper here, so that you need not worry about money,' M'sieur Hugo said, holding my hands.

'Oh, m'sieur! How can I thank you? You've been more than generous...' My eyes pricked with tears at his continued kindness.

'Nonsense, you are too dear to me to abandon you completely. And I cannot leave my godson in precarious circumstances, can I?'

M'dame chimed in with, 'You have more than earned what is offered to you, *ma chère*, and M'sieur Hugo's right to say we can't and won't abandon you. We will stay in touch and if ever you are in need of help, please contact us.'

This time I am too upset to see them off at the harbour and busy myself helping Sophie clean the house from top to bottom. My only consolation over the months, and possibly years, to come will be the letters we will exchange.

January 1874

Ill news from France — M'sieur's son Victor has finally succumbed to the renal-tuberculosis that has plagued him these past few years. He died on Christmas Day, his father wrote:

'*I drew aside the curtains. Victor appeared to be sleeping. I lifted his hand and kissed it. It was warm and supple. He had just passed away, and though the breath had left his lips, his soul was on his face...*'

I shed a few tears for the son, and the father. Only poor, mad Adèle was still alive and could bring no comfort to her father. The grandchildren were his delight and are constantly mentioned in his letters.

'I played in the garden with the little ones, who are adorable. Jeanne said to me, "I left my drawers at Gaston's place". Gaston is her boyfriend, five years old'.

Life for me goes on as before. Victor is a fine little boy who will soon be ready for school and is showing signs of great intelligence. I dream of him becoming a doctor or a lawyer and it's a dream which keeps me going. Pierre has reverted to his old behaviour and been violent towards me when drunk. He is careful to avoid marking my face but punches and kicks my body so that I'm close to fainting. Sophie does her best to help me, letting me stay in bed to recover while she tends to my son and her chores. Thank God for my pension! We can still manage even when Pierre drinks away our money.

July 1878

M'sieur Hugo has had a stroke and m'dame has brought him here to recover. I'm so happy to see them but sad to see his deterioration. He is now in his late seventies and for the first time shows his age. He's not writing at the moment but goes out for drives around the island in the little carriage and walks little. M'dame Drouet shows the strain of nursing him but is fierce in her devotion to him. She has hinted he has been unfaithful since their return to Paris and this has caused her some pain. To my knowledge she has never known about the maids he has slept with. M'sieur now appears too unwell to indulge in such behaviour, the fire which has always burned so bright in him seems to have been quenched and his mood is often sullen. M'dame tells me he is a little brighter when I am there, but I find it hard to see.

November 1878

M'dame has given up hoping Guernsey will heal M'sieur Hugo's ills and they have departed for France. Apparently they are now to live in a different apartment which adjoins that of Alice, the children and her new husband. At least m'sieur will be close to the children he adores. In my heart I know I will never see my friends again and, after knowing them for sixteen years, the pain rips me apart. We will write and m'sieur has assured me my pension is to continue and he made a fuss of Victor, now eight years old and progressing well at the College. Impressed by my son's intelligence, he offered to pay the cost of his education, including university if he wishes to train for a profession. I am overwhelmed with love and gratitude towards him.

My body is showing the signs of my ill-treatment, but I'm reluctant to consult a doctor. I'm afraid some of Pierre's punches have damaged my vital organs and my monthlies have stopped flowing. Sophie has found an old nurse who does her best for me, making up potions of herbs to help with the pain and to heal the bruises. I doubt if I shall live to old age and can only pray my son is a man before I succumb. At least I was spared while my friends were here, but now...

Anne Allen

CHAPTER 38

Eugénie's Diary – Late May 1883

I am distraught to learn that my dear friend M'dame Drouet died on 11th May after suffering great pain in her stomach for some time. Since receiving the letter from M'sieur Hugo I have barely stopped weeping. She was as a mother to me and will be missed by many. M'sieur says he was so heartbroken he took to his bed for two weeks and was too overtaken to attend the funeral or pen any letters. She is buried with her daughter. His pain is evident from what he writes, and in spite of his indiscretions, I know he truly loved her and she devoted her life to him. I cannot but wonder how such a blow will affect his health. Now in his eighties, his strength must be waning. In his letter, he quoted the epitaph they had chosen for her grave.

When I am nothing but cold ashes,
When my weary eyes are closed to the light,
Say to yourself, if my memory is engraved in your heart,
The world has his thoughts
But I had his love!

His last words sent a chill through my heart:

'It is true what they say, you only realise how important someone is to you when you lose them. Juliette was my confidante, my muse, my love and I am now lost without her. It cannot be long before I shall be with my beloved'.

Although I am not religious, I went to the Town church to say a prayer for her, taking my son with me. He has fond memories of her, too, being the grandmother he never had and he shed a tear at the news. Pierre offered appropriate words of condolences but showed no real emotion, which I have come to expect from him.

23rd May 1885
What I have been dreading has happened. My beloved Victor Hugo died yesterday and the newspapers are full of the news,

277

with his photo splashed across the front pages as the world mourns the loss of one they call the greatest poet and writer of the century. To me he was that and so much more. I cannot put into words what I have felt for him and how much pain I suffer knowing he is dead. Sophie alerted me to the news when she brought me the English newspaper and held me as I cried. Since this morning I have lain in my bed, unable to sleep, and unable to face anyone but her. My body has been growing weaker these past few years and I have little strength to deal with this loss. I allowed Victor to see me when he came home from school and we hugged each other in our mutual sorrow. Pierre no longer shares my bed since Victor, now a tall and muscular young man of fifteen, threatened to harm him if he lays a finger on me again. He had seen some of my bruises and I was forced to tell him the truth about his father. At the time he was ready to fight with him and would have won as Pierre has become bloated and out of condition, but I convinced him to desist, afraid he would lose his place at the College.

June 1885

I have received a letter from dear Alice, who even in her own grief has found the time to write to me. She assumed I would have heard about Victor's death but wanted to offer her condolences, knowing how close we were. She describes the State funeral which took place some days ago now and how it seemed the whole of France had turned out to mourn her father-in-law. Amongst all the pageantry the incongruous sight of a pauper's hearse caused the most astonishment, she wrote. But it had been his wish, in keeping with his reputation as a philanthropist, and no-one had dared to deny it. Alice said how affected Georges and Jeanne were, but both had been very brave. They are his main heirs and have inherited, among other assets, Hauteville House and I would love to see them here again. I know M'sieur Hugo spoilt them, but surely that is the right of a grandfather? Alice tells me I, together with my son, have been left a bequest in his will, which is to remain unknown to my husband. She does not query this and I wonder if she suspected what had been going on in my marriage. The bequest is generous and will see Victor through university and beyond and my portion will provide the few comforts I need for many years. More years than I am likely to live.

May 1888

I am dying. Much against my will, Victor called for a doctor to attend me after I collapsed yesterday. The doctor is newly arrived from England and knows nothing of me and my history and I was obliged, under his kind but firm questioning, to tell him everything. He examined me with Sophie present and his face grew grave as the gentle touch of his hands caused me to cry out in pain.

'Mrs Blondel, I am sorry to tell you that your organs have been damaged by the constant physical abuse you've received and are now failing. Even your heart is weak. I'm afraid there is little I can do except relieve your pain.'

Sophie gasped and clutched my hand. .

The doctor's verdict is not a shock for me, I have long suspected I am gravely ill.

'How long am I likely to live, Doctor?'

He coughed and found it difficult to look me in the eyes. He's young and will need to become tougher if he is to succeed in his profession.

'It's hard for me to say, but I think only…weeks.'

'I see.' Not long then. Perhaps it's for the best as the pain has been particularly bad lately. My beautiful son, Victor, is eighteen and off to university soon and his future is assured. He is to study the law and plans to be an advocate in Guernsey. I can do little more for him.

Sophie started to cry and I tried to comfort her.

'Don't be upset, dear Sophie. I'm resigned to die and wish only to be free of pain.'

'I can give you injections of morphine for the pain, Mrs Blondel, using the new hypodermic needle. We can increase the dose as necessary. Shall I prepare some now?' The doctor lifted out a steel contraption with a long needle at one end and I agreed. I felt a sharp pain as the needle went into my arm, but it soon subsided. I began to feel woozy and must have fallen asleep.

The Inheritance

I woke today to find Sophie and Victor beside my bed, both with tear-stained faces. The pain in my body is much reduced.

'Oh, Mama, I cannot believe I'm to lose you. Please tell me the doctor is wrong.' Victor raised my hand to his lips and his eyes pleaded with me to live.

'My dear son, I'm afraid the doctor's right. My body is worn out after…and it's only my love for you which has helped me go on until now. I'm so proud of you and know you will do great things in your life. When the time comes I shall die in peace.'

I remember little of the rest of the day, except the doctor appearing with his hypodermic syringe filled with morphine.

This becomes the routine for days. I stay in bed and Sophie attends to my needs and shops and cooks when I sleep. I am never alone, as Victor takes it in turn to sit with me and my friend Florence calls round most days. I manage to continue writing my journal with Sophie's help as she props me up in the bed, but do little else. Florence and Victor read to me when I'm in the mood to listen, but they tell me I often fall asleep.

Pierre knows I'm dying but I refuse to see him. The doctor says I could press charges against him, but what would be the point? Why bring disgrace on our family now? My husband is slowly drinking himself to death and Victor, although legally a minor still, is financially independent and mature enough to manage his own affairs. My dreams are filled with visions of the old days, when I worked for Victor Hugo and fell under his spell. My life has not turned out as I wished, but I have been blessed to enjoy a unique friendship with a man who was truly a literary genius as well as ahead of his time with his thinking. And dear Juliette! What a force they were together. I do miss them so much.

June 1888

My strength is fading and I can barely write. Sophie has to help me hold my pen. I'm trying not to be afraid, but it is hard. Perhaps after all, I shall meet the loved ones I've lost in some other world. Or there may be nothing. An eternal blackness. I shall soon know. Poor Victor hardly leaves my side and he is the one thing I can be proud of. My son. I hope he marries and has many children and regales them with stories of their grandmother and her friendship with the great Victor Hugo, their father's godfather.

I have asked Sophie to place all my journals, together with everything connected to my time with M'sieur Hugo, in the cupboard in the attic where my desk is stored. My correspondence with M'sieur Hugo and M'dame Drouet and any other connected to the family, I have already hidden in a secret drawer in my desk. The cupboard door is to be plastered over to conceal it. This is to be done in secret and Sophie has arranged for this to be completed when neither Victor nor Pierre are at home. I do not want Pierre, or anyone acting on his behalf, to have access to what is so personal and private to me. On the other hand, I cannot bear the thought of it all being destroyed. My son knows all he needs to know and if, in the future, some descendant of mine or even a stranger should find it, then so be it. If it needs to be found, it will be...

❧ CHAPTER 39 ❧

Tess – August 2012

Shocked, Tess sat rooted to the spot. Eugénie looked different; thinner, broken and her dress was shabby.

'Eugénie,' she called softly.

The figure lifted her head and turned. Tess saw her bruised face wet with tears and instinctively reached out to her. Eugénie didn't seem to see her and the figure slowly dissolved into the air. Tess had to steady her breathing before going to the sink for a glass of water. The memory of Sally's bruised face flashed into her mind as she gulped it down. God, I'm surrounded by battered women! She went downstairs to find Charlotte who, luckily, was on her own in the kitchen making a cup of tea.

'What's happened? You're as white as a sheet.' Charlotte put her arms around her and led her to a chair. Tess told her what she'd read and seen.

'Gosh, no wonder you're upset. Here, have my tea and I'll make another.'

Tess sipped the tea while Charlotte dunked a teabag in another mug and then joined her.

'Poor Eugénie! How unlucky to have got saddled with such a man.'

'Yes, especially as she resisted marrying again for so long. At least she has baby Victor, but at one helluva cost,' Tess said, frowning. 'The weird thing is, I also have my patient who's in a similar situation, except she might be able to support herself if necessary. Eugénie was legally dependent on Pierre.' She shook her head.

'Are you going to read any more tonight?'

'No, I'm not in the mood now. Having to deal with a battered wife in the present is bad enough.'

'I can imagine. If you like I'll carry on tomorrow when I can. I've noticed the entries have become less frequent since her marriage.'

'Please do. And we know from Doris's family tree that poor Eugénie didn't live to old age which is probably a good thing under the circumstances.'

Tess had managed to shake off thoughts of Eugénie and Sally by the next morning and arrived at work in a cheerful mood. The day seemed to rush by and it was late afternoon before she had a chance to phone Paul at La Folie.

'Hi, Tess, you'll be pleased to hear Sally had a good session with Molly and they're meeting again tomorrow. I get the impression Sally's coming round to the idea of leaving her husband under certain conditions. So, it's wait and see. In the meantime she looks better and says she's enjoying the chance to be looked after, but misses Rupert. As we're strictly child-free here, I'm arranging for Sally to spend a couple of hours at our house with her mother and the baby tomorrow morning. Louisa will stay with her. Happy with that?'

'Yes, sounds a good idea. I'd wondered how she'd cope without him. And vice versa. Thanks, Paul, I'll stay in touch.'

Pleased some progress was being made by Sally, Tess's thoughts turned to Eugénie. She guessed there was no happy ending for her great-great-great-grandmother, but was anxious to learn what *did* happen to her.

'Hi, Tess, have a good day?' Charlotte asked as she arrived home.

'Yes, thanks. Certainly better than Friday! And you?' Tess squatted down to join James who was on the floor playing with giant Lego bricks. He gave her a toothy smile and she dropped a kiss on his cheek. Charlotte, stretched out on the sofa, looked tired.

'Good but exhausting. This little chap has had me running around in the garden this afternoon and I've only just sat down. Where do they get their energy from?' She gave an exaggerated groan.

Tess laughed.

'The joys of motherhood, eh? I'm led to believe it gets better by the time they're eighteen, so you simply have to hang on in there.' She picked up James and gave him a cuddle, saying, 'Your mummy says you're wearing her out. Can you slow down a bit, please? I think she's feeling her age.' Tess grinned as her friend threw a cushion at her, making James gurgle with laughter.

'I can see I'll get no sympathy from *Doctor* Tess, so I might as well go and make a cup of tea while you entertain my son. Want one?' Charlotte stretched and stood, slipping her feet into her sandals.

'Please.'

Tess helped James build the walls of a house, admiring his complete concentration on the task. When Charlotte reappeared with two mugs of tea, she left him to carry on and joined her on the sofa.

'Ah, that's better.' Charlotte sighed contentedly as she sipped her tea. 'He's a good little boy, really, so I shouldn't complain. And when he had a nap earlier I managed to fit in some reading.'

'Anything interesting?'

Charlotte described the events of the early 1870s, adding, 'You know, I would have liked to meet your Eugénie. She comes across as a caring person, not just concerned with herself. In fact, she played down her own problems, which at times were pretty bad.'

'I agree, I think she's someone to be proud of. Did you read any further?' Tess sipped her tea, the image of a sobbing Eugénie in her head.

'The return of Adèle to Paris. I bet that caused quite a stir! Thanks to her poor mental state she's confined in a nursing home. In her shoes, I think I'd have stayed in Barbados.' Charlotte grinned wickedly.

'Poor thing. Her life was ruined by unrequited love and a mental disorder which apparently ran in the family. It's just as well I'm not related to Hugo or heaven knows how I'd have turned out,' Tess said, pulling a face.

'Fair point. I've marked the page where I finished if you want to carry on.'

'Thanks, I do.' Tess drained her mug and stood. 'I'll leave you in peace as it must be Master James's supper time soon.' She picked him up for a cuddle just as Andy arrived.

'Hello, one and all.'

'Dadda!' James wriggled out of her arms and reached up to Andy, who, laughing, picked him up and swung him round.

Tess collected the diary, gave a quick wave, and left. The little family scene brought into sharp relief the different circumstances of Eugénie's and Sally's lives, leaving her somewhat pensive.

After a shower and change of clothes Tess ate her supper of chicken salad, poured a glass of wine and sprawled on the sofa with the diary. Tess pursed her lips as she carried on reading about the rest of 1872 and into 1873 when Hugo and Juliette returned to Paris once more and was cheered by Hugo's generous offer of a pension, providing Eugénie some financial security.

Tess put the book down and rubbed her eyes. Enough for now. Time for a bit of TV before bed.

A couple of days later Tess received a call from Paul, to say Sally would like to see her at La Folie after surgery, if she could spare the time. Tess was happy to agree and drove across to Torteval that evening. The building, with Gothic towers and heavy granite walls was, in Tess's view, quite ugly, but once inside it was transformed into a place of beauty. She sniffed the lightly scented air as she waited for Sally in the entrance hall, quite content to be still for a while. A woman in a white towelling robe came towards her and for a moment Tess didn't recognise her.

'Sally! You're looking better. How do you feel?' Sally's once bruised face now glowed, whether with make-up or not, Tess wasn't sure, and her hair looked freshly washed and styled.

'Much better, thanks, Doctor. Sorry to drag you out here, but I'm not ready to go out in public yet. Shall we go into the garden? We can find somewhere private to talk.'

Tess agreed and followed her down a corridor leading to the back of the building and a door onto the garden. Tess looked around at the stunning flower beds, shrubs and trees leading towards the cliff and a view of the sea. To the right was a glass-domed structure housing a swimming pool and along the back of the property was a deep terrace scattered with tables and chairs.

'Gorgeous, isn't it? Someone worked hard to create a garden like this,' Sally said, with a smile.

'They sure did. Where shall we sit?'

Sally led her to the far corner, where a bench was set facing over the cliff.

As they sat down, Sally began twisting her fingers.

'I can't tell you how much it's meant to me to be here. Not only has my body had a chance to heal, but I've been able to gain a new perspective on my…marriage and what I've been putting up with. The counsellor's been great and helped me to see I do have choices.'

'I'm glad, Sally. Have you been able to reach any conclusion?'

Sally let out a deep breath.

'Yes. I've decided not to pursue charges against Don. On certain conditions.'

'And they are?' Tess held her breath.

'That he agrees to a legal separation, prior to divorce, setting out his commitment to support me and Rupert financially, but to stay away from me. If he were to threaten me or try and hurt me, I'd go to the police. He'd go to prison and his reputation and career in the States would be finished.' She paused, her hands still twisting. 'I…I've seen my advocate and she's drawing up an agreement for him to sign.'

Tess breathed again.

'That sounds good, Sally. And you can go through with it? I remember you saying you loved him…'

She nodded.

'I know, and part of me does love him. But I can't go on living like I was and it's not fair on Rupert is it? In a few years' time, he might see Don hurt me and what sort of message does that send to a little boy? I was always scared no-one would believe me, Don's such a powerful and well-liked man, but you believed me and so do the people who have helped me here. I see now I was simply too afraid to pull away and start again.' She smiled shyly. 'And I have you to thank for giving me this chance, Doctor.'

'Well, I'm glad I was able to help. Do you think Don will accept your conditions?'

Sally frowned.

'He doesn't have any choice if he wants to stay out of prison. My advocate assured me that's what would happen if I went to the police. And Don would hate that.'

'For sure. And what about Rupert? Will you allow him contact?'

'Yes, but again with conditions. He could see him at my mother's or at his parents'. I wouldn't want to be there.'

'Sounds like you've thought of everything. Well done. So, when's Don going to be told?'

'Tomorrow. I can't leave it much longer as I want to be with my son, but it's not safe for me to leave here until we reach an agreement.'

'I understand. I think you've been very brave and you're doing the right thing for you and your baby. You deserve to enjoy a new life free of fear and pain.' Tess clasped Sally's hands.

Sally stood, her eyes bright with unshed tears.

'Thank you, Doctor, I'll let you know what happens. And even if I move from the Vale, I still would like you as my GP.'

Tess nodded and they walked together back inside before saying goodbye. She sat in her car, taking a few deep breaths before starting the engine. It was wonderful if it did work out for Sally the way she hoped, and it looked promising. So that was one battered wife escaping abuse, but Tess had a horrible feeling things were not looking good for Eugénie.

❧ CHAPTER 40 ❧

Tess – July/August 2012

Charlotte's eyebrows rose in enquiry as Tess entered the kitchen.

'Evening. You're very late, everything okay?'

Tess threw her bag on the table before pouring herself a glass of water.

'Yes, I think so. Had to see a patient after surgery and now I'm starving. Anything to report before I go upstairs?' Tess drank greedily, feeling hot as well as hungry.

'I managed to squeeze in some reading and there's not much left now. I covered 1878…' She filled her in with the details, finishing with, 'Pierre was still hitting her and her health wasn't good.'

'Oh, no.' Tess bit her lip.

The next day her father arrived and this time stayed at the Pandora in Hauteville. They arranged to meet at *St Michel* with Jack during her lunch hour.

'It's great to see you, Dad, and looking so well.' Ken looked fitter and had a healthy colour and Tess was relieved, glad he looked his old self again.

'And you look pretty bonny yourself, love. Something must be agreeing with you, eh?' He tilted his head, his eyes twinkling.

She felt herself redden.

'If you must know it's going quite well with Jack but please don't pump him will you? It's early days and we're taking it slowly.'

'Understood. Right, are we going in, then?' They had met outside the front door and Tess pushed it open. She hadn't been round for several days and was keen to see the progress.

'My, what an improvement,' Ken said, as they stood in the hallway. Tess smiled as she took in the painted walls and the newly fitted lights. The mahogany staircase and panelling gleamed and the wooden floor glowed with fresh polish.

'Glad you approve, Dad, I'm looking forward to moving in. Let's see if Jack's around.'

She led the way into the front room and found the painter working on the walls, the wooden floor covered with dust sheets. She had chosen a pale creamy yellow for most of the walls and a deep green for the fireplace wall in the front room. And without the chimney breast the dining area looked much bigger.

'Hi, is Jack here, please?'

'In the kitchen, Tess,' replied the painter, barely glancing her way.

She went back into the hall and through the door leading downstairs, her father following. Jack was talking to the electrician, finishing off the complicated electrics in the kitchen now the tiling was completed. Jack came over to say hello, kissing Tess and shaking hands with Ken.

'Well, young man, you seem to have done a grand job for my daughter. I'm impressed with what I've seen so far.'

'Thanks, Ken, I'm only happy if my client's happy,' Jack said, squeezing Tess's hand. She had to avoid her father's eyes in case she blushed and moved over to see what Sparks was doing. He explained how he was wiring up the appliances to switches above the worktop. Tess nodded and walked round, leaving Jack and Ken to chat. This was the first time she'd seen the kitchen looking more or less finished and as she ran her fingers along the granite worktops she admired the understated matt cream units. Her big extravagance was the range cooker, a sleek black and silver contraption with a double oven and grill and topped with an extra-large hob. It would, she hoped, encourage her to improve her culinary skills to match those of her friends. Other appliances were hiding behind unit doors and in the centre of the room was an old farmhouse table and chairs to soften the blandness of the units. The old downstairs loo was now a functional utility room and another door led directly to the garden. New, bigger windows and clever lighting made the whole area look and feel bright and airy.

'Everything okay?' Jack said, joining her.

'More than okay, thanks. I love it.' She nodded towards the jungle outside. 'I'll need to organise some help with that if I'm to enjoy sitting outside this summer.'

'No worries. I've arranged for a lad to come and clear it next week. Then you can see what's worth keeping or whether to start from scratch.'

'Thanks, that's thoughtful of you.' She turned to her father and suggested they check out the rest of the house before she ran out of time.

The first floor bedrooms were ready to be painted and looked light and airy with fitted wardrobes and the master bedroom now boasted a small en suite, complete with shower cubicle, loo and basin. Tess and Ken admired the workmanship before checking out the main bathroom, now fully tiled with a roll-top bath, walk-in shower, loo, bidet and vanity unit.

'It's just like a five-star hotel, love. I can't believe how much you've transformed the old place.'

'Well, I have had a lot of help, Dad. And when I can afford it, I'm going to add a conservatory on the back of the kitchen, like my neighbour. Come and have a quick look at the attic rooms. We've smartened them up, but not doing too much yet as I don't need them and have run out of money, anyway.'

She showed him the two rooms, now with new larger windows, newly plastered walls and boasting central heating like the rest of the house.

'It's a big house, alright, love. Going to be a bit big for you on your own, isn't it?' Ken said, with a sly glance at her and Jack.

'For the moment, maybe, but who knows?' She shrugged, avoiding looking at Jack. 'Now, I must run and we'll see you tonight at eight for dinner, okay?' Ken nodded and they retraced their steps downstairs with Tess dashing to her car, leaving the men to say their goodbyes. She'd known her father wouldn't be able to resist saying something about her relationship with Jack and could only hope he'd behave when they ate together. With a heavy sigh, she started the car and drove back to the surgery.

Jack had suggested they dine at The Wellington Boot, known affectionately as the Welly Boot, the restaurant of the

Hotel de Havelet, yards from her father's hotel and with the same superb views of the bay and islands. Tess enjoyed the meal, though was still feeling less relaxed around Jack. He appeared a great guy, ticking all the boxes on the list of what she wanted in a partner, but…it was all happening so quickly. And the examples of poor Eugénie and Sally kept pushing their way into her mind. Unnerving. Ken, meanwhile, was quite chirpy, looking forward to moving to Guernsey when he found the right property. Tess was going with him to view his choices after work the next day and he showed them copies of the agent's details.

'They both look great, Dad, particularly the new development with views over La Salerie.' She handed the details to Jack, who promptly laughed.

'I'm flattered you've chosen this, Ken, as it's one of mine. Will be interesting to see what you think of it.'

'So you're the vendor?'

'That's right. There are only two units left as they've been very popular.'

Ken grinned. 'If you've finished them to the same standard as Tess's house I'll be very tempted. It's dearer than the other one near Castel Church, but I like the idea of being on the edge of Town.'

'Tell you what, why don't I come with you tomorrow? I can answer any questions you might have better than the agent.'

'Good idea, lad, especially if I can negotiate a discount, eh?' Ken chuckled.

Tess picked up her father the following day at six thirty and drove out to Castel to view the first apartment. Ken was disappointed with its dated condition and they then met Jack at the development not far from Les Cotils, perched on a hill and with clear sea views. Once inside, Tess knew Ken would love it. More contemporary than their family home, it offered a luxury open-plan kitchen and living area, a spacious en suite bedroom, separate bathroom and a small terrace and garden with views to match those of her own house.

'Well, Dad? What do you think?' Noting the gleam in his eye, she didn't really need to ask.

'It ticks the boxes, all right. It's just the price...' He gave Jack a sly look.

'Okay, let's talk about that, shall we?' Jack winked at Tess as he led Ken onto the terrace. A few minutes later they returned, shaking hands.

'I've bought my new home, love. And Jack says I can move in as soon as the advocates sort the paperwork, which shouldn't take long for a cash sale.' Ken beamed at her and she gave him a hug.

'I'm so pleased, Dad, it'll be lovely to have you here. Did you drive a hard bargain?' She looked from him to Jack, who shrugged his shoulders.

'Let's say we're both happy.'

After returning Ken to his hotel, where he was meeting up with an old friend, Tess returned home in thoughtful mood. Had Jack given her father a discount because of her? If so, and it didn't work out between them, would he be annoyed? And he was definitely going above and beyond on her house. She reminded herself that it was his responsibility, not hers. No-one could guarantee the smooth path of a new relationship. Not that Tess wanted to finish with him, she was just a bit scared. There, she had admitted it! Not necessarily scared Jack would turn out to be a drunken, violent partner, but scared to commit to another human being. Losing some control. Oh...the ringing of her phone interrupted her thoughts. It was Paul, phoning to say although Sally was still at La Folie, her husband had grudgingly agreed to her terms and she was awaiting his signed acceptance. She would then move in with her mother until she bought a new home. Tess thanked him for the update, heaving a sigh of relief. Result!

She was spending the evening at home instead of Jack's. It had been her idea, telling him she had things to catch up on, and would see him on Saturday night after taking her father to the airport. Jack had looked a bit put-out but offered to cook dinner for them on Saturday. In truth, Tess wanted a chance to both stand back a little and to finish the diaries. After enjoying a plate of pasta she settled down with the final part, beginning with Juliette's death in 1883. Tess had grown to like the sound of her and understood Eugénie's sense of loss and also wasn't surprised how deeply Hugo's death had affected her two years later. She had loved him for over twenty years and suffered so much. Reading on, Tess was pleased to see young Victor had stood up to his father who now left Eugénie alone. About time! She was even more cheered by the news of Hugo's bequest. The entry dated May 1888, '*I am dying*' made her cry out, 'Oh, no!' Her eyes filled with tears as she continued reading. Pain relief. Morphine injections. Sophie's tears. Victor's tear-stained face. Eugénie's calm acceptance of her fate. Then the final entry, June 1888. Shaky writing. Forthcoming death. Son. Journals…attic cupboard. Secret drawer…desk. Tess gasped, looking at the desk behind her. Door…plastered over. Secret. '*If it needs to be found, it will be…*'

Wiping her eyes, Tess stumbled over to the desk, wondering where on earth the secret drawer could be. She opened the lid and started pushing and pressing various panels and knobs. Nothing. Perhaps Charlotte could help, she was more used to antiques. She ran downstairs and found her in the sitting room with Andy watching television. Charlotte looked up in surprise as Tess gabbled on about the diary, Eugénie dying and a secret drawer in the desk.

'Oh, I see. There's a secret drawer? Right, I'm coming.' Andy was left staring after them as they ran upstairs.

'I don't know what I'm looking for, and thought you might know more about antiques.' Tess showed Charlotte the last entry in the diary and her eyes widened.

'Isn't it sad? And she would be so pleased to know you've found it, Tess. Her direct descendant. Now, the drawer.'

Charlotte frowned as they stood in front of the desk.

'My father had a secret drawer in his desk but it was a different design. You have to look for something not quite right…' She pulled out drawers and compared their depth to that of the desk. One was much shorter. They looked at each other with round eyes. Charlotte pushed her fingers into the space. 'There should be a spring or a panel.' They heard a click and she pulled out another, much smaller drawer, crammed with old letters.

'Oh! Fantastic! Let me see…yes, they're all addressed to Eugénie and posted from abroad.' Tess opened the top one but struggled to read the writing and passed it to Charlotte.

'It's from Alice, written after Hugo's death. It must be the last letter Eugénie received from the family.'

'So there'll be letters from Hugo and Juliette in here, too. Wow!' Tess cried, spreading the letters on the table.

Charlotte picked one up.

'This is his handwriting. May I?'

Tess nodded and Charlotte started reading the letter. 'It's the one he sent after Juliette's death. What a wonderful collection. These are even more precious than the diaries. So poor Eugénie left quite a legacy.'

'Yes, she certainly did. And I have to decide what to do with it.' Tess chewed her lip, still reeling from the poignant account of Eugénie's death.

Charlotte threw her arms around her.

'Hey, I can see it's upset you. She got under my skin too and I'm not related. Sit down for a minute. Do you have any wine?'

'Yes, there's an open bottle in the fridge. Pour us both a glass.' Charlotte filled two glasses and sat beside her.

'Cheers! To Eugénie and may she rest in peace.'

Tess repeated the toast and took a sip of wine.

'It's been quite a journey and I only wish Aunt Doris hadn't wasted all those years looking for the answers which were upstairs all along. I'll probably be able to chuck away all those papers,' she said, nodding towards the boxes in the corner.

'Maybe. But at least now you do know the truth and can relax and enjoy your beautiful home.'

Tess nodded, taking another sip.

'I wonder how long that awful husband of hers lived after she died. Not long I hope.'

'Don't you have the family tree Doris drew up? That will tell you.'

'Of course! It's in the desk.' Tess searched one of the drawers and pulled out a large sheet of paper. She scanned the names near the top. 'Yes, Pierre died in 1891, in his early fifties. Good, that means Victor was free of him when he was only twenty-one.'

'And what happened to Victor?'

Tess read a bit more.

'He married at twenty-five, had a son and a daughter but the daughter died young. Victor died in his forties.' Tess frowned. 'My mother said those who lived in the house tended to die young, but people did in those days. And Doris proved her wrong, didn't she?'

'Yes, and I'm sure you'll live to a grand old age, surrounded by your children and grandchildren.'

'That's my life mapped out, then,' Tess said, laughing.

Charlotte joined in, before saying, 'Look, why don't I leave you alone now? See you in the morning, okay?' Charlotte stood, glass in hand.

'Okay, thanks.'

Her father left for Exeter on Saturday, planning to clear the house prior to completion and expected to be back within two or three weeks, ready to move into his new apartment. Tess still hadn't heard from her mother and Ken said he'd encourage Elaine to get in touch.

'I don't want you two falling out because of what's happened, love. She's your mother after all and didn't make a bad job of bringing you up, did she?' her father had remarked as they said their goodbyes at the airport. Tess had to agree with him. But at the moment her priority was Jack and their budding love affair.

'Hi, did Ken get off all right?' Jack greeted her as she arrived at his cottage.

'Yes, thanks.' He pulled her into his arms and kissed her. It felt good, but she found herself pulling back, with a tentative smile. For the moment the spontaneity had gone.

'What's wrong? And don't tell me there isn't anything, because I won't believe you.' Jack's brow was furrowed as he held her arms.

'Let's have a drink and we can talk. Okay?'

He nodded and, after dumping her bag in the hall, she followed him outside. Now early August the evenings were staying hotter and the cottage doors and windows were wide open to encourage a breeze to flow through. On the patio the table was set with two glasses and a bottle of white wine in ice. Jack poured the wine and sat beside her.

Tess took a large swallow of wine.

'It's not you, it's me.' He went to say something, but she stopped him. 'Let me finish. My feelings for you haven't changed. It's…it's I'm a bit scared of rushing things. I've had to deal with a nasty case of domestic violence this week and it made me very angry. Angry with the husband for the way he's treated his wife, and angry with her for letting him. I've calmed down now and, thankfully, the wife is leaving him. Added to this, I've been reading Eugénie's diaries and she was also abused, to the extent that she died relatively young.' She saw Jack's face harden and hastened to add, 'I'm not saying I think you would be abusive, but it's touched a nerve in me and made me aware how scared I am of commitment. Of letting someone else play a big part in my life. Does this make sense?'

'I guess. As a man it's not something I've had to worry about, for myself, that is. Although I understand how awful it must have been for you dealing with this, you are one tough cookie, Tess, and I can't see you ever being under any man's thumb, literally or figuratively. And, speaking for myself, I would never, ever want to harm you. The opposite in fact. If anyone threatened to hurt you in any way, I'd be there for you.' He reached out and stroked her hand, his eyes locked on hers.

She felt her heartbeat quicken.

'Thank you. I think it's all happened a bit fast with us, and we need to get to know each other better. Don't you agree?'

'Sure, I'm happy with that. I know you've had a lot going on and there's no rush, is there? Let's enjoy ourselves, starting with dinner, which is ready, if you are.'

'Yes, please.'

With two weeks to go before the house was due to be ready, Tess became increasingly excited about the move. It had been a relief to clear the air with Jack and her former joy at being with him had reappeared. And once settled in her own home, she would feel more in control of her life. And could see Jack as much or as little as she wanted. In the meantime she had to go through Doris's papers and decide what to do with Eugénie's diaries, letters and Hugo memorabilia.

She discussed it with Charlotte one evening.

'I think you have three choices, Tess. One, keep everything in your house; two, copy the letters and offer the originals to Hauteville House, together with the more valuable memorabilia; or three, keep the originals and offer copies to Hauteville,' she said, ticking them off her fingers. 'We could talk to Stéphanie once you've made a decision. My only thought is, you'd need to have appropriate security and insurance to keep anything original at home.'

Tess frowned.

'That's what bothers me. Do I want that worry? No-one will be interested in the diaries so I'll hang onto them, it's everything else that's a problem. What would you do?'

'Much as I'd be tempted to hang on to everything, I'd have to accept it's not practical and would be depriving the public of a glimpse into Hugo's life here.'

'You're right. Once I've moved let's ask Stéphanie if she'd like to come round and see what I have and go from there.'

'Good idea. She can see the original hiding place as well.'

By the following week Tess had worked her way through Doris's collection of papers, keeping only a handful of interest. The rest were binned. Now all she had to take to her house were Doris's books and what she had brought from Exeter. While she had been at Jack's at the weekend he had offered to help with her move.

'That's great, thanks, but are you sure you don't have an ulterior motive?' she'd asked as they lay curled up in bed.

'What possible ulterior motive could I have for helping my gorgeous, sexy girlfriend sort out her new home? Unpacking boxes, shifting furniture, setting up the TV, making the bed…'

Tess had burst into giggles, spluttering, 'Exactly!' before he'd stopped her with a lingering kiss.

One evening Tess was in the kitchen with Charlotte, who offered her a glass of wine.

'Andy and I would like you and Jack to have dinner with us here on Friday, seeing as it's your last night. And he's welcome to stay over,' she said, with a grin.

'Thanks, I'll ask him. I'm sure he'll be only too happy to accept.'

He was, and on Friday Tess left work looking forward to what promised to be a memorable weekend. She walked into the house to be met by a wonderful aroma of garlic and herbs and found Charlotte in the kitchen watching James eat while she prepared vegetables.

'Hi, I thought you'd sworn off cooking hot meals and was expecting a salad,' Tess said, giving James a kiss on his forehead, the only clean part of his face.

Charlotte grimaced

'We've had a few this week and I've really missed proper food. And so has Andy. I loaded up the slow-cooker this morning so haven't been near a hot stove. I'm aiming for eight, and we can have a drink and nibbles in the garden first. Are you ready for tomorrow?'

'Yes, some smaller items were delivered today and Jack was there to sign for them. The big stuff will arrive tomorrow and then it's all systems go.' Tess nicked a carrot and started chewing on it. 'Right, I'll shower and change and be down soon.'

August was getting steadily hotter and she was glad to cool down and change into a short cotton dress. She tidied the rooms ready for her overnight guest as best she could, considering the piles of stacked boxes and cases.

Downstairs she joined Charlotte and Andy in a cold lager and a few minutes later Jack arrived. Tess experienced a strong flick of desire as he kissed her. It promised to be a great evening.

It was. The next morning Tess struggled to wake when the alarm went off at eight.

'C'mon, sleepyhead. We have to get a move on, literally.' Jack's laughing face greeted her as she slowly opened her eyes. Move! Yes, it was moving day. She was taking possession of *St Michel* in all its new glory. Within minutes she was showered and dressed in shorts and T-shirt, as was Jack, and after a quick breakfast of coffee and toast it was time to load up the cars with her possessions. Andy lent a hand with the desk, placed carefully in the back of the Range Rover and Tess and Jack managed everything else. Once the cars were full Tess hugged Charlotte, Andy and James goodbye and they stood and waved them off.

Tess opened the front door of *St Michel*, to be met with the strong smell of fresh paint. She laughed and Jack asked what was funny.

'I was thinking what a huge improvement the smell of paint is compared to the awful smell when I first got the keys.'

'Right. Now, let's empty the cars before any furniture arrives, which won't be long.'

Tess hadn't seen the house completely empty of workmen and equipment and it was a joy to walk around the rooms glowing with fresh colour ready to welcome her. They loaded everything into the sitting room first before Jack moved the cars to leave space for the delivery vans. While Jack was outside Tess carried her cases upstairs and stood in her bedroom with a big smile on her face. The freshly polished four-poster now had a new mattress and muslin hangings and looked gorgeous. All she had to do was unpack the bed linen. She checked out the en suite; good. A quick look at the other bedrooms and bathroom confirmed everything was spotless. A pleasant surprise after so much building work.

Downstairs Jack had returned and together they positioned the desk in the sitting room, where Tess thought Eugénie had originally placed it. The big dining table was in place by the far window waiting for the new chairs.

Jack put his arms round her.

'Happy?'

'Oh, yes. And it's going to look even better when the sofa and chairs arrive. And the other bits like the TV. Thanks, Jack, you and your men have done brilliantly. It's better than I'd ever imagined.' She smiled up at him and his mouth came down on hers. The doorbell rang and they moved apart, laughing.

'Looks like you'll have to thank me later. Come on, let's see what's arrived.'

By the end of the afternoon Tess would willingly have crept upstairs for a nap in the inviting bed. Every muscle ached from lifting and unpacking boxes and arranging the new furniture. She took a break and, leaving Jack setting up her new LED television, slipped into the garden for some fresh air. The grass had been cut right back and she could see the old shrubs and planting along the borders. They would need work, but Tess saw it as a labour of love to recreate what was once a pretty garden. Taking deep breaths of paint-free air, she walked down towards the far boundary and stood in front of the tall eucalyptus tree, offering shade on a hot day. A passage from Eugénie's diary came to mind '*he was laid to rest under a eucalyptus tree at the bottom of the garden*'. Tess knelt down and touched the bare earth. 'I'm going to plant a camellia here for you, Arnaud, so you and your mother won't be forgotten.' Feeling a movement behind her she said, not turning round, 'Have you finished setting up the TV?' When there was no reply, she turned and watched as the hazy figure of Eugénie looked at her, smiling. Then, with a nod of her head, she was gone.

Tess found herself waving at the disappearing figure, knowing she wouldn't be back. But their bond would always be there.

'Who were you waving at?' Jack came out of the back door.

'Oh, it was a pesky wasp.' She had yet to tell him about seeing Eugénie. Perhaps later...

He came up and holding her head still, gave her a long, lingering kiss.

Coming up for air, she said, 'What was that for?'

'It's my way of saying I love you, idiot girl. You may be a clever doctor, but I'm not sure how well you understand the workings of the heart.'

She smiled, her own heart racing with joy.

'Oh, I do understand, Jack, I do.'

The End

Author's Note

The Inheritance was inspired by Victor Hugo's home in Guernsey, Hauteville House. Having been on a couple of guided tours I found it gave a fascinating insight into the man himself. I then began to read various biographies, particularly focusing on Hugo's fifteen years in Guernsey. An idea for my book began to take shape, and *voila!* Eugénie was born. She is in fact loosely based on another French girl who worked as Hugo's copyist around this time, and one of the few fictional characters in this part of the story. Her family is fictional, but all those mentioned as part of the Hugo household, his acquaintances and the named local shopkeepers were real people. Many actual events are mentioned, but I have used my imagination when describing characters' reactions and emotions.

I offer my heartfelt thanks to those who have helped me with information for this book and patiently answered my questions. Particular mention goes to the Priaulx Library, which offers a wealth of information concerning Victor Hugo, his family and his works. I am especially grateful to Dinah Bott, who was both helpful and encouraging. Another thank you goes to Stéphanie Duluc at Hauteville House who very kindly not only answered my questions, but picked up some errors in my original draft. Also thanks to Dr Susan Taylor for background medical information.

Bibliography
Victor Hugo by Graham Robb
Victor Hugo and his world by W.J.L. Hugo
Victor Hugo by Samuel Edwards
Hauteville House Museum Guide
Victor Hugo's St Peter Port by Gregory Stevens Cox
Victor Hugo in the Channel Islands by Gregory Stevens Cox
Victor Hugo's Guernsey Neighbours by Gregory Stevens Cox
Les Travailleurs de la Mer – some Guernsey perspectives by Gregory Stevens Cox
Les Misérables by Victor Hugo

The Inheritance

Anne Allen lives in Devon by her beloved sea, near her daughter and grandchildren. Her restless spirit has meant a number of moves, the longest stay being in Guernsey for fourteen years after falling in love with the island and the people. She contrived to leave one son behind to ensure a valid reason for frequent returns. Another son is based in London, ideal for her city breaks. A retired psychotherapist, Anne has now published seven novels. Find her website at www.anneallen.co.uk

Praise for Anne Allen

Dangerous Waters - A wonderfully crafted story with a perfect balance of intrigue and romance.' *The Wishing Shelf Awards, 22 July 2013 – Dangerous Waters*

Finding Mother - A sensitive, heart-felt novel about family relationships, identity, adoption, second chances at love With romance, weddings, boat trips, lovely gardens and more, Finding Mother is a dazzle of a book, a perfect holiday read. *Lindsay Townsend, author of The Snow Bride*

Guernsey Retreat- I enjoyed the descriptive tour while following the lives of strangers as their worlds collide, when the discovery of a body and the death of a relative draw them into links with the past. A most pleasurable, intriguing read. *Glynis Smy, author of Maggies Child.*

The Family Divided - A poignant and heart-warming love story. *Gilli Allan, author of Fly or Fall*

Echoes of Time - Not only is the plot packed full of twists and turns, but the setting – and the characters – are lovingly described. *Wishing Shelf Review*

The Betrayal – All in all, totally unputdownable! *thewsa.co.uk*

The Inheritance -A gorgeously intriguing story set in a beautiful location. I completely identified with contemporary heroine Tess and Victorian heroine Eugénie. *Margaret James, author of The Final Reckoning.*

Also by Anne Allen

Dangerous Waters

Finding Mother

Guernsey Retreat

The Family Divided

Echoes of Time

The Betrayal